THE CRACK

THE CRACK

Christopher Radmann

ONEWORLD

A Oneworld Book

First published in North America, Great Britain &
Australia by Oneworld Publications, 2014

ISBN: 978-1-78074-528-2 (Hardback)
ISBN: 978-1-78074-399-8 (Paperback)
eBook ISBN: 978-1-78074-427-8

Cover design by Katya Mezhibovskaya

Printed and bound by CPI Group (UK) Ltd, Croydon,CR0 4YY

Oneworld Publications
10 Bloomsbury Street
London WC1B 3SR
England

FOR CHRIS AND JENNY PARKER

A glossary of certain Afrikaans words/phrases is appended (page 325).

Everyone who is born holds dual citizenship, in the kingdom of the well and in the kingdom of the sick. Although we all prefer to use only the good passport, sooner or later each of us is obliged, at least for a spell, to identify ourselves as citizens of that other place.

— Susan Sontag

To fill a Gap
Insert the Thing that caused it –
Block it up
With Other – and 'twill yawn the more –
You cannot solder an Abyss
With Air.

— Emily Dickinson

1MM

The Soweto Uprising, 1976

At about 7 a.m. on 16 June 1976, thousands of African school students in Soweto gathered at prearranged assembly points for a demonstration. They launched a movement that began in opposition to the imposition of Afrikaans as a medium of instruction (in African schools), and developed, over twenty months, into a countrywide youth uprising against the apartheid regime.

This movement cost the lives of more than a thousand youths. But, like an earthquake, it opened up a huge fissure in South African history, separating one era from another. It politicised a whole new generation of youth, and consigned beyond recall the era of defeats in the 1960s. It announced the determination of the youth to end one of the most barbaric examples of modern capitalist slavery.

> – **Weizmann Hamilton** writing in *Inqaba Ya Basebenzi (Fortress of the Revolution)*

> The police garage was next to the mortuary, and the bodies of soldiers who had died in police or army operations came in daily. We began to keep score. I soon got used to the idea that a human life had very little value.

> – Johan Marais, *Time Bomb: A Policeman's True Story*

T he crack appeared at the bottom of the swimming pool on 1 January 1976.

Or, possibly more accurately, it was on 1 January 1976 that Janet first noticed the crack at the bottom of the swimming pool.

It was not a big crack as far as cracks go. In fact, it went nowhere. It simply shimmered beneath the wobbling water as her three children lay on the slasto at the pool's edge. Did she even see it.

The children lay panting and glistening like oiled seals in the midsummer sun. Beads of water sparkled on their brown backs. Even from behind her sunglasses, Janet's eyes winced at the brightness of their silvery-brown skin. They lay recovering from a game of Marco Polo that had descended into Sharky and the swallowing of great gasps of chlorinated water by the boy in the middle.

Janet had come across from her deep oasis beneath the willow tree, summoned from her uncomfortable doze by the sounds of Pieter's sisters berating his attempts at drowning. Her haven, a heaven of soft-lime striations, had yielded to their impetuous squeals. She had burst through the shroud of branches straight into the light.

Sis, man, the girls shrieked in that high-tensile, female way.

Ag, sis, man.

Ma, Ma, look at Pieter.

Their shrill cries had hooked her out of the limbo into which she was sinking. Into which she had been sinking these last eleven years.

One moment she was drifting into the haze of steaming pine scent that seeped across from the neighbour's garden. Then she was on her feet and moving fast across the big lawn as Pieter spewed his lunch over the side of the pool.

She was in time to see the carrots she had chopped so finely lend a colourful sheen to the slasto beside the pool. Offset by the red and white of the radishes.

Gross, man, Pieter's sisters screamed with the addition of gagging sounds.

Gross, squealed the older.

That's quite enough, Shelley, she snapped.

Gross, echoed the younger.

Be quiet, Sylvia, her mouth opened and slammed shut.

Pieter knelt at her feet like a dog. Or a piggy, in the middle of two very vocal sisters. He seemed to be studying his reconfigured lunch with some surprise. He raised a hand and for a moment his mother wondered whether he was going to poke it, to play with his food that shone in the viscous sun, neatly filling the cracks in the crazy paving. Instead, he wiped his mouth and raised his little face to her.

Sorry, Mommy, he said.

I said that you should not go mad in the pool after lunch.

His face fell.

She was scolding herself, for letting them go berserk so soon after eating, but his little face fell.

All their faces fell.

It wasn't the vomit that was ruining their game. It was her sharp voice. Her voice that cut through their childish fun and frolics. So what if Marco Polo had discovered the skill of projectile vomiting. Who really cared if Sharky now surfed through an acidic salad. Her sharp voice had snipped off the fringe of their fun and games. They were silly children now. Shelley. Pieter. And Sylvia. Three blonde heads and lithe bodies. Perfect little bodies gathered around the sick at the side of the pool.

She gave commands.

All shrieking stopped and they began to splash water from the pool so that it gushed over the vomit and sent it coursing to the edge of the slasto and onto the grass. The little bits of carrot, radish and lettuce lay wilting in the ferocious sun. Of the thick slices of wholemeal bread, oddly, there seemed no trace.

Then they moved off to one side where the slasto was lovely and hot, and lay panting and glistening like oiled seals in the midsummer sun. Beads of water sparkled on their brown backs. Even from behind her sunglasses, Janet's eyes winced at the brightness of their silvery-brown skin. Then her eyes were drawn to the wobbling water that lassoed the sun into strange rings and coils. And there, beneath it all, was the crack.

For a moment, she thought that there was no crack. Surely if there were a crack, the water level would have dipped. Surely, she would have noticed if the water level had dipped. Or Solomon would have said something about the water level dropping. Nothing had been said or noticed. Until now.

She stood there. Her three little silver darlings shivered in the heat and murmured to one side. She slid her sunglasses onto the top of her head. She stood over the pool, leaning out as far as she dared. Still the water looped and coiled the glinting light. It would take time for the waves to settle.

But she had time.

Of that commodity she had an abundance.

Always that sense of time on her hands. As though time were some sticky substance that clung to her fingers and had to be carefully scoured off. Rubbed off with care and Sunlight soap so that it did not stick under her wedding ring or catch in the gap between the white gold of that ring and its little neighbour – the more recent eternity ring presented to her by Hektor-Jan after the birth of their third child, precious little Sylvia. Well done, said the ring. Well done on securing the next generation of white South African children, but enough, now, no more. The future is safe as the eternal circle of the ring suggests, but enough, too, as the white gold zero urgently implies. For ever and now. It felt strange accepting, for a second time, such a ring from such a man. Everything and nothing.

Janet found herself looking down at her hands that rubbed themselves all the time in a silent ritual even though there was no sticky substance that clung to her skin. She quietly folded her arms and stood there, looking down. Trying to peer through the azure gleam of the water, like a priestess trying to divine the heavens. Yet in Janet's case, her lips thinned as she smiled a tight smile, the heavens were an 8 × 5 metre swimming pool that reeked of chlorine and responsibility and was stuck at the far end of a suburban garden in the heart of the East Rand, in the town, Benoni, on this, the first day of another new year, 1976.

She waited for the waves to subside. They must eventually settle down to a flat rectangle of blue that would present the world with one hot sun on its calm surface. And then she could move along the edge of the pool and find a spot that did not blind her, and then she could see to the bottom of the pool. She could see where the leaves lurked. Where moths and grasshoppers lay in the sapphire depths dreaming that they were flying free instead of being suspended in their 8 x 5 metre liquid tomb and going nowhere. Nowhere but up the coiled length of the Kreepy Krauly that would switch on at night and go chugging around the pool sucking up the leaves and the little dead bodies. Janet would lie awake and listen to the heartbeat coming from the swimming pool at the other end of the long garden. Sometimes it sounded like Hektor-Jan's heartbeat or her own, but she knew that the timer had clicked and that the new Kreepy Krauly had begun its circuit of precisely random cleaning of the pool. That as they slept through the insistent chirping of crickets and the howl of a hunting mosquito, the little bodies at the bottom of the pool would disappear up the jerking, pulsing funnel of the Kreepy Krauly. In the morning, they would be gone, all those foetal corpses, and the pool would be ready for another day: fresh, blank and blue. It was the opposite of birth. It was a beautiful obliteration.

But now there was the crack.

Somewhere.

Somewhere beneath the mass of shifting water she had seen, had sensed possibly, the crack. Janet almost wondered whether it was that that had awoken her in the early hours between 1975 and 1976. Whether she had, in fact, heard the smooth concrete split and had murmured in her half-awake, half-asleep dwaal. Murmured to Hektor-Jan that there was something out there.

But she couldn't have murmured anything. Certainly Hektor-Jan could not have heard anything, as he would have been up like a shot, switching on the emergency torch and getting the gun and leaving his wife gasping.

You never mess around with things like that, he would have said. Better to be safe than sorry. And he would have gone prowling through the deep house with his torch and his gun. Checking doors and windows. Ready to defend hearth and home. And the children would have been noisily sleeping in that messy way children have, she prayed. All snores and snufflings, please, dear God. Pieter in his own little room and Shelley and Sylvia together in theirs. Please, oh please. And every lock and burglar bar would be safe and secure and the children still squirming from the excesses of Christmas and not yet ready for school. He would wander to the spare bedroom, the one that looked out over the little courtyard to the maid's quarters, the kaya that abutted the double garage, and check that there were no comings and goings there. Janet held her breath. Then Hektor-Jan would have returned with his hand over his torch so as not to blind her and would have hidden his gun. With a playful slap where her nightie just about covered her bottom, he would sink into bed and perhaps into her again as she lay in fear of what might have been out there. Hektor-Jan would try to continue celebrating the start of the new year in style. They had had a busy night of it. They had gone round for drinks at the neighbours to their left, but then straight home and to bed for the children, who would be starting school in a week's time. The playful slap after the playful clinking of glasses to usher in 1976. It was going to be a good one. To continue the economic recovery after the grim times. That's what Doug had said as he raised yet another glass of 5th Avenue Cold Duck sparkling wine and refilled theirs and Noreen had quacked away with flushed cheeks and they had all said, Cheers! once more. And Hektor-Jan had made a lovely speech. Surprising, impromptu, but a sweet speech. Yes, 1976 was set to be a good one.

And just before the stroke of midnight, after they had returned home and put the murmuring children to bed, she and Hektor-Jan had escaped from the house into the cool depths of the garden. And bubbling after the third bottle of 5th Avenue Cold Duck, they had giggled their clothes to the ground and slipped into the coolness of the pool. When last had they skinny-dipped. When last had Hektor-Jan been free of his uniform, and Janet so uninhibited. The booze made them brave. The chlorinated water made their skin hard and Janet had said Goodness me, it was happening so unexpectedly and Hektor-Jan had whispered Happy New Year and had made another pass at her. But there was moonlight and the black water shone very brightly and Hektor-Jan had said The children – and Janet had remembered and she had playfully pulled him. Out of the pool she pulled him and he could not resist as 1975 slipped aside and in flooded 1976. They kissed beside the pampas grass. They kissed beneath the willow tree, but the moonlight was bright and the windows of the house were watchful. They were alone, but the children – the children. So Hektor-Jan bent his strong arms and she was lifted as light as a fluted glass brimming with bubbles and, like the sparkling wine, she was swept off her feet to the side of the house. Shhh, breathed Hektor-Jan as she chuckled and tried not to snort in an unladylike way, and then they were at the double garage which adjoined the maid's quarters, but Alice was not back yet. And Hektor-Jan wiggled his eyebrows in the moonlight and before she knew it they were in the garage and there was the smell of oil and paint and soft sawdust. The concrete floor was cold as he let her down slowly, slowly down the length of his burly body. And her husband was warm and he turned her and she leaned on the smooth metal of the parked car and Hektor-Jan took charge from behind. But then you could not tell who was leading and who was following as they struggled together over the cold bonnet of the Fiat – which had the habit of backfiring. Janet almost heard the car as Hektor-Jan crashed behind her. There was a warm bang, the gasp of a sound as something metal fell, some big tool, and then it was just their laughter as she bucked and called, Hektor, my Hektor-Jan, and Hektor-Jan cried, Janet, Janet, right beside her ear. And all her senses were arrested as her policeman husband held her, overwhelmed her, with his great love. And then she turned and kissed him.

They were so close. Locked together in the oily garage with their wet skin and warm kisses. Gentle and rough, loud and quiet.

That was 1975. Or was it 1976.

It will be different, he whispered. New. A brave new year.

And now, already, the crack. Tomorrow, next year, was already today. And it was the first of January – definitely a very bright, new day –

Still the water wobbled. But the many, many suns were slowly reducing in number. It would not be long before the water lay calm and yielded up the bottom of the pool. And Janet had time. Great, generous dollops of sticky time.

Alice would be back soon. Helping to clear up the mess as all that time melted and dripped through her fingers. Ah, the luxury of a live-in maid. So many in white South Africa had a live-in maid. What was life without a black live-in maid. Her Alice. Who helped her to make and preserve a wonderland.

Last night Noreen had gone on about life without her girl, her Emily. About the mysterious pregnancy, as Emily was not supposed to have gentlemen callers while she was there in the kaya working for them full time. Her Emily had given notice and Doug and Noreen were looking for a new maid. Emily had gone back to Daveyton, the sprawling township a train-ride away from Benoni, and from there back to Zululand, apparently. Now they were looking for a new maid. And Janet had tried not to let Hektor-Jan's hand on her shoulder distract her – his fingers were the size of fists – while Noreen asked, Did Janet's Alice know anyone. Or Alice's mother, the old but legendary Lettie. Surely she would know someone, or have another daughter or niece or whatever who needed work.

Her Alice, Janet was sure, would know several young women keen to escape into a kaya that lay adjoined to the back of a double garage. A neat retreat from life in the townships of the East Rand. To be yoked to a white family from morning until night with the odd afternoon off. To be spared the multifarious claims of one's own family by being pressed into service of another family and paid for it. To become a domestic servant. To suspend yourself in domestic servitude until the Kreepy Krauly of life sucked you up and out. Isn't that what happened to Noreen's Emily. Her womb, like the pulsing funnel of the Kreepy Krauly, had sucked her up and out of her old way of life. Now she was gone. Their pool was clean. Clean, but somehow bare. Noreen had said, That was one way of looking at it, yes, for sure, if you put it like that, and Hektor-Jan had secretly pinched Janet softly on the bottom, just there, right where her bottom began.

And there was the crack on this, the bold, blue 1 January 1976. In the heart of the swimming pool and running along its entire length. A hairline fracture in the concrete scalp of the pool. Not much to look at. Indeed, barely noticed. In fact, completely unnoticed were it not for the game of Marco Polo followed rather too soon by Sharky and Pieter's vomiting.

Janet stood with her arms folded, looking down. She could be a bird in the sky, looking down from the heavens on the world far below. Perceiving some divinest sense – to a discerning eye, or perhaps amazing sense – from ordinary meanings. Her delicate hands lay resting on her arms. They were her wings, and folded, so she did not fly and she could not be a bird. Then she unfolded her arms and knelt down at the edge of the pool for an even closer look. Maybe she was a giraffe now, her limbs splayed out to support her weight as she peered over the edge of the pool, straining ever further to see what was shimmering there at the bottom of the pool. She bit her lip. It was a crack, of that there was no doubt. Why had the children not said. They played in the pool incessantly. It was their second home. Why had Solomon the gardener not said. He basically lived in the garden, both in the front and the back garden. Surely someone should have noticed and raised the alarm. Come running to her to say Mommy or Madam, there is a crack at the bottom of the pool in this the year of our Lord, 1976. The children should have called Mommy! And Solomon could have spoken softly, his shaven head respectfully bowed as he clutched his rake for support and said, Madam, the swimming pool, eish.

She did not need this in her life. Not at this juncture. Not with Hektor-Jan about to start working a new shift and certainly not with the play that they hoped to put on, the great drama scheduled for the end of the summer. They had only a few months.

Maybe it would go away.

Janet stood there on the edge of the pool.

She could feel the house in the background, squatting prettily within the newish cement-slab walls that bounded the property and already hidden by big, established shrubs. She felt the fierce green grass, the lawn that seethed from the house all the way to the pool at the far end of the garden. And she could feel the shrubs and trees and flowers and insects all buzzing and bursting in the midsummer sun. Everything that kept Solomon busy like a ragged black bee three days a week whilst Doug and Noreen next door had him only for two. And the unexplained absence of Wednesdays, the gap in the middle of the week when who knows where Solomon went. The bee, the bee is not afraid of me, she thought as she tried to swat away the humming sound that persisted on the edge of sense.

Today, Solomon was not hers. His stern body with his lithe limbs and shaven head would not be servicing the garden. Grass would not be mown, shrubs trimmed, flower beds weeded nor cracks noticed by Solomon. Solomon would not hum and sing as he worked.

Today was Thursday, and New Year's Day.

And Hektor-Jan had to disappear. Even on this first day of 1976. His promotion demanded such things of him. No longer would he wear a uniform. Now he was in plain clothes and he was going to have to rely even more on his wife to keep the home fires burning, their little ship on even keel. Janet was left holding the fort and now there was a crack in one of the surrounding walls, a chink in their armour.

Like a giraffe, she lowered her elegant neck to the surface of the water. Her sunglasses stayed perched on the top of her head. Be still, be still, she silently commanded the waves. It would not be long now.

Crouched there, she suddenly sensed, as she sensed the house and surrounding garden – her home, her motherly, wifely, womanly domain – that she was being watched. Just as her short neat dress crept up her slim thighs and exposed the backs of her legs to the sun, Janet felt the prickle of a male gaze. She knew without looking that it was coming from the neighbours to the left. That once again, it was Doug, Douglas van Deventer, and that Noreen was no doubt buried somewhere in the house, possibly incapacitated by one of her migraines, lying in state in her bedroom with the curtains drawn. That would leave Doug free to grasp his shears and a little ladder and edge along the wall that bounded their properties. He would be pruning. Even at this stage of the summer, there would be the snip-snip of wayward branches being cut back, brought under control. And Doug's head would bob along the boundary. Like a dog at the wall, leaping to look up and over and into their lives. Doug the dog. And if he clambered to the top of that little A-frame ladder, he could peer through the bushes and tangled foliage into their garden, right across the lawn and almost, but not quite, up Janet's dress.

The backs of Janet's legs stung in the sun.

Now she was caught between propriety, her own at least, and the urgent need to confirm the existence of the terrible crack that seemed to split the bottom of the pool. In a moment the water would finally be still. If she leaned out a little further, just a fraction further –

Janet did not lean just yet. She sent one hand to the back of her dress and gave it a modest tug. It was high, but hopefully not too high. Her hand came back around. She leaned out as far as she dared and held her breath.

Ma, came the urgent whisper from her eldest. Ma, hissed Shelley.

Janet froze. She could not move. She could not look back now.

He's at it again, Ma, whispered Shelley and she knew that the children had spotted Desperate Doug amongst the trembling foliage.

It's Uncle Doug, Pieter's piping voice confirmed. Like he was proud. Like he was unwrapping yet another Christmas present. Janet closed her eyes. In no way was Doug van Deventer related to them; they were just polite kids.

His older sister shushed him. Not so loud, she hissed.

They all knew Mr Doug van Deventer. Uncle Doug. His strange habits. The way the little man managed to do lots of gardening when Mommy lay in the sun, or when Mommy occasionally swam or when Mommy patrolled the garden checking that Solomon the garden boy had done a good job. Uncle Doug was very friendly, but there were times when he gave them the creeps, when they wished that he was less friendly and that he would stop pretending to cut branches and peering in on their lives. He was a bit like the giant in Jack and the Beanstalk, hey. Even though he was a shorty-pants, a small man, hey. More like Rumpelstiltskin, if you wanted to get all technical.

Janet did not want to get all technical. One did not get technical when one was about to fall into the pool with one's skirt hitched up almost beyond the bounds of modesty in front of a leering horticul-turist and one's three young offspring. And there was the crack. It was surely about to reveal itself when the tiresome water finally ceased shimmering.

There, there. Now. Almost now. If she waited for just another second or two, leaned out another fraction of an inch, there it would be. She could be sure. Possibly, absolutely certain. Many things in this life are uncertain. Janet wanted at least to be certain of that one thing. It is not often that one discovers a crack in the bottom of the pool on New Year's Day. She leaned forward another fraction.

Yippee! screamed Pieter as she toppled into the pool.

One moment she was suspended above the water. Then she was a living splash.

Yippee! yelled Pieter and then they were all in the pool, all three of them like puppies or seals, wriggling and thrashing beside her, on top of her, kicking up water in her face and making her gasp and choke. They were laughing. Hanging from her, pulling at her arms and legs. She would lose her dress. She was fighting for breath, then she was laughing too. Clutching them to her like a watery mother hen as they wriggled and squealed like electric eels. Brown worms. They were wriggling worms and she was the early bird.

Marco Polo, Sylvia shouted. The memory of the recent game still fresh and sharp.

Sharky, shrieked Pieter, his recent vomiting forgotten.

Janet threw back her head and laughed.

She wiped her hair that instantly had plastered her face. She swept clear the brown, slick curtain and peeped across the garden before the children renewed their attack. She laughed and laughed as the thick rhododendrons wriggled against the neighbour's wall and then were still.

Suddenly, she too, was still.

The shock pulsed right through her.

She felt it black and swift and certain. There was no mistake.

It was a mistake.

She went rigid.

She was standing on the crack at the bottom of the pool.

He slept and dreamed and his dreams mocked his sleep. In the heat of his midday bed, he turned and cursed himself. In the house of his father-in-law were many rooms. But not one he could call his own. He did not feel at ease. He felt his children, the fruit of his loins, twisting and turning. It was a long hot night and now it was well past midday. He lay asleep, but waiting. From within the four warm walls of his mind came the Roepstem, came the Call. The voices were urgent and unquiet. He knew what to do. He always knew what to do. He reached under his pillow for his gun. It was at the ready. His knife was hidden, but his gun was always waiting. For who should descend into the deep but him. And with each uncomfortable sigh, he breathed in the certainty. With each breath he blessed the Lord his strength, which taught his hands to war and his fingers to fight. There was the thud of subdued flesh and the slap of recognition. There was the crunch of bone and the silent seeping of blood. Contusions and joint-popping contortions. Internal bleeding and hopeless screaming. But he blessed his God, his goodness and his fortress, his high tower and his deliverer, his shield and he in whom he trusted, who would subdue his people under him. He was fond of the psalms. But out in the darkness the monster began to walk, and the warrior slept. He was terrified.

2MM

The poverty in which most African families lived had far-reaching implications for many children. As a result, the boundaries were not always clear between childhood, adolescence and adulthood. The youth of 'school-going age' spent their days on the streets doing odd jobs and playing, but mostly taking responsibility for their siblings and homes while their parents were at work from early morning until late at night. Many had to raise cash for their families as hawkers (selling fruit, peanuts and other goods on trains and at various railway stations) and others worked full time as providers. Child labourers included 'spanner boys' who helped to fix cars and those who sold coal and firewood, as Soweto had no electricity.

> – Sifiso Mxolisi Ndlovu, *The Soweto Uprisings:*
> *Counter-memories of June 1976*

It is very difficult for me to open up and write about my husband, because it is a pain you can't describe to anyone else. My husband began to suffer from stress after being exposed on a daily basis to scenes where people had been killed, shot or maimed – to people whose decomposed remains he had to take out of the water in the course of his job as an emergency diver for the South African Police Service.

It became so bad that he began to patrol the house at night, getting up at the slightest sound and inspecting the entire house and property.

Our curtains had to be left open so that he had a clear view when he heard a sound. He sat staring through the window for hours and no one could persuade him to sleep.

– Johan Marais, *Time Bomb: A Policeman's True Story*

T he crack did not go away. No. It seemed it was there to stay.
When they trooped inside on that first day of the crack, she sensed the burden that she was going to have to carry to her husband. It seemed as though life was a spell so exquisite that something now was trying to break it.

Despite their laughter and the children's excitement that Mommy had swum in her clothes and had discovered the joys of Marco Polo and Sharky – twice! – they crept into the house.

Daddy was sleeping. Daddy was sleeping so that he could begin his new job that night when he started night shift. Wasn't that strange, she had prepared the children. Wasn't that exciting that Daddy was going to start a new job which meant that as they were going to bed, he was going to work!

Poor Pappie, Sylvia had cried out. Poor Pappie, working in the dark. What would he see but blackness? What would he do but stumble around in the scary darkness when the world was scary and black? She would be scared. She would need to hold on to Teddy and to Golly for dear life and stay warm and snug in her bed. Would she ever have to go on night ships?

Night shift! Pieter threw himself about laughing, holding his sides in a parody of mirth. Shelley prodded him as though he were a small but fairly agreeable animal.

Grow up, she said in that adult way eleven-year-old girls have. Shelley nudged him with her bare foot that had been carefully dried.

Pieter continued to roll around on the kitchen floor, holding his sides, oinking like a little brown pig. His towel came loose to reveal his slender body all muscle and bone.

Grow up, said Shelley again, appealing to her mother to step in.

Night ships, said Sylvia again, provoking arbitration. Her thumb was dangerously close to finding its way into her mouth, despite all their talk of the New Year and Revolutions.

Resolutions, Janet said automatically.

Night ships, countered Sylvia, and then they were all at it again, killing themselves laughing. Children could be brutal little beings; Janet tried to smile at their hilarity. So much energy. So chaotic. So much life and vim and vigour. Sometimes just their sheer energy exhausted her. They drained her like a glass of milk drunk fresh and cold so that all that was left was the hint of condensation on the glass and an ache in the brain from the cold, cold milk.

Would you like some milk, she asked.

Sometimes changing the subject was best. She had become rather adept at changing the subject.

They clamoured around her, including Shelley, for the milk, which she poured into identical glasses to precisely the same point. So even though they were each separated by roughly three years, she dare not distinguish between them by a fraction of a millimetre. That would unleash chaos.

They were silent now. The kitchen resounded with their quiet gulps although before she could say Marco Polo she knew that they would be at it again. Janet leaned against the old kitchen counter with its melamine surface, and savoured the quiet for a few seconds.

How their little throats pulsed with milk. It was terrifying how quickly they could demolish a large glass of icy milk. She could not bear the sterile taste of thick milk, all white and blank. It was like drinking maternal oblivion, a liquid migraine. She wondered if Noreen next door drank too much milk. That would explain things.

Janet tried to explain things. Again. Before they finished their milk.

Remember to be quiet now, she said as their little throats throbbed. Daddy needs his sleep today. Especially today.

Three pairs of eyes watched her around upended glasses. The dregs were being drained. Every last white drop.

I won, said Pieter thumping down his glass so that Janet jumped.

Pieter! scolded Shelley, her rebuke more shrill than the solid crash of his glass.

Shhhh! hissed Sylvia louder than them both.

Janet gripped the towel she had taken from her younger daughter and tightened it around her own belly. Being a mother in a wet dress with knotted brown hair did not help matters. She felt as though she should be on holiday, on the beach, carefree. Not in a wet dress, in the kitchen, playing referee.

Children, her voice snapped like a towel flicked at their damp legs. We are all to be very quiet until two pee em. That's what Daddy asked. Remember. That is expressly why we have spent the day around the pool. We could make a noise around the pool, but –

It is three pee em – Shelley pointed to the kitchen clock.

Pieter leapt in immediately. When the big hand is on the twelve and the small hand –

Pappie! yelled Sylvia –

Janet pressed a hand to her head. Even though she had drunk not a drop of milk. An hour, an entire hour had disappeared, simply slipped through some crack in the day. She could not stop trying to forget about the crack.

Yes, they could all run down the long passage to Mommy and Daddy's bedroom. Yes, go on. Each one of them could charge down to the far end of the house to Daddy and wake him up. He would be cross that they had not woken him up earlier, at two pee em like he said but it could not be helped when you were left in charge of the children, all three of them, for the entire day. Maybe not the entire day, granted, but for a major portion of their waking day. There is just so much Marco Polo and Sharky that one could tolerate before beginning to lose a grip. And the sheer volume of milk that they could drink so enthusiastically –

Janet sighed.

She could hear the rumble of Hektor-Jan down the far end of the house. He sounded fine. One never knew how he might take things. How today, on New Year's Day, after a Rip van Winkle sleep, he might take being awoken an hour late by his chlorinated and slightly sunburnt children. How would he respond if he sensed that they were crammed with cold milk. Never mind what he would do when confronted by the news of the crack. Janet wondered if she could bear to start the year with a crack. And Hektor-Jan beginning his job, no longer in the smart certainty of his uniform, but going undercover. It would have to wait. She had learned that some things would have to wait. Not all things, but some things. Mostly her things. But such is marriage. Such is marriage to a man going undercover. Also, marriage to a man who had come to live in her father's house – which was now hers. And when such a strong man has not built his own house, but lives with his wife and family in a house that his father-in-law paid to have built, then such a marriage might seem uneven, strangely lopsided perhaps. Especially when the husband is a policeman and, unlike the father-in-law, is indeed the law. So to keep the scales of justice finely balanced, she might be inclined to acquiesce too readily, to set her things to one side, to make her man seem strong, to help him to belong.

Janet put on her bright, strong face and strolled down the passage like a woman without a crack in the world. It would have to wait. Surely, it could wait –

Mommy! Sylvia yelled from behind her father as silly Mommy entered the bedroom. Silly Mommy, she announced to the bedroom like the blast of royal fanfare.

What now, her father asked. With mock agitation furrowed in his deep Afrikaans accent.

Hektor-Jan lay in state, propped up on one elbow, his children clustered around him like loyal subjects. The thick curtains dimmed the air, took the sting out of the sun, created a deep pocket in the robe of the house. For a moment Janet thought that her sunglasses had slipped from the top of her head where, magically, they still perched. The children were shadows; Hektor-Jan was a rasping mound of manliness created out of the new duvet, which in turn was a Christmas present to themselves. The air was thick with the fug of her husband's warm body. Janet could scarcely breathe and she inhaled deeply.

You have been for a swim, they tell me, Hektor-Jan's amusement radiated from the bed. Janet had to blink. After the brilliant sun and the bright milk, her eyes were struggling to adjust. She removed the sunglasses from her head and stood there obediently.

More or less, she said.

His voice rumbled from the depths of his children. More or less of a swim, he waved a meaty hand. You're soaking wet.

Janet removed the towel from her waist self-consciously. She turned her head and her back and coiled her hair in the towel, twisting it so that more water was squeezed from her hair. But she could feel drips trickling down her legs. Running in little rivulets, still, and spotting the carpet. If that were the children, she would have a fit. They would be despatched from the house with a curt Will you go and get yourself dry for goodness' sake – how many times must I tell you. Whereas Hektor-Jan urinated standing up and there was no way that she could dismiss him from his own loo with such sudden commands as she mopped up. There were some things one could not leave for Alice even though she was a live-in maid and was paid to clean up after them and had no doubt faced worse challenges in her life. How men could urinate standing up was beyond her: the abandon, the carelessness, the masculine effrontery. It distressed her more than most things and she pressed her lips together.

Janet squeezed and squeezed her hair and glanced in the dressing-table mirror hoping that Hektor-Jan would not notice the hypocritical drops of water that dotted the beige carpet.

He was wrestling with the children now.

She squeezed until her head hurt and the towel was sodden.

Hektor-Jan and Shelley and Pieter and Sylvia were a tangle of dusky limbs and loud grunts. They were trying to pin his arms down so that they could tickle him. But one hand kept escaping and sneaking around to push them off balance so that they fell against him and *he* could tickle *them*. Pap*pie*, they cried. Pap*pie*, they chortled and gurgled and were throttled with excited gasps. They were like one sixteen-limbed creature in the bed. The new duvet was in turmoil; she should never have bothered to iron the cover. Still, Alice would soon be back. And the bizarre, eight-legged human spider thrashed and squealed like an effeminate ventriloquist until one of them would knee Hektor-Jan in the privates. Then his voice would split the dark with a roar. But it was a mock-roar, half pain, half game.

It would not be long before there were tears. Van lekker lag kom lekker huil, Hektor-Jan would always warn. Lovely laughter brings lovely tears, the Afrikaans saying put it well. There were always tears.

Janet thought to escape to the en suite bathroom to fetch another towel as the children renewed their assault on their naked father. Hektor-Jan slept naked. In 1976, Janet did not know of many men who slept stark naked, but Hektor-Jan certainly did. He radiated warmth and hair and manly fumes. She was always aware of his hair. It ran in dark seams across his body. Under his arms, between his legs, up to his belly button, along his spine, across his chest and arms and legs. Lately, even his nostrils and ears had sprouted hair. He was a very hairy man. She grabbed a fresh towel and clung to its clean, dry expanse.

He was also a beautiful man. His strength and his dark good looks. Sometimes she would reach out to touch him as he slept, as though to make sure that this handsome man was indeed hers. And almost to ask the question with her hands, the soft, uncertain tips of her fingers – could this dear man, this dark, handsome man indeed be hers. She who was so ordinary and nondescript. Her figure was fine, of that she was sure. Her face was clear and her eyes – maybe her eyes were too intent. They were light brown, like her mousy hair, nothing to write home about. Not quite hazel eyes, too light for hazel and too penetrating in their utter fixity. That is what her own mother had said. No doubt when Mrs Amelia Ward had performed or uttered something typically outrageous in front of the family and Janet had bitten her tongue, and stared and stared at her bold mother, that had prompted the astringent remark: Child, your eyes. That look. Your funny little eyes so, so penetrating in their utter fixity. Those were her mother's exact words. They cut through time to be as fresh and sharp as when they were first spoken. Maybe her mother had a point. Why, sometimes she felt as though she had to remember to blink. She would gaze unblinking at the beautiful man who was her husband as he slept beside her. Even as that beauty began to be shrouded in more and more brown-black hair. She never recalled him being that hairy.

The children did not seem to mind his hair. For a moment she caught herself fearing that they might get lost in his hair, that they might vanish into all that hair, but then she smiled. Pieter was sitting on his father's head and the girls had got their father's limbs under control. He was trapped. He rumbled beneath his son. The children squealed. They had him now. But then, like a manly and rather hirsute volcano, he erupted in a thunder of ha-has and ho-hos. His children scattered across the bed shrieking with joy and Janet had to escape to the bathroom.

She slipped through the door into the bright light, then shut it. Like turning a page. Suddenly, there was peace and quiet. The peace and quiet so beloved of mothers when their children and their hairy husband were cavorting and when trouble loomed like a pram at the top of a horrible flight of steps. It nudged closer and closer and no one seemed to notice or to care. The baby inside chortled in his glee just as the front wheels tested gravity. The wheels whispered over the top before bumping, bumping down the entire flight of concrete steps. Sheer horror.

Janet sat on the side of the bath and tried to compose herself. Her damp clothes caused her to shiver, even though it was more than thirty degrees out there. The bathroom, with its soft light at the side of the house, was soothing and cool.

She placed an anxious hand on her belly.

Next door, the chaos continued. She could see it happening. Little Pieter caught in the face by a jerking elbow, Hektor-Jan's most likely, his nose blooming with blood. Shelley flying back and bumping her head, breaking her crown. And all fall down: tiny Sylvia shrieking off the edge of the bed like the baby in the pram. Falling through space before lying broken and twisted on the carpet far, far below.

Was he doing this intentionally.

There was a shriek. Then there was silence. Dear God.

Hektor-Jan opened the door of the bathroom and... and evolved into the room. He was a naked chimp. Janet looked up in surprise as he loped in. Then, before her very eyes, he lifted the lid of the loo and sat down. At least he had the nous in the house to sit down. For once.

The children, she whispered. The children.

The silence next door was ominous. Were they all dead. Had he smothered them with his father's love. Had they drowned in his hair and disappeared.

They're hiding, he whispered too, conspiratorially. Like a mocking clown.

Janet opened her mouth.

Hektor-Jan started to gush.

She closed her mouth and squirmed in her makeshift seat.

Hektor-Jan winked at her.

The towel slid from her grasp and pooled at her feet. She could only stare at her hairy husband astride the porcelain throne. Right before her in the bathroom with one hand delving between his legs as he sat there and gushed fulsomely.

Hiding, she said faintly.

Hektor-Jan nodded vaguely. His eyes seemed to turn inward as he strained.

No. He was not going to. Surely not.

It's a new game, Hektor-Jan's voice strained into her loo, which could do with a clean. Alice would be back the following day, thank goodness.

Janet leapt to attention. A new game. Not Marco Polo or Sharky inside the house.

Relax, said Hektor-Jan.

He reached for a strip of toilet paper.

Janet sprinted for the door, except her legs failed to move. She never made it.

Right before her, in the cool depths of her bathroom, Hektor-Jan leaned forward. Dear God. First the gulped milk and now this. Long gone were the days of little ankles pinned in the air by a motherly hand and the careful wiping, such careful wiping, of chubby pink cheeks as Shelley then Pieter then Sylvia cooed. Gone were the buckets of Steri-nappy and the broadsheets of cloth nappies hanging on the line like warning flags. Or a whole series of surrenders. White flags symbolising the sacrifices of body, mind and soul to her three offspring who had used her like a launching pad and had sprung free. Now they were birds flitting through the house. She clutched at her stomach and Hektor-Jan tore yet another strip of toilet paper. Janet mumbled something and again Hektor-Jan winked like it was a big joke. Then he flushed, gave a shocking squirt of air freshener and came over to where she stood, like a bedraggled butterfly – no, a moth – about to take flight.

The sun had turned his skin dark and bronzed. With all his hair and his summer skin he could be a different species. Even a different racial classification in this South Africa obsessed with racial classification. Obsessed like children colouring in with different shades of black, white, yellow and brown. Or kids messing around with pastels labelled white and non-white, blankes and nie-blankes. Or poo and nappies. Crisp white towelling blowing in the breeze or poo on toilet paper or nappies stuck bleaching in a bucket of Steri-nappy. Did that make sense. Goosebumps pricked her flesh and Hektor-Jan knelt before her and placed his warm hands around her back and pulled her towards him. Last night –

The towel lay crumpled on the floor and he pulled her close so that his cheek rested against her belly as he knelt there like a subservient ape, her very own Hektor-Jan, her husband who was about to go on night shift. She could smell him, as though he were turning lavender at the edges, and now his warm face pressed close to her belly through her damp, cool dress, and she stopped standing there like a startled bird and began to stroke his head. There, beneath her fingers, was the one place on his body where there was supposed to be hair and there was now less and less hair. Her Hektor-Jan was growing bald despite the recent sprouting from nose and ears, or perhaps because of it. A sudden shift in the balance of hair.

The new job will help, he said from the depths of her stomach and for a moment she thought that it would help him grow hair. That the new job under the cover of night, his promotion, would somehow promote the growth of hair on the top of his head. Top secret could become toupee secret.

He chuckled as though sensing her confusion. His naked flesh wobbled beneath her and he held her more tightly.

Just over seven months to go, he rumbled below her.

She nodded, which he could not hear. Yes, she said softly, which he did not hear.

What would you like, he said. A boy or another girl.

You just never know, she said.

What's that, he asked.

Just seven months to go, she said. Aren't you glad I kept all those nappies.

He did not move. Just knelt there warm and close as her hand fondled the hair on his thinning scalp. She could not bring herself to mention the crack. Not there. Not then. Not whilst her beautiful grown man knelt like a little lost boy before her and the children were mercifully though suspiciously quiet somewhere in the house. But then she was gripped by fear and a dread of lavender. It was like a sharp screwdriver of scented lavender had been driven between them and she was wedged apart from him. She needed to let go this hairy man no matter how handsome he was. She had to remove the cloying dress that trapped her in its damp folds. For a moment, again, her arms were wings and she had to fly free. She managed not to emit a loud squawk. That would have startled Hektor-Jan. It might have bowled him over or made him instantly bald. You never knew with shock. You just never knew. And she blamed the crack. She feared for her husband and she could not burden him with the crack. She did not want him to get how he got. She would speak to Solomon, see what he said.

Gently but firmly, she extricated herself from his grasp. His warmth peeled away and she was free. Free to escape to the bedroom whilst he knelt there beside the bath, his back to the loo.

The curtains were still closed in the bedroom and the house was in a state of warm hush. If she closed her eyes she could sense her children hiding. They formed part of the fabric of the hot afternoon as Shelley, Pieter and Sylvia fused with the cloth of heavy curtains – hid in the hanging folds – or insinuated themselves under chairs and behind the opacity of doors. Janet was tight-lipped in the gloom.

Whilst Hektor-Jan knelt in silence in the bathroom, she slipped out of the clasp of her dress and quickly freed herself from the moist clutches of her bra and panties. The smell of chlorine suddenly rose from her skin, and she patted her damp flesh that, in the sudden chill of nakedness, did not feel like her skin. It could well be the flesh – goosed, cold, oddly lifeless – of another, as though she inhabited the body of a stranger.

Janet patted her arms and her belly just to make sure, to instil a sense of life, but her hands, too, were cold. She would have to go back into the bathroom where her husband still knelt. Would he remain there until it was time to start work.

Janet crept to the door, slipped in and ran a quick hand to the peg on the other side of the door. Then she was back in the safe gloom, pulling the white towelling gown over her skin so sticky with cold and goosebumps. For a moment she felt as though she were pulling on a large nappy, such was the texture of the gown. She stood, then sat on the edge of the bed, wrapped like a large white present, a baby-adult, in white towelling that scratched with the precise texture of new babies' nappies. More Christmas presents to themselves. A His and Hers towelling robe for moments just like this. Beautifully scratchy and stark white with a firm towelling cord to tie around your belly and keep you safe and secure. Beneath the tight circumference of the belt that kept her together, Janet felt the new life within her begin to move. It was early days yet, she knew, but she fancied that she could feel him move. And she knew, just knew, that it was a he, a boy-child. Sometimes, she pictured him climbing around inside her like his father, a little hairless version of his father, a tiny monkey with precious limbs, and she beamed as he swung from the liana of his umbilical cord and she felt him dangle within her. She smiled to herself and patted her precious cargo beneath the firm belt. Hektor-Jan in the bathroom, and Hektor-Jan inside her. A world of Hektor-Jans. One hairy but going bald, the other bald but soon to grow hair. She held her breath and from deep within her came a tremulous scream. It wavered and warbled. Come and get me, it screamed with a ghoulish voice and she realised that it was Shelley or Pieter, probably, and that they were growing impatient. They expected her to come and get them and, once again, she had confused herself with her house. God knows, she had lived here long enough. But her children were deep within the house, not her. The scream came from them, not from her womb.

Tying her hair back, Janet pulled her face into shape and with a brave mother's smile she pantomimed the exaggerated steps of the huntress. Into the passage she went. I am coming to get you, she called with an actress's voice. She brightened considerably. This could be good practice for the show. When was the first rehearsal. She would need to check the schedule clamped to the fridge door by the magnets Pieter had given her for Christmas. A cluster of metal miracles that clung to the fridge like desperate children – a whole coloured alphabet of scrambled letters that currently spelled words like YEAR, HAPPY, NEW and GOD on the great white coral reef of the fridge. That was Shelley, mocking her little brother's not-so-subtle hints for a DOG. It was his birthday soon. He himself was almost a Christmas present eight years ago. Now he was turning nine and the only thing his little heart desired was a DOG. Some furry puppy to replace old Jock. Jock who had suddenly died the week before Christmas and who was still keenly missed. That was why Shelley was so bitter. How could one replace Jock with another dog – which Pieter, with profound originality, wanted to call Jock – and why did GOD kill their DOG? Did GOD move in mysterious ways? Or was it just like Father Christmas and the Easter Bunny? Someone else all along? Shelley was insistent. There came that look in her eyes, which could be described only as a look of utter fixity. She was too angry to cry. Speak to your father, Janet had said, but Shelley would not speak to her father. Not on that subject. She pestered her mother.

Janet smiled as she crept down the passage that ran like a rich, deep vein through the house, the conduit of all domestic traffic. She felt again the crisp towelling scratch her skin beautifully and she held the simultaneous thoughts of puppy and fridge and Shelley and God and the play and Jock and Pieter in her mother's mind. Anything to escape the sound of smearing excrement and the deeper sense of the crack at the bottom of the pool. Coming to get you, she boomed in her most resonant, theatrical voice and Sylvia squealed away her position under the dining-room table. Comin' ta get ya, Janet put on an American accent, and then an Irish accent. And then she whispered the words, a chilling psychopath.

Gently, she patrolled the perimeter of the table pretending not to hear the tiny squeals of excitement that semaphored Sylvia's position. Where can Sylvia be, she mused aloud like Donald Duck, prompting further smug hilarity whilst Pieter shouted, Come and get me! from behind the lounge door. It was only her older daughter who had the good sense to secrete herself with silence into some dark space. For a shiver of a second, Janet worried that Shelley might have pushed the boundaries of the game and had perhaps gone to the pool and lay hidden in the crevices of the crack. Quickly, she pulled Sylvia from under the table and exposed Pieter in a flash. Aw, man, he squawked his disgust at being the second one to be found yet again – always the second one – and Janet hurried through the rest of the rooms in search of her eldest child. Where could she be.

Shelley! Janet called. Can we have a clue.

Pieter muttered under his breath about his stupid sister always stealing the best spot, and Sylvia giggled uncontrollably. Janet rounded on them. Where is she. She gripped their arms and pulled them close. Where is she. Tell me where she is hiding.

Pieter, it turned out, did not know, and Sylvia was simply giggling because it was just so funny. Crossly, Janet let them go and plunged back into the dining room. This was not good. This was not fun. First Pieter being sick, then the crack, then nosy neighbours, then the milk and now this. What more could go wrong on 1 January 1976. Why couldn't she and her strong husband still be in the intimate garage on the stroke of midnight. If only Alice were back now, instead of the day after tomorrow –

Shelley! Her voice screeched like chalk against the board of the house. Sylvia put her hands to her ears and Pieter chortled all the louder. Why did little boys find maternal distress such fun, Janet wondered for the umpteenth time and thought about the ridiculous calm that Hektor-Jan always displayed when she was at her most fraught, when the situation actually demanded emotion. When Jock choked that time on the bone and almost died. When the dirty sparrow fell down the chimney and squirted distress all over the lounge and it took Janet's piercing scream to drive it out into the entrance hall and then right out through the front door. That time when Pieter stubbed his toe beside the pool and cried himself senseless as the top of his toe flapped loose and leaked dark streams of blood.

Shelley! Janet's voice seemed to want to pierce the walls of the house and prise her loose. Shelley! Each exclamation was a detonation. From room to urgent room, shadowed all the while by a merry Pieter and his paralytic little sister.

Shelley!

And then she was there. Right in front of her. As though she had been standing there all along and saying, Yes, Mom, as cool and insouciant as you like and Janet feeling the palm of her right hand itch and having consciously to restrain her right hand with her left hand as though she was made up of two separate mothers: one wanting to hug her daughter who was safe and sound and found, the other about to knock her cheeky block off.

Instead, Janet stood there in a tangled limbo, and tried very brightly to say, Shelley!

Yes, Mom, said Shelley again. I cannot believe you didn't see me. She actually smiled and put one mocking hand on her little girl's hip.

Janet's right hand whipped free and for an instant she had struck the smirk from Shelley's face. Knocked it clean to the other side of the room.

But jumping back from that fork in the road, Janet instead threw her arm around her daughter and pulled her close into a brutal hug. Shelley, she whispered into the damp on the top of her daughter's head, which was already so close to Janet's chin. As long as you are here, safe and found.

But you didn't find me, Shelley's voice insisted from the painful, towelling embrace. I helped you by coming out. You would never find me. It's my best place ever.

Where? Where? screamed Pieter and Sylvia took up the chant. Where? Where?

Not telling, murmured Shelley. She smiled as she imagined an eleven-year-old sphinx might smile and repeated, You will never guess.

And so Pieter kicked her. Simply raised his right foot, with the thin scar across the top of his big toe, and kicked her hard on the shin. His toe was hard, but Shelley's shin was harder. There was an ugly cracking sound and it was Pieter who fell back howling and clutching his foot in agony. Janet and her youngest child gasped but the sphinx barely blinked and then uttered the brightest, most vatic peal of laughter.

It was some time before the troubled waters subsided: before Shelley emerged from her room to which she had been banished, before Pieter's foot and toe were sufficiently swaddled in bandages to render him silent and satisfied. Sylvia had been gainfully employed with a damp facecloth, which she used to mop Pieter's brow, much to his and her pleasure and Janet was just about to begin to make Hektor-Jan's fried breakfast in earnest.

Isn't this fun, Janet had said as Shelley cracked two eggs into the old saucer and Pieter separated four rashers of bacon.

I want breakfast, Sylvia had countered and the cry had been taken up by the other two, sudden allies in the campaign to eat breakfast with Pappie before he went off into the sunset on his night ships.

The fight quite gone from her heart, Janet relented.

After thirty minutes of domestic carnage which featured broken eggs half-scrambled, half-fried and two rascally rashers of bacon that made a bid for freedom onto the floor, they were ready to eat. There was fried tomato, fried banana, fried bread, and the usual eggs and bacon and toast. Hektor-Jan was summoned and they all sat squashed in the breakfast nook, their plates loaded in front of them.

At last, Janet could sit still. The perpetual motion of motherhood shifted gear and she paused, her food momentarily forgotten. Her thoughts turned to *Brigadoon*, the forthcoming play, and her role as bonnie Jean. And then, as her family chomped and chewed and idly requested more tomato sauce – of which there was none, but now added to the shopping list for tomorrow – rising up from beneath the mists of *Brigadoon*, there came the sense of a fissure. In the very fabric of her mind, in the deepest tissue of herself, there came again the ringing sound of concrete splitting and the image of the crack – which lurked like guilt and fear and things forgotten and not yet bought for the pantry – at the bottom of the swimming pool.

Janet blinked and, like her family, tried to lose herself in the swabbing of yellow blood from the haphazardly fried yolks. She clung to half a slice of toast and smeared the bright chaos around her plate. Thank goodness there was no more tomato sauce. The yellow was garish enough. There was almost the sense of her plate shouting at her, so vivid was the yellow yolk and Janet – as ever – tried not to think that they were all eating the brilliant liquid feathers of chicks which had not been born, little chicks that now would never be born owing to the fact that they were eating them for breakfast – at night. Janet lowered her toast in a trembling hand. There, in a long line down some imagined supermarket aisle, there was now added another neat box of a dozen eggs, twelve more chicks that would never cheep endearments to their mother hen. And there was Hektor-Jan wiping the last yellow blotches from his moustache. Janet wanted to spread her wings – her arms – around her little chicks and hold them close. But it was too late. Hektor-Jan was off. He was off to brush his teeth and then he would be heading into the night on his night ships. Little Sylvia was looking sad and the children got up.

Coffee, said Janet, and Hektor-Jan paused in his flight from the table.

Ja, his voice rumbled with pleasure. Ja, of course. He sat down. With a lordly gesture, he spread his arms wide and placed his hands behind his head. His stomach jutted fiercely from his solid frame and he smiled.

Of course, his new shift could be delayed for another minute or two, however long it took her to pour the oily black coffee into a mug and stir in three spoons of sugar so that the white granules were embraced by the black coffee, were forever fused with the black coffee. And then the white milk turning the stark black liquid a beautiful brown. She handed her husband his mug of coffee and turned to face the gun.

There before her stood Pieter pointing a gun.

It was Hektor-Jan's gun. Heavy and thick and black, it shook in Pieter's little white hand. Pieter might as well be holding a bomb or a black rat or a crack. And it strained, ready to jump and bite her, ready to explode in her face and in her kitchen, ready to shatter her world to smithereens. Her life stood still – the loaded gun –

Stick 'em up, said Pieter with the curt, hostile enthusiasm of a young boy. Stick 'em up, Mommy. I said, stick 'em up.

It was a filthy imperative in such a small, cherubic mouth.

The gun waved in his hands. It leered drunkenly at her. The little boy could not hold the weight of the gun. It lurched and swung in front of her.

Pieter, she tried to gasp. Pieter, her face twisted as she tried to scream. Pieter! But no sound came. And then there was the laughter of Sylvia as well as Pieter as they watched their mother pulling the funniest face and making the strangest noises. And then there was their father's laughter. Their Pa, who was always ready for a laugh. How his barrel chest brought forth deep guffaws. They filled the kitchen now, poured like thunderous waves into the kitchen as Janet seemed to drown.

Gulping, the gun, the guffaws, she was at sea in her own little kitchen.

I don't think Mommy likes that, said Shelley in a soft clear voice. I don't think –

Bang! yelled Pieter. Bang!

Hierso, seun, said Hektor-Jan in his native Afrikaans. Here, son. Gee my die rewolwer. Give me the gun.

Pieter knew when the game was up. Render unto Caesar – he meekly handed over the gun. From his little hand, the ugly weapon passed into his father's meaty paw. Hektor-Jan hefted the weapon thoughtfully. He looked at Janet. Her face slowly settled back into her usual features of motherly calm, a special form of stoicism.

Holster, he said to Pieter. Gaan haal hom. Go and get it. And the bullets.

Again Janet's face twisted as her tiny son returned trailing the dark-brown holster and a fistful of live ammunition. She watched as Pieter handed over one golden bullet after another and his father inserted them into the waiting chamber which he had snapped open from the belly of the gun.

Why this ritual. Why did Hektor-Jan insist on this ridiculous farce every morning – and now, Janet supposed, it would be every night. And she could not stop herself. Each day the shock of the gun. The ghastly paradox of innocent Pieter and the beastly gun. Was it because Hektor-Jan had grown up on the farm with guns and dogs and killing. Hardly a farm. It was more of a smallholding near Springs, further and deeper into the East Rand, past Benoni, further away from the English city of Johannesburg. Hektor-Jan and his rough older brothers had enjoyed free rein of a stretch of veld and scrub and trees, small koppies, little hills and a vlei, a stagnant pool where they shot birds with their .22 rifles, guns that seemed to grow on trees while little birds fell from them. He was only eight for God's sake. He said he was eight years old when he went off alone with a rifle and killed his first tarentaal, a kind of quail, all by himself. Just he and about seven brakke, seven mangy inbred dogs that got in the way, but which also got the injured quail that scuttled into the long grass bleeding to death. On the farm, you were self-reliant. On the farm, if you didn't stand up for yourself your older brothers and their friends would beat you down until you had to stand up for yourself. You grew up quickly: you had to. Was he sad. Was he sad that he missed a childhood of Enid Blyton, of Noddies and Big Earses and Famous Fives. And Hektor-Jan had laughed deeply in her arms and had said, No. He and his brothers were the Famous Four and that they took no kak, no shit, from anyone. And so it seemed natural to join the police after the army. When you were good with guns and used to shooting things and full of camaraderie and excitement, who would not want to join the South African Police Force. And he would like Pieter to get used to handling a gun. So that when it came to shooting a gun he would not shit himself like some Engelse dorpsjapie, like some little English town-boy who could not tell his elbow from his arse, his gun from his bum. Hence the ritual, every day. And every day her shock at the unpalatable heist in her kitchen, held up by her own son every day and every day the jolt got worse, not better. She seemed to shove it deep into some back drawer of her mind with the other cluttered mess of things and so, each day, Pieter and the gun was a shock to be experienced anew. It was something to which she dare not become inured. What would happen if she failed to respond with mordant horror. Janet caught her breath. Sylvia loved the drama but Shelley, older, wiser Shelley, shook her head and tried to be brushing her teeth when it happened. And then Pieter had to be taken down a peg or two once his father left –

Hektor-Jan himself just laughed to see such fun.

Janet's hands trembled under the cover of the dish-towel. It was done for another day. Time to file it away.

Shelley's Secret Journal

Word for the day from Granny's list is INDUBITABLE.
Pieter kicked me and hurt his toe. In some ways God is indubitable but maybe not with animals. We had breakfast for supper as Pappie is starting night shift with no uniform any more. We slept in after a late

night. Mommy and Pappie did some skinny-dipping and played in the garden. I watched them but then Pappie carried Mommy into the garage. It was quiet for a long time. Today Mommy fell in the pool. We played Sharky and Marco Polo. It has been sixteen days since Jock was murdered. I shall not forget. I shall not turn the other cheek as they say in church. I shall keep this journal like you asked me, Granny, but I will try to write more neatly. The indubitable blisters on my hands have now peeled leaving skin that is red and lumpy. That makes me remember and I try not to cry. I still do not know why Jock had to die. It was terrible. He kissed Mommy indubitably right near Jock's grave. Happy New Year. Shelley.

Hektor-Jan lumbered off to do his teeth and to finish getting ready.

When their father returned with clean teeth and his gun snugly secured in his dark-brown holster, they could hug him and hug him. So strange now to have a father no longer in uniform. No longer the crisp, starched sense of their burly father pressed into a uniform with medals and names and a rank on his sleeve. He did not look as if he was going to work. He looked like they should all be going to the drive-in, to see a fliek about *The Island at the Top of the World* or *Escape to Witch Mountain* maybe. They should be going with him to have some fun and so they clung to him like human limpets.

Janet tried yet again not to think about her children and the gun, tried to bury the thoughts in that back drawer and to wipe her hands clean of the memory with the rough dish-towel. She did not want to think about her husband and his gun which clung like a misshapen appendage at his waist. Dangled there for all the world to see. Although that was now to change. No more uniform. All plain clothes now and Hektor-Jan was very likely to get a shoulder-holster he said. Something to hide the gun. So that he could slip amongst the bad guys and not be noticed until it was too late. And then he would get the bad guys, just like that, and Hektor-Jan had snapped his fingers like the sound of concrete cracking and Janet had gasped and had almost bitten her tongue.

And then he had hugged her and had told her to finish all her breakfast like a good girl and he had kissed her on the top of her head and he was gone, walking in slow motion like a great ship covered in barnacles. His barnacles emitted high-pitched laughter that Pappie could be so strong and that they could ride on him all the way to the front door. Then Hektor-Jan began the patient process of scraping them off one by one, peeling off their arms and legs and lowering them to the ground and hardly breathing heavily as they attempted to leap back on to him. Then it was final goodbyes and a soft, Look after your Ma now.

The front door closed with a bang and the car went growling into the distance.

The children were mooching around like morose puppies – no more barnacles at all, but puppies abandoned by their father, the one with whom they had such fun.

Cheer up, she had called loudly, staring at her plate across the kitchen. Her hands worked busily beneath the dish-towel.

Go and get your books, she had called again to their silence. Time for some Secret Sevens and Famous Fives. What about *The Children of Willow Tree Farm* and, Sylvia, I'll read some Noddy to you.

Pieter poked his head into the kitchen and gave her a withering look. From live ammunition and a real gun to Julian and George and dogs with such stupid names and everything set in some old England somewhere and the pictures of stupid curly-haired children who exclaimed Oh, I say and drank lashings of homemade lemonade. Pieter made some disgruntled remark, but his mother let it go.

And so they lay straggled about the lounge, her litter of puppies, all curled up with Enid Blyton and nice, safe stories where everything worked out in the end and the children triumphed and there was a distinct and pleasant dearth of dangerous weapons.

After she tucked them up in bed – no need to bath after a day spent in the pool – Janet kissed them goodnight: first Sylvia and then Pieter, who said he was sorry that he had frightened her, as he said sorry every night and then did exactly the same terrible thing the next day. He said sorry and asked her to kiss his bandaged toe. She kissed his toe and patted him on his tousled head. Night, night, she said. Then, last of all, her sensible daughter Shelley, who put away whatever she was scribbling on and who held her close and whispered encouragement in her mother's ear, as though she was the one to look after her poor, dear mother and that, in the final reckoning, it would be all right in this busy house.

And Janet would blow them kisses and switch off their lights as though she was never going to see them again. Such fond nightly farewells! Their little hot bodies shrouded by a thin sheet in the stifling warmth of a midsummer night, and glasses of water in easy reach and the faint incense of mosquito repellent. And she closed the doors to the little crypt chapels, a votive priestess following some sacred rite. Amen, she breathed as her trinity of tiny warm prayers drifted into heavenly slumber. Amen. Amen.

That night, for the first time on 1 January 1976, Janet was alone.

There was no Hektor-Jan. There was no Alice doing the last of the dishes and asking if they wanted a mug of Milo. And there was no Jock with his doggy dreaming and soft farts in this declension of household routine.

Janet stood alone in the lounge. At her feet, the open wings of Enid Blyton's flights of fancy lay stretched. Janet stood silently for a long while. It seemed that she herself was poised for flight, not ready to rest. She switched off the last of the lights in the house and remained standing in the dark. Her mother's mind went out to her children, both born and unborn. Almost without knowing it, she made her way into the spare bedroom, into the room already set aside for the new baby. In the darkest womb of the house she stood, feeling the squareness of the house, its brick-and-mortar solidity. She needed to feel such certainty. Maybe it was the hormones, maybe an accumulation of the sudden attacks by Pieter and the gun. She sighed. She did not know. She did not want to know. For a long while she stood there, her hand resting on one smooth wall. She thought of her children sleeping peacefully. She thought of the baby brooding just below her heart. And she thought of her largest child of all, Hektor-Jan, heading off into the night, into the darkness of the night with his little gun and his tiny bullets and she smiled a soft, small smile. Hektor-Jan tried. For all his shortcomings, he certainly tried. She returned to the previous night and her lips parted as she felt him again. When they were together she knew who she was and what to do. She did not have to think at all. Her skin did not have to think and his hands and body were immediate and unambiguous. Her hands were sure and certain, swift and secure. The precise opposite of her mother. The bulk of Hektor-Jan dispelled the sense of her mother and she sighed a soft sound, a moan of remembered pleasure. All could be well. She moved with the memory of those warm moments.

And before she knew it, Janet found herself outside in the dull brilliance of the back garden. To one side, she could feel the shadowy fronds of the weeping willow. Then across the black grass there came the sound of the chugging Kreepy Krauly busy swallowing the pool, ingesting all that liquid tarmac. Cleaning-cleaning-cleaning, the heartbeat of the night. The scent of the giant pine tree next door, distilled and coaxed into even more intense life in the humid air, came to her and, once again, Janet stood at the edge of the pool.

The dew fell steadily and the sky reeled with stars. Janet tried to lift her head, but she was afraid that she might end up in the black water. Chug-chug-chug went the Kreepy Krauly beneath her feet. Above her the Southern Cross tilted on its silent axis. Hektor-Jan's belt became Orion's Belt and it slipped loose. Right across the sky, the stars glistened brightly and Janet swooned.

Catching herself, on an impulse, Janet stepped back and out of her clothes. Inexplicably and with such ease, Janet was cloaked in nothing but the night. The soft, warm Highveld air swaddled her and she stood at the foot of the swimming pool. Yes. It was unmistakable. Running down the length of the pool came the certain crack. For a very long time, Janet stood there not knowing what to do. Her feet shuffled apart. Was she a living dowser, a female divining rod made naked and ready to yield to the subtle, teasing pull of such rhabdomantic forces she neither acknowledged nor understood, unlike the very loquacious man they hired before the borehole was drilled. She felt the gentle air whisper through her hair and from the top of her head down to the skin right at the bottom of her toes of her parted feet Janet felt the ground shift. She knew the certainty, the very fact of the crack. It was as though it had split her clothes from her body and rendered her white skin naked to the African night. She dwelt in possibility. The spreading-wide of her narrow hands to gather – yes, to gather – to gather anything. Anything was possible.

For a long time Janet stood there and waited. For what, she had no idea.

When the front door slammed and he stood in front of the house, he paused. His limbs still sang with the warmth of his children. Slowly, his skin cooled. His breathing settled. His children were the three-stroke motor which propelled his life. They and their thin, anxious mother. His own internal dynamo, flesh of his flesh, heart of his heart. He strode to his Ford Cortina, the little family car, and hefted his body inside. It was a snug fit. Then he inserted the key and turned it. The car roared. Briefly, he felt as though he spoke with the throat of the car, that its roar was his roar. God knows, he spent enough time tuning it, trying to squeeze every last bit of power out of it. He reached under the seat and drew out a secret bottle. Glancing left and right, to the shrubbery and to the lawn, he took a long slug of witblits – white lightning. He opened his mouth and again the little car roared. He had to roar for he knew that neither great goodness nor great wickedness could be achieved by a man devoid of courage. He needed courage. One did not work for the South African Police Force in 1975 – now 1976 – without courage. Without conviction. The witblits traced his soul with a finger of fire. He shook at the thought of the night. At the great darkness to come. Ja, sekerheid. Hy het krag nodig. He needed certainty – and courage. For Janet and Shelley and Pieter and Sylvia he was greatly in need of courage. His hands trembled. He tried to stop them. Then he closed his mouth. Then he was gone.

4MM

The Soweto Uprising, 1976

Since February of 1976, anger had been mounting over the regime's enforcement of Afrikaans as a medium of instruction – an anger very rapidly directed against the whole system of 'Bantu Education'. First introduced in 1955, Bantu Education was designed not merely to place every possible obstacle in the way of the intellectual development of black Africans, but consciously to create an enslaved proletariat exploitable as cheap labour.

> – Weizmann Hamilton writing in *Inqaba Ya Basebenzi (Fortress of the Revolution)*

My application was successful, and I was assigned to Riot Unit 6, with its headquarters in Bedford Avenue, Benoni. This unit was one of the first specifically focused on combating riots, and we began to practise new methods and techniques, using new equipment.

Our activities weren't limited to riot control. We were also involved in the combat of urban terror, the penetration of buildings and diving operations, and we provided support to the Security Branch and the Murder and Robbery Unit. Over the next few years, my specialised training at Verdrag and Maleoskop near Groblersdal included dealing with counter-insurgence and urban terror.

– Johan Marais, Time Bomb: A Policeman's True Story

Not knowing when the dawn would come, she opened every door of her father's house. And so it came to pass: the action that would settle itself into solid habit. In the dark hours of the early morning when Hektor-Jan was on night shift, Janet would wander through the house making sure that each door was open, that her children were safe and breathing peacefully. In those summer months she would open the back door too. Open up the house to the deep scents of the garden and the last peals of the ringing crickets. And she would wander the house like a ghost, remembering her childhood.

She had grown up in that house. It was her father's and mother's house, designed and built by them all those years ago. She had arrived in that house as a baby, and here she was, bringing forth more babies into the world. The bedroom where Pieter snuffled in his sleep had been her bedroom as a child. The bedroom where Hektor-Jan made babies on her, indeed with her, had been the very bedroom in which she herself was conceived by a twinkle in her father's eye, as he used to say.

His eyes twinkled less these days. He had given up the family home to the next generation, and to help out his only child who had married a policeman, an Afrikaner policeman, who brought new expressions and blunt thoughts to his house, but not much money. Yes, to give him his due, Hektor-Jan (strange name) did bring forth beautiful children. That Frederick Ward could not deny. And so Frederick Ward had given his thin daughter a surer footing, if being made a mother three times over could be called having a more certain foothold on life. His tiny Nettie became Mrs Janet Snyman and she swelled with life, with Shelley then

Pieter then little Sylvia. And now her belly was beginning to bulge with another one and Janet knew that her father had happily made space by moving into the retirement home on the outskirts of Benoni, into one of the largest set of retirement complexes in the southern hemisphere, it was believed.

Her mother was less retiring.

At first it was rather funny. The onset of Old Timers' Disease. Do all old people get Old Timers'? Sylvia asked her grandmother as only Sylvia could ask. At that stage Janet's mother was able to laugh brightly and scoop Sylvia into her lap. That was only a year ago, or maybe two years ago.

Then Janet watched and her father watched as the little bird of a woman they knew and loved flew away into folds of wrinkled skin and into twisted plots of tangled undergrowth. The sudden penchant for fresh tissues. The children watched in awe as Granny teased a tissue from its box like a wizened magician and then, with a flourish, ate it right in front of them. Do it again! yelled Pieter. Do it again, Gran! And she did. As though partaking of the finest cucumber sandwich, Mrs Amelia – never Millie, only Amelia – Ward lifted another tissue from its lunchbox and ate it. All the while, the children said, she chatted about her life as a lecturer in English Lit. and part-time dance teacher before the Art Writers got her hands and she had to stop. Pieter would not stop laughing. Do it again, Gran. Do it again! And he watched the tissue slowly vanish, until it left a ragged white rim around her lips. As though she was foaming at the mouth. Pieter laughed and laughed.

But it was not so funny when she called him over to her and asked him to escort her around the garden. Hand in hand they strolled across the lawn towards the pool. And then she had stopped and adjusted her dress and had performed a little twirl before him. Beside the wild spray of pampas grass in the far corner of the garden, the razor-sharp pampas grass that hid the giant compost heap, Pieter's dear old granny had tried to kiss him. She had clasped him to her and then had pursed her lips and opened wide her mouth.

I thought she was going to eat me, Pieter said tearfully, trying not to accuse his granny of being the wolf. Her tongue came out and so did her teeth and she tried to suck my lips and lick them and her teeth sucked back into her face and made a gross sound and I screamed and Granny asked haven't you got any balls young man.

Then it was the fixation with peeling carrots.

Then Amelia Ward tried to seduce Solomon the gardener when Janet was at the shops and the kids were at school. Alice said that Solomon asked her what was going on as he was almost dragged inside on the pretext of opening a jammed wardrobe door. Then Amelia Ward made her move and Solomon had to scream for Alice as the old Madam grabbed and would not let him go and Solomon and Alice and Janet swore that they could tell no one, but it was time that her mother received specialised care. Her father knew that, of course. He had been trying to avoid it. He wept the first time they left his dear Amelia in her room in Arendts Care Home situated close to the top of the town along the Atlas Road. Janet was left to hug her father – and to remind him to remove any tissues from her mother's reach whilst Amelia Ward – née Amis MA – danced around her single-room cell, waltzing in a sprightly fashion to the grand symphonies of an imaginary orchestra. Or tartly lectured the somnolent inhabitants of the communal lounge on the finer points of Keats's odes or the lesser-known novels of Henry James.

Janet thought about her neat, trim mother as she wandered through the dawn. The horizon flushed above the neat suburb. There was bird-song and there would be – yes, there it was, she winced – the raucous call of the pair of Hadedas that flew past every morning en route to the Bunny Park, the huge park that lay on the other side of the road, opposite their house. Bring me the sunrise in a cup, Janet thought with longing as she returned to the kitchen – and the kettle boiled and she set up the teapot and the light outside grew bright and bold. She stirred in clouds of milk and a shower of sugar, enough to take the edge off the rough tea, making it soft and smooth.

Then she sat back, alone in the lightening kitchen. One hand held her teacup poised beneath her throat whilst her free hand came to rest on her belly. Her thoughts turned to Alice's welcome return. It would be so good to see her after her fortnight's leave. The children would be overjoyed too. It would be like having Granny back, fit and well. Someone always there, to talk to and to listen. Her lovely Alice – bring me Alice with the sunrise –

She admired Alice. Always so cheerful. Always so happy. Singing as she worked. As she polished the wooden floors of the house on Mondays, did the windows on Tuesdays, washed and ironed the bed linen on Wednesdays, beat all the rugs on Thursdays and had her picnic parties with the other maids under the willow tree during Friday lunchtimes. Always neatly presented in her pink or blue or yellow maid's outfit: the dress, apron and doek all in soothing gingham. Her lovely curves accentuated by the neat pattern, her polished face beautiful above the pastel shades. The children loved her too. Alice! Alice! Alice! They would follow her like a tangle of puppies showing her things and telling her all sorts of childish nonsense, which she never minded. Her demure laughter like the sound of Africa. Full of health and vitality. Fresh and alive. Yes, she had such a soft spot for Alice. Right now, she could do with Alice bustling helpfully in the kitchen, singing. She really could.

Janet put the teacup to her lips but the tea was already finished. She poured herself another cup, but it was cold and not very nice.

Janet set to work on supper.

She had promised Hektor-Jan that, after his first night ship, she would make him his favourite supper. Boerewors with pap and sous: thick, jutting sausages with a maize-meal mash and a sauce made from onions, garlic and tomato. And a big bowl of Angel Delight, the instant dessert – banana flavoured.

As she cooked, she wondered what sort of night he had had. She hoped it was a quiet one. More of a desk job now, Hektor-Jan had said, perhaps more pen-pushing than running around after the criminal element. Janet never tried to peel back the plastic wrapping around that phrase. Unlike the coil of boerewors that she had just liberated from its shop packaging, she did not want to let thoughts of the criminal element loose in her home. And neither did Hektor-Jan.

Janet made the maize-meal pap as the tomato and onion sauce bubbled gently. Checking the kitchen clock, Janet heated the large frying pan and finally looped in the boerewors. There was a stinging hiss which quickly settled into a merry sizzle and Janet placed a large plate in the warming drawer. She set the table and jumped as her three children appeared in the doorway, drawn from their dreams by the smell and sounds of cooking.

I told you, said Shelley.

So what, said Pieter, I don't care.

We thought you were Alice, little Sylvia stumbled into the kitchen. Pieter and me said it's Alice but Shelley was right. It's only you.

Of course it's me, just me, Janet scooped her up and pressed her face into her youngest's sleepy curls. The scent of a tiny blonde girl, just woken up.

Pieter threw himself at the table and chairs. What's for breakfast? he said. What are you cooking for breakfast?

Janet started to point out that it was his father's special breakfast, but then, laughing at his sullen face, she threw the rest of the boerewors into the pan that hissed and spat afresh. Let's all eat supper with Dad, she said and Pieter looked at Shelley and Shelley smiled.

When it was all ready, Hektor-Jan arrived home on perfect cue to a little family gathered in his honour.

And his favourite supper was waiting for him and they were all going to eat it for breakfast just as the previous night they had breakfasted together in this topsy-turvy new routine.

Hektor-Jan went to wash his face and hands, and to store his gun.

How was it, Janet asked as he feasted.

The children had tucked into their unusual breakfasts and were silently chewing their way along the steaming brown snakes of boerewors, attacking them and eating them right back into their lairs of fluffy white pap. Hektor-Jan shook his head. His mouth was full and he never talked work in front of the children. Then he smiled and gave the thumbs up.

And did you all have a good night, he asked once he had swallowed his last mouthful of supper at 6.45 a.m.

He had parked the car in its usual spot, returned the bottle to its hiding place deep beneath the seat, took a big breath and then marched into his father-in-law's house. And as he took more and deeper breaths, there came the cries of his children and the soft smile of their mother. He was home. Safe and sound. He breakfasted on his favourite food. Food from his youth. Food from his innocent past. It was good. And the children still tousled from sleep were beautiful. Then he escaped to the bathroom. In the shower, as the hot and powerful water jetted down on him, he thought about what a baptism of fire that first night had been. The water drilled into his scalp and almost burned him, but it needed to be that way. The bathroom door was closed and the shower door was closed. The white towel lay waiting, its folds ready to receive him. The water beat down and he felt out the scrubbing brush and the block of soap with his powerful, stubby fingers. And then he began to scrub. First those very fingers that held the brush and the soap. There was no blood, no trace of short wiry hair under his nails, but he made sure. There was no blood that had sprayed up onto his arms or his face, but he scrubbed and scrubbed. Even across his eyes and mouth, he sent the scrubbing brush scouring deep red stripes to make absolutely certain. By the precious heat of the water and by the brush, he was washed from his sins. By the balm of Lifebuoy soap he was sure to gain victory over his devils, sure to cleanse his conscience and to deliver unto himself a sense of forgiveness. In the shower, he was made righteous, if not holy. United with water. But he knew the truth. Unless he ate the flesh of the sons of men and drank their blood, so to say, he would have no life in him. He would have no job to sustain him and to feed his tiny children. He stood without moving. For a long time the water beat down on him and the steam rose like hot, moist incense into his nostrils. The memory of his superior officers shouting at him to do it, do it, fokken do it, slowly softened. The thoughts of the small blond major making an example of one of the suspects, showing him how it was done, steadily dissipated. He steam cleaned his mind. And when the shuddering stopped, he switched off the water and opened the door.

The towel was soft and white.

8MM

I once visited the cemetery where the sixty-nine victims of the Sharpeville massacre are buried. They died when police members fired into a crowd of black protestors on 21 March 1960. For some reason I have always been fascinated by this incident. One epitaph reads: 'Here lies my son killed by police dogs'. I was shocked by the realisation that policemen could be such hated figures. In general, however, there was not much time to mull over things. The police were the enemy and we suffered the consequences.

On one occasion, an inexperienced young officer reacted to a radio report that six armed black men had robbed a shop in Ratanda, a dodgy township near Heidelberg. He had a description of the robbers and set out to search for them by himself in a government vehicle. We found the car a few blocks from the shop, parked across an alley filled with rubble. The doors were open and the policeman lay in a pool of blood next to the car – he had been shot and killed with his own service pistol. It was only when we turned him around that we saw how badly he had been assaulted.

– Johan Marais, *Time Bomb: A Policeman's True Story*

Bedtime Story

But why is a bar of soap more slippery than truth, Mama?

Thula wena, child. Your father was in prison and needed to wash himself.

Was he dirty, Mama? Was he covered in soap when he slipped?

Thula wena, child. The facts are hard like concrete walls.

Mama, those walls, those facts, must have been hard to crack his skull
   like that?

Thula wena, child. Be quiet, my child. That is another story.

– Richard Venter

No Alice. There must be some delay.

Friday came and went without the return of Alice. It was a busy
day for Janet.

Once Hektor-Jan had finally emerged from the bathroom, she had
made the kids brush their teeth and then it was out into the garden with
them. Go and play, she had said. Leave your father to sleep in peace. And
she had happily piled the dirty dishes and frying pan, all the utensils
made sticky with fat and maize meal and sous into the sink, as Alice
surely would be back later that day. She had checked that the children
were quietly messing around at the bottom of the garden. They were
hunting for stag beetles and Christmas beetles and songololos apparently,
and then she had run a deep bath. She needed a deep bath. Was it only
last night that she had stood naked in the garden, her skin soaking up
the night, stained by the night.

Whilst Hektor-Jan snored like a man-mountain in the bedroom,
Janet lay in the children's bath. She held up one hand then the other, as
she tended to do. Watching closely should there be any tell-tale trembling
like her mother's hands. No. Not yet. At least, not yet.

Thoughts of *Brigadoon* floated through her, like the bubbles that swelled and frothed about her belly and legs. She would need to look at her words. There were quite a few songs too, and dances. She wished her mother were there to help her with the dances as she had always been – up until recently. Janet would look at her words once Alice got back. No doubt that would be some time in the early afternoon. Yes, it would be lovely to have Alice back. Thoughts of Alice and *Brigadoon* were interrupted by the stealthy arrival of three pairs of grubby hands bearing two stag beetles, a swarm of rose-brown Christmas beetles and a very long songololo that looked like it had found the journey from the bottom of the garden to the ginseng-scented bathroom a little too arduous: it hung motionless from Pieter's hand and was fatally bent in several places along its centipede length.

Lovely, she murmured, well done. Now take them back into the garden – and don't wake your father. Then she had to sit up as the stunned songololo squirmed to sudden life and dropped into the bath to join her. Whilst she and Pieter were scrabbling in the foamy water, a Christmas beetle roused itself on drowsy wings and flew into Janet's hair.

It'll drown, bellowed Pieter as though it were her fault and Sylvia attacked her hair in an attempt to locate the beetle. Shelley offered quiet imprecations in the background and Pieter groped between his mother's legs. Janet felt as though she might be scalped by her younger daughter.

Right, Janet said, leaping to her feet out of the gentle froth and foam, a pregnant, East Rand Aphrodite. Right, just take them back outside. Please. Your father is trying to sleep, and I am trying to bath. She pulled the beetle from her hair. Several of its spiky legs remained lodged close to her scalp and the stump of a thing wriggled crazily.

It's got no legs now, Ma, now it's got no legs! Sylvia seemed about to cry but then Pieter gave a yelp of triumph at having located the longer portion of his songololo. The other bit was nowhere to be found.

Shelley, Janet said with a rising sense of desperation and her eldest child nodded wisely and ushered her noisy siblings from the bathroom.

Janet stood there, pearly bubbles popping along her body as the children's progress muttered through the house and out of the back door. Hektor-Jan snored on. She washed briskly, standing up. There was no way she was sitting on half a songololo and she would have to give her long brown hair an extra brush to tease out the legs of the beetle. Kids.

And still Hektor-Jan slept and still Alice did not come.

As the water drained down the throat of the plughole, Janet knew that she would have to venture into the garden to look at the crack. But, for the time being, she held back, waiting for the little stripe of the songololo to be exposed as the water drained. And there it was. The other half of the poor creature with its bizarre shell-body and tiny legs. It lay in the remnants of the bubbles and water, very dark against the white porcelain of the old bath. Janet fished it out with a few squares of toilet paper and flushed it away. Then she crept into their bedroom and brushed her hair with some vigour. The tiny lines of the Christmas beetle legs were already knotted and tangled, part of her hair.

Kids, she muttered again.

She tiptoed around the snuffling form of Hektor-Jan. He was a noisy sleeper. Mumbling, murmuring. He turned over with a sigh. He seemed to whimper. Janet took her underwear and frock to the baby's bedroom. There, overlooking the back garden, she dressed. It was still early. There was a whole day and Alice would soon be back. Janet could not remember if Alice had mentioned a time. Often it was late afternoon before Alice arrived. There was shopping to do and the dishes could wait for Alice. And Solomon – well, they would see him on Monday.

Sheathed in a comfortable dress, a shift which tended to show off her nice legs and made her feel quite young, Janet put on some old sandals to walk a line across the dewy grass to the bottom of the garden. Even before she got to the pool, she could see that the water level was down. Now, there was no mistaking it. No wondering about it. An ugly black seam ran like a lightning bolt down the length of the pool. It was almost one centipede – centimetre – wide and the water level had dipped.

Oh God, Janet's hand flew to her mouth. Hektor-Jan would go mad. They had never budgeted for something like this. He did not like little surprises like this. Memories of car bumpers she had scratched, jagged rainbows which Shelley had drawn in Khoki pen on the bedroom walls and other domestic setbacks came flooding to her. Guttering that needed replacing, the old fence, splitting as they watched it. Life was a falling apart. It was happening all the time. As a woman, Janet seemed better able than Hektor-Jan to cope with such traumas. Maybe a woman was used to enfolding, enclosing such circumstances. Such insistent intrusions. Was a woman more used to accommodating such things, Janet wondered.

But she found herself clutching her belly, gasping at the pool. This was different. If Janet was not mistaken, she could see that the crack did not simply lie beneath the limpid water. The black fracture did not lurk inertly – passively – at the bottom of the pool. If she was not mistaken, the crack came creeping up each side of the pool.

Janet spun on her heel and almost ran to fetch the hosepipe. It was already attached to the tap at the back door, and a guzzling sound announced that it was, in fact, in use. It stretched across the paving to the maid's quarters, then ran down the van Deventer side of the garden. How had she missed it.

Janet walked quickly. Her flip-flops flapped her concern. Sticky wet grass caught beneath her feet, a terrible sensation. She rounded the pampas grass, the scene of her mother's humiliation, and came upon another drama.

Sylvia stood aghast as Pieter and Shelley fought. Shelley had the hosepipe stuck down a hole in the ground. Pieter was trying to get at the hosepipe, to remove it from the hole. Shelley would not let him. He had just gone flying onto his back. He was making shuddering, growling sounds, just like when his grandmother had tried to kiss him. But now he was on the attack.

Pieter! Janet shouted as he threw himself at Shelley. Shelley was tall and strong. She easily brushed him aside and again he landed on his bottom with an amplified gurning noise from deep inside his throat.

Pieter! Shelley! Janet shouted again and then Pieter saw her and lurched sobbing to her.

She's trying to kill them, he blubbered. She's going to drown them. He threw himself like a dog at her.

Shelley looked steadfastly at the hosepipe that pumped water into the hole in the ground.

Moles! little Sylvia shouted aggressively. Moles in the holes.

She's going to drown them! Pieter screamed, his little boy's voice high and effeminate.

Janet held on to his clutching form. Shelley did not look up.

Shelley, is that what you're doing. Janet's voice was sharp.

Shelley looked down at the pulsing pipe. Water shuddered into the ground and started to bubble up from the hole. Whatever was down there was now swamped with water.

Shelley, Janet's voice was sharper.

Pa hates moles, Shelley said. She glanced up at her mother. You know that. Pa nearly went mad last time we had a mole.

That was true. How could Janet have forgotten. Hektor-Jan nearly drove them all mad when he thought the back garden was going to be overrun with moles. He had poured poison down their little holes, he had tried wet cement and gassing them and had even stood over the little mound with his gun at the ready, waiting to blast a mole to oblivion. But the mole mountains had kept coming. Nothing would stop them. Then before Hektor-Jan could dig up the garden or blow them all to smithereens, they had vanished. Gone to ground. Hektor-Jan grimly triumphant. But they were back.

Please don't take it out on your brother, said Janet grabbing the hosepipe. It jerked free and Janet used the gushing water to clean its muddy length. Pieter still clung to her.

Let go, Pieter, Janet said. She prised one arm loose from her leg. I said, let go.

Pieter fell back.

Sylvia watched him wipe his nose with his arm. She frowned at her older sister and looked expectantly at her mother. Was this going to be the fun part? Was this where Shelley was chastised and Pieter told to grow up? Was this when, by implication, she was a good girl because her older siblings got shouted at and maybe got a taste of Pappie's belt? It did not happen often, but Pappie's belt held a strange fascination for her. Was this when Shelley and Pieter got dragged off screaming to the house and to the sound of thrashing leather?

Stop picking your nose, Janet was rough with her youngest. And take that silly look off your face. Then she turned on her eldest.

Shelley, take this to the pool; make yourself useful.

Then it was Pieter's turn. Go and wash your face. Have you brushed your teeth. Have any of you brushed your teeth.

There were no belts; just Janet's quick voice that slapped them into shape.

Silly children. Fighting over moles. Whatever next. Whatever was down there moved silently. A bubble popped on the tiny surface of the water. It rippled. Then it was still.

Janet stared at it. Dragging at her mind, nagging at her, was the crack in the pool.

They all turned away. Under threat of the wooden spoon, Janet's version of the dreaded belt, the children went in to brush their teeth. Janet marched with the spouting hosepipe. Like a strange knight with a very floppy lance, she charged at the pool and plunged in the hosepipe. It smacked the water, writhed for a moment and then lay still. Janet looked at her watch. Maybe an hour. She would let the water run for an hour. That should do it. Then she would go shopping.

One by one, the children joined her. Janet did not want to mention the crack because before she could stop them, one of them would have blurted it out to their father. Janet would rather he discovered the crack himself – or maybe it would somehow close up as mysteriously as it had opened. Maybe whatever shifted in the ground would move back again. It was a desperate hope, a naïve hope, but it was all she had at the time. Things would change. Of course they would.

She played at being boring Mommy. Look at the clear blue sky, she said, and they looked. How many agapanthus are blossoming along that bed, she asked, and they went to count whilst she just stood there and the water level rose imperceptibly. Then she wandered back across the lawn and entered the bower made by the sighing branches of the willow tree. The lounger was beneath the tree, in the heart of the shade. The morning sun was already stinging the sky and Janet took her headache beneath the gentle branches.

Fetch Mommy her pen and notepad she instructed Sylvia, who had followed her. Then go and do something with Shelley and Pieter.

Sylvia was gone a long while. What could she be up to. You send them on a simple errand and –

Janet half lay back on the lounger. The brisk whir of a weedeater started up at Noreen and Doug's. Impressive. Getting on with the garden before Solomon came back. Doug would never let him use the weedeater. On New Year's Eve, Doug had dramatically shown them his new weedeater. They had been obliged to ooh and aah as he waved the appliance before them. Then he had plugged it in and there, in the lounge, had pressed the grip that made the little nylon thread go whizzing around like a savage wasp. Noreen's dear old spaniel had yelped in terror and shot from the room, much to the children's delight. They were always amazed at how Noreen spoilt her only child, Nesbitt the spaniel, who was just a dog.

Janet had wondered whether they should get a weedeater. Whether that would free up Solomon to do more things once he had tackled the edges so speedily with the new appliance. No, no, Doug had corrected her. Not if you want it broken. You know what kaffirs are like.

Before you know it, it will be broken. Janet had protested Solomon's expertise but Doug was having none of it. Look at your lawnmower, he had said. How long did that last when Solomon started using it. Hektor-Jan had smiled as Janet waded into deeper water. It was a very old lawnmower, Janet had said, my father had it for ages before Solomon used it. Exactly my point, was Doug's easy riposte. You looked after it, it worked fine for years. Then give it to a black and before you know it, it's buggered.

Doug, Noreen had remonstrated. Doug, watch your language. No b word in front of the children. What's wrong with blacks, Doug had joked with a wolfish smile.

You know what I mean, said Noreen, holding a hand to her head that was no doubt beginning to ache.

Kaffirs, Doug had shaken his head. Bloody kaffirs, said with a sigh.

Sylvia arrived beneath the willow tree with the pad and pen. Thanks, darling, said Janet. Now go and play with Shelley and Pieter.

She was left to her list.

To allay some of her anxiety, she corralled the items in neat columns on the page. She worked hard on her catalogue of provisions, running her mind along the length of her kitchen and through all the rooms in the house. What was needed. What were they about to run out of. What was almost used up. Could it wait or should she get more toothpaste, more peanut butter, more bacon, more Brillo pads – she wondered when Shelley would need a training bra. Should she get some sanitary pads just in case. From the mundane to the motherly. Her mind skipped over the myriad fragments that made up a mother's world, over the hairline fissures between those fragments, and her love pulled it all together, kept it all from breaking apart.

The hour passed quickly. The children were quiet. They were good children really. The pool was restored to its former fullness. In fact, the water lapped just below the rim of the pool. There was plenty. No need to panic just yet.

Janet lay back for a moment under the striped heaven of green and brown. Occasional slits of the yellow-blue sky glared through the branches, but it was cool and quiet beneath the willow tree. Not a breath of wind. Already the air outside was hot and sticky. It was going to be a stinker. Janet sighed. The willow tree was a living bell jar, a giant wig. She suddenly thought that she might like to try and write some poetry. It had been ages since she had written a poem. When last had she written a poem. When last had her mother stood over her, making her write a poem. Like she had sometimes stood over her tiny daughter waiting for her to wee in the toilet. Come on, Janet's mother had said. For God's sake, for the love of Christ, when oh when will you pee – poo – excrete a poem – or words to that effect. In situations that were horribly similar. The memories were too sharp, too harshly defined. If she turned to look at them directly they burned her eyes and became instantly blurred. She could see them clearly but it was not possible to look at them.

Janet held the notepad and pen. The pen was poised above the page, but no poem came. For a long time, Janet just sat there, her eyes watering.

Then she took a deep breath and the pencil twirled through her fingers like the drum majorette's baton she had never been allowed to pick up. Another deep breath and she tried to silence the little voice that repeated ad nauseam the line, There once was a housewife named Janet. And to ignore the little voice that tripped along the thought of what on earth would rhyme with Janet. Net, it went. Fret. No, those were off-rhymes. Sit, bit, grit, hit, kit, lit, mitt, nit, pit, slit and then she was back at the pit, the slit, the crack in the pool. She sat up. Got up. She pushed the hanging branches aside and stepped out into the solid sunshine. It hit her squarely between the eyes. The morning heat was a hammer blow.

The children were back at the bottom of the garden. They were crouched around the hole in the lawn, the one that had recently been filled with water.

Come along, Janet said, her voice not unkind. Three squatting children in the harsh sun. She must put some cream on them. They were getting more and more tanned before her eyes. They looked a picture of rude health, but she did not want any more jokes from next door. Your kids are far more black than fair would be Doug's likely joke. He found the strangest things amusing.

They did not hear her. They remained squatting, peering at the hole. For a second, Janet wondered whether she had indeed uttered a sound.

Come along, Janet said again, louder this time. The sun glinted through the shards of grass.

Shhhhh, whispered Pieter without looking up.

There's something down there, Shelley spoke in a hushed voice.

Sylvia squirmed backwards. I'm scared. Her hand reached for Pieter but he brushed it aside, unable to pull his eyes from the hole.

Shelley, Janet appealed to the eldest.

It took an age for Shelley to look up. She seemed to see her mother for the first time.

It could be a mole, said Pieter breathlessly. Or a rat. I bet it's a rat. I could put my hand into –

Pieter, Janet's voice was cross now.

Ma, he looked up. He shook his head impatiently. Then he saw the look on her face and he stood up with a sigh.

Okay, he said, okay. Keep your broeks on.

The short trip to the brand-new Northmead Mall gave Janet a chance to lecture her captive son. He squirmed in the back of the old Fiat whilst Janet lectured him via the rear-view mirror.

Sorry Mommy, he said in his clear voice as they got out of the little car. Sorry, Mommy, he said even more clearly as they dragged after her and the shopping trolley. Then she let it rest. He did not have to apologise a third time. One did not say keep one's broeks on. Broeks, female underwear, were not a topic for polite conversation, even if it was meant as a joke. They did not use the b word. He must learn. He was getting older now. He must grow up.

Noreen was shopping too. The whole world seemed to have run out of things to eat over the festive period. They chatted briefly then continued down the broad aisles of the Mona Lisa mini-hypermarket, as it was called. Janet sent them off on errands, like little satellites breaking free from the mothership to fetch Brillo pads and toothpaste and baked beans. She found a pair of training bras for Shelley and some tiny sanitary towels too. Best to be prepared.

Shelley's Secret Journal

Word for the day from Granny's list is INVETERATE.
The moles are back. They are inveterate. If we don't kill them gently Pappie will get them indubitably with his gun or maybe he will beat them to death in the night or wring their bloody necks. That's what he says. The moles do not realise this. They are very inveterate. They are also vertebrates and have nervous systems. Drowning is like falling asleep in water so I shall drown them before he kills them. Pieter does not understand this. You have to be cruel to be kind just like Grandad says about you Granny. God does not love dogs but I hope he cares about moles. I still love you inveterately Granny. Shelley.

He stumbled from one dream to the next. If there were many rooms in his father-in-law's house, there were even more in the depths of his own mind. He stood back in wonder as his thoughts clambered from one chamber to the next. It was not the darkness that set his teeth on edge. No. It was the sounds. The sound of lips splitting, right inside his head. The sound of a sigh as breath came shuddering back into a body after the solar plexus had been carefully punched a minute or two before. The screams of men. Men made into women by the sudden understanding that fingernails ripped from their soft warm beds offer up a bright pain, a loud, searing hurt that has breadth and depth and length and colour and takes your breath away. That agony has dimensions and weight and texture and – personality. That pain can be sly, that pain can be frank and honest too. Blunt, sincere, gentle, insidious, gregarious pain. Who would have believed that torture could be so sociable. The stunned subject, waiting for the next move in the interminable minuet. The admiring gasps of the onlookers, an audience captivated by blood and squeals, the crunch of living flesh, the ingenuity of the torturer who might discover an impromptu method, another way, of hurting a fellow human. Yes, it was a dance, a performance. And who would have thought that he, Hektor-Jan Snyman, could have such a capacity for pain. That he could, like a dervish of perverse delight, spin such sounds, such gagging, squealing, gurning sounds and send such signals down the network of human nerves. That his large, square body could be so delicate, so brutally delicate. That he could honour his subject and his audience and his new-found art by drawing out such exquisite pain. It was a screaming sonnet sequence, a neat triptych of terror, an aria of horror. He got carried away. It was quite beautiful.

Hektor-Jan twisted in his sleep. Why was he so restless. What need, what hunger drove him. Was it the obligation to feed his family. Was it the pressure of his peers, the whoops of encouragement and even of wonder. Did he simply play to the audience. Hektor-Jan twisted and turned alone in his bed. My magtig. Allawereld. Liewe hemel.

In his heart, Shelley watched him as only a child can watch. She stood awkwardly, twisting one foot to the side and fiddling with her hair. But her eyes were wide and steadfast. Somewhere, a dog barked. Shelley's eyes were very wide indeed.

Hektor-Jan twisted again in his sleep, and turned.

Outside, the sun shrieked until blue in the face of heaven and doves exploded with guttural coos.

1.6CM

Dog, talk not to me neither of knees nor parents; would that I could be as sure of being able to cut your flesh into pieces and eat it raw, for the ill you have done me, as I am that nothing shall save you from the dogs – it shall not be, though they bring ten- or twenty-fold ransom and weigh it out for me on the spot, with promise of yet more hereafter. Though Priam son of Dardanos should bid them offer me your weight in gold, even so your mother shall never lay you out and make lament over the son she bore, but dogs and vultures shall eat you up utterly.

– Homer, *Iliad, 22.344*

The next morning Rynard and I were ordered to burn the bodies in the bush, using wood and diesel. Fingerprints had been taken for identification purposes. We argued that it didn't matter whether we burnt or blew up the corpses, as long as we got rid of them. Burning seemed like hard work, so we decided to place explosives under the bodies and blow them up. It turned out to be a bad idea, for when the dust settled, body parts lay scattered over a large area.

About a week later, a dog came running into the base with part of a human arm in his mouth. Rynard and I were called in. We confessed that we had blown up the bodies instead of burning them as we had been ordered. Van der Westhuizen sent us back under supervision to

collect all the body parts we could find. The remains were set alight and
we had to stay there until everything had been burnt.

– Johan Marais, *Time Bomb: A Policeman's True Story*

A nd still Alice did not come.
The weekend came and went, and the kaya remained dark and
silent and there was no cheery, Good morning, Madam, good morning
Master. How is the Madam? How is the Master? Eish it is hot today, ne?
It is too much hot. I am bringing you more tea. The Madam, the Master
is wanting more tea, ja?

Janet cooked Hektor-Jan another full English breakfast. He set
off into Friday night. While the rest of South Africa was enjoying an
extension to its New Year celebrations, her husband had to abandon his
family and head off to work. Night ships.

But these night ships meant that he did not go near the pool. He did
not have to face what was there and he did not have to go crazy about
the cost of having to repair the swimming pool that he had not paid for
in the first place. Janet knew how his mind worked. If things went well,
that was his idea; if things did not go well, it was someone else's fault.
Most often her father's. How could that Engelsman – that Englishman –
do X or Y or Z. Then Janet realised that lurking beneath the surface of
her husband's Afrikaner brusqueness and good cheer was a world of the
bitter past: the Anglo-Boer wars, the sense of Great Trek entitlement to
the land, an inbred suspicion of the English, those tweegatjakkals and
the soutpiele. Hektor-Jan's expressive terms of not-quite-endearment:
the English, the double-hole jackals and the salt penises. The jackals who
had two holes where they kept separate wives, not be trusted, and the
men with one foot in Africa and one in England, their reproductive bits
dangling in the deep briny sea. Janet sighed as she tucked the children

into bed. She waited for the day when Pieter would trot out such terms. She had the soap at the ready – the children knew that. For more serious occasions, her wooden spoon would come in very handy.

And then she went through the ritual; what was quickly becoming a ritual. She waited in the lounge until the children were sure to be fast asleep. Then she got up and switched off all the lights. She waited in the baby's bedroom until the warm night flooded into every corner of the house, lapping up against her ankles, knees and throat. She breathed it in, the soft black air and waited. When she could resist the pull no longer, she went out into the garden, past the willow tree and across the dew-wet lawn. The waxing crescent moon had long since set. The tiny slice of moon pie had crumbled into the horizon before 6 p.m., even before Hektor-Jan had set off on his night ships. Now it was dark, with just the bright crumbs of the stars.

To her relief, Janet found the water level unchanged. It lay flat and black, without a ripple, a dull eye at the far end of the garden. Janet did not fall out of her clothes. She stood there immobile.

That was just as well. For across the garden came a hiss.

As far as her dental name could be rendered in urgent sibilance, there came a hiss that was definitely Janet.

Janet turned against the dark cheek of the night. Her children.

No, it came again, from the van Deventer side of the garden. From their wall. Yes, the rhododendrons were rustling too. She stepped closer. It was Doug. Doug was leaning over the wall.

Janet, he whispered.

Janet stopped on the dewy grass. The willow tree was to her right, the line of the flower bed that ran along the length of the van Deventer wall lay in front of her. And there, rising over the crest of the wall, was Doug. He peered down at her through the thick branches of the rhododendrons. For a second, Janet wanted to giggle. At least he was not looking up her skirt as she knelt over the pool. Thank God she had not repeated what she did last night. With such a neighbour, what had inspired her to slip out of her nightie by the side of the pool. Now, here she was with Desperate Doug leaning like some reverse Romeo from his balcony of rhododendrons. Doug's shape seemed to look anxiously from side to side. His stepladder appeared to wobble as he had to grab a branch.

Then Janet was struck by a chilling thought. Suppose Doug had in fact been lurking along the wall last night. Suppose he was now waiting for a reprise, for a repeat performance of her solitary striptease. She clutched the sides of her dress, as though to pull it closer around her. Poor old Desperate Doug.

Yes, she said.

The darkness waited with warm intimacy.

She could not stand there all night.

What are you doing, she said.

Janet, Doug whispered.

Why are you whispering, Janet said, her voice clear and firm in the night.

From the other side of the wall came a bluff bark.

Nesbitt, whispered Doug. Then he paused. Actually, I don't know why I am whispering, he said, his voice suddenly deep and clear, and rather less penetrating.

They stood there, facing each other. Janet was level with the concrete panel that hid Doug's lower half. Doug peered at the dark penumbra, the top of Janet's head.

Nesbitt's poodling bark had found an echo in the neighbourhood. A short round robin of barking wheeled about them, gruff and warbling, big and small, and finally a little howl from a tiny dog somewhere to Janet's left.

How is H-J's night shift treating you, Doug said. He used the Afrikaans pronunciation of H-J: Haa-yeer, so it sounded strangely like Higher. How is Higher's night shift treating you, Doug's voice came from above.

Janet looked up in the darkness. It was odd. Doug's voice was more present than himself. His body was a vague blur in the surrounding gloom, but his voice had emerged from its whispering chrysalis and now was clear. She seemed to be speaking to a voice. Voices in the night.

Fine, she said. But that sounded a little rude. Too blunt.

It's not too bad, she said. Breakfast at night and supper in the morning: it's all a bit topsy-turvy actually.

The kids, said Doug. How are the kids.

The children don't mind, said Janet. They hardly seem to have noticed. You know children.

Immediately, she wished she had not said that. Doug and Noreen did not know children. They did not have children. They had tried for too long to have children and now they had just a dog. A Nesbitt.

We shall see, Janet said quickly. We shall see how it all turns out.

They stood there. Roses by any other name might smell more romantic, but that was Doug and this was Janet and Janet tried not to smile at the squirming, shrieking disgust of her imaginary children right behind her. Yes, if they were there, witnessing the scene – well, there would be a scene. In fact, they were there. In Janet's mind, they were just behind her, poised in the house, their needy wakefulness but a hair-trigger away. All it would take was a moth, the silent flitter of a bad dream or a night terror to set them off. They were little landmines of love. Waiting to explode into calls of Mommy! Mom! Ma!

She looked up at where Doug's voice came through the darkness and the blackest leaves.

I don't know how you do it, said Doug.

Janet did not know how to respond. There was another silence.

Doug reached for his wife. Noreen takes her hat off to you. That's what she said. Just this night she said, I take my hat off to Janet.

Thank you, said Janet to the darkness.

I just wanted you to know.

Thank you, said Janet again. She turned to go inside.

Before you go, said Doug.

Obviously, he could see better in the dark than she could.

Before you go, I just wanted to say that if you need anything, I mean anything at all, whilst Higher is on night shift, well, you know –

Janet was caught trying to walk, trying to step away into the house. Doug's voice held her back. His hesitation pulled her back.

You know who to call on: call on me, Doug's voice blurted from the rhododendron bush. It shot over the wall and seemed to splash onto the grass. Janet was released.

Thanks, she said over her shoulder as she stepped towards the house, as she stepped over the puddle of Doug's imperative, one step closer to her children. Thanks, Doug, and she was inside and the door was closed and locked and Desperate Doug was outside, still leaning over the wall in the darkness and the crack lay hidden at the bottom of the pool.

The children slept. Janet checked and their noisy breathing made the silence in the house more intense.

Janet finally tackled the washing-up. As she scoured the plates and pots and pans, she thought of Noreen and Doug. She thought of Noreen fondly, and smiled when she pictured Doug. When she had finally finished, she went to shower. Janet shook her head in the shower as the water thundered on her plastic shower cap and smiled. Thank goodness the children were not outside that night to witness the scene. Doug meant well. Well, who knew what Doug meant.

She slept eventually and was up when Hektor-Jan came home.

He wanted to shower first so Janet carried on cooking his supper, making dirty everything she had cleaned the night before. It was a simple meal: steak and chips and peas, with a monkey-gland sauce that Janet made herself. No monkey, no glands, just garlic, onions, tomatoes, chutney, brown sugar, Worcestershire sauce, Tabasco sauce, tomato sauce and vinegar. The kitchen was a spice den by the time Hektor-Jan appeared. The children slept and she and Hektor-Jan could enjoy a companionable silence at the breakfast nook.

Janet knew better than to ask how the new shift, the new job was going.

She placed a soft hand on his knee as he powered his way through the steak and chips. Good sauce, he muttered, heaping great mounds of it onto the shovel of his steak. Then he was off again, munching and chewing with gusto.

Janet almost mentioned Doug's late-night hovering, but thought better of it. Sometimes Hektor-Jan saw the funny side of things; sometimes not. Janet did not want to say good night so early in the morning to a sullen husband. When he had taken things the wrong way. Living in the house, married, yet with her parents, she had grown used to giving in. Keeping the peace. Keeping her mother's queries, her father's anxiety at bay. Now, she thought that she would let him sleep in peace. He certainly looked like he needed a good night's – day's – sleep.

Hektor-Jan leant back in his seat. He folded his hands behind his head and gave a long sigh. Dit was lekker, he said, heerlik. His Afrikaans purred in the kitchen. So much more expressive than saying that was nice, that was wonderful. Such a manly language, Afrikaans. Even the name, Af-ri-kaans. Longer and more resonant than the sharp, pinched Ing-lish, all little 'i' sounds – the narrow Ing and the little lash of -lish. Whereas the big continent Afrika was embedded in Hektor-Jan's language, rolled right into it with its resonant 'r' sound, as well as the -kaans, almost like chance, kans, the Afrikaans word for chance. Take a chance on Afrika seemed to be the very essence of the language. Hektor-Jan was speaking to her; Janet shook the thoughts from the tablecloth of her mind and smiled at him.

Dankie, vrou, Hektor-Jan, grinned at her, again using his native tongue. Thank you, wife. And again wife would have sounded somehow skew and aslant, too much like the old Cockney rhyming slang of trouble and strife. Vrou, pronounced fro, was gentler, less cutting, rocking gently to and fro.

And Hektor-Jan waggled his eyebrows at her.

Tomorrow is a day of rest, he said. I shall take the children to kerk, of course.

Of course, that's what Hektor-Jan always did. The children's weekly dose of church. An essential bit of Afrikanerdom, so that they were not simply the heathen offspring of an Engelse oupa called Ward. No. They could be brought into the laager of Afrikanerdom, even though they spoke mostly English like klein rooinekke, like little rednecks. But that would leave Janet free, her morning of freedom on Sunday when she would have the entire house to herself. When she would leave Alice to do the tidying up and she would lie back under the willow tree and learn her lines for the first rehearsal of *Brigadoon* that was coming up all too soon. Too soon, *Brigadoon*.

Hektor-Jan waggled his eyebrows again.

Are those kids still vas aan die slaap, he asked. Are they fast asleep.

Janet held his humorous gaze. It was pleasant to have a husband in playful mood. She knew what was coming.

We read a lot last night, Janet said. She started to list the Blyton books.

Hektor-Jan placed a warm hand on hers.

Janet's voice stopped. *Five on Kirrin Island Again. Kirrin Island*, she said, and stopped as her husband again reached out to suggest that no man is an island –

His eyebrows jived a third time and he stood up. His body was burly in his t-shirt and shorts. Tufts of hair sprung out of his shirt at the neck and his arms were dark with it and strong. Despite his apparel, his bare feet and his five o'clock shadow at seven in the morning, Hektor-Jan bowed and seemed to be inviting Janet to dance. Janet smiled.

Kom vrou, said Hektor-Jan, and he led her by the hand to the bedroom.

The passage was quiet and dreamy, the children sound asleep.

In their bedroom, the curtains were drawn, as though they were backstage. Janet felt an actor's thrill and more thoughts of *Brigadoon* skipped before her. Hektor-Jan stood on something on the carpet and hopped on his bare foot. Not one of the children's toys, Janet was about to say, but then Hektor-Jan closed the bedroom door and locked it.

Usually, if the children woke up and knocked or tried to open the door, they knew what to do. Shelley and Pieter and Sylvia would find Alice and chat to her until Mommy and Pa appeared, tousled and slightly breathless and oddly solicitous, with a small smile on Pa's face and Mommy freshly scented with a dash of perfume.

Sometimes Janet wondered if the children stood on the other side of the door and heard anything. Not that there was much to hear. Hektor-Jan's passion was quick. But it was also intense and occasionally the bed would leap in surprise and thump against the wall. Like a bucking bronco, it would arch and jump as Hektor-Jan rode it like a squat cowboy and then he might cry out. Call her name as though he had just lost her in the gloom of the room, and whisper to her, urgent whispers in his gruff Afrikaans voice that spoke to the darkness right in the nape of her neck and filled her ears as he filled her too, filled her with his big, blunt love.

Hektor-Jan, she would respond, all thoughts of the children now driven from her. H-J, she might say, her voice urgent, the only time she might use the Afrikaans abbreviation of his name, an intimate diminutive of his name, but with the hint of a thrilling imperative: Higher.

Here she was with her husband relying on her more and more heavily. She could feel it. Her womb throbbed with it.

And the bed would come to rest and the door would still be closed. And then Hektor-Jan would lie on her, breathless, his breath catching in his throat before he summoned more manly resolve and withdrew to open the curtains with dramatic finality. And Janet would imagine now an audience, not on the other side of the locked door, but seated in a vast auditorium revealed by the pulling back of those curtains. The hush was expectant; they were waiting for her to perform.

Shhhhhh, went someone in the front row – the hiss of the shower as Hektor-Jan began to clean himself all over again. And then came the overture – Hektor-Jan in the shower, singing. And then Janet raised herself on one elbow and squinted into the crowd. Before they could become restless, she would get up and curtsey as her nightie slipped down to cover her, and then she would turn theatrically and promenade to the bedroom door like a chestnut-brown Elizabeth Taylor, small but as saucy as you like, and unlock the door. Dramatically she would pull open the door to check if any or all of the children were waiting there, perhaps ready to gasp or to applaud. Usually they were not there; usually their voices came from the kitchen where they were chatting away to Alice, a soft, familiar murmur punctuated by Alice's good-natured expressions of surprise or encouragement. The black background music to white suburban South Africa.

Janet turned back to the bedroom, to the chaotic bed and to the audience, which held its breath. But then the bathroom door would burst open and it was her chance to shower. Hektor-Jan would take centre-stage and get dressed, or in this instance, make ready to go to bed. She would exit stage left. Then she would shower dreamily.

When she got dressed, usually in a simple frock. Hektor-Jan would watch her, another member of the large audience, so quiet and appreciative. Or maybe he would observe her like a member of the cast, whilst she, the darling of the show, trod the boards and held the audience captive.

Janet would let the towel drop. It was bunched and knotted over her chest, but she would let it quickly slip down in a rough shimmer to her feet and she would step aside like a small, neat goddess, yielded up by the ripples and woollen foam of the towel. And Hektor-Jan would gaze at her breasts, still firm and fresh despite feeding three children and the prospect of nourishing a fourth. And her trim waist – less severe now – and soft thighs. She might turn to her dressing table and catch a glimpse of her comely midriff in the mirror as she reached for her creams. Hektor-Jan might mumble something as she rubbed the lotions into her body. He might be especially attentive, when, like now, her tanned body was dramatically contrasted by a pair of startlingly white breasts and bottom. It was as though, all the time, she was wearing a swimming costume made of creamy flesh. No doubt, the body that filled the costume was what encouraged Desperate Doug to patrol the border of the gardens with such diligence and enthusiasm. Again, Janet almost mentioned Doug to Hektor-Jan, but then there were children's voices and Janet slipped on her broekie and bra, nylon stockings and dress. And she was ready, smiling maternally as her three children flocked in to say good morning to Pa even though it was once again actually good-night-and-sleep-tight for him. And then it was Janet's turn to watch as the action moved upstage, more of a pantomime now, as they all threw themselves onto the bed and onto their father yet again. And Hektor-Jan became a sea monster or a gorilla or a twisting, rumbling earthquake and the game of pin-down-Pa began in earnest. Janet would again open her mouth to warn, to offer motherly remonstrations of gentle caution, but it would all get a bit wild and then, yes, as feared, there would be a bump or a knock and someone would end up in tears for a brief, loud moment. Janet did not mind sharing the stage. But she could sense the restlessness in the audience and one by one, she knew they trickled out, a bit like Hektor-Jan's warm seed within her. No more *Brigadoon*; no more Janet Snyman née Ward. The auditorium slowly emptied and instead of murmurs of appreciation or gasps of awe, Janet heard a fly buzz. In the auditorium, somewhere out there as the children snorted and their pa squealed – or was it the other way around – there was a blue, uncertain, stumbling buzz between the daylight and Janet. And then, it seemed, the windows failed and she could not see to C. From row C, the last person sauntered off and the fly buzzed and Janet closed her eyes and put her arms around herself and hugged herself. It was just a fly. She would stroll across the stretch of carpet and open the window. She could not do what Hektor-Jan did and crush the fly with a sudden, startling finger so that its innards squirted like a yellow-white headache across the glass and the poor thing crunched and died in a dirty spilling of itself. No, she would open the window and the fly could buzz off, out across the veranda and into the auditorium of the front garden and over the road and beyond to the Bunny Park where creaking children played on swings and chased the relentless rabbits in the quarter of a square mile of the local park.

Janet could not see the fly as it rocketed off into grateful oblivion. The fresh warm air touched her cheek.

Nee, nee, jou blikskotteltjie, roared Hektor-Jan as Pieter started tickling his toes, aided and abetted by his sisters. The rumpus was reaching its final stages. Janet could scuttle from the room knowing that it would all end in a few more minutes. She could run to Alice before any of her Humpty Dumpties fell and broke their crowns. And Alice would shake her head and utter an expressive Hau! as they both raised their eyebrows at the folly of the Master, the Baas, who always got the children so excited. The two women would share a moment of head-shaking disbelief in the Baas – such daring disbelief – as his operatic baritone thundered from the bedroom and seemed to mock them all the way down the corridor.

Too late, Janet remembered that Alice was not back yet and that another pile of washing-up would greet her in the kitchen. She would need to cream her hands as soon as she finished doing the dishes once the children had had their breakfast. She must remember to get the cream out of the bedroom before Hektor-Jan dropped off and it was too late to enter Bluebeard's lair as he rumbled in his sleep like a submarine in the deep or a human bomb made of large muscles and hair.

Janet sat down in the breakfast nook. Like the fly, her mind roamed free. She wondered what had happened to Alice. Solomon was due back on Monday. Maybe he would know. Now there was no Emily next door to ask. Janet wondered whether she had had her baby yet, and where.

Zululand, perhaps.

And from the Valley of a Thousand Hills in Zululand, her thoughts flew inward and she felt for her own child blossoming within her. And then she gave a small start. How easy it was to live with the crack. It was the first time that day that she had remembered the crack. Janet sat stunned. Her flesh turned cold and she gave a slight shiver. One hand reached instinctively for her belly, to hold and to protect. Even as she sat there, she knew. She knew that it was getting worse, that the crack was not going to go away. And then it came.

As inevitable as gravity, as ineluctable as water or as certain as the buzz of flies came the cry of a child hurt in the rough and tumble of a silly game. She knew it. She could have told them so. There was Hektor-Jan's gruffly whispered appeal not to upset Mommy, but there was the insistence of Pieter's pain. Or was it Shelley's. How a child will scoop up its agony in shaking hands, holding it up like a bright badge to pin to its chest and loudly proclaim what a bad, naughty, poo-thing the universe is. Look! Look, Mommy – why was it always Mommy – look what has happened to me, poor me, poor little me! And there she was – Mommy – having to lavish sympathy on the bearer of such proud pain.

Janet stood up. The sobs came limping down the passage. Let it be just a bump, or a small scratch from a loose and careless nail. No breaks. Please. No bent limbs or cracked crowns. Janet did not feel that she could face a broken bone so early in the morning, so early in the year. This was supposed to be a good year. Hadn't Hektor-Jan said so, but a few days before, at Doug and Noreen's. Had he not raised his glass of 5th Avenue Cold Duck and toasted 1976. Had he not raised a glass to no more oil crises. Had he not welcomed the birth of Essay Beesee – SABC – and the infancy of South African television. And hailed the country that had given them life and a big blue sky and healthy children – although Janet had wished that he had not been quite so explicit about the healthiness of their children when Doug and Noreen had but a dog. That was a little awkward, but otherwise it was a good speech. And now there was Pieter, crying his heart out and holding his hands over his jaw. And there, too, was Sylvia, a satisfied shadow as her older brother was mewling like a baby and she was not.

Pieter. Janet mustered all her sympathy to wrap around her son.

Pieter sobbed into his hands.

Let me see, said Janet. But he would not remove his hands from his face.

Let me have a look, she said patiently. I can't help you if you don't let me have a look.

Sylvia stared at her brother, her mouth open and beginning to frame a smile. Janet tugged at Pieter's arms. That provoked a horrible squealing sound. Sylvia was beaming by now. Janet could just tell that she was grinning from ear to ear.

Pieter, Janet was getting cross. Pieter!

He let her tug his hands from his jaw. He was strong, surprisingly strong, but he let her move his hands from his face and there was his swollen jaw and his weeping eyes, smeared with tears. His face was red from all his rubbing.

It wath ath athki – it wath ath anthkident – it wath a mithtake, explained Sylvia's voice from around her thumb.

Thumb out, thank you, said Janet as she bent and grimaced at Pieter's jaw.

What happened, she asked him. Can you open it.

Pa, he started to wail again, Pa –

Pappie hit Pieter's mouth, came the helpful clarification from behind Janet's knees. By mistake. Sylvia was surreptitiously trying to peer up at her brother's injury – as well as making a poor show of hiding her joy and her thumb.

Thank you, Sylvia, Janet snapped as she tried to prise open his mouth. It really was swollen.

He wouldn't stop, Shelley's measured, older-girl voice spoke. Pa told him to stop, but he didn't stop. It's his own fault. Now Pa is upset. He has shut himself in the loo.

Open your mouth. Janet gripped Pieter by the shoulders. I said open your mouth.

With a shuddering moan that drew gasps of appreciation from Sylvia, Pieter opened his mouth. Shelley withdrew silently.

More. Much more, Janet inserted an initial finger and felt for fragments of teeth, any sudden splinters or the slippery gush of blood.

There, Pieter gagged a sound. Dere.

Janet stopped. There it was: a loose tooth. Of course, it may already have been loose, although the little boy did seem to be in some pain. And there was some blood.

Pa, spluttered Pieter. Pa.

Your father did this, Janet said.

Are you going to thmack Pappie? Sylvia said. Are you going to get the wooden thpoon? Are you going to teach Pappie a lethon he will never forget? Are you going to – ?

Sylvia, Janet used her time-to-shut-your-mouth-or-die voice. It did the trick.

Pieter's mouth jerked open and Sylvia's snapped closed.

Yes. One of Pieter's little molars was oddly loose. If she touched and wiggled it – Pieter let out a magnificent scream. A scream worthy of the end of civilisation. If Alice was anywhere this side of Zululand she would have heard him. She would be hurrying back home to them.

Sylvia's mouth opened once again and her thumb fell free. Shelley came running back.

Pieter sat down on the floor, a deflated husk of a boy – all that remained after the almighty scream.

Try to rest it, said Janet wondering where she kept the bottle of TCP. Stay there, she said to Pieter as she went in search of the medication. It was going to be a long day. She could tell it was going to be a long day. Pieter would milk his injury for all it was worth. He would require love, solicitous wads of her cottonwool love packed around his lithe body for the rest of the day. Her tiny son. And now her husband trapped in the bathroom, imprisoning himself in the bathroom. As soon as she had given Pieter the medicine, she would coax Hektor-Jan out of his little prison. All this, and not a line, not a word had she learnt for *Brigadoon*. Janet stopped.

For a second she did not know how, why. She almost scratched her head. She inhaled sharply.

She was standing at the foot of the pool.

She was standing, muttering, staring at the pool.

Did she think that the medicine for Pieter's pain lurked in the crack at the bottom of the pool. Why had she made her way here. It seemed as though it were some compendium of ills, a seam of distress, which ran through her life, her day, her pool.

Janet did scratch her head. It was whole, complete.

She looked at her toes. And at the water level which again had dipped. And at the crack that lay sullenly at the bottom of the pool. And yes, it was starting to come even further up the sides. Dear God, it seemed even wider and was definitely longer.

Janet turned away from its magnetic pull. It was a compass needle pointing to true horror. No matter where she was, she felt her insides turn and realign with the crack in the pool. Yes, it was going to be a long day. And, no, she had never forgotten about the crack.

The Lord is my shepherd. I shall not want. He leadeth me in green pastures and into the en suite bathroom where the quiet waters lie. Ja, man, though I walk in the valley of the shadow of death, yet I fear no ill. For Thou art with me and my Beretta and bullets comfort me still. And the knife rests securely between the Old and the New Testaments.

He hunts down sleep like a wounded animal. The ambiguity disturbs him: it is sleep which is wounded. It is a scurrying tarentaal freshly shot, and it runs and bleeds in the thick mielie field, not to be caught. He has no dogs with him. No Voetsek or Bliksem or Boggeroff or Moffie or Swart Gevaar or any of the others. Dogs from the good old days. Dogged by his past and by the present. Hektor-Jan sighs. His right hand is still clenched. That was close. Just before he and Janet got intimate, when they entered the bedroom, he had stood on it. Dank die Here – Thank God – he had stood on it, not she. How would he explain away the adult tooth that lay on the bedroom carpet with its bloody roots, a shred of gum still trailing from its long, cracked roots. It was one of the back teeth. Fed up to the back teeth. This tooth had followed him home. How the hell had this tooth followed him all the way home. He could only assume that it had spat through the air and had fallen into the turn-ups of his trousers. It had hitched a ride home. And when he got changed, it must have jumped out. And there it had lain, chewing on the beige carpet, lying in wait for the unsuspecting foot so that it could bite back. Inflict some pain of its own. Allawereld. Liewe hemel. What was the world coming to when you are hunted down by stray teeth in your own home. He had scooped it up just in time. He had held it tightly in his fist, even as they had had sex. Even as the children romped on his ribs and attacked his toes. And then, in the chaos of fun, he had tried to escape Pieter's clutches, the fumbling of his son who sensed something in his father's hand and had tried to get it. Nee, Hektor-Jan had rumbled. Nee, my seun. But little Pietertjie had insisted like a stupid puppy. He had laughed. Laughed in his father's face and panted and lusted after the fist with the tooth trapped inside and Hektor-Jan had shouted and writhed and flailed and had caught his own son on the jaw. It was almost as though the tooth was seeking out a new jaw. A new day, a new dawn, a new jaw. It wanted to go home. But he held it. In his hand he had the whole tooth; nothing but the tooth in his hand. He would not let it go. He had never wanted it to fly from that poor bastard's mouth. Or had he. Had he tried to impress the little major, the quiet man with the soft voice and merciless, pale-blue eyes. Indeed, had he teased it from its original owner, had he coaxed it from him in a paroxysm of blood and rasping phlegm. His knuckles ached from the effort. A human face is surprisingly hard and resilient. And now those self-same knuckles were still tightened whitely around the tooth. It was going nowhere. And he was not going to sleep. Janet had come to knock on the bathroom door. At first he thought it was a pounding headache or an echo of the knocking, the ironic knocking that he used to warn the men that he was coming, coming to get them and that they had better be ready to tell him, tell him all that he wanted to *know. Not to waste his fucking time. On this earth we have but three-score years and ten and he did not for one moment want to spend any more time than was necessary. But that was a lie, a white lie. For this, he had all the time in the world. He was made for this. Why, had not the Lord his God given him a body that was indeed a battering ram. Was he not the proud possessor of the biggest biceps and – magnificently – the greatest capacity to induce terror. Was he not the vanguard of civilisation. Did he not carry in his mighty hands the precious flame of white South Africa, of law and order and civilisation amidst these savages. He saw what they did with their pangas, their assegaaie and their sharpened bicycle spokes. He knew what the ANC could do to Inkatha, what Inkatha did to the ANC. He knew the hostels and the townships. As a policeman, he had patrolled them. They had been on his beat – and beat was the operative word. These savages needed to be beaten. Without the strong arm of the law, there would be chaos. What he now did in the interrogation rooms of the HQ of the Boksburg-Benoni Riot Squad, well, it was absolutely bloody necessary. No fear, no respect. No respect, then chaos is come again. The riders of the apocalypse would howl through the white suburbs. There would be looting and pillaging and raping. So, in his right hand, in some strange way, the bloody molar comforted and disturbed him in equal measure. Like the witblits in the car which both quickened his heart and dulled his nerves. In his restless sleep, he wondered where he might hide it. The children put their teeth under their pillows. The tooth fairy took the tooth and transformed it into a shiny silver ten-cent piece. He would bury it under the mattress with his stash of magazines. Maybe some tooth fairy would oblige. But, when he got up and raised the mattress, he could not let go of the tooth. He stood for a long time in the dark room staring at his tight fist. It could have been Pieter's tooth. It could have been the tooth of his very own son. But for the grace of God, he might have hit his son's jaw and knocked loose a little white tooth. The colour drained from his face. His hand ached. The tooth bit into his rough palm and now his jaw began to throb. For the life of him, he could not think what to do.*

Shelley's Secret Journal

Word for the day from Granny's list is INVIOLABLE

Pieter's face is not inviolable. Dogs are not inviolable. I hope moles are either inviolable or quickly violable. Mommy was creeping around the garden last night. What is she looking for? Jock is buried and will become part of the soil, flowers and so on till he is almost inviolable. Pieter and Sylvia and I do not like it when they lock the bedroom door to have sex although the little ones do not know about sex yet. Granny you have not told them yet and I have kept my promise not to tell Pieter or Sylvia. Granny you called it the sex act. Mommy is going to act in a musical. I have to act like I don't know what is going on. Sometimes I wish I had not seen what happened to Jock and I don't like to think about the sex act either. Even if you said indubitably it makes you feel inviolable. Granny try not to eat any more tissues. Love, Shelley.

3.2CM

Allied to the blacks' appalling conditions in both town and country, the constant harassment by police and the consciousness of political and social paralysis, the inevitability of violence was stark. Three weeks before the [Sowetan Uprising] massacre the Anglican Bishop of Johannesburg, Desmond Tutu, who was emerging as one of the most influential black leaders, had written an open letter to [State President] Vorster expressing his 'nightmarish fear that unless something drastic is done very soon, then bloodshed and violence are going to happen … almost inevitably … A people made desperate by despair and injustice and oppression will use desperate means.'

– Frank Welsh, *A History of South Africa, Chapter 18: Disintegration*

The Poor Man

Pity the poor man buried in white skin.

There is nothing thicker, more weighty than white skin.

Just like steel-reinforced concrete and armour plating and bullet-proof
     glass,

Nothing seems to penetrate such a tough carapace.

Neither guilt, remorse nor the pangs of conscience.

The poor man must carry it with him to confession,

Drag it about the city streets, lug it along the corridors of power.

How it must distend and distort his face as he peers in the mirror.

No, there is nothing thicker, more weighty, than white, white skin.

– **Abraham Nkosi**

I ndeed, it was a long weekend. But, at the end of it, Alice did return. It was Sunday afternoon.

Hektor-Jan was out the front, fiddling with the car and waited on hand and foot by his faithful Pieter and watched by Sylvia of the piercing voice and disquieting perceptions. Shelley was somewhere inside, reading no doubt.

The back garden was a haze of thick, aromatic scent. Invisibly, it poured from the giant pine next door and seemed to fill the garden from wall to wall in the hot, still air. The garden filled like a pool, filled with thick liquid scent and Janet sank into it, drowning happily.

Janet lay under the willow tree.

Her script, dangled limply from her hand, slowly licked up the sweat which trickled from her fingers. The mists of Brigadoon soaked up the sweat pulled from her pores by the heat of Benoni.

Once in a hundred years, the magical town of Brigadoon would appear, intact and inviolable. Out of the Highland mists it would come, an enchanted place, a hallowed place. Forever free from the threat of disruption or change. Quaint customs were eternally preserved and the villagers sang of home and bonnie Jean. Here there was no crack. Janet could hardly wait for the first rehearsal. To leave the merciless blue of the Highveld sky and enter the more maternal mists of the Scottish Highlands. To set aside Janet for a few hours and to become the celebrated and vivacious bonnie Jean. To sing and be sung to, and to dance. Hektor-Jan did not dance. He did a lot of things, but he did not dance.

He had taken the children off to kerk that morning. All dressed in their Sunday best. Hektor-Jan in his suit which fitted him like a leash, which held back the power and strength of his square body, just about containing his big muscles and thick neck. He looked ready to explode and he ran a blunt finger under his collar. Too much of the good life, he muttered as his children were assembled before him. Janet watched him straighten his tie, which bulged in a dark line over his chest and stomach.

The children were finally ready.

Janet had fielded with absent-minded equanimity the weekly questions.

Why was she allowed to stay at home? Why did they have to go? Kerk is boring, Mommy. Can someone die of boredom? They have come close to death by boredom every week. Dominee speaks funny, Mommy. He shakes his fist at me, Mommy, and when he reads from Die Bybel, his voice starts to shake and we can see his spit. It collects in the corners of his mouth, it really does. I swear it does. When the sun comes in the back window I can see the dust in the air, Mommy: it's like he is swimming in all the dust in the air, like it is pouring down on him and he spits. We can see the spit flying out of his mouth into the shining dust. It almost gets us, Mommy. One day it's going to hit us, isn't it, Shelley? Didn't you get some on your cheek last week? You said you got some on your cheek last week. I got some on my cheek. I am not a liar, you said you got some –

And when they were gone in the throb of a freshly tuned Ford Cortina, Janet would remain standing on the pavement, a small figure beside the line of plane trees that ran down the length of the road. Her hand would be raised in a motherly salute. Or perhaps it was a gesture of submission or maybe even of protest. After a few moments, she would look up at her hand, as though wondering who had set it there at such an angle above her head. And she would bring it down, bring it back down to hang at her side as she turned and made her way into the silent house. Usually, she would leave the beds and the breakfast things for Alice to tidy up before Alice, too, would head off for the rest of the day to her church events and whatever she did on a Sunday afternoon in an East Rand suburb.

And then Janet, tingling with pleasurable anticipation, would walk slowly to the lounge. She would walk across to her favourite piece of furniture, her childhood, it seemed, memorialised in glowing wood and perched on four beautifully curved short legs, each culminating in a wonderfully orbed, clawed foot. It was like having a lion in the lounge, an Aslan in smooth, honeyed wood all gleaming and shining from Alice's devoted polishing. There it stood, wreathed in the soft flames of the morning sunshine that streamed into the north-facing house. The radiogram.

Janet would make sure that it was switched on, and then she would gently open the pair of doors which glided down to bring with them the record player on the one side and the dials and volume knobs and radio-station tuner on the other side. Then she found her favourite record in the neat drawer at the top of the radiogram. And before long, the black wheel, the glossy whirlpool of the LP began to spin, began to rotate and the grooves which contained all the wonderful music lilted up and down almost sinuously. Janet might watch those many, many lines spin with promise as the record undulated before her eyes and the subtle hiss came from the speakers. Then, finally, unable to resist the pleasure any longer, Janet raised the white arm with the hooked needle and gently lowered it onto the outer edge of the record. It might hesitate for a tiny second, but then it caught a groove and took. And Janet would step back as though in a dream, and feel her way to the low couch onto which she would sink as the liquid, clear and mellow voice of Karen Carpenter filled the room.

Alone, she could have the volume as loud as she liked, and she liked it loud. With her children and their father neatly seated in the dusty

Christopher Radmann

kerk before the spitting Dominee, Janet could sink into golden sounds of the Carpenters that glowed in the sunlight and filled her with such feeling. (They Long to be) Close to You and We've Only Just Begun washed over her. Please Mr Postman and Love is Surrender called to her soul and she moved her lips to the lyrics of As Time Goes By and Only Yesterday before singing along to The Night Has a Thousand Eyes, Desperado and Solitaire., For several hours, LP after LP, Janet could be swept along by the beautiful harmonising of the sister and brother. It was the call of the woman with the hair the same colour as Janet's but the voice and the looks of an angel, so thin and so delicate, that tugged at her heartstrings and let her weep with joy.

But that morning she had to search the house for her script. No Karen or Richard Carpenter for her. No time spent crooning on the couch.

She had to find her words. Brigadoon did not just vanish in the mists of Scotland, it seemed. How often did she have to hunt it down in her own home. Very strange. She wondered if the rest of the merry cast had the same problem. She tried not to think about her mother's dementia, how it started with the little things. Spectacles lost on the top of her head. The tasty tissues. Starting to go to the loo in the lounge. Attacking her own grandson. And all those other things from long ago. Too many things from long ago. Janet would rush from the house with the relieved and gasping script clutched firmly in her hand and sink back with a shudder under the willow tree. This was a profound sacrifice. To forsake Karen Carpenter for the script of *Brigadoon* was a terrible sacrifice indeed.

Before she plunged in, Janet lay back and marvelled again at the tree whose branches knew to grow to a precise length, just long enough to arc from the main branches above, and to cascade down to kiss the ground. No branch grew too long. Whatever the fall of each frond, it did not go too far to lie wastefully on the ground. No, each tip stopped just short, or merely touched the ground. Janet lay back, overwhelmed by such chaotic precision. The tangled order, the cluttered symmetry of the tree shrouded her and she raised the damp script of *Brigadoon* to her eyes that stared up at the mesmerising, living lines above her.

Then it was at least an hour of focusing on the printed page. Making sure that those lines now started to fill her head. Janet could be pushed a little to one side. The clamour of domestic duties and insistent children who feared death by boredom and the dangers of excessively expectorant dominees could be set to one side. Janet could become Jean. And bonnie Jean to boot. In her mind's eye, she danced gracefully on stage. Ready for every cue, she responded with quick and fluid timing. No longueurs, no ghastly gaps whilst the audience stared embarrassed and the whole show fell apart. Oh no. They were too good for that. They might be an amateur dramatic society on the East Rand, but they had their pride.

And as a little reward, after at least two-dozen lines were learnt, Janet might slip from her brown and lime bower and into her favourite bikini. Then she would grab a swimming towel and drag the old lounger from beneath the tree and she would lie in the morning sun. It was hot but not too frazzling. Bonnie Jean would soak up the Benoni sun. And as she went through the lines, now a shifting set of words and emotions in her mind, she might be aware on the edge, on the periphery of consciousness, of the rustle of the rhododendrons or even the glint from somewhere in their neighbourly depths of a pair of cautious binoculars. Usually the children would tell her. Sidle up to her and whisper, Uncle Doug is at it again. Except on Sundays, when there were no children and Doug could spy away with impunity.

Janet wondered whether she should make a scene. She was half-conscious of the irony that here she was, preparing to expose herself on stage, to be viewed by a school hall of watching eyes, and the fact that she might be a little squeamish about a neighbour – a good friend – admiring her from the very depths of his rhododendrons. He was just one set of eyes. But then she thought of the glinting binoculars, the power-assisted scrutiny. Part of her wondered how close Doug got. What part of her filled his secret vision. Then did she become angry on Noreen's behalf. Did she feel some feminist revulsion, some outrage at a not-so-subtle form of male exploitation or implicit degradation. Or was she somehow flattered that her body, which had yielded up three children and was preparing to launch a fourth, could still arouse male interest. After all, was that not the very reason she loved the idea of performing on stage. To be noticed. To be applauded. Were Doug's frequent fumblings in the foliage not simply a rather welcome form of applause.

She lay there with the sun stinging her skin.

That was simpler. To forget about the complexities of motive and morality. Probably preferable to let the sun bleach those dark thoughts. To render them translucent and gleaming and white. Leached of all insidious intent. Just thoughts. She was here. He was there. The sun was hot. The sun stung her skin with beautiful heat. Doug was their neighbour. He liked looking at her. Life could be simple. Life could be brilliantly clear and simple. Indeed, the sun was hot.

And out of the blinding heat, Alice came home. It seemed as though the white sun and the vast sky had finally yielded her up. There was the metal squeal of the side door that led from the alleyway between the garage and the house, from the front garden to the back. Out of the Sunday morning there was the shriek of iron as though the sun had sheared off a slice of the day, and there was Alice. Alice in her beautiful Jet Store – or Edgars – outfit. Chic and smiling and waiting to greet her Madam, who lay as though murdered by the sun.

After all this time, and Janet did not seem to register Alice's return. The rhododendrons twitched in her mind and the sun sang. The day seemed to creak metallically and a dark shadow appeared. Janet lay dead still. Then she lifted her head and peered behind her.

Alice!

Janet sprang from her towel with touching abandon, like a child forgetful of propriety in the enthusiasm to greet its Alice.

Alice!

She stood before Alice, her skin silver with a film of sweat that sparkled in the sun. And Alice smiled at her.

Janet laughed, now suddenly aware of her tight bikini, of the possibly startling conjunction of maternal curves barely captured by little triangles of bright cloth.

Alice! she said, laughing and raising a hand to her mouth. Alice, we were so worried. We wondered what happened. We thought you were coming back on Friday. Is everything all right. Nothing went wrong.

Alice lowered her two big bags to the ground. She rubbed her hands and then placed them on her hips. She was a tall woman, statuesque. She was dressed in the latest fashion and her hair was set free – swept away from her face and clipped at the back. Her lipstick was a beautiful plum and now her teeth gleamed as she smiled.

Here I am, she said. She spoke such good English, clear and precise, although her accent had not managed to break free of the townships. Heh I em, she said – music to Janet's ears.

Thank goodness, said Janet. We were so worried; I was so worried.

Busy, busy, busy, said Alice, her favourite and most familiar phrase. Then the taxi – eish. She shook her head.

Janet could only imagine. The crowded minibus taxi, stuffed to the rafters, packed like sardines.

Ja, said Alice. The minibus taxi broke down. They had to wait at the side of the road for the whole day, and then they had to sleep in the taxi. Hau, it was bad, very much too bad. A catastrophe. She aired that word with a gleam of her impossible teeth.

Janet shook her head.

I am so glad that you are back safe and sound, she said. The children will be delighted. They are at –

Kerk, said Alice.

And Janet nodded. It is just us, she said. Go and unpack, she said, not quite yet the white Madam. Go and unpack and I'll make us a nice cup of tea.

Alice looked once more around the garden. Set Janet carefully in the context of the unkempt lawn that leapt up to demand attention, set her against the backdrop of weeping willow and lounger that lay stunned in the sun. And there was the bright brickwork of the garage and the adjoining kaya, and then beyond that the neighbour's wall and the profusion of pampas hiding the compost mound and the small vegetable garden. Then the back wall and the pool and the neighbours to their right as they faced the back garden. There were signs of the children too. The chaotic hosepipe, no doubt stuffed down a mole hole, the brown leather rugby ball and the pair of hula hoops. But no little landmines left by Jock. No, Jock lay buried in his own patch behind the pampas grass with a tiny, troubled cross fashioned by small hands. That was December; this was January. And the crack. If Alice sensed the crack she gave no sign at all. And Janet took one of Alice's hands in her own and gave it a squeeze. Welcome home.

So this was home.

They had finished their tea and Janet had told Alice all about *Brigadoon* by the time the children returned. Alice was back in her maid's outfit, her pink shift, apron and doek and standing doing the dishes when the children burst in, freed for another week from the hell of kerk.

Alice! they shrieked in triplicate surprise and joy. Alice! and they ran helter-skelter to her and engulfed her with hugs and squeals. And Janet smiled as Alice hugged them back, clasped them to her, her little white brood, so smart in their Sunday best that their father made them wear. The children so smart and Alice so maternal and pink in her familiar uniform as it were.

And then Hektor-Jan appeared and they were all together again, one big happy family.

Welkom terug, boomed Hektor-Jan. And he beamed and freed his neck from the bursting top button and whipped off his tie.

Alice bobbed a curtsey – tried to bob a curtsey with her cargo of Shelley, Pieter and Sylvia and said, Dankie, Baas, thank you, Master, with a smile.

How was Zululand, Hektor-Jan switched to English.

Janet beamed and it did not matter where her somewhat peripatetic script was now, or that there was a crack. With Alice back, things immediately looked much better. It was just so nice being all together once again. It was not the same without Alice. Just look at the children. Sylvia still squeaking, Shelley laughing as Alice tried to tell Hektor-Jan about the wedding feast in Zululand, about the ridiculous lobola, the dowry charged in cows for Alice's cousin, and there was little Pieter, believe it or not, with tears in his eyes and just clinging to Alice's apron. Janet breathed in deeply and smiled and smiled.

Everything would be fine. Absolutely fine. Janet could feel it in her bones.

But later that afternoon, she had the strangest conversation with Douglas van Deventer.

Hektor-Jan was asleep, in a single day trying to readjust to normal routines – and not succeeding. Alice had caught up on the dishes and was now tidying her own room, the kaya. The children were in the pool – where else – and had mercifully given no sign of noticing the crack. Janet need not have been surprised. She knew too well how unobservant, how casually – if not how wilfully – obtuse children could be. Sometimes she wished that she could be like them. So hermetically sealed inside their silver skins that bounced back the sun and turned golden brown with no trouble at all. To be so inviolable, to be so fine! So rude of health and so aggressively well! She distracted herself by wandering right across the garden, inspecting every plant and patch of grass, making mental notes for Solomon, who was due back tomorrow. Dear God, please let him be back on time. Janet did not think she could face another setback to the fragile balance of her blessed routine. And then, once the restless lawn was mown, cut down to size and the bushes trimmed and the edges of the flower beds seen to, then she could show Solomon the crack and see what he thought. Thank goodness Hektor-Jan had not been near the pool. And, for once, the children had not said a thing, had not blurted out to the world the stark and brutal fact that there was a crack at the bottom of the pool and that before long the water would leak out. They did not shout out that their mother simply could not keep topping up and adjusting the watery betrayal of their very own pool.

Janet was close to tears at the edge of the garden when Doug's head rose into view. He seemed to emerge from the leaves themselves. Doug the dog now Doug the dryad. He glanced down as though amazed that she stood there, apparently straight from the froth of the pool where Sharky rang out and there were terrible shrieks of fun.

The kids are having a great time as usual. His opening gambit played safe: kids, great time, all as per usual – the familiar and the familial.

Janet made some reply, equally innocuous no doubt.

Noreen said that your Alice is back.

Doug had the tender temerity to mention his wife, even as his eyes slid along Janet's body and came to rest on her left breast, no, her right, no, in the middle of her generous cleavage that ran like a fleshy valley down the centre of her bronzed chest.

Janet blushed and clasped her hands in front of her. Doug, Doug, Doug.

Yes, she said, Alice is back. Thank goodness, she is back.

You must be pleased, Doug smiled. He shifted a branch that rose up to his chin. His voice seemed to be filtered by the rhododendrons, a feat of vegetative ventriloquism. Janet smiled.

Oh yes, she said.

The children must be glad, Doug dwelt on such gladness. The children must be glad.

Janet nodded.

And Higher must be glad too. He must be really glad.

The children are delighted, said Janet and then she paused. Of course Hektor-Jan was glad. Why would he not be glad. He was as glad as the rest of them. They all loved Alice; she was part of the family.

Because you all love your Alice, she is part of your family, said Doug and Janet had the disconcerting sense that Doug was speaking inside her head. Or, at the very least, he was somehow articulating her thoughts. Her own thoughts were speaking in a soft manly way from the depths of the rhododendrons.

We all love Alice, said Janet to reassure herself. Yes, it was her own voice coming from her own mouth.

Of course, Doug nodded and the rhododendrons danced merrily in their leafy tangles. You, Shelley-Pieter-Sylvia and Higher, you all love Alice to bits.

Janet smiled up at Doug and her arms pulled more tightly around her.

It is important to love one's maid, Doug was like a dog with a bone, or an insistent crack at the bottom of a pool. He did not seem to know when to stop. The happiness of the home depends on the love of a maid. Depends on just how she is taken to the heart of the children, and the wife and the husband. I bet you found yourselves missing her over Christmas. I bet you even spoke about her on the day itself, wondering what she was doing, wondering if she was going to be having turkey too.

Janet stared up at the fluttering leaves as Doug spoke with his hands. Sometimes he uttered such nonsense. And there was no Noreen here. There was no Noreen to haul the conversation back onto safe and familiar cracks – or rather, tracks. No. Doug was roaming free in the conversational sense. Perhaps he had been drinking – yet more 5th Avenue Cold Duck. Janet, down below, could not smell anything and he seemed steady enough. He did not look as though he would fall out of the rhododendrons and splash in a brown tangle of thin man's limbs at her feet. She seemed safe enough.

Yes, we missed her. Have you had any luck on your part with a new maid.

Doug stared down at her for a long while and Janet found herself seriously wondering whether or not she had in fact uttered a word.

She repeated the friendly query, her voice cheerful and bright and she moved her hands to behind her back: far more confident and assertive that way.

Doug suddenly smiled, his eyes again full of her chest, and shook his head. No such luck, he said. No, we have not been lucky in the maid department. Unlike you and Higher. Higher has been very lucky as far as maids are concerned, has he not. Very lucky indeed.

Janet watched Doug's mouth. The way his lips pursed pinkly and the words popped into her head. Words loaded with freight. Words carrying thoughts of Alice and their family. Of a happy Hektor-Jan. And she stared at the beaming Doug whose lips were so pink and oddly moist, almost waxen like camellias and not the spittle-spray of rhododendron flowers at all. Janet began to wonder desperately where Noreen could be, that surely she could not again be poleaxed on her bed with a meat-cleaver migraine. Then she flinched at the violent thoughts – why axes and cleavers. How disconcerting and how pink and wet was Doug's mouth that even now was wrinkled with yet more words that her mind was desperately trying to avoid, like an umbrella fending off sprinkles of sharp knives.

But there is more to life than Alice, surely, Doug seemed to be saying. Something more about Alice. Alice, Alice, Alice. A town like Alice, he seemed ready to shoot off his mouth, or to carol or yodel on about Alice in wonderland. But then he glanced behind him, back into the rhododendrons as though he had seen a snake or sensed a voice that had come from the green flames of the leaves.

Gotta go, he turned to her even as he slid down the ladder, his shoulders, neck and head descending behind the grey curtain of solid concrete and then all that was left was the blank wall, the shrieking of her children and a nagging sense of something on the edge of thought. After a long while, Janet continued her circumnavigation of the garden. She somehow managed to retrieve the list of things for Solomon to do from the depths of her mind even as she wondered what made Doug clamber up the wall to say such things. And all the king's horses and all the king's men couldn't put Humpty together again. Her head hurt and the rhododendrons on the other side of the wall seemed to taunt her with their dark-green vigour.

But everything settled down that evening. Hektor-Jan woke up after a short sleep and they had an early supper cooked by Alice. Toad in the hole with a large side plate of salad each. And custard and tinned pears to follow. They sat in state at the dining-room table. The children were well behaved, no one mentioned the crack and the talk centred on going back to school.

Standard One, Janet said to Pieter, I can't believe you'll be in Standard One already.

Pieter tried to fit half a sausage in his mouth at once. He nodded with the weight of the world on his small shoulders.

Standard One, he muttered to himself in the same tones that he had heard the Oh Peck Oil Cry Sis mentioned and the Shark of Iran. Or the plight of the Aye Zhins under Eddy Amen, which had been much discussed at the dinner table a while back. Let them just try that here with the whites, his Pappie had said darkly, and Pieter had tried to frown and to scowl in the same dark way. Just let the baddy called Eddy try to mess with his Pappie then it would be Amen for him indeed. And he pictured dark figures lurking at the bottom of the front garden, trying to get them, but afraid to come any closer because Pieter's Pappie had a gun and was a policeman. But more serious was the approach of Standard One – yet another year of school after the long age of Grade One and Grade Two. His world of summer holidays was falling apart, but Pieter could intone the deep seriousness of his advancing years in the direction of his younger sister who still frolicked with such innocence in nursery school. Standard One. I, your older brother, am about to face the total onslaught not of Grade One, not even Grade Two, you hear, but Standard One. Trump that, you little squirt.

Pieter has a bogey in his nose. Sylvia knew how to strike back, how to haul Pieter Pieter the Pumpkin-eater back into the nursery. I can see it. It's right there sticking out his nose. It's green. Sis, man, and she made a gagging sound, garnished with salad giggles, as she taunted him with her mouth full.

Sylvia.

Both Janet and Hektor-Jan fired the warning shot at the same time.

Standard One, Pieter repeated darkly making an international incident out of the three syllables.

Bogey, mouthed Sylvia. Bogey, bogey, bogey.

When do we get our new uniforms? said Shelley.

We go shopping tomorrow, said Janet. Once I have shown Solomon what to do, we shall go shopping.

Do we have to? Pieter continued to send the ballistic missile of his stare right into his younger sister's face. Do we have to? It's our last day of holidays. He tried not to grin as Sylvia's face was obliterated by a double mushroom-cloud. That would teach her, her and her stupid bogeys.

Absent-mindedly, Janet stroked Sylvia's cheek through the thermo-nuclear flames. She did not even flinch.

Do we have to? Pieter repeated more urgently.

Pieter, she said. Pieter, you know the answer, and Alice smiled as she cleared the plates and the side plates.

The smooth custard and floating pears appeared before them. Janet nodded her thanks to Alice. So nice to have Alice back. What had she done without her. How had she coped without her. And Janet knew the answer.

Listen to your ma, Hektor-Jan's voice offered manly support and certainty. New uniforms tomorrow and ready for school the next day. Got that.

All three children nodded vigorously, even Sylvia who did not need a uniform and who was not going to get one.

The Crack

The pears disappeared in bite-sized segments and the evening was scraped to a close with the last smears of the custard.

It's nice to have Alice back, said Shelley voicing every thought as they stared up at Alice and beamed as she cleared away their plates.

Shelley's Secret Journal

Word for the day from Granny's list is INVOLUNTARY.

I wish kerk was not involuntary. It is long and Dominee thinks he is indubitable. He makes me feel very violable. Your plan is working Granny. I like your words. I am also glad that Alice is back and Mommy can calm down. I am very glad that we are finally going to get new school uniforms that fit us properly. Pieter is being silly again. I have told him to mind his own business and not to go creeping about in Mommy and Pappie's room or in Alice's kaya. Alice held me involuntary when I said good night. She said she had to hold me because she won't see her own little daughter in Zululand until Easter. I have not seen you this year Granny. I will try to show you our secret journal when we visit. I shall remember to wink three times with my left eye and I will hold you and kiss you even if you have been at the tissues. Love, Shelley.

The Lord is my shepherd, I shall not want. He maketh me to lie down in green pastures: He leadeth me beside the still waters. He restoreth my soul: He leadeth me in the paths of righteousness for His name's sake. Yea, though I walk through the valley of the shadow of death, I will fear no evil: for Thou art with me; Thy rod and Thy staff they comfort me. Thou preparest a table before me in the presence of mine enemies; Thou anointest my head with oil; my cup runneth over. Surely goodness and mercy shall follow me all the days of my life and I will dwell in the house of the Lord forever.

It was no joke, that valley of the shadow of death. To become a God-fearing man, just try putting the fear of God into men. Now, I am become death, the destroyer of worlds. With the rod and the staff – just try getting good, reliable staff – and the flex of the electric cord and perhaps a machete, but definitely a pistol, how easy it was to comfort the confessions from his flock. No flogging the flock. No fucking the flock. Just a table prepared. Things to anoint the human body until the tears and the bladder and the bowels runneth over and the confession was spilled. Then there could be goodness and mercy. And then they could all emerge from the valley of the shadow of death and not become death, the destroyer of worlds and fragile skulls, whole universes of individual thought and perception and experience. Even in terror, there was such individuality. Such a unique response to his ministrations. Never mind fingerprints: the response to pain was unique, characteristic and telling. There was no knowing just when the cup would runneth over, and how. But with such shepherds, runneth over it would. He could not lie down in green pastures as he had slept that afternoon. And he needed to remain awake well into the night so that he could sleep during the following day and be ready for night shift. Be ready, and perhaps as well rested as that valley with its distinctive shadow which beckoned like a lover. Dark and comely, soft and exciting. He would descend with pleasure into that valley – how oddly sexual. Wait, I am coming, he wanted to call out. But he was silent in the dark house as his family slept. He made not a sound as he sat with the Bible, his Louis L'Amours and his James Micheners in the dark, his lips moving silently as he recited the psalms. In his palms, he held the human molar as though he were praying at its miniature ivory altar which perched in four-legged steadiness on his clean skin. Big things were going happen. That had been the final briefing for the week, and the one to set the tone for the new year. Yes, things were on the move. They would have to stand firm when the time came because it would come. As night follows day, so the night, which they knew was coming, would certainly follow the day. The blacks of night were coming for the whites of day. The psalms spilled from his lips in counterpoint to the molar that his hands held so tightly. If he held that tooth any more fiercely, there would be blood. Of that, he was certain. It would bite into the muscle and sinew of his hands and so wreak its revenge. In many ways, he longed for the clarity and purpose of blood, the bright point of pain that might lock his desperate thoughts into the here and now. He gripped the tooth even more loudly and whispered his psalms even more tightly: The Lord is my shepherd, I shall not want. He maketh me to lie down in green pastures: He leadeth me beside the still waters. He restoreth my soul: He leadeth me in the paths of righteousness for His name's sake. Yea, though I walk through the valley of the shadow of death, I will fear –

6.4CM

The game soon got out of hand. Everyone cut themselves, on the thigh and shoulder, but mostly on the forearm, and after a while everyone was covered in blood. Suddenly the men noticed that I was sitting quietly in a corner and they fell upon me. I protested for all I was worth, but finally agreed to cut myself. The men stood aside and watched as I took out my pocketknife, pushed the point into my left arm and cut.

The cut wasn't deep enough to their liking. I was held down and two gaping wounds were slashed into my left arm. At first there was no blood, but then it started gushing. The prolonged drinking had thinned my blood, and I was afraid I might bleed to death.

Our bloodthirst having been triggered, we went to the adjacent bar, where we started a fight and very nearly demolished the place.

– Johan Marais, *Time Bomb: A Policeman's True Story*

Sowetan Heimweh

She calls to me
with her broken mouth.
My name she lisps
through bloody lips,
each syllable a shattered tooth.
Why is my name so long?

– Gabriel Tshabalala

A lice was back and now Solomon was back. Janet could feel more complete than she had felt for most of December and early January. She was up and dressed and ready well before Hektor-Jan would arise and even before Alice came in to do the tea.

The sky was blue and bright, the grass fresh and green with promise. The air was yellow in the soft sunshine – oh, it promised to be a good day. Not too hot. Just right. Like Goldilocks and the three bears.

Janet wanted to fling open all the windows of the house and shout out with joy, Be gone, you crack. Go away, we do not want to play today!

In her favourite house dress, she sat waiting for Solomon, for the creak at the gate as he came into the back garden and got changed into his work clothes in Alice's toilet, the tiny room beside her bathroom which, in turn, was beside her bedroom. He would hang his smart clothes on a nail behind the door and change into his overalls. He would remove his polished shoes and put on his dilapidated takkies. Solomon the man about town would transform into Solomon the garden boy. Old Jock used to bark and snarl at the black man who arrived with the dawn, and then wag his stump of a tail and shadow his fine friend who mowed the lawn, cut the edges and trimmed the plants and picked up his poo.

To keep from becoming too distracted, Janet tried to make her lines for bonnie Jean run through her head. Instead, there resounded Charlie's song with its insistent rhythm, the urgent panegyric about being a roving lad, about the wandering life he had had. The song shifted to reflect more selfishly how he prized his freedom, how he would not be tied down by any silly lass. But then one day he saw her: bonnie Jean. And he knew with such sweet certainty that he would have to go home with bonnie Jean.

And then, as Janet sat there in her quiet kitchen with the back door open and waiting expectantly for Alice to appear to do their tea and to make breakfast for Solomon, his great pot of steaming white pap, there came the call of the townsfolk of Brigadoon, urging on the delightful Charlie to do just that, to go home with bonnie Jean. Go home with her. The gentle euphemism, the innocent enthusiasm tumbled into the kitchen. They all chorused and celebrated Charlie's going home with bonnie Jean. Home, they sang, home, home, home and the wonderful sentiments all hinged on the domestic joy promised by bonnie Jean.

And Janet smiled and shifted in her seat. She was home. She was bonnie Jean. She was the maid who had held out her hand and he now stayed to be with her. Forever together in Brigadoon. The beauty and simplicity of the notion, the feeling of the beckoning song and the comfort of true love almost brought tears to her eyes. And she sat in the kitchen alone in the morning light, her children and her husband asleep, whilst outside Alice and Solomon made ready to service this Brigadoon of theirs and yes, there they came, the pair of Hadedas en route to the Bunny Park, the morning fly-past of the two big ibises with the shimmering emerald-brown feathers and sharp curved bills which cut the sky with their insistent cries. Were their calls, which clattered through the morning blue, soulful or mocking, tragic or menacing. Janet could never make up her mind as the echoes faded across the road and came to rest in the heart of the park opposite the house. Charlie's song to bonnie Jean was gone from her head and she sat in the silence, the aftershock of the Ha-Ha-Hadedas. How she dreaded those first Hadedas so.

And then there was Alice's beaming face, the clarity of her white teeth in her beautiful shining black face and the cup of tea on its silly little saucer appeared before her. Janet had no idea how long Alice had glided about the kitchen whilst she, Janet, bonnie Jean, had sat stunned by a pair of birds.

Thank you, Alice, said Janet.

The tea was lovely and hot. A nice cup of tea. The warmth of it coursed down her throat and welled up around her heart.

I can't tell you how glad we are to have you back, Janet said between sips.

Alice smiled and said how good it was to be back.

And how is old Lettie, asked Janet. Lettie, Alice's mother. Lettie who had helped to raise Janet, probably more than Janet's own mother had – and probably more than Lettie had actually raised her own Alice. In asking the question, in asking with such fondness, Janet could not know the depth of feeling, the longing in Alice's reply.

My mother, she said. The funeral – the singing, the crying, the singing – the funeral – my mother.

I miss old Lettie, Janet now trod even deeper down that overgrown path fringed by black-jacks, those weeds that sent their spiked seeds stabbing into your socks and clothes, which pricked and bit you like guilt and regret and longing and loss made flesh. Seeds with claws that tried to burrow into that flesh.

Alice brushed her arm and smiled.

The pap was starting to bubble and flop about in the pot. It needed constant stirring now and Alice turned to beat it back, to make sure that the lumps that threatened never materialised. Solomon was not afraid to make sarcastic comments about women who could not even cook his pap properly.

And then the pap was ready and poured into the big enamel bowl like the one they used for Jock's food except Jock's was blue and Solomon's was green and pocked with black scars. And there was the big enamel mug with its pint of tea and countless sugars. For Solomon had a sweet tooth and so it took a long time to stir his tea and to stir his porridge.

And Janet realised that, despite sitting and waiting, she had somehow missed the call of the metal door which announced Solomon's arrival. Maybe he came with the Hadedas or perhaps Charlie's song had poured into her head and drowned him out. But he was here!

Alice disappeared with the food and the tea. When she returned she had a question.

Solomon, he is wanting to know what is happening to old Jock.

Janet's eyes turned to the fridge. The magnets still formed GOD instead of DOG in chaotic technicolour. The sadness of Jock's death seemed oddly to seep from their bright shapes and drip down the white surface of the fridge. Janet tried to expunge the image of their old friend, splayed out in the middle of the lawn, his tongue swollen, his dead eyes bulging and his neck well and truly broken. Killed by the night; strangled by the stars. Who knows, they had no clue. Even her policeman husband was shaken by the sight. Old Jock, as strong as an ox, a Rottweiler robust and true, felled by the soft night. A mystery. Shrouded by the dew-soaked lawn and not a sound. Jock the guard dog had made not a peep. Whatever it was that came in the night had killed him quickly and silently. It was not rabies or distemper. No other disease was to blame, it appeared. Jock did indeed seem to have been strangled by the overwhelming darkness. For a moment, Janet wondered about the crack. Could it have slid like a snake across the lawn and wound itself around Jock's throat as he kept guard. Could it have swallowed his anguished barks and yelps, engulfed his distress like a chasm, broken his neck. Janet ran a soft hand around the back of her own neck and around the memory like a collar that was too tight. The poor children. And poor Hektor-Jan, who had dug the great hole behind the pampas grass, but away from the compost heap. Shelley had helped him. Janet could not forget how her elder daughter had silently taken one of the children's spades brought back from a beach holiday and had helped to dig the hole without a word. Just soil heaped to one side, preparing to make Jock part of the garden itself, the garden he had patrolled with such care, the territory which he had marked with stiff-legged enterprise in his old age and which, trembling on frail haunches, he had fertilised with the food that had passed through his body. And the hole had had to be a big hole, Hektor-Jan had whispered to her. Old Jock was already stiff and Hektor-Jan could not bend his legs or break them just to fit them inside a smaller grave. The deed was done as Janet kept Pieter and Sylvia inside so that they would not wail as their father and their older sister dragged Jock and let him slip with a dusty thud into the earth. Shelley did not seem to notice her blistered hands that took an age to heal. She and her father had covered their old friend with soil and stones and had patted it flat as gently as they could, but it was a lot of soil. Janet and the little ones had made the slightly wonky cross in the dining room which had JOCK our DOG in sincere and babyish letters in black Khoki pen thanks to Pieter – and his mother who had rescued JOCK our DOG from the initial JOK ow DOG. The cross still stood, as did the fresh flowers placed there by little hands throughout the Christmas holidays. Janet had had to ask them not to pick the biggest and best roses and agapanthus. She had had to suggest that Jock would be more than happy with bright but small verbena blooms – technically a weed – which grew in profusion behind the compost heap and against the back wall. The morning glory blossoms were also encouraged as fair game. And all the while the kikuyu grass sent energetic tendrils across the bare patch at the foot of the little cross like a spider's web of shooting green. The cross seemed slowly to be sinking into the sea of green. Janet would have to have a word with Solomon. Let him know not to mow over the memorial to faithful Jock.

Janet made her tea last a little longer. Soon there would be the quiet knock on the kitchen door and Solomon would deliver his scraped-clean bowl, his rinsed mug and his quiet thanks.

The knock came and there was Solomon. If he was surprised to hand the tin bowl and mug to the Madam, he did not show it.

Hello, Solomon, Janet said receiving the breakfast things.

Madam, said Solomon his eyes respectfully fixed to the kitchen floor that Alice was about to sweep.

Have you had a good holiday, Janet said.

Thank you, my Madam, said Solomon without looking up. His powerful arms hung by his sides and he shifted on his feet. He seemed to be straining against an invisible leash. Or perhaps he heard the call of the garden, the wild grass, the busy beds in the hot sun. Or possibly, he, too, was disquieted by the line that lurked so urgently in the pool.

With a deep breath, and the metal utensils still incongruously in her hands, Janet stepped towards Solomon. He moved backwards out of the door, making space, and Janet slid past. Come, she said simply.

For a second, her eyes had to be shielded against the stabbing light. She made the mistake of squinting up at the sun and that sent harsh lines dancing across her vision. For a second, what was dark was bright and what was light became dark. Momentarily, Solomon shone like an angel and her shadow glowed. Janet stumbled across the lawn.

Glancing back at the house beyond the expanse of grass across which they had just trekked, Janet turned to Solomon. He stood just behind her, now dark and serious. He watched her. She turned to the pool. With an aching heart, as though confronting grief and loss and a lifetime of quiet desperation, Janet beheld the crack.

See, she pointed, but no word came from her mouth, her throat, her heart. Look, Solomon. Look, there. There it is. Can you believe it. In our pool. In the very pool that has been in this garden for years. Suddenly it has sprung a crack. It has split. There. The smooth blue surface now scarred by a jagged line as thick as my wrist. An artery of ugliness now pulses in the pool.

And Solomon stood there looking at the Madam and looking at her free hand that pointed tremulously at the pool. Her other hand clutched the metal mug and bowl and spoon. They rattled with emotion.

Solomon, Janet said. Look.

And he squatted down beside the edge of the pool, his loose arms now wrapped around his knees, and Solomon watched the pool. The water wobbled with a life of its own. The sun throbbed and the leaves and every blade of grass seemed to strain towards it, seemed to crane upwards in juicy green lines. In this fecund Eden, Janet pointed to the black serpent in the pool of knowledge. At the bottom of the garden was oblivion, chaos, despair.

Solomon slowly shook his head.

Now Janet turned to look down at him as he shook his shaved head and let out a low whistle. He sent a hand towards the edge of the pool. He paused and Janet held her breath. Then he touched the surface of the water, stroked the face of the pool, ran his fingers through its clear blue hair. The water shimmered under his searching caress, eddied and yielded so that the crack was dispelled into a moment of whirling doubt. Still Solomon stroked the pool and eased the nightmare vision. Then he raised his hand to his nose and sniffed.

What do we do, Janet said urgently. What do we do.

And Solomon looked at her from where he was squatting beside the pool. Then he got up. With his long certain stride he fetched the hosepipe and turned the tap so that he brought its gushing length to her feet and the pool. Then he went to the hook on the back wall, just above the pump where the long net was lodged and the brush. With expert hands he pulled the long silver pole with its brush crown from its hiding place and brought it to the pool. Janet held her breath. Solomon never even hesitated. As though spearing a fish like some tribal fisherman, Solomon plunged the long pole into the pool. Down the sides it slid. Solomon frowned with concentration and effort as he slid the pole up and down, up and down. Janet could hear the bristles scraping the sides of the white concrete with a rasping cry. She opened her mouth and there came the synchronous gasp of the scraping bristles, as though she too rasped with busy strokes of the brush.

Solomon, she choked on the scraping sibilance of his name. S-S-Shhhhhhh.

The gleaming bristles of the brush were now about to touch the crack. Janet did not know what to do. She could not stand there clutching at metal desperation and wincing her anxiety. She could not remain there shifting from one foot to the other as she felt the brush scrape her very insides like she was the pool and nightmare was about to spring loose, triggered by the brush and the crack. As though the brush was levering out all the pain from every crack in the world. Through the surging water and the splashing and the pumping silver brush, Janet's cry was lost and the tin utensils, all Solomon's breakfast things, fell from her grasp and clattered to the paving. With a ping, a stinging sound, Solomon's bowl bounded into the pool and leapt like a fish through the water towards the crack. Janet fell back in fright and then she was scrabbling, all left feet and numb arms as she tried to scramble back to the house. But she never made it. Again she was compelled to behold the brush as it surged closer and closer to the crack. It seemed that Solomon was testing the water. Janet was drawn to return to the edge of the pool, but she had to do more. Before Solomon could jab the crack, before the brush and the pole and maybe even Solomon himself could be electrified by the shocking chasm, Janet reached out a trembling hand and touched Solomon's arm.

The brush and pole were suddenly still. Solomon's eyes remained fixed on the pool, as though he had been touched by the water itself – or by the crack which had insinuated its supple length right out of the pool.

There was a long pause.

We cannot tell the Master, Janet's voice came urgently. I do not know what the Baas will do. We must make sure that we fix it and that he does not know. He must not know.

And even as Janet was telling Solomon and even as Solomon stepped away from her touch on his arm and moved uncomfortably closer and closer to the edge of the water, Janet knew that the bark she could hear on the brink of thought was indeed Nesbitt and that Desperate Doug was watching them from his tiresome haven of leaves. For a moment, Janet wondered whether she could confront him with the crack – tell him what was in their pool. But she knew that he had enough on his plate what with Noreen and no Emily. And she knew that he might just spill the beans to Hektor-Jan and then where would they be with Hektor-Jan on night ships and on edge and having to cope with such bad news. No, far better that they try to solve it themselves. They could do it, surely. Ban the children from the pool, drain it while Hektor-Jan was asleep and get some cement to close the crack.

Whilst Hektor-Jan bravely worked at his new job, Janet would keep the home together. She would fix the pool.

You see, Solomon, Janet said, that is what we shall do. The children go back to school tomorrow, all of them, and we can drain the pool and close the crack.

Janet was strangely grateful to Doug. Her annoyance with him had saved her. Pulled her back from the brink. She could instruct Solomon like a more sensible Madam.

And Solomon nodded wisely and began again to move the brush and Janet turned with real defiance and stared long and hard at the patch of rustling rhododendrons. She felt her eyes go out on a hard line that hit through the morning air and struck the trembling bush. She wondered momentarily what bonnie Jean would do and then whether Eve had felt as persecuted by the tempting snake – and it was not even that Doug was tempting in any shape or form. Strange man. She would have to have a more direct word. Soon, when Noreen was better and they had a new maid she would say something to Doug.

She left Solomon fishing out his bowl and striving to brush away the crack. It would not work. You did not simply erase a crack from concrete, not one as wide as that.

Janet tried to think of the children, and Hektor-Jan and the first rehearsal the following evening when the children had been to school and life returned to its usual rhythms. Maybe the crack would close. Maybe it would disappear as mysteriously as it had appeared in the pool. As she thought that, in idle hope, she knew she was being a fool.

Janet did spend the rest of the day in hope though. New uniforms and new shoes were purchased in the chaos of the shops. Why did she always leave it so late. She should do all this before Christmas, not afterwards and she bought the children an ice-cream cone to cool them down and to soothe her too as the creamy coils dissolved into thoughts of the crack. She licked it like a determined child. Her mother used to treat the children to such things. Ice creams and waffles. Little treats that made the shopping bearable. Janet felt as though she should have a permanent ice-cream cone fixed in her hand, ready to lick and to soothe every moment of the day. That would be very nice, agreed Sylvia, having already demolished her ice cream, setting a new record. Did she even taste the thing. How did her brain not freeze from the cold. No, she could not ask Pieter for a lick of his.

Then they returned home. Hektor-Jan ate the meal prepared by Alice and set off to work. Solomon did not break the replacement lawnmower and the grass looked infinitely better – neat and trim, like a park. Solomon said not a word about the crack, and the pool was full again and Janet managed to persuade the children to play in the kempt garden not the sparkling water on this, their last day of the holidays.

Janet wandered aimlessly about, learning her words, her script held to her face, trying not to bump into things. It was a relief in many ways to spend a pleasant hour or two in Brigadoon. There were no cracks in Brigadoon. Just enthusiastic men in kilts and scrumptious Scottish accents.

They all slept well that night. Everything was returning to normal.

Then the children were dragged out of bed and into their new uniforms. Their warm limbs were pressed into the stiff fabric, still crisscrossed with the creases from the packaging and Janet wished that she had remembered to wash the new shirts and Shelley's tidy pinafore. But it would have to do and she tried not to let Alice's reproachful glances upset her. Bonnie Jean did not want to notice the black hands with the soft pink palms gently tugging at Pieter's shirt and Shelley's dress, trying surreptitiously to pull them straight before they were bundled into the car and driven up the road to school. They were dispatched, creases and all, and Sylvia sent off to nursery school amidst the wails of the very new children clinging to the masts of their mothers' legs, not wanting to set sail on such strange seas. Janet always remembered Sylvia's matter-of-fact goodbye. Don't cry, Mommy, she said, before expressing the fervent hope that there would be peanut butter and syrup sandwiches for lunch. At that stage, Sylvia lived on peanut butter and golden syrup. With her brown skin and golden hair, she herself looked like she was made out of peanut butter and syrup. It was a delicious sight as she trotted off.

Janet drove home swiftly. She needed to look at more lines before she set off again to become bonnie Jean and meet the rest of the cast that evening. A thrill of excitement ran through her. How glad she was that Eileen Wilson from next door, bold, brassy Eileen, her neighbour on the other side, had casually said, What about *Brigadoon*. They were putting on *Brigadoon*, a lovely musical, a most delightful story, and that there would surely be a part for her. And so she had auditioned before the holidays. On a hot November night, she had gone with Eileen up to the primary school to audition. What an exciting word! Audition! How they had giggled like two schoolgirls as Eileen squinted at the dark road ahead, refusing to wear her spectacles on this the night of the audition. Her husband, Phil the pilot, was away again having flown the coop and Eileen felt free as a lark. Her enthusiasm had caught Janet up in its warm wings and had swept her all the way up the road to the primary school and into the arms of ERADS, the East Rand Amateur Dramatic Society, formed in 1974 and ready to set sail on a second voyage after its maiden success with *A Midsummer Night's Dream*. From Shakespeare to the Highlands of Scotland, ERADS was looking to entertain, to take as many minds as possible off the worries of those tough years in the early seventies. How fortunate that they had chosen Rynfield Primary School as their base, in the heart of suburban Benoni, within easy striking distance of Boksburg, Brakpan – and even Springs and Kempton Park on the other side. Housewives and busy white professionals were all most welcome.

You will be most welcome, Eileen said as they drove the short distance up Nestadt Street. Phil loves to think of me on stage, I know he does. He talks about it. Men like that, their wives –

And Janet could never have guessed. At that stage, she just hoped. It seemed like fun. Something different. Hektor-Jan in his uniform, their lives rather regimented. This was a complete break in routine. She had not yet thought about the make-up, the spotlights, an entire cast. But it was a change, a welcome distraction.

You are most welcome, said Derek-just-call-me-Derek the director of the show when Eileen, so tall and impressive and sure of herself, had done the introductions.

And they had thrown themselves with fits of giggles onto the tiny wooden chairs purloined from a neighbouring classroom and carried to the hall as there had been such a response off the back of that year's theatrical success. And Janet had the strange sense she might indeed be sitting on one of the chairs on which her children had been ensconced that day. And the hard wood and stiff back of the chair became suddenly warm and soft and Janet felt as though she, too, might rediscover some of her youth. Maybe it was a chair on which she herself had sat as a child, for she had gone to little Rynfield Primary School from the ages of six to thirteen. She was in Stanley House – the white house – just as her children were now, not in Rhodes – red – or Livingstone – grey. It was wonderful how secure she felt letting those recollections wash over her, the sights and sounds of her childhood, though it was more the smell of the hall, the very essence of the place, that had not changed in almost twenty years. She could just about be one of those explorers mentioned. With Eileen chortling beside her, Janet felt as though she had plonked a pith helmet on her head and was merrily feeling her way back through the long grass of her past and then Eileen dug an excited elbow into her ribs and they all hushed as Just-call-me-Derek had clapped his soft hands and was earnestly clearing his throat in their direction.

They were quiet, like an audience themselves. About thirty men and women, Eileen whispered. Janet could feel the lights almost dim and she shivered. Just-call-me-Derek rocked forwards onto his toes as though he was going to jump theatrically at them. He had a sheaf of papers wedged under his arm and he cleared his throat a second time. Eileen turned and beamed at Janet. You'll love him, she whispered and Janet stared at the soft, important man who did not look like his spiky name – Derek – at all. More of a Francis, for he was lightly freckled too and Dereks should not be freckled, surely. Janet stifled another giggle and Eileen grinned as the director delivered his speech.

His words spread like hopeful syrup across the peanut butter of the hall with its sepia light and soft brown tones of the brick walls and wooden floorboards. Janet only partially heard them as she kept thinking, This is like being in a sandwich, this is just like being in a peanut butter sandwich. Here I am, seated like a child on a tiny chair between Eileen and a little pixie of a man, caught between the slices of my youth and the onset of middle age. Here I am, back in my old school hall, which is suddenly so warm and so small, stuck between rows of East Rand adults, the merry gang of the ERADS. He who dares, ERADS, came strangely to her and she struggled not to chortle out loud as Derek-who-should-be-Francis built up to a rousing murmur – or sigh even – He who dares, wins, and we plan to win, which almost sent his little body catapulting lightly into the first row, so enthusiastically did he rock forwards on his feet.

There was applause, polite, genteel applause and murmurs of appreciation. Yes, they dared, yes, they would win. Bring on *Brigadoon*, they could do this, of course they could. And then, like a miniature teacher, Derek-Francis flourished a great sheaf of papers and they were passed along the rows and all the way to the back. Everyone got one. On one side were the female lines – a dialogue between Jean and her sister Fiona, on the other side was the manly repartee of the two Americans, Tommy and Jeff. And there was a snippet of song at the bottom of each page too. Gently, Derek-Francis explained how they would be given ten minutes to pair up and to practise the lines of both characters. They might be asked to play the part of Jean or Fiona – the women, Tommy or Jeff – the men. And she and Eileen were swept up in the hilarity that scattered them all across different parts of the hall so that they could throw themselves into becoming someone else.

I'll do Fiona first, said Eileen and Janet was Jean. Eileen gripped the script and seemed ready to throttle every single line. It was as though she had Fiona by the throat and was going to wring each word from her lips. Janet looked at her friend in surprise. She knew that Eileen had played only Robin in *Midsummer* – as Eileen blithely called it – and had doubled up as Wall, and that she was desperate to land a better part this time. And Janet had the quiet sense that Eileen had asked to be her audition-buddy, perhaps in the secret hope that not only was she being nice and neighbourly, but that she would certainly not suffer by comparison with the more restrained and possibly – here Janet felt ashamed of her suspicions – more dowdy Janet. She was certainly not as long of limb as Eileen, nor was her hair quite as brassy. Eileen had kept certain features of a beehive but had added golden bits, rather like streaks of honey. And Eileen's voice, coming down from on high, possessed an amazing, resonant quality, like someone about to yodel but deciding not to only at the last moment. That was certainly the case when Eileen put on her stage voice and began to do unexpected things with her mouth and limbs. Janet waited for her cue with a sense of wonderment – there was more to acting than she ever thought possible. Just behold the strange change that came over her neighbour. Janet did not know whether to reach out and pinch her, or to pinch herself. Instead, she buried her nose in her script and tried to breathe normally.

And then there came the little buzz of adrenalin, like another fly suddenly up against a pane of glass, and Janet felt that she was up against it, and, as the fly buzzed in her stomach, with a clear voice and a sudden, marvellous sense of urgency, she threw herself into being bonnie Jean, the bonnie Jean that all the men of the village of Brigadoon might sing to, about coming home, coming home to bonnie Jean. And as the words poured from her lips she kept thinking about her Hektor-Jan and that she was the reason that he came home every night – the following year it would be every morning, how odd – from his hard day with his warm strength and hairiness and that she, little Janet, was his fortress and his tiny strong tower. That was she. And Janet now transformed like a butterfly from a small suburban chrysalis to become bonnie Jean calling all her dear men to her so that they might sing and be strong because she, she was so bonnie and bright. A butterfly on fire. Aflame with tartan colour and Celtic vivacity.

There. It was done. Derek-Francis and Eileen stared at her with open mouths. The rest of the performers, by now tired and jaded, looked up in surprise. What an audition. What a performance. Janet, little Janet, had stepped right into the shoes of bonnie Jean, just like that. Amazing. They were amazed. Who would have thought. Honestly, where did that come from and Eileen was full of praise for her friend who had landed a small but important role just like that, while she, Eileen, a veteran of *Midsummer*, had been given another chorus part, with two lines of dialogue as some old crone selling rustic Highland treats in the village market.

Amazing, repeated Eileen in the car on the way back home, amazing. And she patted Janet maternally on the knee as though she were her child and had brought home an entirely unexpected piece of good fortune, as though she had won the best prize at a tombola stall or had pulled a giant rabbit out of someone else's hat. Amazing.

And when she had dropped Janet off at the bottom of the short drive, before heading home to the empty house next door, Eileen had leaned across and again had patted Janet on the knee. With a voice almost choked with emotion, Eileen had said that this could be the making of Janet. That she must give it her best shot. She must just be strong and go for it. And should she ever have any doubts, then her understudy, Eileen, could always step in if she ever needed her to.

And Janet had almost reached out and patted Eileen-the-Understudy, too, but had kept her hands to herself at the last moment and had simply murmured her appreciation and that she was sure that there would be at least one night when Eileen might step into the shoes of bonnie Jean. And then she had escaped from the car calling her cheery thanks just before the possible onset of tears because Eileen did not have a proper part and her husband was hardly ever at home and she had no beautiful children like Janet who now, on top of it all, had an important – though fairly small – part in the play.

Brigadoon, Janet had whispered to herself as Eileen's car had stumbled off, choked up with guttural emotion, its headlights searching the way back to next door. And Janet stood there whispering Brigadoon to herself, sounding out each syllable in a Scottish accent which she would have to practise. Brig – a – doooon, as Eileen's car shuddered to halt next door and the lights dimmed. Brig – a – doooon, Janet whispered to the warm night and to the streetlight that filtered through the leafy silhouettes of the plane trees on the broad street and scattered a wonderful mosaic of yellow and greeny-black shadows all over the pavement. And she danced a little jig, a neat Highland fling, there in the dark. Only as she made her way to her front door, up the steps to the veranda and towards the house, did she hear Eileen get out of her car and slam the car door. Of course, those were the days before the crack.

And so, on the evening of the first rehearsal in January, there was a little hoot, a quick jovial toot on the drive to let Janet know that Eileen-the-Understudy was ready.

Bye, called Janet softly to Alice who was doing the dishes in the kitchen and who was going to sit up with the radio after making sure that Pieter and Shelley brushed their teeth properly, and took their tiny fluoride tablet to keep their teeth strong and healthy and white. That seemed to be the latest craze in responsible parenting: fluoride tablets. Another thing to worry about. Motherhood – it seemed – was a never-ending series of anxieties and little concerns. Janet was almost relieved to be heading out, to be leaving her capable Alice in charge. Goodbye, Alice, she said, as Eileen hooted softly a second time. Janet flung herself with her script from the front door.

Shelley's Secret Journal

Today's word from Granny's list is INTERMINABLE.

The interminable wait for school is over. I love school. I am twenty-second on the class list and I sit by the window in each classroom and even in the laboratory. You know exactly where you are with school. The teachers are in charge and know things. They tell you things and you write them down in nice books that smell so clean. You underline the date with a ruler and rule off after each piece of work. I understand Granny why you liked university better than being stuck at home. Mommy and Pappie have also decided not to be stuck at home tonight. Its only us children, Alice and Jock in the ground. He will never leave home. Mommy sent us to school in uniforms still with stupid lines from the packaging. Did you ever do that Granny? I promise I will indubitably never ever do that to my children. I will also look after my husband and my dog and maybe only have two children two boys called Jack and Jock. They might be twins with red hair. No one will be able to tell them apart except for me. They shall have puppies as pets and be able to swim whenever they want to and I shall love them inviolably. I have warned Pieter. I told him not to. It is his last chance but I don't think that he will learn the easy way. He is a bit like Mommy. I am more like you Granny. Love, Shelley.

Happy New Year! rang out amongst the cast as each new arrival was embraced. They had not seen each other since the November auditions. From all over the East Rand they came, and there, beside her tall friend, was Janet who was bonnie Jean. Was she well. Had she had a lovely Christmas. Goodness me, who could forget her audition. Was it truly her first audition ever. No ways. And Janet smiled with aching cheeks as though she were a new bride and tried to deflect some attention towards Eileen-the-Understudy whose idea it had been in the first place and who had played such a magnificent, such a solid Wall last year.

And then Janet was swept away by the soft, guiding arm of Derek-Francis to meet her fiancé – her energetic whippersnapper of a Highland Jock, young Charlie who was going to sing all about coming home to bonnie Jean.

Heads turned and there was a sudden hush, not because Eileen-the-Understudy was having a coughing fit but because there was Janet Snyman standing before her man, Frank van Zyl, and they could have been brother and sister. In fact, they could have been twins. Remarkable. There was actually an intake of breath, quite simultaneous, they agreed later, when Frank held out his hand and shook Janet's. It was as though he were reaching out through the looking-glass to touch himself. The same slim features, the same chestnut hair with the same waves. And no one had spotted that before. Had Derek meant to cast this pigeon pair, this mirror image, but Derek was as stunned as the next person. Why had they not thought of *Twelfth Night*. It was, what was her name, Violet – no – Viola and her brother, presumed lost at sea. Uncanny. Almost spooky. But *Brigadoon* it had to be. Come home to Brigadoon.

And the first rehearsal went swimmingly, on the night of Tuesday, 6 January 1976, in the peanut-butter hall where the air was as thick as syrup and humid as could be. The shriek and whine of crickets came piercingly when they threw open the doors, and the moths fluttered inside and Christmas beetles zithered about madly, and things began to fall into place. Despite the mayhem of insects and the barometric tightening of the air as thunder clouds gathered, and despite the dark circles of sweat under armpits and oiliness of brows and the stickiness of feet in nylon stockings and pinching shoes, it all went most swimmingly.

Janet just dived into her role as though she were to *Brigadoon* born. Derek-Francis began by blocking the first scenes. It took an age to walk the cast through the opening number where the village woke up after a hundred years' slumber. The director made them all lie down and then in waves of sudden wakefulness they had to stretch and yawn and peer blearily about them, as though seeing light for the first time in an age, realising, after the protracted snooze, just where they were and how they had come to be there. And just as they were trying to do it again, as Derek-Francis had shaken his head and breathlessly requested Verisimilitude folks, I want ver-i-sim-i-li-tude please, the school caretaker, a grumpy black man with a soothsayer beard and an aggressive bunch of keys, had come to ask when he might lock up for the night as it was getting late. He was quite unpleasant about it all and actually raised his voice to Derek-Francis who was very patient when they came to think about it, but some of the men got involved and the caretaker was despatched with a flea in his ear. Actually several fleas to remind him that Hey, my boy, just remember your place, okay, and that You should not try to get too white, all right. And Derek-Francis had told the men that it was fine, that there was no need to get involved and that he had said they would be done by nine-thirty and it was, in fact, already five past ten. And so they had called it a day, or a night at least. And there were cheery goodbyes, with some real yawns, and some had a fair distance to travel home but they agreed that they had made great progress even though the incident with that black had been a bit off. A bit of an intrusion. And so they stumbled from *Brigadoon* back to lives in Benoni and Boksburg and Brakpan and Springs and there was also a couple from Sunward Park and even a man called Nigel from the small town, Nigel.

Eileen was very vocal in the car and threw herself about in the confined space with frantic good humour when remarking again just how amazing it was that Janet had a twin brother and had told no one and how could she keep such a secret to herself the silly, silly girl. And Janet had smiled with lots of patience and understanding and had asked whether Eileen-the-Understudy really thought so and Eileen-the-Understudy barked with laughter and had said, You mampara, you silly, silly mampara.

They parted on good terms and Janet waited at the front door until Eileen-the-Understudy's car stuttered to silence next door. It was a while before Eileen-the-Understudy's car door slammed, and there came the far-off rumble of thunder. It was going to rain. They needed the rain. Janet unlocked the front door and went through to find Alice asleep with her radio arguing softly with itself and Alice's head in her arms, leaning against the hard wood of the kitchen table. Janet watched her for a brief moment. She leaned close to her and took in the soapy scent, the strange soap that Alice used, and gazed at the wiry strands of her hair that escaped from beneath her covering doek, strands that coiled coarsely and thickly, so different from her own soft brown hair. Janet reached out, perhaps to touch Alice's hair, but then she was gently shaking Alice's shoulders and telling her that she, Janet, was home and Alice could go outside now. Thank you, said Janet as Alice took her murmuring, disputatious radio with its Zulu or Xhosa or Sotho or Shangaan or whatever the voices were back to her kaya outside. The children, they being good, were Alice's last words for the night.

The children! It took a moment for bonnie Jean to remember that she had children. That she was indeed married with children: there was the cautious girl, the eldest, Shelley, followed by little Pieter, the brave boy, and then chaos on two legs, the youngest, the little Sylvia. Was that the right order. Of course it was. Bonnie Jean was banished from her mind and it was just Janet. Married to Hektor-Jan and not to Frank her twin brother from Illyria.

Despite the heat and the thick humidity, Janet treated herself to a deep bath and emerged pink and perspiring. It was very late, and Janet could not bear the rasp of her nightie. So she threw herself onto the bed and lay there naked. Her skin throbbed with the heat of the bath and Janet felt the sweat ooze from her, a film of moisture and it welled in her navel and ran between her legs which she spread wide in an attempt to get cool. But it was impossible.

She got up, but the bedroom windows were already open, and the air did not move a midnight muscle. Janet stood there, and the thunder growled closer. The storm seemed to be skirting the house, circling it somehow. Janet hoped that it would not pass them by. The air needed to break; this stifling heat needed to be split so that the heavens would open and pour down some cooling rain.

And as she thought about the heavens splitting, Janet knew that she would not be able to help herself and before she could grip the edge of the bed, she had opened the back door and was standing once again at the foot of the pool.

The horizon winked with lightning and the thunder lumbered closer, heavy and rough and slouching. What beast was it that was coming to Benoni. The air grew thicker and ever more expectant. Janet stood with her arms stretched wide, her legs apart, trying not to touch herself as it was just too hot, too humid. Such sweltering and sweating – even outdoors. She should never have had that bath. And Janet knew that she was going to have to. She was going to have to step forward. It made sense, as the air bulged so heavily pregnant with the storm. It made sense but oh the horror as she stepped into the baby section of the pool where the water swallowed her ankles with a soft, cool mouth. But she was going to have to descend deeper into the pool or die of heatstroke.

In slow motion, as though the water were black syrup in the midnight air, a pool of deep molasses, Janet waded down one step, then the other, to stand in the shallow end, the beautiful coolness flooding between her legs as well as into her belly button. Bliss. She gasped and all the while she felt with her nervous foot to see if she was anywhere near the crack. She tried to keep to the left-hand side of the pool as she waded deeper and the gorgeous balm of cooling black crept up to her breasts, her shoulders, her neck and chin. And as the proper lightning came, quick and jagged like an electric fracture in the sky, Janet sank beneath the water and never heard the giant, throat-clearing cough of thunder. As she had done as a child, Janet pulled her feet up beneath her and clutched them with her looping arms to form a human ball which gently rotated underwater, buoyed up by the air in her lungs. And as she let the air slowly bubble out of her nostrils, she began to sink – now a human balloon. She could not bear to touch the floor of the pool though and there was the sudden shooting fear that she might put a foot wrong and end up – or down – in the gap in the bottom of the pool. Disappear through the crack to God knows where. Janet uncoiled and threw back her head to the dark air just as the thunder crashed again – crashed as though she had jolted from the water and bashed her head against the pressing sky. Ow, that hurt. Such a big sound and then Janet remembered her mother's fixation with Highveld thunderstorms. Never shelter under a tree. Janet had to promise never to seek shelter under a tree during a storm. Never stand alone in an open field where the lightning might strike. Janet promised that too. And never ever be anywhere near the pool – that self-same pool – because, Janet, dearest Janet, are you listening, water – conducts – electricity. Electricity is to water what guilt is to marriage, and little Janet had to repeat water – conducts – electricity and to promise – never – to – swim – when – there – is – a – storm and yet here she was a quarter of a century later, a woman stunned by her broken promise that lay shattered at the bottom of the pool like the deep crack.

Janet leapt out of the pool before the dark crack or the blinding lightning or her broken promise could get her. She stood again at the pool's edge, breathing shakily, a small child filled with shame.

And even as she stood there, bearing in her womb her fourth child, she needed to hold the hand of Lettie, the gentle Lettie whose strong fingers had gripped hers when Janet first learned to walk and whose voice – sometimes sharp, often stern, but always ready to break into gales of laughter – had been the one, telling constant in her growing-up. Her own mother was too busy travelling from the East Rand to Johannesburg, from the old mining town to the big city of gold where the university was, the University of the Witwatersrand. And there Amelia Amis – never Mrs Ward, always Amelia Amis MA Cantab – lectured on the Enlightenment and on Nineteenth and Twentieth Century Female Poets and on the novels of William Makepeace Thackeray, Anthony Trollope and George Eliot. And she would come home late and Janet would have to pit her small strength and ingenuity against a pile of essays for her mother's attention. Janet took to bouts of tummy ache, sore heads and once a rash of lipstick spots but to no avail whatsoever. Mummy, in Amelia Amis MA mode, would sigh over the top of the neat, stapled pages and perhaps pat her daughter's head whilst the red pen tick, ticked away or jabbed dismissive comments in the margins. And if Janet kicked up a fuss, perhaps began to sob, then her mother's eyes would peer over her half-moon spectacles and her hand would be withdrawn and she would sigh her daughter's name. If Janet persisted, the red pen might make its way behind Amelia Amis MA's right ear and both hands, unencumbered, would reach down and grip her shoulders, not unkindly, just uncertainly, as though trying to get to grips with a living argument or a sobbing thesis that did not quite make sense and that by holding on to it, she might be able to work out what it was or in which direction it led. But if the tummy ache or the headache made her cry still more loudly or persistently then the hands would turn her away and the sharp, English-accented voice would sound over the top of her head as it summoned Lettie. Lettie, I give up, was the implication. Lettie, this little conundrum is too tricky. Where is its central and lucid structure, its governing argument. Where the coherent analysis. Instead, I have in my hands rather too much raw and wilful emotion. And behold, the salty tears and coursing mucus. And the mess of lipstick smears. Where did she find the lipstick. I never use lipstick.

So old Lettie would appear from nowhere where she had no doubt been waiting in hope and she would receive little Janet once again in her soft, pink-palmed hands that were a burnished and beautiful brown on the other side, just the opposite of Janet's own hands, so often grubby on the inside and pink on the outside. And Janet would try not to cry as her tummy ache or headache or, that once, her lipstick spots, were soothed by Lettie's cuddles and soft hands. And Janet would find herself a while later wielding a dustpan and little brush or watching a loaf rise in the oven or helping Lettie to sing a song and little Janet had quite forgotten to bend over her make-pretend tummy ache or to grimace through a phantom migraine.

Where was Lettie now. Janet struggled to remember. Lettie lived on in Alice. She was in the old kaya that adjoined the garage, no doubt fast asleep, not naked before the pool and facing alone the mayhem of the Highveld storm.

As the sky split above her and the heavens opened, Janet was a child once again. With no thoughts of her own children snuggled deep inside the house, Janet ran wildly to Alice's room. She could not stop her fist from pounding on the metal door with a thunder all of its own. And Alice must have thought it was thunder too as it was a long time – after yet more frantic bashing on the resonant metal – before the handle turned and the door peeled open to reveal her white, startled eyes.

Lettie, Janet cried, I am so sorry. Alice.

And Alice opened the door a fraction more, with a murmured, Madam.

The rain thundered down on the metal roof of the kaya. Janet could barely hear her own voice cry out Alice's name again. How did Alice ever manage to sleep out here. It sounded like the end of the world. The air fizzed with lightning, tasted of lightning, it was that close, and the crack of thunder was instantaneous. This was the heart of the storm. It was useless to shout. Janet could not shout.

She reached out and took Alice's hand that clutched the edge of the door. She pulled each of Alice's fingers loose from the chilly metal and took them in her hand. Alice, she shouted again through the pelting rain, and then she was dragging Alice through the gap, pulling her from her cosy kaya out into the wet-teeming garden.

As she was urgently walking with Alice's hand, the rest of startled Alice followed in a ghostly nightie, and the rain gushed down cold and hard.

Madam, shouted Alice again but did not pull away her hand. Madam.

Janet led her through the crashing rain. Their hair ran into their eyes, the wet grass clung to their soles, their shoulders stung. Janet could not stop.

Alice's hand was warm in her own. It was the only warm thing in the world and Janet was not letting go. And then they were standing on the slasto at the pool's edge and Janet was pointing with her free hand at the leaping surface of the water that splashed like a living salmon and she was shouting out to Alice, The crack, the crack. Alice looked wildly around, as though for the end of the world, and Janet pointed again, The crack, oh God, the crack, as Alice pulled the sodden nightie about herself with her free hand. Then the light bulb of the heavens flashed once before exploding and Janet could scream, There, there, did you see that, and point wildly at the dark fist which had smashed the bottom of the pool. Janet was on her knees, as though dragged down by some vortex, as though beaten down by the rain, and her hand quivered out in front of her, a part of some terrible scarecrow or a divining rod that trembled with the knowledge of the fault, the fissure. And as the night exploded into lightning, and the slick wetness burnished their skin to deep black or brilliant white, it was impossible in the heart of the storm to see who was the Madam and who the maid. They flickered and shone, like lights, like ghosts, soaking wet but on fire.

It took all of Alice's strength to pull her to her feet, to pull the sobbing little Madam up to her chest and to hold her there as she struggled and fought and tried to turn back to the pool. The rain shrouded them both and the lightning struck again and again, but the storm was wheeling off and it would not be long before the rain softened and the thunder was a murmur from the lips of the sky. And so it came to pass that as she held the Madam, held her so tightly with her wet nightie that it quickly became warm, the rain did indeed sigh to a gentle drizzle and the Madam stopped shaking and fighting and trying to point to the swimming pool.

And like her mother before her, the legendary Lettie, Alice knew precisely what to do. It was not long before Janet was tucked up in bed, her big double bed now, with her feet carefully wiped and freed from the strips of grass that stuck between her toes. And Lettie, no it was Alice, held the glass of warm, sweet Milo to her lips as she sipped, her head secure in a nest of pillows, just how she liked it. Her hair was dry and stroked by Lettie's pink palms and the soft brush, and the silken sounds of Lettie's soft voice came singing the lullaby Tula Tu Tula baba Tula sana, Tul'umam 'uzobuya ekuseni, Tula Tu Tula baba Tula sana, Tul'umam 'uzobuya ekuseni, Hush my baby close your eyes, Time to fly to paradise, Till the sunlight brings you home, You must dream your dreams alone, Tula Tu Tula baba Tula sana, Tul'umam 'uzobuya ekuseni, Tula Tu Tula baba Tula sana, Tul'umam 'uzobuya ekuseni, Hush my baby go to sleep, I'll be with you counting sheep, Dreams will take you far away, Sleep until the break of the day, Tula Tu Tula baba Tula sana, Tul'umam 'uzobuya ekuseni, Tula Tu Tula baba Tula sana, Tul'umam 'uzobuya ekuseni. And Lettie – Alice – held her gently as she burped after draining every last drop of Milo and then she could sink back into slumber as Alice-Lettie switched off the light. Unbidden, in the dreamless dark, her thumb found its way to her mouth.

And then Alice checked on the children who had stood peering from the dark caves of their rooms as Mommy was led past in her birthday suit. Everything was all right. Everything was going to be fine. No more storms. And Mommy would be dressed in the morning and ready to take them to school just like all the other mothers who drove their neat cars and who were all, invariably, indubitably, fully clothed and entirely respectable.

He knew that she would be awake, as was her wont. He would return after the heavenly mayhem to find her, a watchtower, a beacon of wakefulness, waiting for him, to nourish his body and to replenish his soul.

And he wondered with all his might and main, just how he might stand before her, in her father's house, and answer her truthfully when she turned her head into his neck and whispered, How did it go, my love. Or the even trickier, How are you.

Could he lie. Could he lie directly and blatantly and just say, Fine, all is fine, when everything was anything but fine. Unless you counted the fine attention to detail, the fines imposed on living flesh, the ironic, but you are such a fine fellow, or the paradoxically fine grains of degradation, the opposite of the coarse, the obvious.

And so he could not tell her as a man might tell his wife about all he had done that night when he had sailed forth on his night ships.

He could not describe the briefing of the major. The finger-jabbing, chin-thrusting imparting of the latest security status by the station commander. The very latest on the Swart Gevaar, the Black Danger, which was but one arm in the Total Onslaught against their God-fearing, Christian nationhood. He could not cuddle her and say we are at war with a Communist anti-Christ the likes of which biblical pestilences and plagues are nothing. That they, that beacon of white light on the southern tip of Africa, the land of their covenant with God, their Vaderland and their refuge, was under attack from without and from within. He could not tell her about the arms caches they would discover after his Tuesday night interrogation of those men.

How he, Hektor-Jan, so recently promoted, had already proved his worth. How his great gift to be able to sniff out the truth from a miasma of untruths, evasions and obfuscations had brought such fine success.

He could never tell her how instinctively he went about his work. How he divided his day, his night, into shifts and made sure that he had his tea breaks and stopped when his shift was over so that he might come home on time.

Christopher Radmann

He could not tell her about this man, Mokoene or his boy, his friend, Rapele. And the third member of their little gang, Mujabe. How they were brought into the holding cells already in a bit of a bad way. How he had pretended to be a doctor. All that was needed was a white coat and a stethoscope, so easily borrowed. It was a neat reversal as usually the stethoscope was brought out near the end to check whether they were dead or not, not at the beginning, even before he had begun. And he was so kind. So solicitous. Had they had access to a lawyer – when he knew they would never see a lawyer. And did they feel well, when he was about to make them feel a whole lot worse. Let me look into your eyes. Let me listen to your heart. My goodness me, he said in English so as not to terrify them with his Boer-urgent, Boer-brutal Afrikaans. My goodness me, he said in softer English, how black and wide your pupils seem, how dilated, and he tried not to emphasise the first ominous syllable of dilated, but moved on gently to remark, How your heart is thumping so. How it is going boom-diddy-boom, boom-diddy-boom. That cannot be good. Have you been hurt. Has anyone been unkind. Can I get you a glass of water, a Disprin. Do you have a headache. Maybe a warm mug of tea with lots of sugar. And how they tried to hold on to him, almost not believing their good fortune, almost hoping that not all policemen were dogs, almost not believing that this was some sort of sick joke at their profound expense. And he had gone to get their Disprins and to make them their tea just as the blacks drank their tea – white and sweet. The very opposite of the tired joke in the canteen – Johan/Willem/Sarel/Freddie likes his coffee/tea just as he likes his women – black and strong. And they would laugh again just like they had laughed the last time. And even the men who had been known to take an active interest in some of the black female prisoners, and who, it was known, had actually been willing to help out with the interrogations with parts of their own anatomy, well, they laughed maybe even louder and longer than most.

But he kept a straight face and delivered the Disprins and the steaming tea. He even let them take them. Let them swallow their Disprins for the relief of pain and drink their tea as act of communion. Possibly they even smiled briefly at him, this square man in the tight white coat who looked like a doctor and who did not look like a doctor. But he had brought them some pain relief and the nicest mug of tea. And they sipped their tea out of the police mugs, and tried to make their tea last as long as possible because they knew in their hearts that this tea break from pain and terror could not last. When you are branded a terrorist, you must be prepared for terror. And, as each second passed, and as this white man, who looked like a Boer and sounded like a settler, who appeared so hard yet seemed so soft, asked them yet another gentle question, they knew in their heart of hearts what was coming.

And he knew that they knew. He felt their sick certainty. For it was reciprocated by the pounding of his own heart, the constricting of his own pupils, and the light sweating of his palms. He slurped his tea as noisily as they did theirs. He was watchful in a way which was not watchful or wary, but in his very seeming gentleness and guilelessness, he knew that he terrified them. For what white man would spend time in their cell with no gun. Even if their hands were cuffed and their ankles hobbled. This white doctor ran a careful finger under the warm steel to see if they were hurt and did not glance suddenly over his shoulder even as the uniformed guards patrolled the corridor or as the sounds came muffled from behind closed doors, the soft portent of the pain to come. These Boers were famous for it. What marvellous adversaries they made. What wonderful foes in this battle over the centuries between Boer and black and British. So whilst there was no pain yet, they sipped their tea and quietly spat out the white tablets which they had not swallowed in case they were not Disprins and exchanged secret glances behind his back.

He let those glances continue for a while, and ignored the soft patter of the tiny tablets dropped behind the steel bench, but then their tea had to come to an end. The dregs had to be drained and he finally sighed and removed their mugs. He placed them through the bars, four neat mugs as his was with theirs. They made a neat square and some of the sweet sugary sediment lay in the bottom of each mug and he saw how the white sugar was mixed with the brown tea and stained so that it too was a dull brown and could not be separated from the insidious tea. And he felt oddly moved by the ineffable fact of the brown crystals that were once a pure and refined white, almost translucent. And then were stained by the tea.

The bars of the cell pressed against his forehead.

He turned to them and came before them, where they were perched on the low steel bench that was fixed into the concrete floor and which could not be raised as battering ram or a big bludgeon. He squatted before them and regarded them earnestly, even sadly. As though he were genuinely sorry that they had finished their tea and now it had come to this. The white coat trailed down on either side of his strong haunches. The very edges of it kissed the concrete floor. His deep voice welled up. Is there anything you need to tell me, he asked. Anything at all that will make it easier, that will make things better. Informants have told my colleagues that you have been a little bit naughty.

They stared at him. Naughty. Where did this word come from? Children were naughty. They were not children. And yet he squatted, a bit like a child before them, and told them that they had been naughty.

He cleared his throat, as though embarrassed. It was getting to that delicate stage. When push came to shove. But he sensed that the fulcrum was yet to find its precise place. That if you were to move the earth, shift heaven and hell with a lever of infinite length, you had to be certain where to place it, where to find that all-important fulcrum. And that was precisely why he had been promoted. For he was a past master of patience and of knowing exactly where to insert that lever and what to use as a fine point, a moment about which worlds would tilt and spin.

Very naughty, very bad, he clarified. Which was not good. He let the negative numb the air. He watched them swallow as perhaps the last slight taste of the rejected Disprins wore off. Nothing would dull the pain that was to come.

You see, he said, still squatting sympathetically at their level, *each of you has someone who is important to you. You,* he nodded genially – even sorrowfully – at Mokoene, *you have a wife – Grace. And you,* to Mujabe, *also have a wife. The youngest man, almost a boy, Rapele, has but a girlfriend, but she is very pretty, very pretty indeed. She is so pretty. Her name is Gloria Ngubane, if he was not mistaken.* And the youngest man started as though stung. How did he know, how did this big Boer know?

And he watched the boy jump. He jumped and his eyes widened helplessly, a complete giveaway. And his eyes widened and he flinched fractionally, and his fists clenched even tighter. And the smell of the young man came to him through the flinch and the fists, the smell that was all the more acrid, an amalgam of wood-fire, and toil, and now fear. He saw, he sensed all of that as a complete picture of guilt and rude surprise. The portrait was revealed to him; he was aware of each constituent part, yet it was his appreciation of the whole that was so masterly. He was profoundly aware of how his subject leapt to artistic life without having to peer at the component strokes. No, the portrait was revealed in its organic completeness and its resonant simplicity. The others were better liars. The others were hardened and more professional. He always knew that this boy would be the one to crack, but it would be a while yet, though the signs were there to be read. It could not be more obvious. And he stood up and called the guards, still gentle and sorrowful all the while, as though saddened by the curtailment of their little tea party. And the uniformed guards came at his soft call and took away the two older men so that it was just he and his sweating friend. It would need to be a solo performance. Or maybe more of a duet if you counted himself. He did not want the youngest of the men to feel that he, Rapele, needed to put on a brave performance for his friends. Oh no. It had to be just the two of them. Mano a mano. If this boy, this terrorist they called Rapele, were to sing his song, it would be for his ears only. That much respect and distance the major had accorded him from the start. After that first performance late last year, they had *not raised a single objection or even dared to refer to official procedure. It was just he and Rapele in the small, intimate space.*

And yet they were out in the open now. The cell opened up to encompass heaven and hell. There was life and death crammed into that small space and he could feel it as though it were a shape and he could smell it and hear it as though it were a ripe fart and so could the boy. They looked at those things that filled the space between them in the cell. They did not look at each other just yet. That would come. They both knew that would come.

And Hektor-Jan let the silence grow. The silence that was filled with more wails and screams than it was possible to catalogue crammed their ears and quite deafened them. He had to wait for the resounding white noise to settle.

He circled the impossible things in the very centre, the heart of the cell. He seemed to measure out, pace out the perimeter of the horror to come and then at last, after making absolutely certain, it seemed, he turned to the boy.

Rapele did not look up. It appeared as though his bare feet had suddenly become the most fascinating things in the entire universe. Hektor-Jan also examined the calloused feet, the yellow toenails in need of a cut and the oddly serried ranks of the toes, uneven with two long and two short beside the blunt big toe. The boy knew that he was being circled. Even though the large Boer stood before him in his white coat, he knew that something dark and dangerous was stalking his very breath, his innermost thoughts and feelings and there was nothing he could do about it. And Hektor-Jan knew that his mere proximity had tugged at the heart of the boy's sphincter as there came the scent of warm piss, a tiny gushing like a sudden smear across the canvas. The poor boy.

Then he laid a hand on the boy's shoulder. It did not have to be like this. He told the boy with real sorrow and a tragic certainty that it did not have to be like this. Could he not just play along. Help him. Help him help himself. It could be so simple. Please, asseblief, please let it be a simple matter of letting him help him.

The boy stiffened beneath his touch.

We are informed, he told the boy quietly, that you have hidden the weapons in Kwa-Thema.

The township of Kwa-Thema was not too far away from where they were now. In half an hour they could be standing in Kwa-Thema, locating the weapons.

It would be so helpful, so helpful if you told us where the weapons are hidden.

It was like a child's game. You have hidden the sweeties that we want. Now, where are those sweeties, which you have hidden. We want to find them, right now, please.

But the boy was obliged not to play along. As much as he swallowed and fidgeted, as much as he would like to get this over and done with, he had to look obtuse and overtly innocent and say that he did not know what this man was talking about, that he had no idea, no idea whatsoever. He had to say that as he waded deeper and deeper into the darkness and the warm wetness spread over his crotch and he stewed angrily in his own embarrassment and fear. No idea whatsoever.

Whatsoever, Hektor-Jan repeated thoughtfully. Whatsoever is a big word, a profound compression of three words but it did not leave much room to hide. Hektor-Jan unpicked the word, dismantled it into its three smaller cogs: what-so-ever. If he had no idea what-so-ever, that did not help very much at all. Did he not have just the tiniest inkling. What. So. Ever. That would be so helpful if he had even the slightest idea. Did he not overhear someone saying something. Maybe one of the others. Did he not have an address to which he might send his friends to find the weapons. Then all would be well. No harm would befall him whatsoever. Did he really and truly not want to tell him.

But the boy could only stare at his feet.

The big Boer sighed. It was a soft sound. So very incongruous.

The young man would have felt a lot better if the big Boer had just shouted and stamped his foot, ranted and railed, carped and cursed. Not that gentleness, that terrible tenderness. That sadness. That reluctance. Because if it made that terrible Boer so sad, what on earth was going to happen to him, the prisoner, the black, die swarte, die kaffir, in that tiny cell.

And then it came.

Gloria, Gloria, Gloria, her name rolled from the Boer's tongue like a hymn.

And the boy reeled with the triple blow. Of course.

Gloria, repeated the Boer, his mouth making her filthy. Glo-ri-ah.

He offered the dying fall of her name, the boy's girlfriend's name. How it sank beneath the weight of its own syllables. Glo-ri-ah. But hidden within it there lurked the threat of gore. Gloria. Gore to come. Glorious gore. But for the moment he let her name sigh to silence – ah.

No, screamed the boy suddenly. Nee, asseblief nee. No, please no. Perhaps he thought that if he addressed the Boer in his native Afrikaans, it would help. How could it help.

The hiding place of the weapons, the Boer asked quietly and the boy knew that that was his last chance. He hesitated, Hektor-Jan granted him that. But it was not enough. No idea whatsoever, said the boy, in polite, formal English with his eyes screwed shut.

In the stifling silence of the cell, the Boer's voice came quietly. It was some signal, and the Boer's voice did tremble, the boy might have granted him that.

And a door clanked open and into the corridor two uniformed guards brought his Gloria. She did not come quietly. She was sobbing and struggling and it took a while for the policemen to handcuff her wrists to the outer bars of the cell so that she was spread before him, her arms wide as though about to embrace him but instead she reached out to cold metal, the bars that were sheer and vertical and unyielding. And the Boer nodded to the men in uniform and their shoes squeaked like mice, like rats, down the corridor and then were gone behind the closed door.

Hektor-Jan moved to one side of the cell. This was awkward. He was the uncomfortable go-between. There was the boy on one side of the cell, clamped to the low, steel bench. And opposite him, outside the cell, her arms stretched wide, was his girlfriend who looked as though she had spread her wings and was about to fly into his arms. But she was sobbing and her eyes were swollen and snot ran down into her mouth and she could not flap her wings.

Hektor-Jan ran a hand over his brow. Then he looked at the boy. He had opened his eyes all right. There was a fruitful pause. The boy finally tore his eyes from his Gloria and looked at Hektor-Jan and then in a help-less instant he spat. A sudden reflex, a sodden reflux. The gob of spit that came from his mouth was large and loose, surprisingly gelatinous and it landed with a streak on Hektor-Jan's right shoe. Hektor-Jan looked down at his soiled shoe and shook his head.

The walls and the bars of the cell opened up and fell away. No more was it the claustrophobic cavern of the whale's belly. No longer did the functions of suck and swallow apply. It was as though all laws of gravity and motion had fallen away and they were in the bright realm of infinite possibility. He could strike the boy in the mouth for that. He could send the pile-driver of his fist smashing through the boy's face for that. He could kick the boy. He could rupture the boy's groin and explode his balls with one well-judged, vicious kick. He could crush his toes with the heel of his soiled shoe. He could take a short step and break his kneecap. He could grasp the boy's head by the ears and bring his face smashing into his rising knee. All these things were now possible and Hektor-Jan knew what had happened countless times in this cell, and his penis, a stiff tuning fork, an urgent divining rod of terrible tension, had already responded to those seductive echoes, to the aphrodisiac of power that saturated the cell. But he knew better than to trust his own base nature. This was not sex; this was not even art. Hektor-Jan despised the hardness in his trousers, a stiff, creased tangent, so disturbing and dis-tracting. Hektor-Jan sighed. Spare the rod. Thy rod and staff comfort me still.

And even as he began to remove his spit-smeared shoe, slowly, almost reluctantly, he knew that it was a job, a job that he did well, sublimely well, and the faces of his beloved children came to him just as the salary that his job supplied brought food to the table and nourishment to their tiny bodies. And even as he slipped off the shoe to reveal the intimacy of his socked foot, last seen at home in his bedroom, so his actions carried sustenance to the solid wood table in the homely kitchen. And as he took the shoe to Gloria's face, so it was also a loaf of bread that fed Shelley and Pieter and little Sylvia. And as he smeared the stringy mucus in Gloria's wet face, so his actions by simple extension brought food to the sweet, sweet mouths of his children. He did not have to do it, it was true. He did not have to wipe her boyfriend's spit in her face. What had she done. But someone would have to do it and at least he did it gently, tenderly.

He put his shoe back on. They were both very quiet now.

He gave the boy every chance, one last chance. Please, he said again, asseblief, just tell me. Because, wragtig, when I call those dogs back again, it will not be a good thing for your Gloria. And even as he sent out the final overture, Hektor-Jan knew that the boy would stare sullenly, the artery in his throat pulsing with the quaint effort, the heroic stupidity, to remain morose and silent.

And Hektor-Jan had to turn to the girl. She was pretty. Despite the swollen, tearful, smeared face she was a pretty woman, maybe a little older than the boy, her body shapely. She would make a lovely mother; her body would nourish little mouths in years to come, if only he would speak. But he would not and Hektor-Jan was left with no choice. There was so much riding on the boy's voice. Lack of a voice.

The boy would never know that it hurt Hektor-Jan as much if not more than it maimed and injured the victim. Did not the psalmist say, Let a righteous man strike me – it is a kindness; let him rebuke me – it is oil on my head. My head will not refuse it. Yet my prayer is ever against the deeds of evildoers. And did not our Lord say, Thou preparest a table before me in the presence of mine enemies: thou anointest my head with oil; my cup runneth over. How much oil could Hektor-Jan spare. How much could it hurt him, did it cost him. The boy was safe in the here and now. Yes, Hektor-Jan was pincered in the present, too, but he was also caught between the terrible weight of the past and the future. He knew exactly what it was like, and what it would be like. It was and would be dreadful. And it could so easily have been stopped. With just a word.

And with a heavy heart Hektor-Jan uttered the words that he did not want anyone to hear.

Thus summoned, the two men returned. The dogs that he had mentioned, against whom he had tried so clearly to warn. They were unleashed now; there would be no stopping them now.

They were the dogs who, before the young man's very eyes, slowly stripped his Gloria. With her arms stretched like a dark Jesus before him, they carefully undid each button, buckle, clasp and zip so that she was prised free from every last stitch of dignity. They did not hear Gloria's gurgling gasps, the clanking of her wrists that tried to shake the very foundations of the bars but which succeeded only in letting the blood slip from the delicate skin of her wrists so that her clenched fists seemed to rise like buds, like flowers, from their slender stems of blood. And they folded her clothes, her dress, her nylon stockings, her panties and her bra and placed them on top her shoes, off the floor, neatly out of the way. And then they each took a leg by the calf and, as she turned frantically to see what they were up to, they spread her legs gently wider and wider so that she sank a little closer to the floor and her fists now slipped back in time, now bulged like buds about to burst into bloom against the added, downward pressure. Then they cable-strapped her ankles to the bars so she became a dark dove spread-eagled and as her voice choked in her throat, she became Da Vinci's Everyman. But she was most palpably and certainly a woman. For her female space was aired, was most obstetrically vaunted. Flaunted. They were making her flirt.

Hektor-Jan could not bear to look. The sight of those firm white hands squeezing her dark flesh as her legs were stretched. The terrible teething sound as the cable-straps zithered closed then locked. They set his own teeth on edge and the breath rasped in his throat. For a full minute he stood there immobile and slowly became aware that his hand had reached out, was touching the boy on the shoulder, was heaving up and down as the boy's chest and shoulders heaved up and down.

Asseblief, he whispered through his dry mouth even as he heard the sound of the dogs. The two white men were getting ready.

Were the syllables too soft. Was the Afrikaans word for please too frail for the freight it had to carry. Asseblief, sighed from his ashen lips and died almost before it was born.

Still Hektor-Jan could not look at the naked woman stretched behind him. Still he could not move his gentle hand from the boy's shoulder. Every emotion played itself out beneath the young man's skin. His face contorted, fought, struggled and yielded to every emotion there could be. That Rapele loved this woman there was no doubt. That he would die for her was certain. That he could tear down the heavens to save her was obvious, that he could not utter a single, helpful word was his profound, acknowledged undoing.

Hektor-Jan could not tell him that there were strict protocols in the South African Police Force concerning the fucking of suspects to elicit information. In careful accordance with the laws of the land, whites did not fuck blacks. This was the South Africa of Apartheid after all, of Separate Development, of Christian National Education, of the Pass Laws, of Manifest Destiny, of the Immorality Act and, very recently, of the Bantu Education Bill. However, they were not in Parliament. What went on in these cells, in this space, well, wragtig, no one knew what went on in these cells. Any political system, any belief system, is underpinned by a thousand million little private acts, secret gestures, implicit nuances that bring it to life. Yes, there were clear protocols concerning the fucking of suspects, but that did not stop suspects from being ceremoniously fucked within an inch of their lives. Besides, she was not a suspect. An accomplice, perhaps, but that was all.

From the boy's face, Hektor-Jan could tell that at least one of the dogs had lowered his trousers and that, in full view, his hunting snout was sniffing close. And from the fearful inhalations, the gasping acceleration of the woman's breathing, she knew that the hunt for her cunt was on. And that she stood no chance. For she stood spreadeagled, her private spaces terribly exposed and she could only twist and try to turn to peer frantically behind her as the dog drew closer, actually knocked his cock like a little truncheon against her angled thigh. Little pig, little pig, let me come in. It was not a children's rhyme, but the dog was crooning something. Hektor-Jan's skin went cold.

For then she could do nothing but stare at the boy, her lover, as the places that he had found so recently within her warm flesh were now suddenly explored, were rooted out by an unyielding rod of white iron.

The pulse of all the boy's tortured feelings shook Hektor-Jan's hand that still rested on his shoulder. He felt the sickening squirm, he felt the almost synaptic shock of the woman's gasp as the dog grasped her flanks and drove his ramrod will deep within her, the dreadful pain that shot across the tiny space from her to him, then right up Hektor-Jan's arm like lightning.

It was Hektor-Jan who seemed to crack. Stop, he shouted. Stop. And still he could not bring himself to look at the sweating dog or the lolling woman tied to the cold, steel bars. The other dog had to stop the first dog. Physically had to restrain him and pull him back so that, snorting, he came out of the woman panting with the effort to extract his pounding flesh. Stop, whispered Hektor-Jan.

And his eyes searched the face of the boy. Do you not see, Hektor-Jan tried to say. Do you not see what will happen. How one will have his way, and how the other waits ready, standing to attention. With a penis so paraat. These dogs are privates. With their privates on public display. The blood drained from his head and he felt dizzy. And that will not be the end. It goes on. Do you not see that it will go on and on. They might do it again, both of them. They might decide that the short rubber truncheons are much more fun. They might call their friends, make it an office party. Do you not see. For God's sake, you must see. Why will you not see. This is only the very beginning.

In the downstairs cells beneath the town of Benoni, there was no sense of the soaking rain that fell that night or of the rumbling thunder or even of the brilliant display of lightning. But there were other storms.

12.8CM

The Cabinet has [...] approved in principle the introduction of staturily controlled television service for South Africa, which will form an integral part of the Republic's broad educational system as a whole and which will be based on a foundation designed to ensure that the Christian values of this country and the social structure of its various communities are respected.

– Senator van der Spuy, *Hansard*, 27 April 1971, col. 5288

The World again challenged the government. In its editorial on 25 February 1976, it declared that, 'whether the South African government likes it or not, many urban African parents are bitterly opposed to their children being forced to learn in Afrikaans'. The newspaper dismissed 'God-like decisions made by white officials – even Cabinet members – on matters of vital importance to blacks' and rejected the old racist dictum that 'whites know what is best for blacks'.

– Sifiso Mxolisi Ndlovu, *The Road to Democracy in South Africa: 1970–1980*, Volume 2, Chapter 7

D oug has invited us around tonight to show off his TV, Janet said to Hektor-Jan as he peered at his plate of food. He seemed to be waiting for a signal prior to picking up his knife and fork. He transferred his gaze from his plate to her.

Janet tried not to yawn. She had overslept and yet felt exhausted.

Hektor-Jan, now at the end of his day, looked similarly spent.

Janet had not awoken with the dawn chorus. Nor had the Hadedas split her fragile shell of sleep with their harsh cries. The storm had wheeled off into the night and the children had slept through. It was Alice's warm cup of tea that trembled slightly in the saucer that had summoned Janet to consciousness. Her eyes seemed to creak open to discern vaguely Alice's kindly face bent over her, exactly as she had hovered over her the previous night. But the air was washed clean. It was a new day, minted freshly by the storm. Why, Janet could barely recollect how she came to feel so stiff and why her limbs ached. Her throat was dry. She never slept on her back. She must have snored.

And before she could move, before she could practise waking up as they had rehearsed waking up last night for Derek-Francis as citizens of Brigadoon, Hektor-Jan was home and holding her. Bending solicitously over her and lifting her partially out of her snug bed to hold her. He held her and held her. He rarely just held her. She felt his warmth through his shirt. She felt his hair beneath his shirt, springy and coiled, quite soft. And between them, their warmth yielded up the familiar scent of their bed, and Hektor-Jan's sweat. And there was also another smell. On the cusp of his manly smell was the hint of other odours. Quite pungent they seemed, and complex: layers of smells which in her sleepy state she noticed, but barely knew that she had noticed. Certainly nothing to remember as she dressed and he showered vigorously, showered for ages but without singing, and then they were seated together. She sipped her second cup of tea whilst he sat and stared at the plate of food dished up from the oven by Alice. It was last night's macaroni cheese with its decorative slices of tomato curling upwards in crisp despair, and the shredded beetroot salad seeped loud colour into the creamy, cheese-smeared worms that were spilled in such heaps on his plate. To be fair, it was not Alice's finest hour. Janet had left her in charge during the rehearsal and the two-tone meal was quite startling. Cream and crimson. Hektor-Jan certainly appeared quite perplexed by his plate. Now he raised his knife and fork, then carefully lowered his knife. Certainly, the macaroni seemed already to have been stabbed quite enough. It seemed to have bled profusely whereas Janet knew, if she concentrated, that it was the lurid beetroot that was doing all the damage. Alice disappeared from the culinary crash site. The hoover started up far away in the main bedroom. That's right – Alice was going to do the noisy jobs first so that the Baas could sleep uninterrupted. It was time that the children were up anyway. Hektor-Jan put down his fork. He said something but Janet was listening for the sound of scampering feet. Yes, no. It would not be long.

Don't expect us to get one, said Hektor-Jan and for a blank moment Janet watched him rise from the table and carry his plate to the sink. Is it a colour, or black and white, asked Hektor-Jan and as Janet was about to answer, realisation dawning on her face, he supplied the answer. It will be colour, of course; he shook his head. Only the best, only the very best for Meneer van Deventer. And with that he turned from his plate and came over to her. He held her face in his hands and kissed the top of her head. Janet closed her eyes as his warm hands held her face so firmly and the smack of his kiss was rooted on her scalp.

Darling, she said as he disappeared off to bed. Then she heard him hugging the children. He attacked them in their rooms and their delighted squeals pierced the background thunder of the hoovering Alice. They would come to her soon enough. Pulling on bits and pieces of their uniforms, they would amble into the kitchen and find her staring at the loaded plate that squatted beside the sink, the macaroni now blood-red. Unable to bear the waste, Janet got up and reached for the tasty mayhem. It was still warm, hot. There was no Solomon that day – he had done his mid-week vanishing act and so there was no one else to eat the food. Janet waited for her children, chewing thoughtfully.

Another day passed.

That night, with Hektor-Jan full to bursting with a fried breakfast, and the children having eaten and fresh and clean in their pyjamas, they popped across to behold the television of the van Deventers. We can't stay long, Janet had warned. Daddy must go to work and you have school tomorrow. And Pieter, we might need to practise your seven times table in the morning. I think you still don't have the hang of it and Pieter rolled his eyes behind her back and she knew that he also stuck his tongue out at her. But they had arrived.

Doug must have been waiting for he immediately threw open the door with a hearty laugh. Hektor-Jan and Pieter were greeted with great manly handshakes which left Pieter rubbing his crushed hand in surprise and grimacing. The girls each got a loud kiss which Sylvia made no secret of wiping away with the back of her hand and a slight gagging sound. Shhhhhhhh, Janet nudged her as they were led into the lounge to greet Noreen and the colour television, which stood in pride of place with all the furniture and Noreen facing in its direction.

Noreen looked lovely, a picture of stately decorum, not a hair out of place. She beamed and hugged them gently and precisely, whilst Doug assumed a proprietorial position beside the magic box. Douglas is so excited, murmured Noreen and her gaze lingered on the children.

Nesbitt? asked Sylvia and Noreen smiled and whispered as though imparting a secret. Outside, she said. Uncle Douglas, you know Uncle Douglas.

And they turned where they stood and Doug van Deventer waved his hands and said Take a seat, grab a pew, come on, come on, make yourselves comfortable, just as he always did although this time he seemed even more energetic. He was almost hopping from one foot to the other. Noreen and Janet perched on the settee; Hektor-Jan was ushered to the fancy armchair which Pieter was sometimes allowed to make lean backwards by pulling a little lever. But not tonight. The children settled down on the floor, pulling their dressing gowns about them. And Doug beamed at them yet again and asked if they were ready. They all nodded furiously – though Hektor-Jan managed to sneak a glance at his watch. He could not stay for long.

This, announced Doug even though they were no more than ten feet from him, this is a BarlowVision 200, Full-Spectrum Colour Televisual Domestic Appliance. He beamed at them as he touched it, his hands lingered on it and he stroked it. They stared back.

TV, squealed Sylvia suddenly and clapped her hands.

Janet smiled and reached down a restraining hand. Shhhhhhhhh, darling, she said, Uncle Doug –

The On button is located to the right of the control panel, Doug continued undeterred. Are you ready.

There was a round of nods. They were ready. Boy oh boy, were they ready.

Yay, shrieked Sylvia and Shelley added another restraining hand to her sister's shoulder. Outside there came the beagle volley of Nesbitt's yipping. Noreen smiled thinly.

I shall now proceed to fire her up. Doug was on a roll. His face was flushed as he performed for Janet and he tried to remember to include the others. Noreen, his own wife, Hektor-Jan, her husband. The children.

Here goes, he said redundantly and theatrically as he thrust his bantam weight onto his tiptoes and reached an arm across to the large box rimmed with a faux-wooden panel. He pushed the button. Nothing happened. Then it began to snow. Then there came the sound of Americans, a drawling hiss out of which could be discerned the cries of Paw, and Hoss or Horse, and Li'l Joe.

Yeeha, cried Sylvia and Pieter as a cactus-strewn landscape loomed out of the snow, and yielded to swathes of high chaparral. There were horses and neckerchiefs and sweating cowboys and ranch fences and spitting. For a moment Janet had to blink and look away before she was pulled back by the box into the slightly lurid world that gushed into the living room. It was indeed amazing. The colour that filled the room, the sound that overwhelmed them. The galloping horses, the chirping cowboys. A neighbour who needed help but whom no one wanted to help. The wise old Paw, a wrinkled patriarch with broad cheeks and bulging eyes. Janet thought how he would make a wonderful Toad of Toad Hall, and then felt strangely guilty that she was somehow missing the point. Even Hektor-Jan seemed impressed. The children stared open-mouthed, it was true to say. Luckily, there were no flies in the room. One did not expect to find flies in Noreen's perfect home. And there were certainly no flies on Doug. He remained standing beside the television as though it somehow needed his presence in order to work properly, as though his touching it and peering round at it were strangely crucial to its successful functioning, this televisual domestic appliance. Janet knew that Doug was watching her too, was enjoying the television through her startled eyes and Janet tried not to glance at Noreen. But she had to. Noreen, Janet started, was staring at her, not the television. Their eyes met to the sound of thundering hooves and they smiled, as though indulgently, as their men and the children remained transfixed.

Darling, Janet had to turn and whisper to Hektor-Jan. Darling. He responded, looked briefly at her but did not see her. Then he was back with the cowboys, the exuberant brotherhood filled with joshing and laughter. Darling, she said again and this time he saw her. She pointed to her watch. She did not want him to be cross when he suddenly realised what the time was. He was up in a flash.

Doug, he said, Man, Doug. Then he said, Don't worry, I'll find my own way out, and he kissed his children who saw through him, peered around him, and he kissed Janet who saw only him, and then he was gone to the sound of more frantic yelping from Nesbitt the cocker spaniel.

Doug finally left his position beside the television and moved to sit where Hektor-Jan had sat.

Not bad, hey, he said to Janet and Janet nodded at him but kept her eyes on the television. She knew that dear old Doug continued to watch her watching, and also that Noreen was watching Doug watch her. She wished she could be a child again, a child scooped up into the world of chivalrous cowboys whose simple honour was pinned to their sweaty sleeves and who would honestly cross their hearts and hope to die in a matter of easy seconds. Outside, Nesbitt simply would not shut up. And the music swelled as the neighbour in the television wept with gratitude and the other townsfolk learned a lesson in philanthropy, and then the credits rolled and Janet said, Right, let us leave Uncle Doug and Auntie Noreen in peace.

Predictably, the children kicked up a great fuss. Pieter most of all, despite Janet's warnings prior to their arrival, and that hardened her resolve. She prodded him sharply and then they were thanking their hosts for a lovely time.

You must come again, said Doug ostensibly to the children, but actually to Janet. You *must* come again, and Doug pumped Pieter's hand up and down and kissed Shelley and scooped up Sylvia into his arms. Noreen kissed Janet as Doug careered around the living room, making cowboy sounds as though he, too, had just been visiting the Ponderosa Ranch on *Bonanza*. Sylvia shrieked. She needed no encouragement. She was a shriek waiting to happen. Both Noreen and Janet put their hands to their ears and said Enough, Douglas, enough for goodness' sake, please. And Noreen added, Let these poor people go home; the children have school tomorrow. And Doug finally lowered Sylvia and for a moment Janet thought that he might scoop her up, Janet herself, and go waltzing around the room with her in his arms and what would the children think and how could she ever face Noreen's genteel dismay. But Doug just escorted them to the door as Noreen pulled the cushions straight in the living room and readjusted the furniture no doubt. But, as the children filed out past Uncle Doug, he did lay a cool hand on her arm and held her back.

There was no playfulness in his eyes as he quickly murmured two short sentences. From the side of his mouth, the words came squeezed and compressed with a strange urgency and Janet kept walking against the tug of his hand and his voice. She kept walking and thanking Doug who broke his fierce gaze and quickly looked back over his shoulder into the house. He followed her out onto the patio and down the steps to the front gate. I mean it, he said. Think about it. Promise me you will think about it and Janet nodded and smiled and was pulled onto the pavement and across to their front drive by the children who – Shelley excepted – had started to whinny like horses and gallop.

Then they were home and Alice was being updated by three excited voices and there were requests for a colour TV. In fact, any TV would do. The appeals came flooding from their lips. Ag, please Mommy. I'll learn all my tables. I'll be good. Pappie loves cowboy shows!

And all Janet could do was smile and nod and say, Perhaps one day when they had saved a lot of money. And that they could not spend all of Daddy's salary on gadgets and toys like Uncle Doug, who did not have any children who needed school uniforms and all sorts of things that cost money – never mind the time spent doing their homework. Now, into bed, chop chop, and yes, Shelley could read for a little bit whilst she settled other two.

Where's Pappie's knife? The red penknife? Pieter was asking, already an Indian sharpening the ends of arrows or a cowboy cutting strips of beef jerky – the biltong – they seemed to chew as they spoke. One of them had thrown a knife and pinned back the arm of a baddy who was about to harm Paw, or was it Li'l Joe?

No, Janet warned him. Oh, no. And her finger waved in admonishment before his naughty eyes and she reached over and closed them and kissed his eyelids.

Mommy, he groaned, and she murmured to him and switched off the light.

In the darkness he complained, but she did not hear him as all the while Doug's words were whispering in her mind. They were lent an odd weight by the intensity, even the anxiety of his eyes. Look after your husband, he had said. And how is Alice, he had said before repeating, Look after your husband.

And Janet shook her head to herself and wondered what on earth Doug could mean and why he would choose that moment to impart such heartfelt concerns. As she tucked Sylvia then Pieter into bed and kissed them goodnight, she saw only Doug's anxious eyes and heard his whispering words, Look – Husband – Alice. How very strange. And she knew that if she went outside later, once Sylvia was settled and the house was quiet with Alice asleep in the kaya, she would feel Nesbitt's heavy breathing and hear Doug peering out of his ridiculous rhododendrons. She sensed that he was there, now, waiting. Just like she knew what to expect at the bottom of the pool. And she was certain that neither was going to go away. The black crack was lodged deep in the pool and Doug lurked along the fringes of their garden. It was most disconcerting. She was dog tired. After her late and disturbed night, she longed to be able to sink back into bed, and not to feel this buzzing behind her eyes, this buzzing inside her head, as though a horrible, hairy fly had somehow managed to squeeze in through her ears or into her throat whilst she had snored on her back with her mouth open the previous night. She should never have slept on her back, she knew that now, knew it always when it was too late.

Salary comes from the word salt, Shelley's voice said behind her and Janet jumped. And television is made up of words from different languages, said Shelley. One meaning far and one meaning to see. It means far-seer. We did it in school today. The tall girl clutched her Enid Blyton close to her chest and looked fixedly at her mother. Janet swatted the air in front of her and frowned. Then she smiled at her elder daughter.

That's just the sort of thing your grandmother would say, Janet said to Shelley.

Television? said Shelley sounding surprised.

No, things about words, said Janet. Your grandmother knew a lot about words and writers, you know. She liked to use words, she said vaguely.

How? said Shelley in her persistent way that did not mean to be persistent. We all use words. Even Nesbitt knows some words: sit, stay, she qualified unhelpfully. Jock used to know what chocolate meant.

So he did, said Janet. The thought of Jock and her mother and Nesbitt made her even more tired. She frowned down the dimly lit passage.

How? repeated Shelley.

How, said Janet.

How does Granny use words? said Shelley shifting the Enid Blyton from one hand to the other as though to wave words at her mother, her slow mother.

Prickly, said Janet with some feeling as the fly disappeared. Your grandmother liked to make words very prickly.

Shelley stared at her. Was there a ghost of a smile. Prickly.

I mean that your grandmother tended to use sharp words, sharpen even the softest words to make them like black-jacks that would stick in your socks and scratch your skin and you would do your best to try to forget them, but then you would finally have to take off your socks and put on new ones with no black-jacks. That's what she did.

Janet was suddenly breathless.

Black-jacks, said Shelley seeming to savour the sharp rhyme and completely miss the point concerning her grandmother. Black-jacks. Indubitable, interminable, inviolable black-jacks.

Janet tried to smile. She grasped her eldest child by the shoulders, gently. She peered at Shelley and wondered if her mind was now running along black-jack-strewn paths, whether she now had stuck in her mind the thought or the sound of black-jacks and whether she was going to pursue that thought and its associations to the end of the path no matter how far it took her. Just like her grandmother.

Time for bed, said Janet.

Shelley shifted the book to her left hand. What did Uncle Doug want? she asked quietly.

Uncle Doug, said Janet.

She looked sharply at Shelley. Why was her daughter so full of awkward questions this night.

When we left, said Shelley. He looked like he wanted to tell you something very important.

Black-jacks, said Janet.

Was this even vaguely related to her daughter's question – or to her grandmother. Were they talking about the same thing. Words, grandmother, black-jacks, Uncle Doug.

Then the lie came easily as though she were slipping out of a pair of prickly socks.

He wanted to warn me about black-jacks in the back garden, said Janet feeling bad, but relieved when her daughter smiled and gave her a good-night kiss.

Don't forget to brush your teeth, Janet said softly and Shelley vanished into the bathroom. She was left standing in the long passageway with her skin itching.

They had been talking about the same thing. Those things all made Janet feel as though she was very small and did not quite grasp what was happening. It was a powerful, unpleasant sensation. She was a small, lost child. It was terrible that she could feel like that in an instant. She blamed her mother. She cursed herself.

Shelley's Secret Journal

Today's word from Granny's list is INDEFINITE.

Why is Mommy so indefinite? Last night she was bare again. It was the storm this time. Poor Alice had to go and fetch her. I told Sylvia and

Pieter that Mommy was checking that Jock was fine. I was as indefinite as I could be but I made them swear on Jock's grave not to say anything otherwise we will never get a television. Uncle Doug has the best television. I wish we had a television. Sometimes books are not enough. Did you use sharp words? Mommy says that you did and I don't know if that is another one of her ideas. How young can you be to get old timers disease? (I know its not really called old timers.) I worry ~~indubitably~~ interminably. Last night Pieter had a nightmare in the storm. Mommy was in bed but Pieter was screaming in the passage that the blacks were coming to get him and he needed the knife. He wanted to run and tell Mommy but I stopped him. I think his screaming was involuntary but I had to push him down and then we fought and he ran into Alice as she was coming out of Mommy's room. And he held on to her and cried and cried that the blacks were coming to get him. Alice hugged him and told him that the news on the radio was not good. But Pieter just screamed about the blacks the blacks the bloody blacks. I was going to get the soap but Pieter would not let go of Alice and Alice put Pieter to bed because Pappie is on night shift and Mommy was naked and in bed. I asked Alice about the news on the radio but she shook her head and put her finger on her lips and made me go to bed. I covered my ears so that I could indubitably not hear Pieter or the storm or Alice's radio. I also just hoped Mommy would stay in bed indefinitely. I hope tonight is a better night. Love, Shelley.

Janet sent Alice back to her kaya for an early night and for a long time she wandered the house in the dark. She listened at her children's doors and tried to breathe in time to their peaceful inhalations and exhalations. All the lights were off. The house was a lung, humid and dark in the deep-breathing night and Janet tried not to hold her breath but to breathe gently, keep breathing normally.

The back door was locked and she resisted the pull of the pool. She could not face the thought of standing there whilst to her right lurked desperate Doug with his disquieting perceptions and his strange, intense ways. Janet listened, rather, to the rhythmical sleep of her children. As she breathed and they breathed, she found that she had wandered over to Hektor-Jan's side of the bed, and had slid open his bedside drawer to reveal the old Bible and, buried in its pages, his Swiss Army knife – blood-red with its golden cross. Pieter had not taken it. It was safe and hidden. Her breathing was deep, as deep as her children's breathing and, after a long time she, too, was sinking into bed and into a heavy slumber. But her skin itched the entire night as every black-jack in the entire world seemed spitefully to nip and bite at her legs and ankles – and the sharp penknife prodded and poked, just out of sight.

She was up before the dawn and was ready to receive Hektor-Jan. She showered and gently soaped her raw legs where she had scratched them in her sleep. She dressed whilst running through more of her lines for bonnie Jean. She found herself whispering the word Brigadoon – emphasising the long final syllable perhaps as a soft antidote to the harsh black-jacks that had plagued her dreams. Brigadoon. There may be picturesque thistles in Brigadoon but there were certainly no black-jacks. Of that she was certain. Black-jacks seemed to be a peculiarly South African experience.

Hektor-Jan was home slightly earlier than usual. He came into the house quietly and urgently, and then into her in the same intense manner. As Janet held her heaving man and rolled with him, she tried to forgive his desperate way with her. She tried to understand that there must be black-jacks that pricked his soul at work, that a new job, new routines, new ways of doing things would make strenuous demands, would no doubt scratch at his self-confidence. Black-jacks, black-jacks, she found herself repeating in the poke and thrust of his love. And then it was one silly step to thinking about that prodding part of his person as a pink black-jack, spiking, scratching away at her innermoist, most tender self. And then, with conscious effort, she found refuge in the softer, rounder thoughts of *Brigadoon* once again. Come home, come home, come home to bonnie Jean, she heard the Highland chorus calling from afar with such misty longing, so gentle and yearning, and she mouthed the secret words into Hektor-Jan's neck where his hair grew down in thick curls if he forgot to shave it. And as Hektor-Jan flooded her, so she was filled with the famous song and she lay there, the lyrics welling up and sure to overwhelm her, pour out of her, drown them both. And Charlie's smooth tenor subsided just as Hektor-Jan panted into her ear and whispered desperate endearments. And before she could reply, there came the answering call of the assembled townsfolk. Three times they urged him to go home with his bonnie Jean. Then twice more, just in case he even thought about hesitating. With double reassurance they sang on about going home with bonnie Jean. And as Janet pillowed the full weight of her husband like a living mattress, again she heard Charlie's excited declaration of love and domestic intent. And his song flowed on, unstoppable, leaping over a series of exclamations and rhyming on about the romantic setting – the glen at ten – and linking bonnie Jean with the village green. And Janet made a throaty, chuckling sound at the silly lyrics, the childish rhymes, but before she knew it, she was mouthing the chorus again, like the jubilant townsfolk, repeatedly urging Charlie to go home to bonnie Jean. And Charlie responded so promptly with his fervent desire to do just that, to abandon all the married men and their lovely wives, to forsake all those lovely women and to go home with bonnie Jean, just bonnie Jean, safe in the knowledge that with her his days would fly by till the day he would die – and again came the exclamations, and the simple rhymes of indeed and need, fly and die, green and bonnie Jean! And Janet wondered how green was that green, and how anyone could fly anywhere when their large powerful husband lay at full stretch on top of them as though felled like a giant pine tree of passion. She was finding it difficult to breathe now, but there was something almost comforting in her helplessness. She could do nothing, not move a limb, only blink and whisper, and her entire self seemed to be expressed now in her writhing lips that mouthed the urgent chorus with Charlie, repeating the happy injunction about going home, home, home, to be with bonnie Jean, Jean, Jean! And, as those words and Hektor-Jan's semen whispered out of her, she found that she had no more strength to inhale or to close her legs. Hektor-Jan was home, was he not; she was bonnie Jean, wasn't she. Janet had been compressed to Jean and it was most bonnie. But the spell was broken, the enchantment ended as Hektor-Jan jerked in query.

Wat sê jy, he said in startled Afrikaans. His head lifted from the pillow and he arched himself to peer at Janet in the deep gloaming of the room. What are you saying, he asked again.

Janet took a long shuddering inhalation as her chest was freed. For a moment, tartan spots danced before her eyes and she could not be sure what was Brigadoon and what was Benoni. But then she peered up into her husband's face.

Darling, she said with her first free breath.

You said something, said Hektor-Jan. You were saying something.

Was I, asked Janet, and then she said declaratively, I was.

Pressing down with his hips, Hektor-Jan waited. Janet realised by his silence and his stare that he was waiting.

What should she say. That she was singing with Charlie and the cast of phantom Scottish Highlanders about love, about hearts and hearths. About the silly iniquities and attractions of the village green and of a woman called Jean. And how she had wondered if rhododendrons flowered on the edges of the village green, and if black-jacks might spear the odd sporran and how they would meet every night at ten. But most of all, she wondered if she could ever confess that the life of bonnie Jean sounded so very inviting and that if she had the chance, if anyone gave her the chance, it would be so very easy to say, yes, I'll head home with bonnie Jean, for I am bonnie Jean.

I am bonnie Jean, she whispered and smiled into his face.

He squirmed inside her but the rest of him did not move.

You are bonnie Jean, his deep voice felt its way around and into the consonants and vowels of the sentence, as though plumbing it, mining it for meaning. The process transformed her hopeful declaration into much more of an interrogative. *You* are bonnie Jean. You *are* bonnie Jean. You are *bonnie* Jean. You are bonnie *Jean*.

Janet blinked. The warm tickle, the trickle between her legs had become a gush.

The bed, she whispered. We're messing on the bonnie bed, and Hektor-Jan rolled away from his surprised query and clutched at himself and felt for his underpants. And bonnie Janet stretched back, able to breathe freely at last and smile. She laid a hand on Hektor-Jan as he pawed at himself and dabbed at the bed. The bed could wait. She just wanted to lie back and grin. Hektor-Jan would not mind. He would surely misattribute that satisfied smile and think that her languid pose was a direct result of his husbandly ministrations, and, for the most part, he would be right. Janet did feel refreshed. Her ankles had stopped itching, but at the thought of her ankles she frowned. Hektor-Jan sat dozily on the bed. Maybe he was watching her. Tracing her nakedness in the dark as she lay back, seeking out the darker patches of her body, between her legs and the circles of her nipples. Those familiar parts of her that he treasured, that comforted him so marvellous much.

Bonnie Jean, he murmured, running a huge hand along her thigh and hip.

Alice, said Janet and she started at the sound of her own voice, and at the word. Where did that come from – her raw ankles perhaps.

Too early, Hektor-Jan replied. Alice will be in in ten minutes.

Alice, said Janet again and she felt the word well up, as she opened her mouth. A-lice.

Hektor-Jan kept stroking her. Ten minutes, he repeated as his hand hovered close to her pelvis and its quiet expanse of hair.

And she said the name again. Named the maid, made the name in the dark as she breathed in the A and breathed out the -liss. What was going on: A-lice.

I am going to shower, Hektor-Jan stood up abruptly and was gone. The doorway glimmered as he opened and closed the bathroom door and then there was the hiss of water after the gush of the loo.

Janet lay there trying to recover the last strains of *Brigadoon* but all the while breathing the disyllabic A-lice, A-lice, A-lice. It was most trying.

Janet felt better after a shower, and even better when Hektor-Jan was safely tucked up in bed and the children delivered to school and nursery school.

Alice was busy ironing the bed linen in the laundry room with her radio going crazy with voices – if it was news, it sounded dramatic, if it was a drama, it sounded like the news. Solomon had the day off, so Janet had the garden to herself. She had gone shopping after the school run and the house was freshly stocked. That was one worry fewer. She wondered if at this stage of her life, she was going to have to get used to surviving a catalogue of concerns, that as a mother and a wife, never mind as a woman, one simply survived a series of never-ending anxieties. There was Pieter's birthday coming up on Saturday. He would almost be turning double figures, he kept reminding them by waving all but one of his fingers and thumbs at them, and they had been invited to the farm, to Hektor-Jan's dreadful family, as it was Pieter, the only grandson, who was going to verjaar, as they put it. And all he wanted was another Jock. As though they could pull a puppy out of the air and make it just like old Jock. Hektor-Jan had said not to worry, that he had a plan, and that made her worry all the more.

Janet looked out of the kitchen window at the pull of the willow tree. It gleamed with green gold in the morning sunshine and the deep shade looked lovely and cool beneath it, within its simple heart. It would be so easy to lie back in its healing shade and forget the silly hints, the silly business with Desperate Doug and Alice and Hektor-Jan, and forget the crack in the pool and simply go over her words for *Brigadoon*. It was Noreen who had said that there was actually a tiny town in the Eastern Cape called Brigadoon. Who would have thought that in South Africa, as far away from the Scottish Highlands as you could possibly get, there would be a dear little Brigadoon. Maybe they could go there one day. Maybe when the pool was fixed –

And Janet found her feet walking her out into the harsh sun, across the garden and towards the pool. She knew what she would find, and she duly found it. The crack had doubled in width and the pool was almost empty. The Kreepy Krauly was gulping crazily and had almost keeled over with the effort. The pump strained in its little housing and the water sprayed in a single jet from the inlet back into the pool. The jagged crack had ruptured the pool into two distinct halves, although the surrounding slasto had not been split. Even as Janet stared with an open mouth, the water level dipped again. The Kreepy Krauly throbbed and Janet suddenly strode to the pump housing, lifted it, and switched off the pump. With a gurgling sigh of relief from the bottom of the pool, the little Kreepy Krauly shuddered to a standstill, then collapsed on its side.

Janet had to sit down too. Her legs felt useless and she tucked them up beneath her, well out of the way of the pool. And as she sat there, she felt the last of Hektor-Jan's love ooze from her. She stared at the crack. Water disappeared into it whereas from her crack there came another life-giving liquid. It was an odd perception and she shifted her position, which was now warm and moist.

She would have to go inside and change. She would have to go with Solomon tomorrow and buy cement to fix the pool. Just as she spared her husband the finer details of her inner workings – although he knew when it was her period, and when to keep his distance – so, too, she spared him the vexation, the tragedy of the pool. And she knew that she would have to be strong and put thoughts of Desperate Doug and Alice out of her mind. That was another seam which she did not want to mine if she could help it. At least, not until the pool was fixed and she went inside, angrily casting a glance at the shimmering rhododendrons that flared up on the other side of the wall. Desperate Doug should learn to keep his mouth shut. Just look at Noreen. Her heart went out to her super-refined neighbour whose strained smile and gentle ways compensated for so much. These men, these men, she thought and she picked out a clean, neat pair of broekies from the dried washing that Alice had not yet packed away.

Wednesday seeped into Thursday.

Thursday was going to be a big day. First the pool and then the Second Rehearsal.

Whilst Alice beat the rugs outside then polished the wooden floors inside, Hektor-Jan slept after another bout of urgent passion and the children were at school – no doubt learning about the Great Trek as she had had to learn about the Great Trek year after year, studying all about those intrepid Dutchmen crossing rivers and escarpments and defending themselves against wave after wave of marauding impis of the various tribes – Janet made her own small trek to the hardware store on the outskirts of Benoni. With her was her own, domesticated impi.

She had flown out in the early morning at the squeak of the door to intercept Solomon to tell him not to change just yet, that she needed him to go with her to the hardware store to get whatever they needed to fix the pool – the pool was empty now. She had banished the children to the small front garden and Hektor-Jan had gone off to work again without inspecting the back garden. And it was only as you approached the pool that you saw the gleaming white concrete skull split into two hemispheres. Now it did give her a headache just to behold it. The bright, white concave shell, stark and fiercely brilliant with reflected light and heat. It almost sang in the sun and the crack gaped filthily, a jagged mouth that sucked in the light and her heart and there was no telling how deep it was or where it went. Thankfully, it was confined to the bottom of the pool and the sides; it had not shot beyond the edges of the pool. Janet could not bear to think what she would do if it escaped the concrete confines of the pool –

Solomon, she greeted him urgently. Solomon, we go to the hardware store today. She spoke in that odd, clipped way with which white women addressed their garden boys. Sentences simplified to the basics: Solomon, that is you, we, that is you and I, go, that is drive, to hardware store, well, self-explanatory. Why. We fix the pool today. Okay.

Yes, Madam.

So keep your smart clothes on. We go in the car. After breakfast.

And they went. Janet's father had recommended the best hardware store in town and told her where to find it. Why, what for, what are you up to now, how can I help, he had pressed, but Janet had thanked him and said it was something she knew that she must do – alone. And please not to breathe a word of it to anyone. It was going to be a surprise. She knew how he hated surprises, having been surprised and shocked all his life married to her mother. But he would not mutter a word, she was sure. She put down the phone quietly.

Whilst her husband slept in the darkness, they set off in the blinding light. It felt a little odd, to be sure, having Solomon beside her in the car. Her box-like Fiat was cosy at the best of times and they sat squashed together with Solomon's lanky legs and arms awkwardly folded and tangled in his side of the car and she tried not to brush his leg as she shifted the gear lever.

Solomon, have you been in a motor car before, she asked.

Solomon smiled broadly; she could feel the gleam of his teeth.

Yes, Madam, he said. My sister's brother, he is having a car. A big one.

Janet felt her little Fiat constrict and she smiled too.

This is a very small car, she agreed and Solomon acknowledged that it was a small car, and did she want to sell it.

No, she replied shortly. As though to compensate for its lack of size, the Fiat thundered up the road and backfired only once. It was the most throaty and unpredictable of vehicles: she would have to ask

Hektor-Jan to look at it. She would do that once the pool was fixed, when there was one less problem in their life. Hektor-Jan did not mind fixing cars; he was great with cars. Now, Janet would do her bit with the pool. Cars were so masculine; pools were feminine. Hektor-Jan was born to fix cars – his strong hands wielded a bewildering array of tools with exotic names: monkey wrenches, she thought she heard him tell Pieter. Bobbejaan spanner, that was it. Phillips screwdrivers, shifting spanners, angle grinders, slide rules, star-spangled banners, iron maidens, who knew what equipment Hektor-Jan commanded with greasy concentration and grunting effort as he lay beneath the car, suddenly a truncated pair of hairy legs. It was as though he had entered the body of the car, was making love to metal, or was taking obstetrical charge of changing her oil, cleaning her carburettor, replacing her sparkplugs. He always referred to the car in the feminine.

Pools were simpler. A cavity in the ground filled with pliant, yielding liquid. True blue. Receptive. The umbilical cord of the Kreepy Krauly, invented by a man around the corner in the optimistic town of Springs, fresh and coiled with possibility, like a womb. How apt. And all Janet had to do to maintain lovely and clear water was to keep a floating plastic container filled with chlorine tablets. The receptacle looked like a giant tampon. And she used the little testing kit to ascertain the pH balance of the pool so that the water did not cloud with thrush or become menstrually dark in any way. Yes, pools were definitely feminine.

The Fiat backfired again.

Hau, said Solomon and glanced in surprise behind them.

It did sound like a gunshot, thought Janet. I shall have to tell the Master, she said to Solomon. He likes to fix cars, you know.

Solomon absorbed the information in silence.

We are fixing the pool, he suddenly said.

He seemed happy, almost proud. It was a statement of satisfied intent. We are fixing the pool, he repeated.

Yes, said Janet, changing gear. She was pleased that Solomon seemed so pleased. It must be a nice change from mowing lawns, trimming edges, cutting, snipping, chopping. Always having to hurl oneself at the onslaught of green. For a moment she lost sight of the snaking road and all she could see was a sea of heaving verdure, emerald coils of kikuyu grass writhing across paths and over edges, trembling shoots of leaves all of a fluster, and the horizon, like a lawn, shimmered with terrible growth. All sprouting, budding, stretching out, reaching out ineluctably towards them with the urgent sound of Desperate Doug in the rhododendrons. What did her mother say, quoting the Bible perhaps – all grass is flesh – and Janet swerved to avoid a cyclist whilst Solomon went rigid beside her.

He did not even say his customary, emotive Hau. But she felt his glance – tense and amazed.

Sorry, Solomon, she said leaning forward in her seat and frowning through the windscreen as though to bring herself into more certain contact with the unfolding, unwinding road. Her show of greater concentration seemed to work. Solomon removed his hands from the dashboard, his slender, strong hands which had been preparing for a certain collision and he clutched his seatbelt instead.

They were almost there.

Janet thought about her mother, how she had got to the stage where to put her behind the wheel of a car was simply to invite death. She hoped that she would never get like that. Suddenly she was sitting where Solomon was sitting – it was the same car after all. Her mother was driving her somewhere and talking. But not talking to her, rather telling her, telling her about, telling her off, always telling her. And so, she just stuck her head in the gas oven, her mother told her as she sailed through the red lights. Or, she simply strolled into the River Ouse with her pockets packed with stones, she said as the car wandered onto the wrong side of the road. Or, parataxis is not the same as periphrasis, I do wish that they would remember, she told her paralysed daughter as

Christopher Radmann

she swerved around a corner, the engine thundering because it was not in gear and it appeared that she was attempting to accelerate towards oblivion. Oh, do not raise your voice at me, she yelled when she had removed the bumper of the motorist in front of her and there was what she called a moment of quite unnecessary contretemps. Spelled with a final tee ee em pee es, did you know, she later told the tiny, tear-stricken Janet. It's French from the Latin, meaning against time, both literally and, I suppose, figuratively. Now, blow your nose.

Janet brought the car to an abrupt halt. Her fingers were cramping against the steering wheel, she held it so tightly, and her neck ached from the way she poked her head out towards the windscreen.

Solomon leapt from the car. Janet joined him, clutching her handbag. She was going to use her own money, she had decided. The money that her father had transferred into her name, just in case, as he said. Just in case of what, Janet was not sure, but it was very useful if she ever wanted to treat herself or the kids when they were out shopping and she did not have to account for every cent to Hektor-Jan when they went through the household expenditure at the end of the month. It also came in useful when their budget did not stretch far enough with new school shoes too. Her children did not know that they were walking on Granny's earnings, that they were walking on her words, her lectures, treading not so gently on her dreams. Janet shook her head and she and Solomon entered the hardware store beside the yard that clanked and scraped with manly enterprise.

The place was bustling. The air had its sleeves rolled up and it bristled with hairy forearms and strong sweat. There was aftershave too, quite sweet and surprising like a tweak of the nose. Janet blinked and Solomon stood behind her. A bit like the royal couple. There was a tangle of shelves and, to one side, a counter where most of the men were waiting, orders in hand, whilst a man behind the counter barked out instructions to unseen assistants. Janet felt for a moment as though she had walked into Doug's new television, straight onto the ranch where men were men, and there was banter and a great brotherhood of shared jokes and where these strange beings called each other odd names. She wanted to reach out and take Solomon's hand. He was making a quiet sound in the back of his throat it seemed, like old Jock used to do when Hektor-Jan started cursing the car, which had somehow cut his hand or skinned his knuckles.

What do we need, said Janet moving towards a shelf that seemed to feature only a fantastic array of screws and bolts.

The cement eh the washed sand eh the white paint, Solomon whispered in her ear as though Hektor-Jan were lurking behind the shelf and they were going to be caught out. Janet looked up at him and saw that he was staring at the knot of men at the counter. Some had sideburns that were too big for them. One scratched his crotch and turned around. He kept scratching. He must have said something out of the side of his mouth, or maybe it just fell out from beneath his rather precocious moustache as the three men beside him swivelled towards the shelf with the screws and the bewildering bolts.

Janet turned to the pegs with their hanging, pregnant packets. One inch, two inch, three inch, four inch, wood, wall – interior, exterior – with plugs and without, the gold and silver screws dangled before her sharply. The bolts and nuts were even more unsettling with their blunt, bold look. She almost reached out but then thought she would not. Her hand hung in the air, a graceful wave and for a moment the man, Mr Scratchy she christened him, caught between the clamp of his sideburns and hemmed in by his moustache, looked as though he was going to wave too. But he gave his crotch a final yank and leaned back against the counter.

Janet returned her gaze to the shelves and adjusted her bag. She clung to her feminine bag filled with all her familiar things. She drifted to a different shelf, Solomon pulled behind her like an obedient shadow. That shelf displayed tufts of paint brushes ranging from the incy-wincy ones made of spiders' legs to the great clumps of bristles surely pulled straight from the side of Mr Scratchy's face or from beneath his nose.

Solomon, she turned her serious eyes to him, we shall have to ask at the counter.

Eish, Solomon looked past her to the men, one of whom was holding what looked like a mallet with a six-foot handle. It was almost as big as he was and Janet started to giggle. He looked like a miniature Thor, made all the more puny by his monstrous hammer. He paid and strolled past them. Mr Scratchy began again to confirm his unspoken moniker. Gripping her bag, Janet lifted her chin and strode towards the men and the counter.

Like a miniature, feminine Moses, she parted the sea of men. Their banter caught in their throats and there was a cough. Janet stared straight ahead at the huge Italian man behind the counter. His pleasant face sprouted out of an open collar, a thick gold chain and an exuberant welter of chest hair.

Yes, his voice was pleasant and enthusiastic like his hair. It rolled down from the seven hills of Rome. He spoke to Janet and did not seem to notice Solomon, who was standing very close behind Janet. She could feel the warmth of Solomon's tough body; his breath came quickly on the top of her head. If she took a step backwards, she would stand on his feet. Mr Scratchy beside her decided to become Mr Clutch-and-Stare-Without-Moving. Janet's bag gasped.

Good morning, she found her mother's voice saying. Good morning, my good man, it almost said. We are going to be fixing a crack – in a pool, in the bottom of a swimming pool. I wonder if you can advise us. Her voice was lovely and cool. She felt almost proud, like spelling embarrassment correctly for her mother – yes, two Rs and two Ss and two As, I am sure, Mommy, just like address has two Ds and two Ss, isn't that so – but the man seemed confused.

Jislaaik, he said. The Afrikaans word turned Italian around the edges. So you are a-wanting to fixa a pool, hey. His glance took in the other men and there were growls of consternation. Mr Clutch clutched.

Janet nodded, careful not to bump Solomon.

Mr Clutch murmured something that caught in the thick bristles of his moustache. The Italian man glanced at him and then his eyes returned to Janet. He seemed embarrassed. Did he not supply the things she required.

Cement, she said, trying out the workaday words: cement, washed sand and some white paint, waterproof I imagine. Is that right, Solomon.

She turned her head and Solomon stiffened. Ja, he barely breathed. Ja, just about warmed the back of her neck.

The giant Italian man glanced at the other men. He leaned forward. Was he about to tell her a secret. His eyes flickered conspiratorially. Maybe the crack was worse than she had ever suspected. Her breath caught in her throat. She, too, leaned forward.

You aska, maybe you aska you smart black to waita outside, he said. We senda the stuff by the side – you can a loada it into you car.

Janet saw his lips stop moving. It took a moment for his meaning to follow. He glanced at the men before him.

Janet stood there, still leaning forward. The Italian man leaned forward too. The other men lounged back. Who knew how Solomon stood on this ground.

My black, said Janet.

She had asked for white paint, had she not, not black. And cement was grey as far as she was aware, and who knew what colour the washed sand would be. Mr Clutch jerked his head to indicate behind her.

My black, she repeated and the bag beneath her arm now felt very small and empty. Her breath was hollow and she felt as though she were slipping beneath an oppressive car, beneath some large vehicle with convoluted interior workings that were suddenly exposed. She was lying down with a headache like Noreen and then this great car just rolled over her and there she was looking up at its underside at all the pipes and grimy parts and the engine was running loudly and dangerously and she was confused. She put a hand to her head.

Solomon, she said faintly. Solomon, she said again. She confirmed the bold fact of his name, his biblical name, named after a wise king who appeared to suggest cutting a baby in half when actually he was uniting a mother and her true child. Solomon kept order in their garden and the van Deventers' garden. He was the one person who was going to help her unite the opposing sides of the pool, to help her fix the crack.

And as she lay beneath the overwhelming car and its dark engine thundered, Janet knew that she would not have to ask Solomon apologetically to wait outside. She would not have to fight on his behalf. From the emptiness behind her she knew that he was already waiting outside. Her black had gone to wait outside in the bright sunshine and Mr Clutch surely could now let go. And as the colour welled up in her cheeks and her breath returned, she felt her mother's voice jump-start in her throat and then out it came, as though her lungs had just backfired.

For goodness' sake, she shot the remark at Mr Clutch, would you just let go. Let go, for Christ's sake.

In the loud bustle of the place with the brash and noisy aftershave and sweat and the radio playing, her shrill voice was lost. Had she merely coughed. Mr Clutch still clutched and stared. The other men did not move. Only the Italian man at the counter responded. Cement, he said, fine washed sand, vinyl paint, your pool is a-white, yes, you have-a a spade, a trowel, a paintbrush.

Janet looked behind her. Solomon had indeed gone to wait outside. She should join him. They should leave. But the crack. This was the best place to come, her father said so. She must fix the crack, fix the crack at all costs. Solomon would understand. She would explain to him.

With trembling white hands, she tried to open her bag then her purse. She took out her mother's money while the Italian man calculated the price with a stub of a pencil on a scrap of paper. She started to count out the green ten-rand notes, each with the face of Jan van Riebeeck on the left-hand side. It was a lot of money. She counted angrily; her face felt hot. She felt the gaze of all the men and beneath her thumb she caught the stare of the Dutch sailor, Jan van Riebeeck. For a moment it was a relief to look into his cool, green face. His neat centre parting, his flowing hair, his high collars. But then she noticed his pursed lips, oddly open. Was he about to whistle. Did he, too, feel stunned. He looked bemused, pensive. Possibly even amazed. His lips were very strange indeed. They made a definite gap in his face, puckered, somehow raised, yet a dark gap nonetheless.

The Italian man told her the price and she paid. Then she could return several notes and a fistful of coins to her purse and snap her bag closed. The Italian man shouted her order through a doorway behind him. He turned back to Janet.

You bringa you car to-a the loading zone, he said. We load-a you car. You fix-a that crack.

Just like that. Janet tried to nod. Tried to nod and say Thank you, yes, I fix-a that crack, but she seemed to have clipped her voice into her bag along with her tight purse. She turned and left the Italian man and Mr Clutch and the staring men. They remained silent behind her, watching her no doubt in the way that men have. She felt her legs and her bottom and her back prickle, just like when Doug peered over the wall. Doug could be very sweet, but it was that look, that male peering that bored through your clothes like black-jacks and crawled into your underwear and made you squirm. Janet squirmed out of the door into the hot light. Solomon was nowhere to be seen. She walked over to her car, key at the ready.

There he was. Crouched in the shadow of the far side of the car, out of the way.

Solomon, she said.

Madam, he said standing up, unfolding his long limbs.

They stood there with the car between them. Its white surface was luminous with heat and light in the polishing sun. Janet had to squint then look away. I am sorry, Solomon, she said facing back towards the store.

Solomon stood on the other side of the car.

Janet wanted to say more. She wanted to describe the underside of that car, which had simply rolled over her. But with Solomon's deadpan stare and in the gasping heat, she stood there, looking away.

We fix that crack, came Solomon's voice.

Janet tried to nod. She stared fiercely and pathetically at the store. She tried to return the penetrating stare of the men that lurked in there surrounded by tools and screws and metal bits and masculine certainty and –

Yes, Solomon, she managed at last, and then they got into the car and Janet drove around to the loading zone. There were more black men to help them and Janet and Solomon stood by as a huge bag of cement and two of washed sand were loaded into the boot of the car. The little vehicle hunkered down on its back wheels with the load. Then came the tin of vinyl paint – brilliant white – and the trowel. They did not need a spade. They had a spade, the one Hektor-Jan had used to bury old Jock. Janet signed the order form. They had got what they wanted, got more than they had bargained for.

Janet climbed slowly into the car. Was it overloaded. Did it have too much to bear. Solomon slipped into the seat beside her. The car felt very low. Janet tried not to breathe.

Here goes, she whispered and she started the gruff engine. It sounded very throaty. As they inched out, avoiding the dips and bumps in the loading zone, the little car growled with effort and its chassis shuddered as it lurched over the kerb onto the road.

Damn it! Janet suddenly shouted. Damn it! Her voice finally cracked as they left the hardware store, the little car struggling with its load and the road ahead black with hot tar and the neat dotted line that stretched straight and white ahead of them as far as the eye could see. Damn it, whispered Janet, one hand clutching her stomach and the other attempting to steer.

Damn it.

Whilst Hektor-Jan slept, they repaired the pool.

Solomon changed into his work clothes and Janet put on her oldest dress. It was long and faded and peculiarly workmanlike. She tied up her hair, removed her hot nylon stockings and found some flat shoes. All that she did in the darkness of the room without Hektor-Jan so much as moving a muscle or making a moan. He slept as silent as the dead. He was exhausted, poor man. Janet paused at the bedroom door and looked back at the soundless mound. She thought of Mr Clutch and the big Italian and the other men, and thanked her lucky stars. Men, she whispered to herself and stole outside to Solomon.

It took a while to drain the pool completely. Water and leaves and dead insects had collected in the corners of the deep end. Solomon had removed his shoes and had climbed into the inverted skull of the pool. He was bailing out the last of its murky thoughts. The scrape and splash, scrape and splash of the bucket and water was profoundly reassuring and Janet watched the remaining liquid disappear.

She fetched the hosepipe for Solomon to squirt clear the rest of the pool so that it gleamed with light. It could have been a monstrous satellite dish, sunk into the garden and signalling white radiance, such sheer hot brilliance to the heavens. Janet had to go back inside for her sunglasses. Solomon just squinted and whistled under his breath.

He fetched the old zinc tub, measured out equal quantities of sand and cement, and mixed the two together with great scraping sounds. The metal of the spade struck the metal sides of the tub with a horrible rasping made worse by the gritty sand. Janet stood there holding the hose, her teeth on edge, goose bumps coursing down her arms and back. She shivered.

Ja, said Solomon pointing to the turgid snake that she held and Janet released the kink in the hosepipe so that water gushed into the tub. Ja, said Solomon more urgently and pushed her hand and the hose aside. That was enough water for now.

The sound of his spade deepened and the scrapes were undercut by the folding, slapping sound of wet cement. Then they were ready.

Janet held the bucket as Solomon shovelled some of the mixture into it. It was very heavy. Janet had to put it down with a gasp. Solomon gripped it, hefted it up onto his shoulder and then walked carefully across the crazy paving, down the steps of the baby area and across to the crack where it reached up into the shallow end. Janet watched without breathing as he slowly, carefully poured the mixture into the crack.

The thin stream of grey was slurped by the jagged gap. It looked as though Solomon was feeding a long and violent mouth which swallowed and swallowed. The bucket-load was finished – the crack could take a whole lot more. As much as they had to give, it would appear. Another bucket of sand and cement disappeared. Then another.

Eish, muttered Solomon as he traipsed up the steps for the fourth bucketful.

Janet lifted her sunglasses onto the top of her head. She stood teetering on the very edge of the pool, peering into the white light with its central black stripe. Where was the grey cement. Only after the seventh bucket did a tongue of grey mixture finally emerge from the lips of the crack. It was a very deep crack indeed.

Well done, Solomon, Janet called in relief. They were getting somewhere. Thank goodness, they were making progress. For a moment Janet had feared that they might continue pouring cement into the pool for the rest of their lives and that it would make no difference at all. The crack would be there to haunt them for ever. What would she say to the family. The children, Hektor-Jan, her poor father, even her hard, demented mother, it just did not bear thinking about at all. Well done Solomon, she said as the tub was emptied and he mixed up the next round of grey, wet goo.

Eish, Solomon muttered and he peered up at the hot sky. He wiped his brow then undid the buttons of his overalls. With a neat wriggle he slipped his arms and chest free of the brown cloth. Using the flapping arms of the old, worn material, he tied them around his waist as though his shadow were hugging him, clinging to him in a knotted embrace.

He grabbed the spade and his strong arms rippled as he dug into the dry mixture.

Ja, he said, without looking up. Ja.

Janet held the hissing hose. She watched his expert use of the spade. So swift and assured. The way the muscles in his shoulders and upper arms bunched with controlled power, and then shot the spade forward, lifting and turning. His body glistened black and silver in the sun.

Ja, he said again, and then stopped and looked up.

Janet started. The water. She let go the hose and the water gushed from her little white fingers and fell sparkling into the grey dust. It drilled deep into the heavy tub. For a second, Janet heard Hektor-Jan at the toilet, gushing away, then Solomon repeated his urgent Ja and she stifled the hose with a quick twist.

A while later, Alice brought them some tea. She handed the little cup on its saucer to Janet and the tin mug to Solomon. Then she looked into the pool.

She said something in Zulu to Solomon and he straightened his back and made a noncommittal reply.

It is working, Alice said to Janet and Janet nodded. It is taking a long time, Alice said. I am watching from the house. And Next-door Baas is watching too. She jerked her head in the direction of the van Deventers'. Janet tried not to look, but it was no good. Standing there with the cup and saucer poised at her lips, whilst the hosepipe lay to one side pouring water onto the thirsty lawn, she glanced up.

Doug was on his ladder and wreathed in rhododendron leaves. As usual, he had some small clippers or shears in his hands. Maybe he had not been peering at Janet and Solomon. Maybe, as he did now, he had been clipping the branches, tidying his side of the wall, manicuring his beloved bushes. Maybe that was what he was doing, but even as Janet wondered at the exaggerated concentration of the man, she knew that it was all a ruse. It was too studied. It was too rehearsed. And did he actually cut a single little branch. She could hear the snip-snip, but did a single leaf fall. She saw again his face in the moonlight. She wondered at his perpetual presence. She heard his strange words which she had tried to forget. Janet glanced at Alice, the teacup remained poised at her lips and the water crept coldly over her burning feet. Janet kicked off her shoes and stood there shivering in the heat from the feet up. Only after a third Ja from Solomon did she gulp the remainder of her tea and hand over the teacup with a sigh. She picked up the hose and directed the water to where Solomon pointed. The snipping shears stopped. No doubt, Desperate Doug was doing what Desperate Doug did best. Janet sighed again. She would have to confront Desperate Doug. She owed it to herself and to her husband. She owed it to Noreen as well. What kind of man –

Ja, repeated Solomon quite forcefully and she twisted the hose so that the water was stifled. But too much had fountained into the zinc tub. Solomon had to add more sand and more cement. He was humming now, no, singing softly to himself. Janet held the hose tightly and whispered to herself.

The next few loads went well and the deep crack was reduced to a two-dimensional stripe after several hours of back-breaking work. The dark grey line of cement quickly lightened. In the hot sun, it dried in no time at all.

I am painting next time, Solomon pointed to an imaginary tomorrow just past his left shoulder. This is drying, one day, then I am painting.

Thank you, Solomon, said Janet. The hose still throbbed in her aching hand but she felt overcome with gratitude. Thank you.

Solomon took the hose from her and went to rinse out the tub and the spade behind the huge spray of pampas grass. He sang louder now, relieved probably that the hard work was done. Alice would be bringing him his lunch in a moment. Janet stepped forward over the paving, right to the edge of the pool. She did not slide her sunglasses over her eyes. She let the ringing white of the pool strike her eyes. After all that shimmering water, after the taunting, lurking crack beneath a veil of water, it was such a relief to have it all exposed. It glowed in the light and made her eyes stream. She was very grateful to Solomon, very grateful indeed. And she felt proud of herself. She had not buckled beneath the burden. She had not needed to be told by her mother to get on with it, to stop standing there like a pudding, like a raisin pudding looking for a *raison d'être*. Janet had never eaten a raisin pudding before and she never wanted to have one. What was it. She had faced up to the crack and no one could deny that. Her mother could not tell her to get a grip. She had got a grip. She sighed and was saddened by the simple irony. She, Janet, the disappointing daughter, had mended the crack in the pool whilst her own mother could do nothing about the fact that she was cracked in the head. No strictures or lectures or sarcasm could alter that fact. Janet, the little lost daughter, had taken charge. She did not have to be marshalled by her mother, browbeaten into a corner. There was no sense of triumph though. How could you celebrate your success over faulty concrete or a tremor in the earth when your own mother sat in a quiet corner of her care-home room peering at her knitting as though it were an obscure text in Sanskrit or a newly discovered set of hieroglyphs. When your blue-stocking mother no longer wore any stockings at all, and her legs were exposed, spindly and naked and with faint hairs that glistened in the morning sunlight. Janet sighed. If it were a triumph over some strange maternal sense of expectation and not just the crack itself, then the victory was decidedly Pyrrhic. Her hands fell to her sides. Her shoulders slackened after the bunched-up tension. Janet sighed.

The children would be overjoyed to be swimming again, once Solomon had painted the pool the next day. It would not be long now before things got back to normal and, as she thought that, Janet raised both hands to the certainty of her head. She balled her hands into fists and pressed them hard against her eyes, which she closed at last. The darkness was a relief now. Now it could become a refuge once again, unassailed by cracks or thoughts of cracks. She breathed deeply, breathed in the green heat of the garden and tried her best, her very best to ignore the call that came from next door. Then she thought how odd it might look, and she lowered her hands and turned a bright face towards Desperate Douglas van Deventer who was leaning over the garden wall and calling her. There was no sign of Alice with Solomon's lunch yet and Solomon was still singing behind the huge spray of pampas grass with its razor-sharp leaves. Slowly, Janet walked over to the wall.

Doug, she made her voice bright and gay. She could have been bonnie Jean. She tried to keep a rather wilful Scottish accent at bay but she did not think she succeeded.

How are you on this fine day, she said as though there had never been a crack – as though there had never been his – surely – wisecrack about her husband and the maid.

Desperate Doug scratched his chin with the open points of his shears. Fine, he said, just fine. Absolutely ginger peachy.

Was that American. Was he picking up on her oddly Scottish accent.

Janet was about to ask after Noreen and Nesbitt, was about to drag his own family into the foreground of any conversation that might result, but Desperate Doug beat her to it.

Have you thought about what I said, he asked, rested his chin with disconcerting abandon on the points of his shears.

All Janet could think about was what would happen if, suddenly, he slipped. What would happen if, right before her, Desperate Doug van Deventer lost his footing on the precarious ladder and drove the twin blades deep into his throat –

The largest artery, the jugular, was it not, pulsed in his throat, carried bright blood to his brain. If he slipped and the shears plunged into his flesh, he would be dead in seconds. He would spray blood like the garden hose sprayed innocent water and he would drop silently behind the wall, for ever stilled, and his rhododendron bushes would no doubt raise their branches in a leafy cheer, finally free from the tyranny of his constant attention, finally released from the snip-snip-snip. Maybe Nesbitt would lick him. Maybe the red setter would set up a red howl from the pool of Desperate Doug's blood. Janet felt as though she must lean against the wall and try her best not to rock the cement slabs that nestled one on top of the other between the two pillars that made up that section of the six-foot wall which separated her from Desperate Doug.

Have you looked after your husband, asked Desperate Doug's voice and Janet was forced to stand tall and to peer up into her neighbour's pensive face. She tried to look him in the eye, tried not to be distracted by the artery that shivered beneath the pair of blades.

She kept her voice light and cheery, as though she were in a *Brigadoon* rehearsal. Och, she said making a dismissive noise in the back of her throat, Och, I thought you were joking.

Desperate Doug eyed her strangely. He did insist on leaning on his shears so that little dents appeared in his neck. Was he crazy.

He smiled.

I worry, he said. I do worry. You know how I worry.

Janet looked up at him. She supposed he must worry. Just look at how he worried the life out of his rhododendrons. Just think about how he worried her, always there, always peering, a human mosquito that whined in the background and would not go away. Yes, he worried all right.

Desperate Doug turned his anxious gaze to her garden. It's like this, he said softly. I look out over your lawn and the flower beds and I see patches of darker green and I think of weeds and I worry about you. Because, he paused, eyeing her over his shears so that his words might carry more weight, because if you let the weeds grow then they will spread.

Desperate Doug pronounced each word separately and cataclysmically: If – you – let – the – weeds – grow – then – they – will – spread.

His warning – it was a warning, not just horticultural hocus-pocus – hung in the midday sun. It came from on high. It was spoken over the blades of his shears. It was wrung from his heart and his lips trembled.

Your life is like a garden, he carried on, and we are like gardeners. His lips twisted at the thought. Ja, man, we are actually like garden boys, believe it or not. We can decide what to let grow, and what to pull out. But we cannot let the weeds take over, can we.

Janet felt it was time to move. A response was being called for. She managed to nod her head. Weeds were bad. Black-jacks were not good.

Desperate Doug glanced towards Janet's house. Do you know what Higher is doing right now, he suddenly asked.

His direct question, almost an attack, came as a shock.

Janet was suddenly a little girl once again, under fire from her fierce mother.

Do I know what Higher is doing right now, she repeated, a favourite stratagem which so infuriated her mother. I asked the question, Amelia Amis would become angry to the point of hissing, like a kettle about to boil over. What I require is an answer and not – she repeated the negative, close to hysteria – not the repetition of my very own interrogative.

Desperate Doug did not become hysterical. He just seemed really sad. He looked like he could take his own life right then and there on the points of his shears and Janet found herself wishing that he would. There, the guilty thought was out. If only –

I suppose he is in the bedroom; Desperate Doug looked at her fiercely. He made it sound somehow filthy, as though Hektor-Jan were skulking or lurking, as though a bedroom were a den of iniquity, a hotbed of filth and sweat and –

I suppose you have been outside with Solomon whilst Higher has been inside alone –

Desperate Doug left the sentence dangling on a precipice. Janet felt giddy with the sense of illicit possibility. They both knew that Hektor-Jan was not alone in the house. That he was in the house and Alice, a housemaid, was also, by very definition, in the house too and had been in the house with her husband all along except when she appeared with their tea.

What time did Alice bring you your cup of tea. Desperate Doug seemed to be echoing her thoughts. He seemed to be inside her head snipping away at the neurons and dendrites – the delicate rhododendrons of her thoughts even as those thoughts branched out in her mind. No, he was spreading weeds, the very weeds he supposedly abhorred.

She stared wordlessly at him. Her voice, when it came, when it made its way out of her soft throat, was her own. There was no sense of bonnie Jean now. Brigadoon was banished; this was Benoni.

Desp-, Doug, she coughed up his name and he immediately took pity.

Look, he said, I just ask. He stood up straight now. He raised the shears in a gesture which was expansive, which seemed to evoke the neighbourhood and embrace them all as though he were performing a civic duty. I just ask. As your neighbour. As someone who cares. I mean, look at Eileen, he nodded across the garden to Janet's other neighbour.

Janet turned, startled. Then she faced Desperate Doug again.

Look, he repeated with passionate emphasis. I just don't want to see you get hurt.

He was almost tearful, or passionate. Look – I – just – do – not – want – to – see – you – get – hurt –

And once again Desperate Doug parsed the sentence into weighty fragments, bits that were almost too heavy to bear and they slipped through her fingers and dropped at her feet and hurt even her toes.

Then Desperate Doug glanced behind him suddenly and said, Sorry, gotta go. And as he was swallowed by the wall in quick sections, his voice still came hissing to her. Look to your husband, he said. For God's sake, look to your husband.

And she was left standing there, peering at the concrete sections of the wall, each panel one foot high, six panels of concrete slotted one on top of the other. She thought that she might have heard Noreen's voice – or was it Nesbitt making a strangled sound.

Before she could ponder this further, Alice appeared in her bright pink apron and matching dress and doek with Solomon's lunch and another mug of steaming tea. She smiled at Janet as she walked past, en route to the singing Solomon whose voice still filtered through the leaves of the pampas grass. Janet tried to return her smile. It was a brave effort, not completely successful, and then Janet had to turn away, back to the large fact of the six-foot wall.

Janet was numb. The grey concrete glared at her. The rhododendrons above her shivered. She had to move. She had to get out of the way so that she did not have to smile at Alice as she returned to the kitchen, to the house –

Janet almost ran across the lawn to the willow tree. She reached out and parted its weeping fronds. She slipped through the soft branches into the haven of delicate green. Her lounger was still there, but she could not sit down. She stood in the perfect bower. If the beautiful tree were a wig, a gorgeous hairdo of silver and lime, then she was hidden within the crown of its thoughts. She lifted her arms, reached up for a moment into the lovely space created by the tree. But then she had to hold the hanging branches; she had to drown in the soft fronds, bury herself in the embrace of their gentle arms. These men, oh, these men. She was showering in those branches, washing herself in the streams of their refreshing green as though to rid herself of the half-fears and suspicions that had sprayed over her, had spouted from Desperate Doug's mouth right into her. Janet clung to the branches, supported by them. Alice would have delivered Solomon his lunch by now. Alice would be back in the house by now. It was getting close to the time when she, Janet, would need to fetch little Sylvia from nursery school and then she would leave the house and her sleeping husband in Alice's care. Alice would be alone in her wonderland. In the streaming, cool, green leaves, Janet tried her best to wash those thoughts from her mind. It was not fair. It was simply not fair on her dear, dear Alice. It was no good.

She stumbled blinking from the tree. Just when the pool was being fixed now another worry nagged at her. Would she never be free. Always this worry. Janet sighed. The tingle in her gut stretched back a long time. Indeed, how long had it taken her own mother to relinquish the aspirations with which she haunted Janet, her little daughter. Amelia Amis had got it into her head one summer holiday – between working on papers reappraising Eliot's social realism – George's rather than T.S.'s – and 'The Narrative Intrusions of Thackeray: a Riposte to Roland Barthes' – that her daughter's poetic sensibilities required developing. That if she was not going to practise her times tables with Lettie, well, then, she would jolly well have to submit to a regime of creativity. If not numeracy, then literacy. How old was Janet, nine, ten –

Eleven, Janet's small voice informed her mother, who said it was about time that Janet learned to express herself in proper alexandrines and to realise that vers libre in actual fact demanded restraint. How she forced her to notice things, to gaze upon the world with a poet's eye. At night, across an indigo sky, a bat is not a bat, it is a shred of torn umbrella, a flitting pipistrella. You did not steal the plums, you were sorry that you ate the plums that you were keeping. You did not eulogise true love but rather did not to the marriage of true minds admit impediments across fourteen lines. Rhythm could be regular or sprung. Amelia Amis and her metronome repeated the admonishment in careful time. Do not, my child, offend me thus, her mother wagged her finger in pointed time. Maybe that is why Janet read English at the University of the Witwatersrand – it was the least offensive option to her mother. Maybe it was a way of trying to understand her mother.

Mother, so what do you think of this essay. Please cast your eye over this essay before I hand it in. Maybe it was just a severe lack of imagination. The wrong rite of passage. One that took her deeper into perplexity which had very little – or everything – to do with poetry. Poetry was a form of paranoia – fear made flesh, it seemed. Her mother was no poet. She was a critic. She and her red pens. Her pile of perpetual essays. Her disdainful sneer, her clear eyes that stared into space, past her daughter, through her daughter. Then back to the flick of ink, red spikes, bloody black-jacks.

What made her mother tick. Did her mother know.

And now, thrown up in her face by a Desperate Doug, there was again the fear – currently so clear and sharp – of being hurt and of hurting and of not understanding. Just like a child. Just like the crack. But, while she had Solomon and they had tackled the crack, what could she do with the seams of doubt, impossible seemings, that now criss-crossed her heart and mind. She was no poet. She was not an academic. She was a housewife married to a policeman. She was the mother of three children.

She stood, unleashed by the gentle willow tree, yet moated by the green lawn. She had to move, she had to change her clothes and fetch Sylvia, and yet she dare not take a single step. What if she stumbled into the bedroom and came across a scene. What if Alice were not hoovering and Hektor-Jan not simply sleeping. What if Alice were sleeping whilst Hektor-Jan were hoovering her. Janet stood in anguish, her body a lonely tower in the garden. What if she, like the Lady of Shallot, peered out – or in – and off flew the web and floated wide and what if the bedroom mirror crack'd from side to side.

Before she could stumble across a Goblin Market – more terrible Tennyson – the back door opened and Lettie – no, Alice – came straight across the grass, her pink apron unsoiled, her dress trim and straight. No sign of Hektor-Jan.

Madam, called Alice, Madam, the little one, Sylvia, and she came right up to Janet and pointed to her wrist, to the watch that she did not have but which signalled time's winged chariot hurrying near. Janet tried to nod. She tried not to throw her arms around Alice in sudden relief, to clasp her to her breast and to beg her forgiveness. With a hasty glance at the brooding rhododendrons, Janet stifled a cry and, instead of reaching out to Alice, raised her hands rather to her own head.

Thank you, Alice, she managed to say as she held her relief intact and tried not to weep. Thank you, Alice.

My Madam, replied Alice gently, still standing there. She would not leave until Janet had begun to move. She knew Janet too well.

With a last glance at the neighbour's wall, Janet stumbled forward guided by Alice. Behind them, Solomon emerged carrying his tin plate and mug, still humming. And from within the dark heart of the rhododendrons, a pair of eyes watched their every move. Janet could feel their amused malevolence.

Even as she and Alice went to fetch Sylvia – Alice agreed to her plea to accompany her – Janet felt the gaze of those eyes. Even as she watched Shelley and Pieter eating their sandwiches after they had walked home from their little school up the road, she knew they were watching. Those eyes called to mind the strange book covers of F. Scott Fitzgerald, George Orwell, Anthony Burgess. Eyes which loomed, which leered, heavy-lidded or brightly, with strange white sclera and black and pointed pupils: constricted or weirdly dilated. Janet realised that eyes were nothing but cracks in the face. They were bright holes which winked to a slit, a fleshy, eyelashed crack, every few seconds. She opened her mouth. She closed her mouth. She tried not to scream.

Hektor-Jan awoke and played with the children.

Alice cooked supper and breakfast.

They ate and refused the children's requests to watch more television at Uncle Doug's.

Hektor-Jan left for work and Janet supervised bathtime and bedtime stories. Pieter remembered some homework he had buried in his schoolbag, but Janet told him to save it for the morning. She closed the last page of the last Enid Blyton and offered up the last kiss. Be good for Alice, she whispered. Mommy is off to her rehearsal again tonight and the children murmured sleepily – except for Pieter who chanced his arm with another request to stay up. But Janet was already on the trembling foothills of the Scottish Highlands and filling her ears were the thick-coming sounds of going home, home, home, going home to bonnie Jean. Ye wee rascal, she patted Pieter's confusion on the head and told him to sleep for a hundred years. Then it was time to freshen up with more make-up, another dab of perfume and to find her bag and her script. What a sudden flurry of seeking! But then she ran into Alice who was holding both her bag and the script.

Dear Alice. Janet laid a grateful hand on her arm. I won't be late, she called quietly as she left, and from the kitchen came the soft sounds of Alice's radio.

Shelley's Secret Journal

Today's word from Granny's list is INDECIPHERABLE.

Mommy is indecipherable. I am sure you agree Granny. I think you told me that not so long ago. She calls Alice Lettie. She jumps when you talk to her. I asked when we can visit you but she did not say when. She can't find things and she won't let us play in the back garden. Alice won't let me ask her why. What do you think Granny? Maybe it's the stupid play? Or maybe she knows what actually happened to Jock? And I am getting really tired of Pieter and his nightmares about the blacks. I think he thinks he is in a play like Mommy's big drama. Love, Shelley.

Janet escaped from the house into the chirping twilight. She scurried next door to Eileen-the-Understudy who was waiting in her car. With excited giggles, they were off. What a relief. After such a day, what a relief. Janet could begin to breathe again.

Have you learned your words, Eileen-the-Understudy asked and Janet nodded furiously in the passenger seat. And you, Janet asked her tall friend. Eileen-the-Understudy grated the gears and rounded a corner quite sharply and Janet wished that she had curbed her enthusiasm a little.

Yes, Eileen-the-Understudy said brightly. I have learned both my lines. I am word perfect!

Janet blushed quietly.

She was grateful for Eileen-the-Understudy's hand on her arm as they skipped into the Rynfield Primary School hall. For the hand which squeezed her arm as Frank van Zyl turned to greet them, and to become Janet's attentive shadow. And Derek-Francis again simpered up to say what a perfect couple they were – Janet and Frank – and wasn't kismet a remarkable force. Why, we pit our strength against oceans of troubles and out of the blue a solution comes – just wonderful. Beautiful kismet. And then Janet was alone with Frank and they stood waiting for the last few members of the cast to arrive.

There was a theatrical cheer as the final person – the bumptious friend of the romantic lead, the one who did an amazing American accent – leapt through the double doors of the little school hall. And then they were off.

Derek-Francis had them start with a run-through of the opening scene when the village awoke after one hundred years had passed, and, apart from the two Americans and the girlfriend back home, they all yawned and stretched and did a very passable impression of collective torpor and stupefaction. They were so caught up in their slumbers and then their languorous stretching, that they did not notice the groundsman who materialised out of the dark night and stood watching them.

It was only Janet, so attuned to the pressure of such scrutiny, who gave a little yelp of surprise as the uniformed black man rattled his keys against his thighs. Then, amidst the knots of white folk waking up from prolonged unconsciousness, the black man stepped into the hall and demanded to know once again of Derek-Francis if it was for two hours that they were going to be busy. There were one or two grunts of surprise – who expected sudden black men in *Brigadoon* for God's sake – and a very thin woman squealed and clasped her hand which the groundsman had almost trodden on.

But Derek-Francis was very good, very firm this time.

Some of the men had a word with him, our director, Eileen-the-Understudy breathed, and it seems to have worked. We can't keep being interrupted can we – we have a show to put on.

And that seemed to be the vocal consensus. No more silly interruptions, who does he think he is. For crying out loud. But no one had to cry out loud. Derek-Francis did a very good job of giving him a flea in his ear. They could all hear the flustered exclamations coming through the open door which let in not only Derek-Francis's hissing, but also a constant flutter of insects too.

Then it was back to *Brigadoon* as the mutterings of the groundsman receded into the night and the double doors were slammed shut.

After the more physical stretching of the waking-up scene – repeated three times – Derek-Francis got them all together to do some elocution practice. He wanted authentic Scottish accents and for the next half-hour they chorused words and phrases like Bairn, Sporran, Och, Do ye not know and Phantasmagorical in rich and rolling voices that exalted every last fruity nuance of the ripe r sounds and made a confection out of every vowel, so different from the flat, more leavened accents of the typical South African. There was hearty laughter and Derek-Francis conducted them with gentle exactitude. Yes! he began to cry as they neared the end of that half-hour, Yes, yes, we are getting somewhere! Now we sound like we are in the Scottish Highlands, yes! And there was a cheer from the men. And the women threw their hands to their mouths and squealed again, but with joy this time. They began to grasp the certainty that the Rynfield Primary School hall would indeed be transformed into Brigadoon. Their little project had legs, someone said, and would walk all the way. There were more giggles and Janet tried to concentrate on the prevailing joy and not the image of the play stumbling uncertainly like Sylvia used to, like a toddler making its way in the dark to the little school hall whilst the black gatekeeper rattled his keys and lurked in the wings. The image of the tiny play, almost plaintive, brought her close to tears, but then Derek-Francis was ushering the chorus and the other main characters to the adjacent music classroom where his friend, a gifted pianist, was waiting. It was Derek-Francis's little surprise and he introduced the neat man, Rupert, with a great flourish and Rupert bowed. Then Rupert sat behind the piano and was still before his fingers attacked the instrument and the opening number burst into the room.

Eileen-the-Understudy watched as Derek-Francis drew Janet and Frank van Zyl out of the ambit of voices and took them back to the hall.

Janet shivered. This was their scene. For an hour they exchanged enthusiastic dialogue whilst Derek-Francis fussed round the frills of their words and expertly trimmed and adjusted their movements, their expressions, their dialogue. Each inflection was tried on for size and pulled straight. Janet was overwhelmed by Derek-Francis's dedication. She and Frank fell into their parts, their initial awkwardness briskly dispelled by Derek-Francis.

As Janet confided to Eileen-the-Understudy in the car on the way home, Derek-Francis had started off their private rehearsal with a command. Kiss her, he had instructed Frank. She and Frank had stared helplessly at each other. I didn't know what to do, Janet said as Eileen-the-Understudy tried to find the ignition in the dark. Eileen-the-Understudy jabbed at the far side of the steering wheel whilst Janet tried to find the right words. I didn't know what to do. Derek-Francis wants *intimacy*, he said. He wants it to be *real*.

What did you do, Eileen-the-Understudy flicked on the little over-head light.

I stood there, Janet said. So did Frank.

Aha, said Eileen-the-Understudy peering at the keys.

Think of someone you love, Derek-Francis said. He was quite forceful. Someone you really love. And it does not have to be your husband or wife.

Sorry, said Eileen-the-Understudy as she picked the keys up from between her legs. Clumsy me.

You don't mind my telling you, Janet said.

Lord, no, said Eileen-the-Understudy. It's fascinating to hear what you principals get up to in those private rehearsals. She started the car. So what did you do. I mean, who did you think of.

Janet waited as Eileen-the-Understudy reversed.

I, Janet said, then stopped. I stood there, and I was sure that one of us was suddenly going to laugh.

Laugh, said Eileen-the-Understudy as the little car skidded forward.

But no one laughed. Our director was quite serious. Frank got quite serious too.

No wonder, said Eileen-the-Understudy as the car slowed at the turn into Nestadt Street that would take them straight down to Davidson Street and then to home. She turned cautiously, drove a little way down the road and then pulled against the kerb and stopped.

It doesn't seem right, Eileen-the-Understudy said. I need to give this my full attention. She jerked the handbrake and turned to Janet. No doubt you were thinking of your husband as groovy Frank got closer.

Eileen-the-Understudy turned the key and the car shuddered to silence. The road stretched out before them, tree-lined, straight and broad.

I tried, Janet said looking through the windscreen at the road. I was still trying when he kissed me.

He kissed you, Eileen-the-Understudy said.

He kissed me, said Janet.

There was a pause.

He kissed you, Eileen-the-Understudy said.

Like he meant it, said Janet. I mean, our director was saying Go on, go on, this isn't a sin for Christ's sake, this is drama, for Christ's sake – he said Christ quite a lot – and we need to cement your relationship. He actually said cement and that's all I could think about then – was grey cement and someone stirring cement with strong arms and a sweating back.

The kiss, said Eileen-the-Understudy. What was the kiss like.

It was long, said Janet. Very long. And complicated.

Long, said Eileen-the-Understudy as she held on to the steering wheel. And I suppose he had luscious lips.

Janet's voice came after a pause. Derek, she said. Derek kept saying, Like you mean it. Kiss her like you mean it for Christ's sake.

And I think both of us just got fed up and so we kissed like we meant it, closed lips then open lips and my tongue and his hands –

My God, his hands – and you were thinking of cement, said Eileen-the-Understudy.

It was shocking, said Janet. Then she turned to her tall friend and her voice shook. And it was – delicious. But I feel sick.

Eileen-the-Understudy was very still in her seat. Cement, she said. Cement.

Exactly, said Janet. And then I was kissing him. Then it was my tongue in his mouth and our director was saying, Yes, yes, that's better. That's much more like it and he clapped his hands.

Janet put a hand to her head. The trees were dark sentinels down both sides of the road. Driveways led to gates and to gardens and houses and lots of lives on both sides of the road. Janet turned to Eileen-the-Understudy.

What have you got me into, Janet said. One moment I am reading Enid Blyton and putting my children to bed and the next I am kissing someone called Frank van Zyl. I have never kissed anyone but my husband like that. My tongue –

Eileen-the-Understudy seemed to be practising a range of dramatic expressions. Her face widened with surprise. Look, she said, look here. I wasn't the one who made you throw yourself into the part. I wasn't the one who grabbed that audition and attacked it like that, was I.

Eileen-the-Understudy's voice took a theatrical turn. Her hands also came alive.

But Janet turned even further towards her and held out her hands. My hands, she said to her pale neighbour. Are my hands shaking. Are they steady.

I wasn't the one who grabbed that audition, was I. Eileen-the-Understudy clapped her own hands over Janet's. They were much bigger and stronger than Janet's hands. Was I.

My hands, Janet almost cried, but she swallowed instead. She breathed. Then she tore her eyes away from her unsteady hands hidden beneath her friend's and answered Eileen-the-Understudy.

No, Janet agreed. And she breathed again and her hands finally broke free and rubbed her face.

What will you do, asked Eileen-the-Understudy.

Janet held out her hands again. She could not help it. His hands are strong, she said as she stared at her own. He loves me. He comes home to me. The new job – it is a demanding job. He holds me so tightly. Her voice shook and so did her outstretched hands. What does Phil –

Phil, Eileen-the-Understudy quickly said as though she were still auditioning.

When Phil comes home, said Janet, trying to make her voice nice and steady.

He flies in, said Eileen-the-Understudy. She made a face and looked significantly at Janet. He brings me perfume. She laughed. He does not realise it, but he comes home to me smelling of perfume.

Janet lowered her hands. She looked at her friend.

I don't wear that kind of perfume, Eileen-the-Understudy whispered.

There was a slight pause.

What does Hektor-Jan smell like when he comes home.

Hektor-Jan, said Janet. Her hands were now on her lap. They were cold and still, quite dead. She wrinkled her nose. She inhaled and there was only the sickly stench of rhododendron flowers, in bold sprays like toilet brushes. How could she describe the stink of rhododendrons after the sweet warmth of the school hall and *Brigadoon*.

Hektor-Jan, Janet said again.

Phil, countered Eileen-the-Understudy. Perfume.

They sat in the car for a long time. Then Eileen-the-Understudy drove them home.

Despite the deep shower at the police station, Hektor-Jan looked forward to the beating water of his shower at home. He longed to step into that glass cubicle and to fill his ears with thundering water and his lungs with purging steam. After an aggressive lathering and scrubbing, he would stand there. The water would beat down on his thinning scalp and his lips could move. He could whisper and curse and call out in that confessional of streaming water. His wife did not have to know. His children did not have to run crying from him. The steam understood. It swirled as opaquely as forgiveness. It flowed as gently as absolution. If he raised his tired arms and adjusted his pose, he felt the water run like hot blood from the holes in his hands, and gush from his side and well up from his torn feet. Christ, he needed to shower.

He was home earlier than usual. It had been a trying night. His patience had been tested to the limit and his body ached. His knuckles were skinned on his right hand. If he flexed it, the plasma oozed to the surface. He closed the car door quietly. Then he stood for a moment. He leaned against the car, facing the house. His home grew lighter and more solid out of the surrounding black then indigo heaven. It was close to dawn.

Something else took shape.

There came the whisper of conscience.

Hektor-Jan frowned.

Higher, came the voice and there was a whine.

Hektor-Jan turned slowly and looked over the car, at the wall behind him. There were two cypress trees on his neighbour's side. They stood very tall and he could make out their darker blackness, deeper than the surrounding darkness. From between them came the voice and the panting. His neighbour and his ridiculous dog.

Higher, said the voice.

Ja, said Hektor-Jan.

And then he could see the paler blur of Douglas van Deventer.

You are up early, said Hektor-Jan.

You are home early, said Doug.

Hektor-Jan's right hand felt tight. His body ached for the shower. He did not wish to chit-chat with his neighbour at this ridiculous time. He was exhausted. He leaned on the bonnet of the car, and looked at his hurt hand in the dark. It was invisible.

I heard the car, said Doug.

Hektor-Jan felt the metal, warm in the cold dawn.

I always hear your car – and, especially, Janet's car.

Hektor-Jan balanced two weights on his shoulders: his home and his neighbour. He was caught in the middle.

You came home dead on time yesterday morning, Doug's voice came softly through the cypresses. Then Janet took the tribe to school, spot on time. But then she went out again after that. I heard her. There was a lot of coming and going yesterday. You, then her with the children, and then with the garden boy. You must have been sleeping, boet.

Hektor-Jan took a while to extract the salient fact. Unusually, for he had been interrogating suspects all night, he let the crucial clue slip through his skinned fingers at first. Doug was silent. He waited. He was rewarded.

The garden boy, said Hektor-Jan.

There was a perfectly calibrated pause.

In her car, said Doug.

Hektor-Jan leaned more heavily on the car. He said something in Afrikaans. Then he stood up. Is jy seker, he said. Are you sure.

It was nothing, said Doug. Probably nothing at all. I saw them.

You saw them.

In passing. I was busy in the front garden. I looked over the wall. The way she held the door open for the black boy. How she bent down and adjusted his seat. He watched her. He watched her bending down. Then they got into the car together and drove off together.

Hektor-Jan looked up at the wall. It grew grey, born out of the black-ness. It came to light.

I am sure it was nothing, said Doug. His voice was kind. Hopeful. It was a glass-is-half-full voice. Your-white-wife-and-the-black-garden-boy-were-separated-by-a-handbrake-and-a-gear-stick kind of voice.

They were only gone for an hour at most.

I heard the car return – it backfired again – and they got out together. She laughed.

She put the seat back the way it was. She bent down again to readjust the seat. No one would ever have known. He watched her bend down by his knees. I think he tried to help her. Lent over her. Man, they struggled with that seat.

You must have been sleeping, boet.

She laughed.

The garden boy was silent.

They took things out of the boot. Together. She helped him.

They went to the back garden.

I watched them. I thought of you, boet. I almost called the police. Then I thought, hell, man, you are the police. I thought, maybe you knew. Maybe you were okay with all this. I didn't want to interfere, man.

I hope you don't mind.

I would want to know, you know.

Man.

Jesus.

Whilst you were sleeping.

Jesus.

Hektor-Jan felt the plasma seep from his hand. He held up his hand to his chest. So often, the truth was difficult to extract. It came slowly. A bit like a tooth. You had to wiggle it this way and that. Tease it a bit. Pretend to do something else. Chaff the bloody liars that you had given up meanwhile you were looping a length of fishing line around the tooth, the truth, before fixing it to the open door. Then you kicked it closed.

Out shot the tooth. It was a lengthy process. Here, now, in the stillness of the dawn, Hektor-Jan shook his head as the fishing lines twanged all about him. It was raining teeth. He raised his hand. He did not want it to get bitten.

Doug was speaking. His voice came through the scent of the cypresses. Hektor-Jan had to concentrate to discern meaning from murmur.

Promise me that you won't do anything silly, man, Doug was mumbling. He leaned out between the trees, pressing out of the violet sky, holding on to the wall.

There is probably no need to get jealous.

No need to get angry.

Keep calm. I find a shot of brandy helps. Takes the burning away by burning your guts. Fights fire with fire. Brandewijn. Fancy a drop.

Hektor-Jan stood there. His teeth were on edge and if he took a step, he knew that he would tread on the teeth that had fallen all around him. He shook his head – this was ridiculous.

I've got a bottle; I'll get two glasses, said Doug. Come on, Higher. Like the old days.

Hektor-Jan stood there.

Don't move, said Doug and he disappeared.

Hektor-Jan stood in the gathering dawn. The world pulled itself together, took a deep breath and stood up straight – and there it was. A new day. Out of the darkness, there came forth light. The heavens were newly created and there was the dewy scent of newborn earth.

This is good, Doug said. He reached over the wall and passed a small glass of sunrise to Hektor-Jan. Are you sure you won't come around.

Hektor-Jan looked at the glass in his hand.

Cheers, said Doug on his ladder and he leaned over the wall. Hektor-Jan turned away from him, to face the lightening sky. The glass glowed in his hand. Still he did not drink.

To the old days, said the voice at his shoulder, just above his head, straight from heaven.

Hektor-Jan's hand tightened painfully around the glass. In a sudden motion, he drained it.

Sun-risers, came Doug's voice with rising humour. We are drinking sun-risers. Another one.

Hektor-Jan raised his glass. He did not have to turn around. The liquid came gurgling and filled his glass.

Doug toasted the sky, Hektor-Jan swallowed and raised his glass again. That's more like it. Doug reached down and patted him on the shoulder.

After the fourth shot, Doug spoke again.

Anything, he whispered. Anything you need, just let me know. You're the expert, but if you need any help, I'm right here, boet. I am right – fucking – here. His voice shook with the brandy.

Hektor-Jan sipped the fifth shot.

I admire your control, Doug said pouring the sixth. I would not have such control. Man, I would be right in there. My wife, for fuck's sake. My fucking wife. I couldn't handle that.

Hektor-Jan grunted.

Sorry, said Doug. I don't mean to jump the gun. Fuck. You wouldn't even have to use a gun. Just give it to the kaffir straight. But I suppose there has to be evidence. You cops like evidence.

Doug's voice came fast like the booze. We need evidence. Got to make sure before we pile in. Fuck. Can't just sommer pile in, can we.

They stopped after the seventh shot. The world was ablaze with light. It was a changed sky, a new dawn. Doug saw that it was good.

Hektor-Jan went inside.

Supper was not good.

Janet was waiting for him. The spaghetti bolognaise looked tired. Janet looked like she had not slept all night. Talking to her was like pulling teeth. Hektor-Jan found that the brandy had loosened his tongue. It seemed also to have dislodged his eyes. He saw differently. In segments.

How was your rehearsal, he said.

Janet winced. She put down the plate. It clattered on the hard table.

Sorry, she said. Don't want to wake the children. Her hands reached out uncertainly, then she folded her hands over her lovely chest. Then she hid them behind her back. She did not seem to know what to do with her hands.

Hektor-Jan found his own hands waving her concern aside. He repeated his question. How was your rehearsal.

Janet closed the kitchen door. She sat down opposite him. Fine, she said.

She inhaled deeply. She seemed to wrinkle her nose as she took a deep breath.

He watched her hand wander up to her earlobe and tug it once. Twice. A dead giveaway. She kept holding her ear. Her other hand was under the table. Absolutely fine, thanks, Janet said. She stared at him. She smiled at him. She inhaled deeply again.

The spaghetti was road-kill. It was maggots. It looked at him and lied to his face. Could he eat those twisted falsehoods that lay coiled like worms in a bed of bloody tomato and sweaty minced lamb. Did she expect him to consume them.

Doug's brandewijn gave him krag, strength. He picked up the fork. It was heavy. It had a trinity of tines. He could use it to stab, twist and eat lies, lies and damned lies. He hefted it. It was small but heavy in his hand. He wielded it.

What else did you get up to, he said. Whilst I was fast asleep.

Janet looked at him. She looked at the waiting fork and the neglected knife and the untouched food.

It was a busy day, she said to the spaghetti and rubbed her nose, once, twice, thrice.

Did she jump when he suddenly speared a loop of tomato-stained string. He teased it out of the plate. Looped around the fork, it kept coming. It was very long. Quite serpentine. He could be in the Garden of Eden. Was his wife not Eve to his Adam. Was she not Eve to this snake. Did not Doug's holy spirit call to him. Had his wife not eaten the forbidden fruit. Hektor-Jan tried to pull his eyes away from the strands of spaghetti. Liewe hemel, seven shots of brandy and three times she rubbed her nose.

Tell me about your busy day, he said.

The spaghetti was too long to coil around the fork. He brought it to his mouth, inserted it and sucked hard.

Janet spoke.

A spaghetto came slurping up from his plate to be chewed, swallowed, digested.

She told him about the children. She told him about Pieter's progress with the eight-times table. What Sylvia's teacher had said about her aptitude with clay. How Shelley was becoming even more quiet and studious and that, dear God, her penetrating questions reminded Janet of her mother. Did Hektor-Jan remember what her mother was like before the, you know, the Alzheimer's.

Hektor-Jan chewed. He chewed on the blasphemy which heralded the reference to penetrating questions. He chewed on the fact that, surely, she knew that he tolerated most things in this broken world, but not blasphemy. And did she find his questions penetrating. What did this Englishwoman really think and feel. He chewed. Could he swallow. He chewed as her mouth moved. There was not a word about the garden boy. Not a whisper about the garden boy fell from her lips. She stopped talking. He stopped chewing. The clock in the kitchen was very loud. Its jerking hand tolled the seconds.

What time on Saturday, Janet said. Her voice jumped at him and he swallowed in surprise. Who would have thought that a single spaghetto could make you choke.

She handed him a glass of water.

He gulped it.

He looked at his plate. Was she changing the topic. He looked at the runes, the twisted hieroglyphs on his plate. She had not told him about her day. Tell me about your day, he said.

Yet again the itchy ear lobe. Again the hunted look. The brittle smile. Then the hand reached out to touch his arm that held the heavy fork. She did not need to utter a word. His heart thumped as loudly as the fokken clock. His skin tightened and went cold. His world of work seemed to be pouring into the little kitchen.

She spoke.

Then she stopped.

What did you say, she said. What did you say, darling.

Had he spoken. If he had, what had he said.

Who is Delilah, she said. Did you say Delilah.

Delilah, he repeated. Had he said Delilah. And he knew that he had. The great Samson, in the height of his power, had been cut down by the treachery of his Delilah. Even her name carried the coil of a lie. And his wife. Did this daughter of an English university lecturer and a soft rooinek, an Engelsman, embody a net. Janet. Delilah.

Net, said Janet. What do you mean, net.

He knew that he shook his head and said, no. Nee. Geen kans nie, not a chance. As ek 'n vraag vra – if I ask a question – do not you dare ask a question.

And the spaghetti that were his intestines tightened and he felt the kitchen slide to Benoni Central, to the holding cells. He clung to the ticking of the kitchen clock. Father, husband, father, husband, ticked the clock. His hands ached against the hard fork; he dared not close his eyes. He dared not raise the fork to her face.

Her hand moved on his arm. It was painfully tender. Jezebel.

A bath, she said. But you have hardly touched –

She would run a deep bath. Lots of foamy bubble bath. The way he liked it.

Of course, she said. I'll run it and get you a fresh towel, nice and crisp. Maybe you are coming down with something. And let me see that poor hand.

She helped to undress him, took the clothes from him.

Like John the Baptist, she helped him to sink into the deep water.

She arranged his arm along the side of the bath on a hand towel so that her neat bandaging did not get wet. Keep it dry, she said. Otherwise it will take much longer to heal. Is that better.

His desk job was more dangerous than she had suspected.

And he lay there in the water.

What time on Saturday, she persisted. You said that you had organised a present for Pieter. You know how much he wants a bike, a Chopper. Did you have a Chopper in mind. It's either that or another dog. He desperately wants a dog, a Jock, too.

Maybe if he slipped beneath the surface of the water all would be quiet. He would not hear her. The black garden boy would be washed away by the white bubbles. He eased himself down so that just his ears were underwater. The world became a murmur.

He cursed Doug and his brandewijn. He cursed his stinging hand and the lying bastards at Benoni Central. He did not know how to curse his wife and the garden boy.

It had come to this.

He had thought that he could keep the world of work separate from his life at home. His private Apartheid. He had prayed that he could keep both worlds running along the lines of separate development. How he had prayed.

He was cast out into a wilderness of white bubbles. Beneath the water, it was quiet. But, like the kitchen clock, he heard the warp and woof of his heart. It was thumping.

It had come to this.

25.6CM

Alexandra,
What are teeth, but the off-shoots of a skull?
What is a smile, but the airing of enamelled tombstones?
And when that blackness splits, why is there such a rictus
Of white, white, white?

– Refilwe Ralapele, from 'Anatomising Alexandra'

One day a woman returning from taking her children to school was ambushed on the Sonnestraal road by a group of angry residents from nearby Duduza hiding in the tall grass on either side of the road. They threw stones at the car, she lost control and the vehicle overturned. The woman, a nurse, was stoned to death inside her car. Our base was about four kilometres from where the incident had taken place but we could do nothing to prevent it. When we arrived at the scene, we found the dark blue Volkswagen Passat lying on its roof. The woman lay halfway out of the window, her blonde hair on the dark surface of the tarred road.

– Johan Marais, *Time Bomb: A Policeman's True Story*

J anet brushed her teeth again. She stood beside her naked husband and
whilst he brushed his teeth, she brushed her teeth. She continued long
after he had sunk naked into bed. She choked on the sterilising foam and
coughed it up. She spat hard. Kept spitting and rinsing for a long time.

There were no snores when she dressed and crept out of the bedroom.
Hektor-Jan lay rigidly asleep.

She knew that he was watching her as she dressed. She did not
know what had happened at work, why he should be so upset about
his skinned hand and why he did not seem able to bear her touch. He
was a very impatient patient.

She dressed slowly, and as quietly as she could whilst his eyes glared
in the curtained dark. She chose the dress that was his favourite, the one
that he loved to unzip and let fall to the ground. Such a simple dress,
except for the never-ending zip at the back. She would need a hand.
Usually she asked him, but he was pretending to be asleep. She would ask
Alice. Or one of the children. She left the room with her back exposed.

Janet shut the door on the screaming silence.

Solomon arrived.

Alice made breakfast.

Pieter hovered behind Alice. His face looked blotched and messy –
and he seemed about to suck his thumb. Before she could say anything,
Alice turned and pressed his hand away from his face. Alice bent over
him and said something softly. Pieter brightened. It had something to
do with his birthday.

Janet took the children to school and negotiated all of Pieter's
attempts to bribe the answer to his birthday present out of her. He offered
her twenty cents and three soft Chappies, his favourite bubblegum. He
promised to be good. He recited his eight-times table, all fine except for
nine and twelve times eight. He said if he got a dog he would pick up
the poo. If it was a Chopper, he would go shopping for her. He had to
know. He would die if he did not know. She smiled at him in the rear-
view mirror. He was such an ardent little chap.

She made the children wait even longer as she hugged them hard and kissed them and then hugged them again.

Let go, Pieter struggled, annoyed that he had another day and night to wait for his birthday. Shelley and Sylvia stood like dolls. Woodenly, they accepted her urgent attention. They were like the dolls she used to have, the much older Shelley and Sylvia hidden from her mother's derision and even from her husband. They were at the bottom of the wardrobe, where she kept her things. She had not played with them for ages. She had not introduced Shelley to Shelley, or Sylvia to Sylvia. She looked in wonder at their fresh skin and kissed their soft mouths again. One more hug, she pleaded, but they were gone. Pieter ran. Shelley also ran, but then turned back once in concern.

After the short drive to the nursery school, Sylvia skipped singing beside her. Then, she too was gone and Janet knew that she had to return home and that after all that, she would have to make her way to the bottom of the garden to peer at the swimming pool. She held the steering wheel hard.

She did not hear the backfiring.

She was home.

The cement would have dried. The crack would be closed. Solomon would be painting the bottom of the pool with the white paint. All would be well.

But Janet knew that it was not so.

Before Nesbitt began his yelping and before Desperate Doug could appear and hiss to her, she knew.

She left the car door open and her fingers flustered the front-door keys. She ran through the house, straight past Lettie and out the kitchen door. She dived across the sea of green grass towards Solomon whose bottom half had been swallowed by the empty pool. He was standing in the shallow end.

He did not look up as she arrived breathlessly. He could have been a solitary black-jack in the white flesh of the pool. He could have been a living crack, so dark against the gleaming basin of the pool. Janet had to prevent herself from falling in.

The crack was back. It was more than a foot wide and it ran down the entire length of the pool and all the way up the sides as well. It was worse than ever. After all that work! They might as well not have bothered at all. It had made no difference. If anything, it might have made it worse. How could that be. But it was. Indubitably. One of her mother's favourite words peeled off the past and surfaced. Janet found her lips moving. Indubitably. The deep syllables welling up and spilling. The crack re-emerging from who knows where. Indubitably.

Solomon, she said.

He did not look up. He seemed transfixed by the crack. Just as she was. She was losing him to the crack.

Solomon, she said again.

He shook his head.

Eish, he said. Madam, eish. All the work, Madam. All the money. The mixing – too much hard work.

His final eish was a sigh.

Janet took a deep breath. We cannot give up, she said. We must – persist. Persistence, and she listened to her mouth in wonder as it spoke another of her mother's sharp words. Amelia Amis, a vicar's daughter from the depths of rural Hampshire, from Long Sutton, South Warnborough and a place called Well, had made her way up to Cambridge through sheer persistence. Newnham College for women. Persistence, her clear, posh voice had repeated. Janet stared at the crack and thought of her mother drowning in the dank smells and cabbage-soup routine of the old-age home. Another kind of collegiate system, mostly for old women. It was always the same, it seemed. Rising up with the crack came pain. Memories and a pitiless sense of loss. It felt as though the crack should be festering with flies, and as she thought that, Solomon did indeed swat away a thick fly and it buzzed down the crack.

Solomon was talking to her. What was he saying. She could hardly ear him. Hear him. The blood beat in her breath and her head came too slowly. She was drowning and he seemed to be saying, cement. More cement. Again. We try again. Is that what he was saying. All the flies in the world seemed to be buzzing from the crack and she had to frown and squint and try to make out what Solomon was saying as he stepped out of the pool.

No. She thought she held up her hand and shouted No. No more cement. No more glistening muscles and naked backs and honest sweat. And her hand brushed her eyes and she called for water. Gushing water. Turn on the tap. Bring the hose. Quickly quickly. And it was almost as though part of herself was gushing into the pool as the water came spurting and she grabbed his strong hands and unpeeled his surprised fingers from the hose and took it from him most persistently and with indubitable purpose she directed the jet of water straight into the depths of the crack. The fly never surfaced. The water frothed and gurgled in the dark depths before welling up. She and Solomon stood there. Side by side they stood in silence as Janet filled the pool. Lettie – Alice – Alice-Lettie brought out some tea but set it down on the grass behind them. It steamed for a while in the sun, but still the water jetted. The hose shuddered and pulsed and, after an hour, Solomon took it from her. His strong hands took the hose and he too directed the stream straight into the hungry mouth of the pool. The water bubbled and shimmered now. It lapped, limpid against the bright sides of the pool and Janet felt a lightening and the promise of cool water, of tender blue, even from the depths of her womb. The pool that her father had built. The womb that her parents had created between them. The pool and her body. And Solomon directed the streaming water that now danced. And the crack shook and became less substantial. Could they drown it. Could they simply leave the water running into it forever.

But other business called.

Alice-Lettie came out and reminded Janet that it was time to fetch the little one. Eish, it was getting much too late and the Madam did not want to hurry, ne.

Janet fetched Sylvia and still the water pumped into the pool.

The doorbell rang deep in the house whilst Alice-Lettie was feeding the little one, and Alice-Lettie brought the Madam from next door, Missies Eileen, so that they could talk outside and not wake up the Master, the Baas, who was sleeping.

Janet started. She left Solomon, who had inserted the hose deep into the pool and was now trimming the grassy edges with his shears. It was strange to see Eileen-the-Understudy in the day. Maybe the sun could be a brilliant spotlight and the lawn a great green stage. She could raise her hand in a gesture of welcome and take her friend by the arm and wheel her round, away from the crack in the pool, towards the lounger under the willow tree. And they could chat with brittle pleasure. Swap little pleasantries concerning the blueness of the lovely day, the loveliness of Janet's blue dress and, oh my goodness, the bold new hairdo that crowned Eileen-the-Understudy and emphasised her features so wonderfully. She could lean back on the extended lounger, and Eileen-the-Understudy could stretch out her long, lovely legs which were indeed longer and lovelier than Janet's legs, even though they were not bad at all. Janet could stand before her friend as though she were on stage, somehow performing. And they could hint at the manly imponderability of their husbands. Hektor-Jan's terribly skinned knuckles and Eileen's pilot husband who was back for a night before flying off again on the Frankfurt route. He was sleeping as they spoke. These men of theirs that worked so hard at night and slept so soundly in the day. Men who came home smelling of perfume or of nothing at all. Men whose hands either wafted exotic scents or had somehow lost all the skin on their knuckles. They could shake their heads and try to smile fondly, and Eileen-the-Understudy could hand over the brown-paper package that her Phil had brought for Janet's Hektor-Jan yet again. And they could look at the flat rectangular package that now lay on Janet's lap and they could shake their heads and laugh. And Eileen-the-Understudy could nudge Janet with a friendly elbow and say, What about last night you naughty, naughty woman. Janet could shift within the shady, striped heart of the willow tree and say, Don't, don't talk about that, and Eileen-the-Understudy could chortle with laughter. And Janet could change the subject and tell Eileen-the-Understudy that it was Pieter's birthday the following day and that Hektor-Jan had taken charge of the present, and Janet still did not know what it was. And Eileen-the-Understudy could hand over the next little package, a brighter one this time, and tell Janet that it was the sweetest piggy bank that Phil had told her that they had in Germany and which she had charged her husband to buy for little Pieter. And Janet could thank her for her never-ending generosity and then they could watch Solomon through the veil of branches, now digging and turning over the flower beds, digging away whilst the long hose shuddered in the pool.

And that is what Janet did even though most of her was pouring into the pool. She was proud of herself. What an actress. That she could be so calm and all the while the pool was churning with the new water that ran raw and cold from the tap at the side of the house, along the length of the hose across the vast lawn, straight into the white depths of the pool. Even as Eileen-the-Understudy spoke and tried to tease her about Frank van Zyl, Janet was plunging into the pool. And when Eileen-the-Understudy rose to go and said, Surely you must be off to fetch the children or do they walk home, Janet remained seated and simply smiled. Then she was alone with a vague sense that Eileen-the-Understudy's little performance had just about matched her own and she almost broke into polite applause. But her hands were too far away and she just sat there, the water gushing and willow tree shivering in the heat. At last, she stood up and looked down in surprise as the two presents slipped to the ground. So Eileen-the-Understudy had visited; it had not been all a dream and she wandered over to the pool and saw that it was half full. She tried to think that it was half full, not half empty. Surely, she was a positive person at heart. Only a positive person could attempt to repair such a pool so as to spare her poor husband the trauma. Instead of halving a sorrow, she was prepared to bear the burden alone, but then she knew Hektor-Jan – possibly better than he did himself. And she could not trouble her father who had so much on his plate, who never made a meal of the fact that her mother took up almost all of his time. Amelia Amis MA was like a child. A demanding, recalcitrant child with a terrible temper and foul mouth. A child with fierce and adult urges. Not a mother or a wife, and certainly not a virgin. Amelia Amis seemed to have entered some fourth estate. No, her father had more than enough to keep him busy.

Shelley and Pieter were already munching Alice-Lettie's lettuce and cheese sandwiches when Janet made her way through the kitchen. After the brilliance of outside, inside seemed dark. Janet smiled at their vague shapes and hid the presents in the radiogram drawers amongst the loose paper and the seven singles. Then she was humming Carpenters' songs, snatches of Karen here and Richard there. She stood in the lounge for a while simply humming and letting her eyes grow accustomed to being inside.

Can we swim? Today, can we swim?

The children found her and banished the last chords of Mr Postman from her mind. Their loudness drowned the beginning of Solitaire and she heard herself asking for patience and calm, and that they were to give it another hour after eating and by that time, the pool would be full enough for a nice swim even though the new water would be very chilly. She spoke whilst they all fidgeted and Pieter's eyes went everywhere.

And they did swim and the water was cold. But the thought that it was Friday afternoon and school was banished again for a brief while made them very excited. And Pieter, whose birthday was but hours away was unbearable and Janet had to call from the willow tree that if he did not stop teasing his sisters there would be no presents and they would not go to the farm the following day. He would not see his oupa and his various ooms. Hektor-Jan's wild brothers. That shut Pieter up. Janet knew how he adored the hearty Afrikaans men, so different from her quiet father. Pieter came to apologise to her. His eyes stared large and wide beneath his wet fringe and he held his towel around his little body. He was a towel on legs, with staring eyes.

All right, said Janet. I know it's exciting. But just take it easy.

I will take it easy, I swear I will take it easy, said Pieter and he went inside to get changed like a good boy.

The girls continued to play in the pool, but Janet called them out before long, before they froze in that fresh water. They lay shivering like seals on the hot slasto beside the pool.

When did she know.

When did she just know what was happening in the heart of the lounge.

Shelley and Sylvia had warmed up quickly and now lay panting in the heat. They would want to leap into the pool soon. As usual, their brown skin gleamed silver in the light.

Shadows rustled in the hot air and Janet sat up in her blue dress like a piece of sudden sky. It was as though she could hear the slither of a secret drawer to the right of the radiogram, then the scuffling of small hands amongst the paper and the seven singles. Then silence as the two gifts were prised from their hiding place and Pieter surely stuck out his tongue with the effort and concentration of such stealth. He may have looked over his shoulder, towards the door and the long passage to the bedroom where Bluebeard slumbered or towards the windows which overlooked the back garden where his mother lurked beneath the willow tree. Maybe he began to perspire, little droplets forming on his anxious brow. His hands must have begun to shake as he stared at the two presents. Should he open the larger or the smaller. The larger was plain and dull; the smaller brightly coloured. But it was smaller.

He opened the brown paper bag with its neat bars of Sellotape.

His little hands slipped into the slight gaps and tore quietly at the paper. He must have hesitated, surely, before the brown paper gave way with a sigh and out it came. Not the piggy bank that ingeniously oinked and demanded Deutsche Marks and Krugerrands. Not the clever contraption that offered a slit for coins or folded paper money. No. But there were slits to be sure. Cunning cracks and orifices which appeared to yearn, to clamour for incisive male attention. Heaving thighs and bouncing breasts and parts which surely not even Mommy seemed to have when she stood up in the bath and reached for a towel. And had he ever seen Mommy in such positions. Could the female form be bent and stretched in such startling ways, splayed and trussed and draped. Pieter must have turned the pages of the German magazine – banned from a moral, conservative, Christian South Africa – and stared in growing wonder. Did his mouth go dry. Did he tremble. Did he think of his little sisters with whom he fought and bathed and played. Did he just think of his mother, or maybe the glistening breasts of Alice that day he walked into her outside bathroom when the door was closed but unlocked and she was sitting in the zinc tub lathered in soap and shining and he had just wanted to see if it was she who was singing so softly and it was she and her breasts glistened like wet cannonballs with large nipples and creamy soap. Did he think of his grandmother's mouth that opened so wide and came to eat him that day behind the pampas grass. Maybe he did not think at all.

Possibly the pages turned themselves and the women – black, white, yellow, with nipples of various colours but the same pink-brown and staring gash where their willies might have been – and the women lay back waiting to be exposed by his little hands.

Janet crashed into the lounge. Pieter did not even hear her footsteps through the kitchen and along the passage. He was falling down strange rabbit holes. Some were shaven and calling with craven mouths. Others bearded and whispering darkly. They were not singing Happy Birthday my sweet boy. Welcome to almost-double figures and we hope that you have a good year. He could not put his finger on what they said. But it cut him. He turned another page in this shocking wonderland and his mother burst into sight. For a moment, she seemed to leap from the pages. He looked from them to her. His breath thundered in his ears and he was stunned by her clothing, the bright blue dress that made her so opaque, so withdrawn and hidden, rather than by her cry. From the immediacy of such flesh and undisguised desire, his mother leapt fully clothed and he dropped the other women with their rude bits at his feet as his mother's voice boxed his ears.

Pieter! came her voice and that's who he was – Pieter.

It was hard.

It was hard to grab her agitated son whose mouth moved but from whom no sound came. Grab him and hold him and not break him in a storm of recrimination and retribution. To hold him and feel his stiff surprise and his hot little face. And then his voice came sobbing up in fear and embarrassment.

What would she say? What would Bluebeard do? A thief and a sneak. He had put his hands into secret drawers and exposed the women with no drawers. And now he was caught out and he had not even opened his real present from Mrs Wilson from next door. Would his birthday be banished?

How should she punish him. He seemed anguished already.

She untied her embrace. She held his shoulders and looked into his eyes.

Pieter, she said.

He could not look her in the eye. His breath shuddered and he was trying to cry but no tears came.

Was it an accident, she said.

Was this the first time.

Had he ever fiddled around his father's side of the bed, looked under his mattress for more presents from Mr Wilson the pilot who travelled the world and came back with such things that Customs at the airport did not check or confiscate.

She held him and he shook his head. Then she picked up the offending magazine that lay splashed at their feet. She held it between two fingers like the bag of dog poo when Solomon did not come and she picked up all of Jock's big stinking poos.

I didn't mean to, he said trying not to look at it. I didn't mean to. I thought it was my present. I swear –

We don't swear in this house, said Janet, and she held the glossy magazine. It hung from her hands, now a bright, dead bird. What was she to do with it. Throw it away, as she wanted to. Fling it from her home and from her son. But men occasionally talk. Phil the pilot would surely ask Hektor-Jan – or possibly expect Hektor-Jan to thank him. Maybe he would wink at her husband and they would laugh. What might men do in such a situation. Then there would be questions. Things would go from bad to worse. What had she done with the German magazine.

Fetch me the paper we used to cover all the school books, said Janet.

Pieter ran away.

He returned with the paper – it was brown.

Scissors and Sellotape, said Janet and those appeared. Pieter was going to be good for a long time, she sensed.

Can I help you? said Pieter.

He will be good for a long time, thought Janet.

Mother and son cut a big rectangle of brown paper and made decent the catalogue of nakedness. They tore loud clear strips to make the same Sellotape bars to reinforce the packaging.

There is nothing wrong with ladies' bodies, Janet tried to say as they Sellotaped the big brown fig leaf. There is nothing wrong with men's bodies. It's just that Mommy doesn't like it when –

When what. What was she trying to say. Janet looked at the flat brown package between them as they knelt on the lounge floor.

Mommy does not like it when ladies are made to look like lumps of meat.

Pieter looked at her.

214

Christopher Radmann

Lumps of meat, said Janet. Ladies are not lumps of meat, are they.
Pieter agreed fervently that no lady was a lump of meat.

They get paid to do that, said Janet. Someone pays them to look like a lump of meat. Then someone buys the magazine and the people who paid them to look like a lump of meat get the money. They do it all for the money. The money ties them all together. It's like this Sellotape.

Mother and son stared at the striped symbol between them. Yuk, said Janet. Lumps of meat.

Pieter nodded. But he was going to nod at whatever she said. She left it at lumps of meat and they returned the magazine in its severe tunic to the drawer of the radiogram. It would lie in wait. Janet might make Hektor-Jan ask for it. Has Phil left anything for me. Usually he asked at the end of the month.

What's that, Janet would love to say. Do you mean the porno mag, the butcher's shop of flesh hooked and hanging on the lens of some German camera. The Erikas and Heidis and Giselas that call to you through the brown shirt of the paper wrapping. Dear God, Hektor-Jan, don't you get enough of me. Must I lie awake at night with those women leering up at me through the mattress where you hide them on your side of the bed. Where you press them down with the weight of your body. Am I not enough. Look here, and here and here. Touch me here.

But she would hand over the little flat package, maybe pass it to him as he munched his breakfast. It would squat between them as he crunched his cornflakes. Then it – they – would go off with Hektor-Jan who might start whistling.

Janet shuddered.

What had her husband got their son for his birthday.

50.12CM

As simple as a jackal,
as tender as the sun,
the offal of my heart
of course belongs to him.

– Heidi Laing, from 'Intimacy', translated from the
Afrikaans by Christina Thompson

After about four years with the Riot Unit, I was at the end of my tether.
During a house penetration in Daveyton one evening, my nerves were
so frayed that I fired a shot through a door without knowing who or
what was on the other side. I realised that I was heading for disaster.
I told my commanding officer what had happened and asked to be
transferred to an administrative post.

– Johan Marais, *Time Bomb: A Policeman's True Story*

The Crack

I t was going to be a long day. It had been a long night shift and it was going to be a very long day.

He sat in the car in the driveway. He was on time. His hand felt tighter. He flexed it again and paused before he opened the door. He expected Doug to be waiting. Doug and his sun-risers that had plagued his dreams. That had done nothing to relax him after work. And still no package from Phil. Promises, promises. How three hundred people sat in a plane and trusted Captain Phil to get them off the ground and back again safely. The Promising Pilot called Phil. He shook his head. His sore hand rested uncomfortably on his crotch.

It was their boy's birthday. Not every day did your son turn nine. Hell, man, it was a special day and he reached for the door handle and got out of the car. He forced himself to breathe deeply and he listened to the sharp twittering in the skies. The dawn chorus. Doug did not add his voice to the growing melee in the trees.

No. There was no Doug with nasty news. Did that make him happy or sad.

He paused at the front door. The birds were wild this morning. And, no, he could not hear the heartbeat of the Kreepy Krauly about which Janet had complained so often. To be fair, she had not mentioned it for a while. Maybe she had forgotten. Maybe she had turned deaf. Maybe she had other things on her mind and he shoved the key into its wrinkled slot and twisted it.

He nearly stood on his son. The heir inside the house was dark and still. He got a real fright. He swore heavily. Fok, dropped from his lips. Jou moer, fell from his heart and mouth as he stumbled over Pieter. Before he knew it, his gun was in his hand. Before he could stop it, it was pointing at the tangle of his warm son, stirring blearily. The shot of adrenalin burst through his body. It was a bullet. Instantly he was ready to attack. His left hand held down his son and the right brought the gun to within an inch of his life.

Fok, he said. Jou moer. And there was the gun. And his head was about to burst. And his finger was tight on the trigger. But there was no explosion. Just Fok and Jou moer shot from his lips and Pieter did not even squeal as the swear words hit him.

How long were they locked in that embrace. When did his finger release the trigger and the burning taste subside in his mouth.

It's my birthday, said little Pieter to the wolf.

It's your birthday, the big wolf said to Pieter.

Then he understood. The words made sense and the gun went slack.

My seun, he said. My son. It's your birthday and his son smiled up at him, he who loomed over his son with Fok and Jou moer shooting from his lips and a gun sticking right into his son's head.

Double figures, Pieter's voice was proud. I'm almost turning double figures, Pappie. He moved slightly and held up two five-pointed stars in the dark. His tiny hands.

The gun clunked to the floor. Pieter's hands. He took his son's hands in his own. Folded them into the meaty strength of his own hands and held them. All ten fingers and thumbs, each a year of his life and one spare. All that had happened in nine years. And Hektor-Jan could not remember his own ninth birthday. But he could remember his tenth. Turning double figures. His older brothers beating him with particular pleasure as he was now ten and could take it – ten times over.

Instead of punching little Pieter in the arm, kneeing him in the thigh or subjecting his wrists to a series of Chinese bangles, Hektor-Jan just held him.

Happy birthday, Gelukkige verjaarsdag, my seun, he said. Nine years old. And he held him in the dark as the house waited around him and the gun sulked behind him. He did not have to do anything to this warm body. It was his son and he could simply hold him. He could just love him. He held his son who had got up early to greet his father and to tell him that he was almost turning ten.

How is the trifle? asked Shelley as the car lurched off the tarred road and hit the dust and grind of the dirt track that led to the small farm.

Fine, called Janet. She held the Tupperware box on her lap. The trifle would be fine.

Be careful, came Shelley's voice.

I will, called Janet as Hektor-Jan frowned his way through the smaller ruts and over the lesser stones.

They need to scrape this clear, he muttered. When last did they scrape the road.

The little car juddered and growled. The ground was sticky after the recent rain but the rocks were as hard as ever.

Pieter sat with his forehead pressed to the vibrating window. Janet could hear him behind her. He made small humming sounds that jumped and jarred as the car bumped along. He was talking to himself, and talking to the car. The car spoke through him.

Almost there, Janet called to the back seat.

Yay, came their voices and Pieter hummed quietly to himself.

Janet turned her attention from the back seat to her husband's hand that fought with the gear lever and the steering wheel.

Then she frowned at the winding, lurching road.

It had been a while.

When last did they visit the farm. It must have been well before Christmas. But warm enough to swim, as the children had come back from the reservoir dripping wet and claiming to have seen a water snake. And Shelley had found a mouse skull picked clean and white and glowing in the sun. The two chisel-shaped front teeth were intact, which was more than could be said for Shelley's own front teeth.

And Oupa had had too much to drink, as always. And so had Willem and Koos and François, if she was not mistaken. One sad old man and his three sad sons. Did they drink to remember his wife, their mother. Did they drink to forget.

I hope no one will get too drunk, said Janet over the trifle and low enough for the children not to hear.

Hektor-Jan negotiated his way around a particularly deep donga and then shrugged. Who knows, he said. I am not my brothers' keeper, or my father's.

Janet frowned at the archaic phrasing and the gruff riposte.

There's nothing wrong with a bit of booze, said Hektor-Jan. Pieter has just turned nine. I might have some, you know.

And before she could reply, there came the excited call.

The picannins! Look, Mommy, Pappie, the picannins!

Ahead of them, on the arc of the red and muddy road, stood a ragged tangle of black children. They appeared to be waiting. They always seemed to be waiting.

They got closer and then, as the car drew level, their faces broke into white smiles. Gap-filled grins and hands windmilling furiously. They called out in excited, bleating voices and a few of the girls thrust out their little hips and bottoms and began a sweet, staggering dance, all a-stamping and a-turning. Often Janet winced when their car trailed a shroud of red dust, but today there was no dust to choke their piping voices. Hektor-Jan concentrated on the road, but Janet and her three children waved from inside the car.

For one compressed second, they were level. Then they were gone. The road snaked before them and Shelley, Pieter and Sylvia were left to turn and twist on the back seat, still waving and peering through the stained rear window, watching the black children shrink, and their hands fall to their sides, and they continued walking in the wake of the car.

I like the picannins, said Sylvia happily, as though they were an ice cream or a favourite biscuit. They always wave, don't they?

Yes, they do, said Janet.

Hektor-Jan muttered something about when they weren't stealing eggs or mielies or getting the dogs all worked up.

Then they were there.

It was Pieter's job to open the gate so that they could drive through.

He brought it clanking closed behind them.

The small house with its sprawl of outbuildings squatted beneath several eucalyptus trees. Their bark peeled in grey strips to reveal the bone of their trunks and the car tyres popped over the fallen pods and dry leaves.

There was the old door on its concrete block where the chickens were slaughtered. Janet still felt the tightening in her throat as all the headless fowls she had seen ran pell-mell into oblivion. They gushed blood as they sprinted then quickly keeled over. She would not let the children see that now.

There came the posse of braks. All tails and teeth and legs and paws. Enthusiasm and obsequiousness all in one. Raise a hand and they fell away. Pat your knees and you were swamped by dogs. A hopeless genetic tangle of brothers, sisters, aunts and uncles.

Wait said Hektor-Jan and he got out of the car and bellowed at the dogs. He raised his hand and they backed off cringing and with cautious tails. There were more dark faces, watching from the windows of the outbuildings, though these were older children. No longer picannins. No longer singing and dancing beside the road.

Hektor-Jan thumped the roof of the car. They could get out.

Why do they wear their school uniforms on a Saturday? asked Pieter.

Do they go to school on a Saturday? asked Sylvia. We don't have to go to school on a Saturday. Today is Saturday. Why are they wearing –

And then the wire-mesh screen door crashed open to emit Oupa and Oom François, Willem and Koos. The old, the good, the bad and the ugly, as Hektor-Jan called them. Four Snyman men who had cut a future for themselves out of a small piece of farmland and acres of time. Hektor-Jan was the only one to have escaped. The only one to have run off with a Engelse vrou – an English woman – and to have three children by her. Drie klein kindertjies. So sag. So snaaks. So soft and strange. Three little townies even though they were burned brown from the sun. But there were no scabs on their knees, no festering wounds and they gazed in wonder at the stupid braks.

There was the skoonsuster, Janet. Standing cautiously, holding a large Tupperware box away from the dogs. She wore a nice dress and a smile. Things you did not see on the farm. There were no white women on the farm.

The Snyman men on the farm were not used to being around white women. There were black women, to be sure, but, wragtig, they rarely saw a white woman at all. Only in town and those women had been too much in the sun. The hair of the Snyman brothers had been recently moistened and lay plastered on their scalps. Janet could make out the furrows of the small combs, two of which peeped out at her from the long socks that the brothers wore. Khaki shorts and long socks and velskoene. Except for Koos, who always went barefoot. Pieter would once again want to go barefoot when they got home. He was fascinated by Oom Koos's hardy feet that were impervious to thorn and stone and which featured an extra toe. He can count to twelve on his feet; Pieter was in awe. Twenty-two with his hands.

The older brothers beamed awkwardly. And then Sylvia threw herself squealing into their arms and all were smiles as they passed her around like a small doll. There were handshakes for Pieter, grave and serious, and for Hektor-Jan, the prodigal youngest brother. Then a kiss for Shelley followed by a quick kiss for her, Janet. Nervous lips fluttered somewhere on her cheek – François, the youngest brother – or in the air, about an inch from her face – Koos, the oldest – or smack on her lips taking her breath away – Willem, the middle brother.

Hallo, hallo, said Oupa from behind his large, thick-set sons. Janet always wanted to laugh. Oupa was so slight, so dusty and wrinkled and slight compared to his barrel-chested sons. It was hard to believe that they had emerged from him. Janet knew from the fuzzy pictures inside how big and strong Mrs Snyman had been. She needed to be. A regte, egte boervrou who had produced four sons on a smallholding near Springs. Four thick, strong men had sprung out of her and three of them still seemed a little bewildered. Only one had leapt beyond the wire fences and dirt roads.

Hullo, Janet, said Oupa, carefully forming the sharp sounds of her name given to her by Amelia Amis. Janet smiled and held out her hands wondering why her mother, all soft vowels and gentle consonants, had given her daughter such a sharp name, so prickly. That was why she now had a Shelley and a Sylvia. So much softer and gentler.

Oupa shook hands with her. Shook hands gently and asked if she was well. And how was it going with her mother, that clever lady who taught at the big university in the city so far away and who was now in the care home and unwell. And was her own father coming to celebrate with them, the turning nine of little Pieter who looked just like his mother, jy weet.

The careful English words sprung rich and earthy from Oupa's thin lips. His face was wrinkled beyond belief and his person small and shrivelled and yet he had given rise to four such strapping sons and his voice was deep and resonant. Maybe he had called them forth, summoned them out of their mother's womb with his voice like a male Lorelei.

Janet let her hand be shaken carefully. I am fine, Pa, she said. Thank you. It's been a while. And he agreed and let go her hand.

Come inside, he said waving aside the dogs that milled about hopefully and pushing past his awkward sons.

Janet turned to the house and clung to the box. She would stay calm. She would not let her eyes get that mad gleam that the chickens got just before they were slaughtered. When their eyes shone with hot beadiness. She took a deep breath. The Tupperware box was hard and square.

They stepped through the wire-mesh door into the square house. The children loved this house. Its brooding dinginess. Its air of waiting. Janet always expected to find a layer of dust and sorrow when she ran her finger along the old wooden furniture, the riempie chairs and ironwood table. But it was polished and clean. None of the men's doing, of course. It was thanks to Dorcas, who looked after them. The old maid even now was summoned, by the deep voice of Oupa.

She appeared wiping her hands. She was one of the fattest women Janet had ever seen and Janet knew that the children were sizing her up: had she got even bigger since they last saw her. Had she sprung an extra chin, another roll around her middle. Janet tried to catch their eyes, but they were transfixed. Pieter's mouth was a perfect O.

Tee, Dorcas, Oupa said curtly.

Dorcas ignored him and nodded at the visitors. Kleinbaas, she said huskily, her voice panting up from her huge chest. Kleinbaas was her name for Hektor-Jan, the youngest of the brothers. Kleinbaas, she said and nodded at Janet. Miesies, she wheezed and then came the moment that the children had been waiting for. Having pretended not to see them, Dorcas turned on nimble toes and threw her hands to her face.

Allawereld, she gasped, her chins shaking with emotion. Allawereld. Kleinbaaspietertjie, Kleinmiesiesshelley, Kleinmiesiessylvia. As ever she turned to Oupa in consternation. Wat vreet hierdie kinders, she said. What do these children eat. Hoe groot. How big, how big they are since the last time. Allawereld, my magtig, and her hand was at her mouth and she was shaking her head and her chins and chest were alive.

Tee, Dorcas, Oupa said again. The ritual was almost at an end. Dorcas would flash him a glance and swat him aside like a fly. Then she turned to Janet and breathed a profound Merrem from deep inside her chest and she took the Tupperware box with its precious contents and she left the room gasping to herself as though distressed that the children had grown, that something was terribly wrong when children could grow so quickly. She shook her head and wobbled and muttered into the kitchen. Baas, she was saying, Miesies and then the roar of the kettle drowned her voice.

We shall sit, said Oupa.

So they sat on the assortment of chairs, some at the table, some dotted around the square room. Janet tried to look at Oupa's face or at Koos's feet, but already the children were staring up at the walls.

There's a new one, said Pieter.

No, said Sylvia. That was there last time. It was. I remember its little nose.

Janet closed her eyes and prayed for tea, for the reassuring presence of the giantess, Dorcas, and her wheezing pleasantries.

Hektor-Jan rumbled into Afrikaans and the brothers hung on his words. But Oupa was watching the children.

Sylvia is right, he said to Pieter. We had that klipspringer six months now. But look over there, behind you over there. And Janet turned with the children to look on the wall and there, with glassy eyes and a tightly stretched grin was the head of a jackal. It was nestled between the heads of a bontebok and a tiny, striped springbok.

And before the children could ask, Oupa stood up and was detaching it from the wall and handing it to them.

Hektor-Jan barely noticed, but the blood pounded in Janet's head as she sat dizzily longing for Dorcas and the tea. The children stroked the mangy thing. They touched its fur and its stiff ears and the horrid gash in its face, all teeth and dark space and they squealed at how sharp the teeth were and said, Look Mommy, look. And she was forced to look or to scream so she looked with all her might and tried not to see, but she saw. And Pieter must have sensed her shock as he leapt forward with the grinning head on its flat plaque.

Hello, Meneer Jakkals! he shouted imitating Oupa's Afrikaans and his voice was a yipping y sound of Hello Meneer Yuckulls and the head leapt at her face.

It was the youngest brother, François, who had been watching and who gently took Pieter's arm and led the jackal away from Janet's face.

Let us sit hom terug, he said mixing up his English and his Afrikaans. He was a man of few words. He sat down again with a smile at Janet as the children were now off, looking in the house for Diepseun the tortoise.

Thank you, François, Janet said and he smiled again and she tried to smile.

The deep Afrikaans voices circled around her like a storm and François shrugged and smiled even more broadly. How is your play, he asked suddenly.

But before Janet could tell him that she had indeed got a part in the play, before she could describe the magical world of *Brigadoon*, Dorcas appeared on the crest of a huge bronze tray. It might have been an old firescreen, such was its size, and she set it down with medley of teaspoons and chattering crockery.

And François stood beside her, a solicitous presence, whilst Meneer Yuckulls leered from the wall and they all gathered around, even Dorcas who sang most sweetly as they raised their voices to Pieter who returned and stood there with his sisters and blushed. Happy birthday, dear Pieter, happy birthday to you. And Sylvia yelled the hip hip hoorays at the end and it was the barefooted Koos who said, Nog 'n piep, for the final hooray.

And that cheer was the signal. Maak toe jou oë, said Francois with a hand on Pieter's shoulder. Close those eyes. He led Pieter to a chair. Pieter, who was already blind with excitement as he sensed what was coming.

Koos flapped from the room with his bare feet and Hektor-Jan winked at Janet. She had no idea what was waiting outside. But then she knew. All the panting animals above her, around her. Of course, she should have known. What a good idea. Was it a good idea – the new baby, and now this. Something else to worry about unlike the old and faithful Jock. You read about babies and –

In came Koos with a squirming bundle of brindle legs and ears. François's hands held Pieter's eyes shut. Oupa let out a cackle and both Shelley and Sylvia gasped. Before Koos could hand over the puppy to Hektor-Jan to present to his son, Oupa was on his feet and pulling at his pocket. He tied the yellow ribbon around the dog's neck. They could see its head now – a Rottweiler, no plaas brak, no farmyard mongrel.

And into Pieter's trembling arms came baby Jock. The new Jock of the bushveld – and from some breeder in Springs whom the brothers knew and who gave them a good deal. It was all gasps and delight, licks and squirms. Janet had to hold Sylvia back so that her brother could hug and hug the GOD who had become DOG, and Janet saw Shelley smile softly and knew that the bright magnets on the fridge would soon spell a different message. Little Pieter remembered to say thank you – a whole round of thank yous to all the Snyman men, as well as to his father and mother. As he brought New-Jock for her to stroke and admire, he whispered, I am so happy, Mommy. I am so happy.

Janet laughed to see such fun and the puppy's fur was softer than midnight. It glowed black and its caramel patches were delicious.

Then Dorcas clapped her hands and proceeded to dish out the cake she had made in Kleinbaaspietertjie's honour whilst Oupa insisted on pouring the tea from the old cracked teapot, tea brewed in honour of the daughter of the English professor who lectured in the city, but who now languished closer to home. Which was presumably where her father was. He was due to join them but Janet had said that something must have come up as it was unlike her father to be late, so do carry on. And they did. And the trifle was kept for later.

Watched over by the heads of various beasts with their glassy eyes and desperate hauteur as well as by the more immediate, more kindly Dorcas, they sipped their tea out of the old tea service. Paper-thin china that rattled in tiny saucers and which became Lilliputian in the meaty hands of Hektor-Jan and his beefy brothers. Their eyes strayed briefly to Janet as they slurped delicately. François even had his baby finger pointed to the ceiling in a little salute to Janet's Englishness and, just like last time, she had to fight back the impulse suddenly to cackle with laughter. It was made worse by the silent chomping of the children as they mowed through the moist slices of chocolate cake and the tense slurps of tiny tea from the men who usually gulped out of big mugs. And Dorcas watched over them all with a tender impatience, as she wanted her chance to pour from the special teapot and to offer around the jug of thick milk. And above Dorcas, around them all, on every wall, like some bizarre tribe, there circled the gaping beasts, slain and staring with

Christopher Radmann

beheaded surprise. It was as though the house had sprung a welter of heads, which strained and pulled each wall towards a facing wall, their eyes bulging with the effort, their mouths gasping. They wheeled around the puppy, which was squirming with life and making nuzzling sounds against Pieter's tummy. Janet wanted to stand up and shoo them away, the laager of dusty old heads. Shout, Be off with you, Go, Voetsek, but more tea was on its way and Sylvia was trying to get onto her lap, maybe already jealous of the tiny New-Jock.

After Dorcas had danced about the room, waltzing tea into their tiny cups and smiling with pride as every drop was drunk and the cake demolished, Oupa muttered something to Koos.

It was a signal to the men, for they all stood up. Teacups were carefully returned to the tray and Dorcas gruffly thanked. Pieter was hauled to his feet – told that he should take his dog. It was old enough and strong enough.

There was a brief hiatus as they all went to the loo like a row of schoolboys. No one hopped from foot to foot but the chain clanked and the toilet flushed loudly in the passage next door and then they all had guns and Sylvia was on the brink of tears as she asked why she could not go too.

Hektor-Jan's eyebrows appealed to Janet and she stepped in.

Sylvia, she said gently. Sylvia. And she could feel the yearning of the creatures above and around her. Their mute appeal. Please, they seemed to say, please, no more. Not another one. Yes, your son might have to aim and shoot, but not your little girl. Surely not your little Sylvia.

Janet caught Sylvia up in her lap. The little girl struggled hotly and Janet held her and seemed to squeeze the tears from her. It did not help that Shelley was tying her laces more tightly and was joining the men. If Janet silently appealed to her older daughter to stay, Shelley ignored her. Maybe she knew that her mother had to remain with Sylvia; maybe she would keep a maternal eye on Pieter who was in the passage already hefting a .22 rifle onto his little shoulder and watching Oupa tie a leather thong around the puppy's neck.

The Crack

Sylvia squirmed violently as the men disappeared. François called goodbye, but the rest departed to the creak of the screen door which closed by itself with a final slam. Janet was left with her daughter on her lap sitting uncomfortably beneath the ranks of dead animals. Out there, out in the veld, they would seek another deer or rodent or little predator-cum-scavenger to kill. She and Sylvia would have to wait like Dorcas, sitting in the quiet cave of the house, whilst the men roamed the veld, hunting. Part of her was terrified; part desperately amused. Sylvia was so hot on her lap, shuddering to herself.

The heavens were clear after the rains. It was all so clear and simple. They walked out into the blue of the sky and the yellow grass, already bleached and bronzed by the sun. Hektor-Jan breathed in the morning air and felt his heart flower with sudden happiness. He was a child again. Instantly, he stepped out of his old, thick body and he felt lithe and he looked at his father leading the way with Koos, Kaalvoet Koos – Barefoot Koos. It was a relief and a joyous sadness to know that nothing had changed and that everything had changed.

The old .22 in his hands. Well, it was a most familiar weight, the heft of the warm wood and the smoothness. It led in a straight line to memories of similar mornings and afternoons and even nights. Like Kaalvoet Koos, they were all kaalvoet back then. The grass springing between their toes, warm and soft. The dogs licking their ankles and panting. Laughing at the way Blikskottel lifted his leg every fifth step even when he was dehydrated and empty. And Bliksem who could sense a tarentaal hiding in the wild grass from fifty yards. And the manliness of his older brothers. And marching with his brothers was his son and his elder daughter. They both had the old rifles, the very ones he had practised on as a child. The cans clinked and leapt in his mind. All the cans he had shot off the rocks like metal salmon leaping. His first guinea fowl. Warm and limp. A thin trickle of purple blood and the spotted feathers. The comical cone on the head like a dunce. Blue and red. And the eyes closed, dreaming it was still alive.

The power he felt. The strength and power that came shooting along the rifle. The bullet burst out one end, but the feeling of invincibility thudded out the other, jarring his shoulder with greatness. He smiled. And Pieter walking without looking. How he had eyes only for his new dog. It was the perfect present and his heart tightened with both fear and joy. But old Jock was buried deep and still in the earth and here was the new Jock, snuffling and panting with a huge smile on his face, the bloody stump of his tail a blur of happiness.

The sun beat down on Hektor-Jan's scalp and drew up memories of all his dogs. He smiled at the silly bow that still fluttered around the puppy's neck, wrapped up with the leather thong that served as a leash. Hektor-Jan's smile broadened. You could not gift-wrap a morning like this.

And then Pa was motioning them to be quiet. The farm buildings were far behind. Their route had taken them through the koppies and towards the vlei. They sank into the long grass, pressed down by Pa's hand. Now they would wait. Despite the mid-morning hour, something was bound to come to the vlei to drink. When the sun was hot, creatures had to drink.

Hektor-Jan snapped a grass stalk and began to chew. Pieter snapped a grass stalk too. Shelley stared at the gun in her hands. The sun gleamed off the polished wood and dark metal of the rifle. François shook his head and murmured something. He tapped Pa on the shoulder, handed him his rifle, crept backwards very quietly and slunk off. Not even Shelley watched him go. The puppy fell asleep in the hot grass.

The inside of the house was dark and cool. Sylvia had quickly run off to be with Dorcas. They were doing something in the kitchen. It sounded complicated. Sylvia was full of English questions. Dorcas matched her in Afrikaans. They seemed to be trading laughter – hilarious misunderstanding.

Janet sat in the chair. Without seeming to move, she gradually slumped till she was half-lying in the seat. The house pressed down on her. She tried not to think of Hektor-Jan living in the house that her own father had had built. She tried not to think what it must have been like growing up in this squat building that Hektor-Jan's father had constructed with his own bare hands. She tried not to think of the dead creatures fixed to the wall above and around her. She tried not to think at all.

What were they doing now. What had they shot. What had they killed. What creature did not know that even now it had but bare seconds to live. What must it be like to know that you had just moments left in this life. Janet thought about her children hunting and she could not think of Pieter and Shelley raising rifles to their small shoulders and taking aim and –

Janet pulled herself upright in the chair. She looked wildly around the room.

She glanced across at the photos of Hektor-Jan's mother. The one with her leaning back with her feet up, something in either hand. Janet looked closer. Was it biltong and a knife. Yes, a strip of biltong – a long stick of dried meat – and, in her other hand, the glinting blade of a stout penknife. Surely the same nostalgic penknife, which Hektor-Jan still used to slice biltong. With its strawberry-red handle and the brave cross of the Swiss Army. Probably the only heirloom, if you could call it that, which came to him when his mother died. A knife for her youngest child. Janet shook her head and Hektor-Jan's mother looked fiercely out of the picture. She seemed to be mid-chew, certainly not making an effort to smile. Her broad face had the oddest expression. Janet dismissed Mrs Snyman as she herself felt dismissed by a sepia mother-in-law wielding bloody stick and blade. Janet found herself peering more at the wooden frames, the polished wood with the grain exposed and glowing. The life that pulsed in the frame and bordered the old brown figures from dead times. The frames seemed alive; the people stuck in the past. The glowing wood throbbed with life and light, thanks no doubt to Dorcas's polishing hands, which so busily burnished things in this odd room.

Presumably, she dusted Meneer Yuckulls and his friends. Against her will, Janet's eyes were drawn upwards and she stared at the sad heads around her. Each animal strained forwards. Each creature yearned, it seemed. Tried to leap from the wall which had become its shoulders and midriff and limbs. Each head tried to burst from the blank wall of its tomb.

Janet held her breath. She could hear them panting. Most of their mouths were open. If she sat very still, Janet would hear their breathing, strained by effort and throttled by the wall. She pulled herself upright again. What was wrong with the chair. She breathed out.

What is wrong with the chair.

Janet did not move. It was Meneer Yuckulls. Of that Janet was sure.

What is wrong with the chair.

The voice was the jackal's voice and yet it spoke inside her head. What is wrong, it said again, this time noting a more general malaise.

Janet tried not to look up at the jackal. She tried to breathe in, and then she had to look up. She narrowed her eyes. She stood up, freeing herself from the chair, and her breath came and she shook her head. Her hand moved to her belly. The glass eyes of the jackal gleamed. They pressed down on her and its panting mouth spoke again.

Ek is 'n twee-gat jakkals. I am a two-burrow jackal, it announced.

And even though its head was fixed to a rough, wooden plaque, it nodded and the whole wall shifted too. A two-burrow jackal. One burrow for wifey, and another burrow. But was that a surreptitious or a blatant other burrow. The way the jackal grinned at her, there could be no doubt that it rejoiced in its second burrow. It seemed to make no bones about another burrow. That is what jackals do, appeared to be the leering implication. One burrow for Janet and a burrow, a disused rabbit hole, maybe, that led to Alice and her wonderland. There, it was thought and it was said and Janet could not breathe. A twee-gat jakkals, with gleaming teeth and a filthy mouth. And the walls of dead animal heads crowded closer. Trapped in Springs – all these creepy crawlies. Their desperation compressed the air, seemed to gasp all the oxygen from the room, leaving Janet reeling, her lungs tight and heaving. Spots danced in front of her eyes and her chest burned. She thought she might pass out, clamped as she was between the bright jaws of Meneer Yuckulls. He could crush her skull in an instant. The pressure was unbearable and her chest burned and burned. Her head was going to split – so was her heart. Then there was a bang.

She fell back into the chair and there was a bang, a gunshot in the house, and François, the youngest brother, burst into the room.

Janet sensed rather than saw him. There was a double flicker in the jackal's glass eyes and there he was, standing in the doorway, the smash of the screen door now healed by silence. In the sad house, the bang simply became a brief scar in the memory of air. Janet seemed to fall back even further in her seat, suddenly released and her chest heaved – she breathed.

François started to come over to her, then stopped. He stood in the no-man's land of the middle of the lounge. Gasping, Janet watched him in duplicate in the jackal's eyes.

I do that also, François said.

You hear the jackal speak. Janet tried to breathe the words, tried to untie her tongue which was glued to the roof of her mouth, tried to turn to her brother-in-law who had given up on the hunt.

François laughed. There is times, when I can't sleep, jy weet. When I come and I lie back in the chair, where you now lie back. And I look at these animals. In the dark, I do that when I can't sleep. Most of these animals would be alive in the dark. Eating, hunting – alive, jy weet.

Janet stood up again – shakily – and took a step back. Such sadness welled up in the old room.

I come and I look at them.

François moved closer and stood beside the trembling Janet, looking up at the jackal and all the other heads on that wall. Janet did not know what to say. The jackal had said it all. Had it spoken. Was she – like her own mother – was she –

Janet turned to François so that she could see his tanned skin, his shy smile and not her mother's pale, taut face. Talking jackals then eating tissues. One surely led straight to the other. She raised her hands before her and looked at them.

That one, I shot. That blesbok, there. François picked out a timid deer. And that meerkat, there. But that's alles, niks meer nie. Not any more.

Janet lowered her hands, knotted them behind her back and turned to his sad face. How the muscles moved in his throat and his confession came to her ears. The jackal had not moved, yet –

Who shot the jackal, she managed to ask.

François's throat and jaw moved, and his hands gestured as he told her. Janet's hands squirmed above her coccyx. They would not remain still.

Meneer Yuckulls, he finished saying.

Meneer Yuckulls, she repeated.

They were still standing there when the screen door smashed open again and Hektor-Jan burst into the room.

He shouted at François. Telefoon. Ambulans. Ongeluk. There has been an accident. Gun. Barrel. Bullet. Bliksem.

Then he was gone and François was on the phone, his thick fingers slipping off the dial with whirring curses and Meneer Yuckulls did not say a word although there was the sudden wink of a smug glass eye and a general air of I told you so. An accident. With a gun, barrel, bullet. Of course. Play with fire. Let your children play with fire. What on earth do you expect.

Janet fell from the house into the light. Pieter. Shelley. She knew something like this would happen. She had seen it in the entrails of the pool all year. An augury of concrete fact. A crack that leapt to instant life and which no amount of cement or wise Solomons could cancel. 1976 was not going to be a good year, no matter how much it was toasted. Why, in the fizzy flight-patterns of 5th Avenue Cold Duck had she not sensed –

There, on the other side of the koppie that swelled at the back of the house, they came carrying a body. Janet ran and could not see. She stopped and put a hand to her brow, to shield her eyes from the beating sun.

The chickens skrawked in their hok and it sounded like the picannins had come home to roost. The mangy chickens chattered and muttered and laughed.

Still, she could not make out who was hurt and, far away, Hektor-Jan's form now joined them on the low hillside and there was a tangle of helping and dogs milling, their barks coming faintly on the air. One jumped up and Hektor-Jan sent it flying with a sudden kick and then a little girl's figure and a little boy's figure appeared at the side of the huddle.

Shelley was fine and Pieter was fine! Her children were alive and sound of limb!

But wait. Pieter had disappeared from sight, somehow swallowed by the dry veld grass and Hektor-Jan was bending down now, and Shelley was beside him, holding something, also looking down. Janet felt her knees buckle in sympathy, felt her motherly tenderness run, pulling out of her, looping from her belly in an anxious arc across the space. Her hands found her face although her voice seemed somehow hooked on the screen door. Janet's mouth hinged open and shut without a sound as Hektor-Jan picked up Pieter, clasped his inert son to his chest and stumbled forward, face raised to the hot sky. Shelley followed – dragging the new puppy and something dangling from her other hand. Koos and Willem carried Oupa between them and François burst from the house.

Nee, he screamed. His voice shrieked high and effeminate. Dorcas steamed through the screen door behind him, but did not catch him as he fell. Janet turned just as Dorcas rumbled past and she saw Sylvia's face pressing against the wire mesh of the outer door. Should she run to Hektor-Jan; should she stay with little Sylvia. Janet twisted where she stood, unable to distinguish between the lesser of two evils, between the devil and the deep blue sky.

1.024ₘ

Who understands a human hand:
Fingertips and tenderness hidden in a fist.

> – Olivia Pretorius, 'Daddy's Hands'

During one of these roadblocks at the northern entrance to Tembisa, I learned an important lesson. Initially everything went peacefully, until a taxi full of passengers approached and the door slid open. A man jumped out and came running towards us, screaming. He had a knife clutched in either hand. I was armed with a shotgun, but when I noticed him, he was almost on top of me. I could not shoot him at such short range without blowing him away.

I was standing slightly to one side, so one of my colleagues pulled out his service pistol and fired two shots into the man's legs. It had no effect. He raised his weapon again and shot him in the chest. At a distance of a metre, the eighth bullet finally struck him in the head. The man fell down dead almost on my colleague's shoes. No one knew why he had attacked us.

The lesson I learned from this was to be on the alert at all times. I also learned that a person who is hit by a 9 mm-bullet does not stagger back ten metres, as the movies would have you believe.

> – Johan Marais, *Time Bomb: A Policeman's True Story*

The Crack

That was Pieter's birthday. An infamous Saturday.

He got more than he could have bargained for. A new DOG, a ride with Oupa in the ambulance, a bristling caterpillar of six stitches that stretched above his right eye – as though about to crawl across his temple – and a whole fistful of memories to punch his dreams into the middle of next week's nightmares ... for years to come.

Janet tried to stroke his brow, but he shrank from her touch.

Too sore, he moaned, his sheet screwed up whitely beneath his chin.

Kiss New-Jock good night, said Janet but Pieter seemed not have heard her, and it was Shelley who took the puppy to the kitchen and rolled up the newspaper in readiness for the night – and who, indeed, rearranged the letters on the fridge to THANK YOU GOD. They remained there for some time, their colourful gratitude squealed to the kitchen, while Oupa had his eye that was pierced by the metal of the exploding rifle taken out, as well as his sinuses and the best part of his left cheekbone. His tattered left ear, what remained of it, was stitched until he looked, by his own assessment, like one of the plaas braks that had been in the wars.

Pieter and the puppy moaned and cried the whole night.

Hektor-Jan cursed the fact that it was Saturday night, and that he had not slept for over thirty hours, and he got up to smack New-Jock with the newspaper every time Janet went to Pieter.

Her small son clung to her, neither awake nor asleep.

It just went bang, he sobbed and tried to punch his pillow away from his face. He kept coughing up Bang, and again Bang, from the depths of his little chest.

An hour later, he writhed through Oupa's blood. Bloody, bloody blood, Pieter wailed and Janet could not tell whether he was cursing or crying. And Oupa's eye, yeye, eye, Pieter almost yodelled the sight of the burst yolk, the gooey egg of Oupa's eye that cracked and ran down the side of his face, what had been the side of his face but was now a dented, shredded messy, messy mess, all hanging muscle and grinning teeth that gaped through the hole in his face and chattered as the eye, yeye, eye-slime ran into his mouth.

That's when he fainted, Shelley said, when she joined her mother at the two o'clock session; when New-Jock's cries had got worse and the sound of the thrashing *Benoni City Times* had woken her up again. Pieter was fine, she said, But then he just sommer fainted, just like that.

Janet stared amazed at Shelley's slender fingers that snapped coolly in front of her, the sudden snap denoting the abrupt felling of little Pieter who had cracked his head on a rock and had begun to bleed like his oupa.

But he was a good deal noisier, said Shelley, and again her mother watched with something approaching fascination. Janet held Pieter tightly, whilst his sister perched on the end of his bed and described how he had kept crying and asking if he was going to go blind with all that blood that was gushing into his eyes. He could not see, and he just kept shouting about going blind, Mommy, Shelley said.

Keep your voice down, Janet managed to whisper as Pieter and his ears shuddered beneath her arm, and she surely smothered Shelley's words.

Fine, said Shelley and went back to her bedroom to watch over the snoring Sylvia, who had remained like a little white picannin dancing behind the wire mesh of the screen door and had been spared most of the anguish. The frantic staunching of Oupa's face with Dorcas's apron that she whipped off, after shoving her doek into the hole in Oupa's cheek. She tied the apron strings around and around his head leaving just his mouth to swear foamy bits of blood and bone. And Dorcas would not let Koos near his father with the brandy bottle because Die dokter sou seker onmiddellik begin opereer – there would be an immediate general anaesthetic and an operation. Surely. Seker. Dorcas knew that. How, no one had any idea.

Hektor-Jan dragged the dazed François off to the bathroom inside, whilst Koos tried to pass around a two-litre Coke bottle of the neighbour's best mampoer and Dorcas cradled Oupa's elevated head in her lap, his body prone in the dust. That would help to reduce the bleeding, if not the blaspheming. Janet clasped Pieter's head in her lap, like Dorcas, and tried to mutter reassurances as stoutly as the meaty maid. Janet's soft right hand pressed down over Pieter's forehead and eye, her left hand supported his neck. Shelley went looking for Sylvia who had disappeared. Then the ambulance arrived.

The paramedics were swift and certain. It was all over in a flash of gurney clips, quick hands and gleaming needles. Oupa in the back of the ambulance, on one side, snuggled into his morphine blanket, and Pieter on the other. With Janet and Dorcas caught in-between the bed-ledges with the one paramedic. An optimist who whistled Boney M tunes through a gap in his teeth whilst asking Pieter if he supported a rugby team.

Pieter's stitches were simple; Oupa's emergency operation took much longer. They needed to send him to the Joburg Gen. Willem sent Hektor-Jan home with his family. François's broken nose could be seen to on Monday, and they would stay with Pa. And Hektor-Jan was to look after the birthday boy and his six stitches.

Shelley's Secret Journal

The word from Granny's list for today is INELUCTABLE.

Today was a ~~busy~~ strange day. Oupa got his eye shot out and the left hand side of his head blown up. I shot a guiny fowl which is now in the fridge. Pieter missed everything he aimed at. Oom Koos said I am a natural. That was before the accident and before Pappie hit Oom Franswa. Oom Franswa had let his rifle scrape the muddy ground. Then he left the rifle with Oupa. The mud dried and blocked the barrel and that made the barrel explode in Oupa's face. Oom Franswa's face was not as bad. A lesson that he will never forget, Pappie said. Pieter never saw Pappie give Oom Franswa that lesson and Pappie said that I am growing up and ~~better~~ must not tell Mommy. That is why I have written it and I know that you can keep a secret, can't you Granny? More secrets. I found the secret store in the big cupboard by the washing machine. All the old newspapers are gone and it is full of tinned food. Mommy has bought all the tinned food from Mona Lisa. There is enough beef, pilchards, sweet corn, beans, pears, powdered milk, sugar and flour to last until Christmas. Are you coming to live with us? No one has said anything. Something ineluctable is happening. Even Alice wouldn't tell me. She just gave me a hug and told me again about her daughter far away in Zululand and how she is worried about her with the trouble that is coming. I thought she would cry but then baby Jock did a little poo right beside us. The new puppy is very adorable! Pappie is hitting it so that we can get some sleep. Maybe if the puppy gets used to that then what happened to Jock won't happen again. If Pappie stops using the newspaper and starts using his hands I will run into the kitchen and scream and make him stop this time to make sure that nothing becomes ineluctable. Ineluctable is not a nice word Granny. Love, Shelley.

They all slept in. No one went to kerk. There was no soothing singing from the Carpenters. New-Jock was paraded around the kitchen for Alice to admire. Alice had always been uncertain about dear old Jock. But that was possibly because Jock was fully grown when they got Alice. Or, as some might say, when old Lettie handed over the family to her daughter, Alice, like a precious white heirloom. Maybe Lettie, Alice, Alice-Lettie would feel more at home with the squirming New-Jock, who now settled peacefully in the far corner of the kitchen after his antics in the night. Alice-Lettie had to feel Pieter's stitches and count them carefully. Janet watched Hektor-Jan watching Alice-Lettie's gentle hands with her pink, intimate palms and her slim fingers as she stroked Pieter's brow and told him to be a brave boy. She gave Pieter a hug, held him for a long while and Hektor-Jan's coffee mug hovered before his lips, seemingly lost in thought. They were all watching Alice-Lettie, it appeared, as Janet tore her eyes away from the stunned mug and her husband's pursed lips, half open, oddly waiting, like Jan van Riebeeck about to arrive at the Cape and discover the strategic port for the Dutch. The girls' hair was a mess; her own a scratchy tangle. Their pyjamas needed a wash too. Janet's toes curled on the cool linoleum and Hektor-Jan's mug waited. When would Alice-Lettie let go of her son. When would Pieter, who never stood still for such a maternal embrace, remember and break free. Janet held her breath. When would Hektor-Jan's mug remember. Janet's heart pounded and, still not breathing, she had to stand suddenly, her legs jerking with a life of their own and propelling her from the kitchen, past New-Jock and into the clear sky of the back garden.

She exhaled in a rush, more spots dancing before her eyes and coffee dripping down her front, her knuckles white and sticky. Then her diaphragm pulled with a shudder and she breathed in the green grass, the giant mauve lollipops of the agapanthus, the late scent of Doug's rhododendrons and the heraldic shimmer of morning glories from the far back wall. The complex symmetry of the verbena blossoms was radiant behind the razor spray of the pampas grass with its assegais of feathery stalks. The garden heaved itself at her. Was she reassured. Was she mocked. Did it terrify or delight. No longer did she seem to know or understand. And all she could hear was the soft sound of Alice-Lettie's voice and the ghastly hiss from the Kreepy Krauly that lay wedged on its side, slurping dry air and sunshine. The desperate suction pulled Janet from where she stood and the garden tilted to roll her towards the pool. Janet yielded. Her legs jolted her across the lawn that pitched with fairground gravity. And there, gasping on its side, a helpless, fatally wounded appliance, was the Kreepy Krauly. It was caught in the mouth of the crack that had drained the pool dry. The crack had a fringe, possibly a moustache, of split and ragged concrete – all of Solomon's handiwork shredded – and it gaped now more than three feet wide. The pump in its safe housing strained as the Kreepy Krauly gulped in air, a dying wildebeest in the implacable jaws of the crack. It was carnage. Janet's half-full mug smashed on the slasto at the edge of the pool, little white fragments sheared off into the gleaming pit, shatteringly, dazzlingly white, before some of them bounced into the crack and were gone for ever. The stain of coffee welled and spread around her bare feet, making her toes sticky with sweet, brown blood. And even as Janet sank to the ground, sitting in the small patch of Nescafé, she saw how the sides of the pool had given way and how the crack was beginning to sidle up to and jab into the ribs of the garden. It could only be hours, minutes before the crazy paving around the pool finally cracked and the dark gap sprang into the lawn itself. Janet pushed herself back, away from the edge and saw the last of her coffee slip into the strained patterns of the slasto and vanish. Quicker than evaporating, more insidious than the tongue of a dog, the coffee drained away, giving up the ghost. With a howl, Janet scrambled backwards and clutched her stained nightie about her, as though the crack might run up her legs. Fighting to her feet, she turned and ran into the gentle embrace of the willow tree. Her hands clasped at the weeping fronds. Her fingers knotted themselves in the pliant strands. She seemed to throw herself into the maternal tree and she hung there, gasping, sobbing. The child within her writhed and dangled too, and, in the background, deeper than any womb, came the black and snaking crack. It was an umbilical cord, was it not. It pulsed with life and death, did it not. Janet buried her head in the soughing branches and cried soft leaves like tears.

She could see it. She knew it. The thoughts branched out wildly.

Solomon's stoical surprise on Monday morning when he was presented with his tea and the crack. The children slipping through her fingers as she tried to tell them to keep away from the bottom of the garden. They would go precisely where she said to keep away. They would take the puppy. New-Jock might leap into the crack and exhume the bones of Jock with a cheery bark. Shelley would stare and stare, fathoming some hidden depths, no doubt, and Alice-Lettie, Alice-Lettie would eish and turn to Hektor-Jan for solace and support. Desperate Doug would have some ripe riposte, a sphinx-like smugness, and Eileen-the-Understudy would be ever so bright and brittle. Her father would be sad that he had never been told and her mother would bristle with some acerbic comment designed to pierce her skin and make her crack. And Hektor-Jan would come home –

That is where Janet faltered. Alice-Lettie would turn, her face tilted upwards as Hektor-Jan came home – and then what.

But it was Sunday. The day of rest and of Karen Carpenter. However, there was neither rest nor the Carpenters.

Hektor-Jan was going to see his father. She should go with him. The children would whine if they could not play with the puppy, and she would have to ask Alice-Lettie to stay behind and not go to her church. Maybe Alice-Lettie could accompany Hektor-Jan whilst Janet lay down in the kaya surrounded by the scent of Lifebuoy soap and dreamed of old maids and a life in Zululand.

But that did not happen.

Alice-Lettie did go to her church, but Janet did not leave the children. Hektor-Jan did visit Oupa and came back much later that night. Janet killed four birds with one stone. She said a fond farewell to Hektor-Jan, dismissed Alice-Lettie and phoned her father. She took the children at long last, for the first time in 1976, to see their grandmother. There was no one, save Doug, to spy on the crack. It could lie there, squirm there, do what it wanted. She was sick of it. She felt that there was every chance it would go away if it was ignored. Perhaps she had been giving it too much attention. Time to fight fire with ire. Put the crack on the rack. Make it go away. To hell with the crack.

With every explosion that the little Fiat produced, Janet's heart lifted. She began to hum Top of the World. What would Karen Carpenter do. What would bonnie Jean say. Life was good, damn it. New-Jock lolled amongst the giggling children in the back of the car. Why, Janet felt that she might even be able to withstand the slings and arrows of her outrageous mother.

The care home was quiet.

It preserved a thick somnolence in the heat of the day. Breakfast trays had long been forgotten and lunchtime not yet remembered. The loo rota was well underway and they stood waiting on the stone corridor for Mrs Ward to be returned to her room. Even the duty sister was nowhere to be seen and they had smuggled in New-Jock with impunity.

Grandpa was visiting too. He was suitably impressed. He held the squirming puppy to his face and giggled like a little Pieter as he was thoroughly washed by New-Jock's pink tongue.

It's been a long time, he kept saying as he helped his grandson to hide with New-Jock behind Granny's curtain. It has been a long time. And his grey hair, which had faded even more and which badly needed a cut, fell over his eyes.

Janet and her girls retired into the corridor again; the boys waited inside.

Where was Granny.

She arrived slowly, as though she were leading the nurse on a grand tour. And here, her manner seemed to suggest, is a room, a fascinating example of a quick conversion from some functional part of a nunnery to my home. Yes, just off this flagstone corridor with its faux-gothic arches and its orange-red brick – vaguely reminiscent of Hampton Court in Middlesex – you will find the sunny cell in which I now reside. I say sunny, but it is only the busy old fool of the morning sun, which peers through my curtains and makes of my room an everywhere, a nowhere. But only for a very short space of time, the sun. Otherwise, there is not much to recommend it at all. In fact, I would advise you to give it a miss. I am only waiting here to be fetched. It will not be long. They will come. Three quick winks of the left eye, that's the signal. Then I shall have to bid you a fond farewell and do keep your sterile hands off me. Off me, I say. I shall brook no argument. Will you let go.

Janet's greeting caught in her throat as her mother was delivered, muttering and unseeing, to her room. Her petticoat trailed from beneath her skirt and one heel had escaped from her special Scholl shoe. She shuffled past them on the arm of a smiling, nodding nurse and she scowled at them as though they were intruders in her corridor, her life.

Granny, Shelley said once the nurse had escaped.

Amelia Amis MA stood beside the chair that crouched next to the bed. She seemed buried in her clothes, as though they were too big. Nothing seemed to fit: not her skirt, not her shoes, not this room. But then she took a breath and tried to draw herself up, as though to begin a lecture on a more difficult perception of Spenser or Smollett or Swift. To gird her loins in the face of undergraduate apathy. Such sportsmen and women, these South Africans, but dear God on high, could they not read a little more widely, a little more deeply. What a rift, a wrench it was to cross the equator, to leave so many dreaming spires in the more cerebral hemisphere –

Janet reached out a hand. She had heard it all, at home and at university. And the curtains twitched, stage left, and into the room sprang Pieter and the puppy, and Grandpa.

Surprise, they yelled, Grandpa every bit as wild as his grandson with the six stitches from his ninth birthday bash.

Sylvia squealed with delight and Mrs Amelia Ward shook. For a moment, Janet thought that she was going to strike Pieter, open up the gash on his forehead, but then the puppy yelped and from somewhere deep inside her mother came an answering call. A smile broke out across her mother's chilly features and her hand leapt to her face in an expression of delight.

My dear boys, she said to her grandson and her husband. My dear chaps, and she blushed and held out her hand to their faces, the puppy unseen and untouched.

Look, Gran, Pieter shrugged off her searching fingertips and shoved New-Jock at her. And then Mrs Ward was all oohs and aahs, stroking the dog and beaming at the boys.

Happy New Year, Mother, Janet said.

It was Pieter's birthday yesterday, and look at his head, said her father.

We've got a puppy, said Sylvia. She took over the holding of New-Jock, while Pieter displayed his wound as though it had been acquired at great expense in battle.

And we have a present for Pieter don't we, Granny, said Grandpa and he produced a neatly wrapped box that he gave to his wife. Mrs Ward peered at the box and then she began plucking at the Sellotape. No, no, said Grandpa and he handed her the card instead and gestured to Pieter.

Pieter reached out and took the card from Mrs Ward, who smiled at him, but may have been a little put out. Her card was gone. Now opened by this small boy.

Then Pieter unwrapped the old Meccano set – the one that belonged to Grandpa and which still was perfect in its faded box.

There were oohs and aahs, and Shelley had to see. Pieter hugged both his grandparents.

Many happy hours, Grandpa said smiling up at Janet. Many happy times.

Pieter wanted to start playing with it immediately. Not in here, said Janet and both boys were crestfallen.

Shelley stood silently. The room was crowded and she looked like she was twitching. She had something in her eye, poor girl, and again Janet offered the silent prayer that her daughter did not follow her grandmother, that she make her own happy way in life.

They all sat down. Janet beside her father on the bed, the children with New-Jock on the floor. Mrs Ward occupied the solitary chair, queen of the sparrows in this parliament of fowls.

She pulled at the skin on the back of her hands as they all chattered and chirped. The news came thick and fast. Janet's voice was part of the chorus. They said what happened to poor Oupa, passed on Pappie's regards, described the previous day's exciting presentation of New-Jock and the drama of Pieter's fall, as well as the birthday cake and even the little picannins that they had seen once again. If Janet were a child, she might have breathlessly imparted the perceptions of Meneer Yuckulls, described his gleaming mouth from whence such unpleasantness came, and maybe she would have spoken of the crack. But she saw her mother's strained face and how the old woman tried to calm the picking, picking of her hands. Hands that picked hands. Her father reached out from the bed and took the closest hand in his own. Mrs Ward looked up at him from the depths of the children's voices, and smiled. She remembered. She seemed to remember. Mr Ward beamed and Janet's heart nearly broke.

The children gabbled on as Janet wondered if it all came to this. The touch of a familiar hand and a soft smile. Did it matter if Doug thought that Alice-Lettie –

Who the hell was Doug.

And even if –

As long as there were hands to touch, loving skin, was that not world and time enough. Eternity in a touch and an answering smile.

New-Jock was now ensconced on Mrs Ward's lap. She looked down in disbelief. Her lap had sprouted a dog that squirmed and shed the finest of hairs, little lines that would run down her skirt for days to come and join the faint blotches and smears of future meals. And the smell of him would remind her of their visit and she might discuss hounds and greyhounds, mongrels, spaniels, curs, shoughs, water-rugs and demi-wolves in the catalogue ye go for men speech with the rather disappointing cluster of old folk whenever they were next taken out and aired in the common room.

We shall definitely visit this coming week, Janet said to her mother.

She would like that – you would like that – her father was eager to say. We always like a visit.

Fine, said Janet. And I shall give you a haircut, Dad. I'll bring my scissors and things next time. Or you could pop around.

I know you are busy, said Mr Ward. And I see Mommy twice a day.

The diminutive pressed at her heart again. Her mother. Mommy.

Saturday, said Janet. With the kids.

Mrs Ward did not get up. She did not look up. She stared at the warm spot on her lap, where New-Jock had wriggled and squirmed and shed his hair.

And Janet wondered why Shelley threw herself into the car and refused to speak all the way home. The strange girl clutched at her buttoned cardigan, silly apparel in the warm weather, and seemed to want to dig herself right into the depths of her seat as though she had stomach cramps, as though her stomach were square and hard. Maybe it was starting. So soon. Becoming a woman. Janet would need to talk to her again.

Later that afternoon, just after Pieter had swallowed his Disprin with great ceremony, and Janet was wondering whether she could sneak a moment on the couch with the Carpenters, the gate in the low front wall creaked and there was Doug – who the hell was Doug – with Noreen in tow. Why. What would Doug like to say now. What would he imply in front of his wife and her children. With a dark vein pulsing in her heart, Janet realised that neither her maid nor her man were at home. They were out. Not together, surely. But both out. She opened the door, her chin set at a careful angle. Whatever he had to say, she would take on that chin. Who the hell was Doug.

They had come with Pieter's birthday present. Doug held up Pieter's bright present like an offering. They had remembered. No one was home yesterday, not until late. They had not wanted to disturb.

How kind of them to remember – even though, and possibly because, they had no child of their own. Janet adjusted her chin. What. No mention of the maid.

Noreen smiled. Doug grinned. The present glowed.

It was a book. They knew just how Janet approved of books. Pieter read the card first – good boy! – and then tore the paper carefully. Look, Ma, he said. He held up the book with the thundering horse on its cover. *Black Beauty*. Look, he showed his sisters. There was a girl on the cover, too. Shelley might want to read it. He may not quite want to, but it was his to have and hold, to wave in front of his sister. To watch her eyes, to negotiate favours in return for a chance to read the book. Or simply to have her ask again and again, safe in the certain proprietorship of the book with the stupid horse and dof girl on the cover.

Thank you, Pieter said, and he kissed Auntie Noreen and shook Uncle Doug's hand.

Then Pieter showed them his stitches and mentioned his medication.

It was a rock. He fell, Sylvia verified. And Oupa hurt his face – bad.

Well I never, Noreen's eyebrows rose to meet her perfect hair as hunting and guns and dried mud in the barrel of the .22 were breathlessly shared.

Doug stood behind Noreen, his hands on the couch.

And then what happened, asked Noreen. Her voice came quietly, in counterpoint to Pieter's and Sylvia's breathlessness.

They told her, whilst Shelley sidled out of the room. Doug's eyes followed her.

Then she was back, in time for the bit about the ambulance.

Noreen was nodding, looking through the children's graphic and gory enthusiasm right at their mother's strange indulgence. Noreen frowned. She raised her eyebrows. That was when Shelley stepped right before her and whipped out the dead guinea fowl from behind her back.

Look what I shot, she said. Oom Koos said that I am a natural.

She held it by its neck. Its blue and red face flopped against her little hand, and it dangled bloody and dead right under Noreen's nose.

She did not make a sound, and Janet managed to squash her yelp of surprise into a sudden gasp of, Shelley –

Where had the bird come from. In all the dreadful business of the weekend, Shelley had never shown her the bird. It dangled, a dead thing, in the lounge. Noreen raised a hand. Would she touch it or push it away. Janet's hands fluttered too. The thing hung dark and heavy from Shelley's hand. Like a human head. Speckled with white thoughts and pondering deeply.

Doug saved the day. He leapt forward before a sudden headache could overwhelm his wife and his neighbour's wife. He took the spotted bird from Shelley's hand and held it, cradled it.

Well I never, he echoed Noreen. A guinea fowl. You hear them in the park, he said, But I have never seen one this close. Look, look at its helmet, and he stroked the conical head gently in case he might cause its closed eyes to flutter suddenly and the firm feathers to squawk to life. Look, he said again, ostensibly to Shelley, perhaps to himself. Like a little doek. And he took the helmet between a forefinger and thumb, and said, Doek, again. He murmured to them all, In the same bold pink, yes, and the face in the same bright blue that Emily used to wear. He smiled back at Noreen, and then turned to Janet. Your Alice wears a pink dress with a pink doek, hey.

Janet brought her hands down and tilted her face. She did not like the way Doug was twisting the bird's head to look at her, its pointed beak curving towards her, its eyes closed as it sought her out with its sharp little mind. And now he was opening its mad eyes. What would he do next, make it squawk out the name of Alice-Lettie like a feathery bagpipe pressed under his arm with the last wheeze in its lungs. Would he leap towards her and shove it in her face and suggest nasty things about her husband. The bird's spots danced in front of her eyes.

Don't be silly, Doug, she said.

Her voice came clearly and quickly. She could not have done a better voice. It was a mother's voice. It expressed patience tried and tested. It was a tired voice. It said, Come on, you silly little boy, that is quite enough, enough now, thank you. Just who do you think you are with your guinea fowl and your stupid imprecations. For goodness' sake, grow up.

And Doug grinned like a little boy.

Had he heard what she said.

He shuffled up to Shelley, a pantomime waltz with the dead bird, and eased it into her hands. You clever girl, he said looking over her head at her mother.

And then the children were calling New-Jock who was trying to get at the bird and Uncle Doug was laughing and pulling Noreen to her feet as though he was going to hold her up and make her squawk too.

Thank you for the present, said Pieter with no prompting from his mother. She could let them go, their neighbours, that man from across the wall, the creature that lurked in rhododendrons and in the corners of her mind. She could rise, force a smile, even peck Noreen on the cheek and have her soft cheek touched in turn by Doug's lips except that, as always, as some men do, they sought her lips and almost tried to taste her surprise.

Give Higher our best, said Doug and he seemed to look around the room, as though noting the fact that Higher was not there and that Alice-Lettie was nowhere to be seen. Both were out. And then, they too were gone and Janet was left to bury the bird in the bin, except Shelley kicked up a fuss and quoted Oom Koos, who said that with a plum sauce the guinea fowl is second to none.

They were going to have to cook the damn thing.

Right, my girl, said Janet. But then you must boil the kettle and pour it over the guinea fowl and pluck out every feather. I suppose Oom Koos told you how to do that, and how to gut it.

He did, said Shelley, and her chin was at precisely the same angle and her tone matched her mother's.

Then I shall fill the kettle, Janet said, and went into the kitchen.

A wise son maketh a glad father: but a foolish son is the heaviness of his mother. Hektor-Jan trusted that he was a wise son. Looking down on his father, he had not wanted to ask if he had made him glad. Not when his father was swaddled like a baby in a manger, his face a white mask of bandaging that buried plastic supports and tubes. A tangle of tubes like thoughts came flowing from his father's face.

He did not want to think about what heaviness he might have caused his mother. His hand strayed to his pocket and the fingers of his right hand enclosed her Swiss Army knife, the very knife she had used for her biltong and for her stubborn corns on the sides of her feet. It was the knife that he was meant to have. He did not need to ask. At her passing, just before she rose up to claim her seat at the right-hand side of God, she had nodded to the bedside drawer and he had opened it. There, beside her small Bybel, was the knife, so red and modern. He was flicking through the complication of gadgets when her cord was cut and she passed. It was a good death, he could appreciate that now. He was older now, much older. Too old. He carried the weight of his mother's soft face, still soft and warm in death as he kissed her after her passing. He remembered how he had carried the implacable softness of his mother outside the square house – and how he held her red knife that sought a kind of revenge. There was a stupid brak. It ran up to him as he emerged with the weight of his mother's passing heavy on his heart and his hands still clutching her knife with its myriad spikes and blades, and the knife had sought new flesh, a life for a life. It had found a secret slit: the artery and lung it ruptured released almost no blood. The dark liquid ran inwards and the dog drowned in its own blood, silently. An old hunter's trick. No other creature need be alarmed.

He had wiped the biggest blade clean afterwards with his own thumb and his blood had mingled with the dog's blood and he could have howled for her passing. Just like a dog. Not their dog, though, for it had died silently. He kept the knife deep in the folds of his mother's Bybel – often buried in Revelations – in the bottom drawer of his bedside table. Except when he visited his childhood home where she died – the plot in Springs. And he had it with him now.

It was getting late. Hektor-Jan wiped his face now as he turned into Davidson Street, the Bunny Park on his right and the neighbourhood on his left. A wise son maketh –

Then he saw the figure on the pavement, waiting beside the plane trees with their peeling bark, mottled and growing ghostly in the dying light. The Ford Cortina rumbled up the road. He disengaged the gears and let the car coast quietly along the empty road before turning in to his driveway, the driveway his father-in-law had paved. All he had to do was press the brakes and switch her off. And the handbrake creaked.

The dark figure stepped forward as though summoned by the handbrake.

Hektor-Jan did not turn to look at the man. He let him stand beside the car, black and silent.

The streetlight from across the road looped a soft halo, lopsided with the angle, around Doug's head. His forehead and the side of his face were brighter, and his nose and chin gleamed. But the rest of his features were dark distortions. Hektor-Jan let him stand there, a chiaroscuro of ambiguous intent.

At last, letting go of his mother's knife, he opened the car door. Doug had to move back, and Hektor-Jan stepped out into the night. The world was speckled. The plane trees filtered the light and scattered darkness across the face of the earth. He saw it and wondered if that was good.

It's no good, Doug shook his shining head, a sad angel.

It's no good, Hektor-Jan repeated.

Goodness in a fallen world. There were shadows, but there were shadows because there was light. The world could be fallen only if there had been goodness, surely. Goodness and mercy. All the days of his life.

What a day, said Doug.

What a day, he said.

On your son's ninth birthday, said Doug.

Ja, his ninth, he said.

Don't you wonder, sometimes, Doug said.

He wondered. How could he not wonder.

All these signs, said Doug.

How could he not wonder when there were all these signs.

Signs, he said.

It makes me so angry, said Doug. His voice shook. He must be angry. He snapped open the metal flask and offered it to Hektor-Jan. A doppie, he said. To drown the anger.

Douse the flames. Swallow their pride.

Hektor-Jan looked at the silver flask, yellow in the shattered streetlight. Doug's eyes gleamed.

I have not forgotten, said Hektor-Jan.

You have had a lot on your plate, said Doug, handing over the flask.

I have not thought of anything else, he said, accepting the drink.

You could try to forget, said Doug.

With the garden boy, he said, wiping his lips and handing back the flask.

Some women – Doug's lips curled around the flask and his voice slipped into the hollow cylinder. He drank. Hektor-Jan waited.

Some women like that, Doug's voice emerged.

Some women, he said. Janet, he said.

The law, Doug said.

It is against the law of the land, he said. She can't just –

Sex across the colour line, said Doug. His hand shook and he handed the last drops to Hektor-Jan.

All their previous and present thinking and murmuring in the darkness of dawn and dusk, their drinking and wondering now came to settle down on the vicious word, sex. There. It was said. Doug said, Sex, and lo, there was sex and Hektor-Jan saw that it was not good. In the beginning was woman, and the woman was with him, and the woman was Janet. But there was a snake and that snake was sex. And scenes from the holding cells came welling up in the whisky and he swallowed so that they settled back into the pit of his stomach, and he swallowed so that he could not think more clearly. He handed the flask to Doug. Then his hand did not go to his concealed shoulder holster to reach for his gun. Instead, the knife sprang to his fingers of his right hand as his left gripped Doug by the throat and held him fast against the black and white bark of the thick tree. He moved so suddenly that he surprised himself.

Be sure, his voice blurred thickly in the dark, his tongue streamed whisky into the night. Be fokken sure, when you say –

Doug did not struggle. Even as the longest blade pressed against the side of his left eye, touched the surface of his shining sclera so that if he blinked he sliced open his eyelid. Doug's eyes stared fixedly in the hollow light. He did not flinch. His eyes did not flicker even as the blade gently dented the left eyeball.

So, you want to see, Doug's voice struggled through the stranglehold. It tried to be matter-of-fact. The facts mattered.

Maak seker, said Hektor-Jan switching to his more urgent Afrikaans. Make sure. Maak baie seker, and he was in the holding cells and even though he was about to insert a Swiss Army lever that would move Doug's world, root out the jelly of his left eye, Hektor-Jan's own foundations shifted. Doug was pressed into the plane tree. Hektor-Jan could fall no further. He leaned into Doug's wiry warmth. The knife dropped to one side and his full weight came to rest on Doug's slender frame. They could have been lovers. The flask clinked to the ground and his breath came in hot spurts in the close night.

For you, Doug sounded almost tearful. I am your neighbour. Anything. Nothing is too much trouble, he wheezed out the words beneath the weight of Hektor-Jan. The man's one great hand crawled up his chest and Doug felt it come to rest around his throat.

His Adam's apple was sharp and hard. It convulsed with a sudden swallow, sliding like one of the strange gadgets in the knife. To break his neighbour's neck, even with Hektor-Jan's left hand, was no trouble at all. Grip tightly and a sudden wrench. That would be all.

Maak baie, baie seker, said Hektor-Jan again and then he forced himself to stand upright whilst breath whispered back into Doug's body.

Jesus, said Doug.

Hektor-Jan let the blasphemy squeeze past.

Jesus Christ, and he cleared his throat. One hand ran to this throat, the other covered his left eye. Jesus Christ.

That is enough, said Hektor-Jan. The knife again flicked out a blade.

What is ever enough. Doug sounded bitter. He rubbed his throat. He wiped the other hand across his left eye and winked experimentally.

They had hugged. Now this thin, skraal mannetjie was winking at him.

Hektor-Jan raised his hand. The knife slid into the heart of the darkness. Bliksem, he swore. Jou moer. And he stepped closer again. Winking at him –

That's your special knife, Doug's voice was quick. His hand reached out and stalled the arm of Hektor-Jan. The one you always use.

Don't make me, said Hektor-Jan.

Doug managed to smile grimly. Don't make you, he said. He paused. She knows that that is your special knife.

She knows. The kids know. They know not to touch it. I keep it safe with my little Bybel. Pietertjie once took it. He has never touched it again.

Right, said Doug. Then he tried the Afrikaans word. Reg, he said. Reg so. His throat rattled with the glottal g.

Hektor-Jan frowned in the darkness. What was –

Leave the knife where she will find it, said Doug. Where only she will see it. And I am telling you, before you know it, your garden boy will be playing with your knife and keeping it deep in his pocket. Just there. And Doug reached out and touched Hektor-Jan close to his groin so that he stepped backwards and looked down at Doug's hand.

Jesus, said Hektor-Jan.

Don't let me say I didn't tell you, said Doug and his hand stayed where it was. It was Hektor-Jan who muttered Jesus again and who stepped back some more.

Doug picked up the fallen flask. There were a few drops left. He tilted the flask and drank them all.

Hektor-Jan's lips moved in the darkness. Thy wife shall be as a fruitful vine by the sides of thine house: thy children like olive plants round thy table, he mouthed.

Something fluttered through the trees and brushed his shoulder. He wiped it away. It was a gun-metal feather, speckled with white.

A black snowflake.

From the wings of what dark angel had it fallen, had it been plucked.

2.048m

On 16 June 1976 fifteen thousand schoolchildren gathered in Soweto to protest at the government's ruling that half of all classes in secondary schools must be taught in Afrikaans. Students did not want to learn and teachers did not want to teach in the language of the oppressor. Pleadings and petitions by parents and teachers had fallen on deaf ears. A detachment of police confronted this army of earnest schoolchildren and without warning opened fire, killing thirteen-year-old Hector Pieterson and many others. The children fought with sticks and stones, and mass chaos ensued, with hundreds of children wounded and killed and two white men stoned to death.

– Nelson Mandela, *Long Walk to Freedom*

Traps and snares are generally easy to construct and may be very useful for survival, by extending your limited rations, as well as for such military purposes as setting alarms and explosive ambushes.

In its simplest form the snare is a wire or cord loop placed on a game path in such a way that the animal puts its head into it and is strangled. It is easy to make and set and is very efficient. It is very frequently used by Africans for killing animals and birds.

The placing of traps and snares is very important. You should look for obvious feeding and watering places, nests or folds, game paths or gaps in fences, frequent use of which is indicated by fresh trails or droppings.

259

The snare should be placed, as far as possible, in some place where the game is forced to pass. If necessary, create such a situation by arranging bush or stones in such a way as to ensure that the victim's head must enter the loop. The size of the loop must be such that the animal's head but not its body will pass through easily. Set as many snares as you can. For bait, use fruits or meat, including entrails from any animal or bird you may have been able to kill.

– Col. D. H. Grainger, *Don't Die in the Bundu*

P regnant, said Derek-Francis, his hand with the script fluttering around his head. Pregnant.

It looked like he was trying desperately to swat away the thought. The very idea of her being pregnant. Filled with a child. She knew her words, everything was blocked and choreographed. She had it all down pat. Now, it threatened to go down the spout. Because she was up the duff. Pregnant.

Janet looked at him.

Eileen-the-Understudy stood in a pose of embarrassment. My God, she murmured, I am so sorry.

Janet's fists hung on the end of her arms. It had been said. Not so much said, but certainly implied. With what skill had Eileen-the-Understudy managed cheerily to say, at the perfect volume and pitch, neither too loudly nor too softly, but with just the precise measure of clarity and projection so that Derek-Francis could not help but hear, How's the bump. And she had actually patted Janet on the belly, in case anyone – Derek-Francis, for instance – had missed the point. The bulge. The bump.

Things that go bump in the night. Janet's tell-tale bump now telling its own sudden tale as the rehearsal bumped to a halt in the night.

Janet stood there, the centre of sudden attention.

Enid Blyton's Noddy – the trouble with Bumpy the dog. Didn't A.A. Milne's Tigger bump into anything and everything. Mr Bump and his bandages. Janet stood there, a caricature, a cartoon figure of shame.

When were you going to tell me. Derek-Francis seemed to shove the script at her as the other actors looked on. Frank van Zyl's face mirrored her own. Embarrassed. Stunned.

I – said Janet.

She – said Eileen-the-Understudy.

We – said Derek-Francis.

When is it due, said Frank. He was living up to his name. Honest and up-front. Like her bump. But wasn't he her other half, her second self.

Early August, said Janet.

Early August, Derek-Francis almost squealed.

They were due to perform mid-June. The show had been scheduled for mid-June, just before the July school holidays.

Eileen-the-Understudy trembled. Her hand sought Janet's hand, but did not find it at first. Derek-Francis's script flapped, like a white fowl in its death throes. Was he going to pluck out her pages, pull her from the part, tear her apart. Janet's breath came quickly and she pulled her hand away from Eileen-the-Understudy as though stung. Janet wanted to grasp her belly, cling to her baby, as the entire cast stared at her, the centre of so much gravity.

Gravely, Derek-Francis said, Well.

The mound of her unborn child swelled. Well, his voice was a deep pit. Would she fit. Would she fall.

You know, said Frank suddenly.

What.

The cast played tennis with their eyes, following the ball from one to the other.

We could –

What –

Well, we could –

Spit it out –

We could use it. Make it part of the performance – her character.

Her character –

Play it for laughs –

Laughs –

Do I have to spell it out, Frank's voice was strong and clear. He moved to stand beside Janet.

People again thought that they were seeing double – mixed doubles.

Don't you see, said Frank. We could ignore it, her condition, entirely. Pretend it wasn't there.

Pretend, said Derek-Francis faintly. Pretend.

Let the audience fill in the gaps, for laughs, said Frank.

Gaps. Laughs, Derek-Francis wavered.

Bonnie Jean, so big and bonnie, would have to get married. Her bounty. Her bountiful nature. But we wouldn't say a word, and yet there it would be, she would be, right in front of them, so obvious, with her big bump.

They were all overdue, said Janet, finding her voice in the burgeoning sense of hope. My other children, all very late. My mother laughed –

It might just be the answer, Frank van Zyl snapped his fingers. This could be really good. *Brigadoon* with a bit of social realism.

The cast gasped at his brilliance. *Brigadoon*. Social realism.

The pages of the script again rose in a fluster and flew to Derek-Francis's temple. They whirled around his head like thoughts.

Frank, he said. Frank. The pages circled, homing pigeons without a coup in the world. I am afraid that is the whole point of the play. *Brigadoon* is not about fucking social realism. It's the very opposite of social fucking realism.

The cast gasped again. This was dramatic. Such swearing.

Frank laughed. His hand reached out and took hold of Janet's hand. He held her.

The pages floated down with Frank's soft laughter.

Derek-Francis's brief tempest was spent. Yes, he said, Okay, yes, I see. It's the 1970s, he said.

Frank squeezed her hand secretly.

Yes, Derek-Francis seemed to be thinking out loud. The audience would see her bump and understand, and all the singing about coming home to bonnie Jean would assume a much broader context.

And, suddenly, after a pause, he was laughing.

The cast caught up. A broader context, and their laughter swelled to become a broader context itself, so broad that it spread its collective arms wide and embraced Janet, and Frank, and Derek-Francis with his script and all Eileen-the-Understudy could do was put in a second-rate performance of oh-how-unexpected-oh-my-goodness-me-didn't-that-turn-out-well-I-am-overjoyed-really-I-am-which-I-shall-demonstrate-by-hugging-Janet-embracing-her-bump-and-bloody-all.

Thank you, Janet was tearful after the commotion. They were all late, she said again. There is no reason why this one should be any different, is there. And they reassured her that no, in all likelihood, this next one would be exactly the same.

The rest of the rehearsal went well. They cracked on. All for one and one for all.

Didn't that go well, said Eileen-the-Understudy in the car as they drove home in the chilly night. It was early May and winter was drawing in. Where had the time gone.

Where does the time go, said Eileen-the-Understudy again, as Janet sat silent beside her, a betraying presence in the passenger seat.

Shelley was late, said Janet. And Pieter. And so was Sylvia. All very, very late.

Just as well, said Eileen-the-Understudy. Just as well.

And they shivered and rubbed the windscreen with their sleek gloves. The glass was almost clear by the time they arrived home.

Do you need a hand, asked Eileen-the-Understudy as Janet eased herself from the car.

You have done quite enough, Janet managed to say as she shut the door.

Janet did not wait for Eileen-the-Understudy to drive off. With her hand clasped to her belly, she almost strode up to the front door and fumbled with her keys before slipping into the warm womb of the house.

Flustered and feeling confused, she followed the strands of Lettie-Alice's – no – Alice-Lettie's muttering radio and said good night. She locked the back door after Alice-Lettie and tried not to think of the pool at the bottom of the garden, the pool, that now lay swaddled like a strange present, a cocoon or a mummy, wrapped in its tarpaulin of sorts. Keeping out the leaves of late autumn, preventing prying eyes, saving the situation for another day. It had been her idea. Aided and abetted by Solomon, and another trip to the Italian hardware store, the best in town. Hektor-Jan had not said a word. He had no time. His job was keeping him so busy. Big things, he muttered sometimes, Big things, man. He did not like Alice-Lettie's radio, even though it spoke in black tongues. The news, when it came, was agitated. Alice-Lettie knew when to switch it off. He did not want that in his home.

But he could not switch off his dreams. And Janet tried not to listen to him talking in his sleep. As she wandered the house in the murmuring mornings, cold now, she often longed to be snuggled up in bed beside the great mound of her husband, wrapped up like the pool in the duvet that was no longer new, but warm and soft and leaking secrets.

Now it was her turn. Hektor-Jan was at work and it was time to climb into bed alone with her bump, and to forgive Eileen-the-Understudy in her silent prayers.

In the dark house, the tiny glow of the bedside light, left on by Alice-Lettie, was the only light. Janet tiptoed down the passage, pausing at each door, making her way like a moth towards that light. Silence floated from the children's rooms. She wished that she could scoop it up, so soft and fluffy, and take it with her to bed. So different from

Hektor-Jan's troubled sleep and her own thick-coming dreams and maternal worries.

Then the light flickered in the passage as someone moved in front of the bedside light. There was someone in the main bedroom.

Janet froze in the cold passage. Was Hektor-Jan home early. Had his nightshift been cancelled. What could be so wrong to change his schedule.

She could not move, not even to send a protective hand to her belly. The light flickered as whoever it was moved about the room. There was a quiet cough. An odd sound.

Her children. Their safety. The only thing instantly within reach that might possibly help was the narrow-but-heavy mirror on the wall down the passage. Sick and suddenly shivering, Janet tried not to stumble. She turned, her legs worked and her hands eased the rectangular mirror off the wall. Her sharp reflection reached up to carry herself. Even in the gloom, her image was true and startlingly clear. Her face was a gash. Her mouth, a wound of surprise. Alice-Lettie was a wonderful maid, but Janet wished that the mirror had not been so highly polished. Like some strange thief, she carried herself to the bedroom, the narrow mirror raised in violent anticipation. She would have to attack. She would have to bring herself smashing down on whoever was lurking, creeping in their bedroom.

As her feet curled along the carpet, silent and fierce past the children's bedrooms, Janet wished that her policeman husband were home. He had a gun. He knew what to do. Hektor-Jan would face this head-on. Not head on as she did, with her face angled in glass, about to smash herself, rising up from the silver pool of the heavy mirror. What if the intruder were armed. She had only the mirror and her two hands. She came to the shuddering rectangle of the light in the doorway.

Janet took a deep breath. Ready to dive in. Her knuckles tightened and she raised the mirror a little further. With the strangest, sickening sense, she tried to throw herself into the room. She thought that she had the element of surprise. But it was she who was surprised. It was she who was shocked. The mirror gasped with fragile glass as she almost brought it smashing down on little Pieter's stunned face.

Mommy!

Pieter!

Their cries – shock – came simultaneously.

Pieter fell back towards his father's side of the bed. He dropped the Bible from the bedside table in a splash of white pages. Janet clung to the mirror that was still raised and ready to smash. Ready to crash down on the intruder's head and give him a thousand pieces of her mind. Sharp and silver, like a shower of cold fish.

Pieter, said Janet with tears in her eyes, and lowered her square face onto the bed. Let her reflected self fall to the bed, a soft ploff onto the duvet so different from the silvery splintering that was going to come. The mirror lay on the bed, a bemused ceiling of rectangular light. Pieter just stood there, petrified.

Mommy, he said again. He said it sorrowfully.

Now Janet could move. Unburdened by the mirror, her silver self, she could walk around to Hektor-Jan's side of the bed and take up her small son in her arms. She could press him to her warm belly, and try to hold him close even as the mound of his unborn sibling pushed him away. They both shuddered.

Pieter, she said again. What are you doing.

Nightmares, dreams, she offered him excuses as her eyes took in the open drawer, the fallen Bible, the side of Hektor-Jan's bed that was never touched. Where his gun was kept when he slept, and where his magazines lay flat beneath the mattress, their images of contorted women pressed down by his weight, their siren mouths silenced by his heavy length, their orifices calling, their orisons unheard. Maybe they had awoken little Pieter. He was nine now. Almost double figures. But he had opened his father's bedside drawer and had taken out the Bible, not the boobs, the bums, the breathless yearning.

Pieter, she repeated.

Uncle Doug, he said. Solomon, he said, and –

And all that spilled from his lips was, Uncle Doug and Solomon. That was all. He did not say the names again, but bit them back, tried to take them back into his mouth by biting his own lips, but they were said.

Popping up in their very own bedroom was Desperate Doug. No rhododendrons required now, it seemed. Just a small boy, vulnerable, impressionable. What. Why.

Uncle Doug, Janet started to say, but then she stopped. It was not fair. She would not interrogate Pieter. She would take it up with Desperate Doug. Tell him how she might have smashed the hall mirror on her own son. How her sudden fear had set her heart racing and how she now felt sick to the pit of her stomach and she could feel the new baby tugging at the line within her, wanting to know why. Why the sudden adrenalin. Why the thumping heart.

Get to bed, she said to Pieter.

He did not need a second invitation. He was gone in a flash, leaving her to pick up Die Bybel and close it. She looked down at the dark seam, the well-thumbed section of the Psalms. Part of her wanted to open the book, to see what her strange husband spent his time reading, and she sat on the bed, on the layers of glossy women, who had sneaked all the way from Germany thanks to Phil Wilson and his Jumbo 747 and the fact that he was not searched by Customs, it seemed.

The Lord fills the earth with His love, Psalm 32 offered in plain Afrikaans.

O blessed are those who fear the Lord, she wiped the pages to Psalm 127.

Love and fear, she almost smiled. Her life in the Psalms at her hands. Was she 32. Would she live to 127. She thought not. She sat with the Bible open along the dark line. Pieter needed tucking into bed. Desperate Doug required careful interrogation. And why Solomon. The mirror must be returned to the wall in the hall. Janet sat there on Hektor-Jan's side of the bed. The mirror lay at her side. Janet put down Die Bybel. She leaned across and peered in at her second self, who looked up at her with a strange expression and a face lined with weariness. Then her eyes turned inward as her unborn child pulled at her, pulled then kicked.

And – his neighbour's voice dangled, enquired, as he came home. It was dark now. Dark and cold with the thin Highveld air chill and sharp. His breath steamed and his fingers ached. He wanted to get inside. How did this thin man-next-door bear the dark mornings. Why did he lie in wait. Hektor-Jan closed the car door quietly.

I have not left it out, he confessed.

Doug's side of the wall was silent. Resentful. Look, his voice came quietly, I am only trying to help. Help, you know.

Hektor-Jan knew. He said so.

So, what are you waiting for, said Doug.

Hektor-Jan's hand felt inside his pocket, searched for the warm knife. Steel, which glowed with the heat from his body.

So, what are you waiting for, said Doug.

Janet and Alice-Lettie watched Solomon from the kitchen window.

What has happened, asked Janet.

Solomon made his way across the garden. The grass was yellow now, killed by the black frosts and as blond as her children's hair. It clung to their shoes with a strange static electricity and was prickly to the touch. It would be a while before the rains came back.

His feet, said Alice-Lettie. His feet are very bad.

I can see that, said Janet.

And she could see the large shadow. Faithful New-Jock loped behind Solomon. He loved the garden boy in that earnest, undiluted way dogs have. Janet sighed.

Solomon limped to the end of the garden and bent over the pool. He made sure that the wide tarpaulin was secure, that the tent pegs that they had fashioned from lengths of bent wire were still in place. Janet noticed that he did not lift the home-made cover. He was careful not to set the crack free. Instead, the pool stayed warm and snug beneath the tarpaulin that kept out the dead grass and any stray leaves. Surely, it had stopped. Surely, with the hard ground and the fierce cold in the June nights, the crack had stopped. Maybe it had even shrunk. But the tarpaulin looked stretched. Even strained. As though it was being pulled apart or about to split with news. Janet pressed her lips together. It seemed as though the pool was pregnant.

They watched Solomon hobble behind the pampas grass and disappear.

His feet, said Alice-Lettie. Something is wrong.

Yes, said Doug.

Ja, said Hektor-Jan.

Are you sure.

I keep it only in two places. Die Bybel. My trouser pocket. It is not in those two places.

Doug was silent. I told you so, the darkness seemed to imply.

Hektor-Jan stood by the car – the door was still open, like a wing.

I am sorry, said Doug. Wragtig. I hoped –

Was Hektor-Jan sorry. He did not say a word. Maybe he was angry. He closed the car door quietly. Firmly.

Today is Tuesday, said Doug. It might be a good Tuesday. You have the garden boy today. Tomorrow he disappears.

We have the boy today, said Hektor-Jan.

Then I tell you what, said Doug. This is what we shall do –

I am not tired, said Hektor-Jan after his breakfast-supper.

Janet sat opposite him, her hands perched on her mound. Alice-Lettie washed the dishes quietly behind her. The crockery made gentle thunks and resonant plonks in the deep sink. Hektor-Jan looked tired. But his mouth said that he was not tired. Today, after a busy week, a week that he had said was a very trying week, he claimed not to be tired. His eyes came down from Alice-Lettie's back, back down to her. She tried to smile.

Darling, said Janet. She wondered whether she should stretch out a gentle hand and touch his hairy arm, stroke his wrist where the hair squeezed out from beneath his favourite tracksuit top and lay squashed under his watch.

He looked down at her hand, which touched him. Then he looked back at her. His mouth smiled, but his eyes were hard and did not smile. His mouth said, I love you, but his eyes said, Who are you.

Janet withdrew her hand, confused.

I have a penknife, his lips were moving now. The sounds came all the way across the kitchen table. She frowned. Finally, an image of a knife, Hektor-Jan's knife, appeared in her head.

Yes, she said. She could see it. She did not like it.

It is gone, he said.

Janet struggled. In her mind's eye, she saw the knife. It was red, blood-red, and within its heart of warm colour, there lurked silver blades, corkscrews, prongs, strange files, scissory things. She could see it so clearly now; she could almost feel the decisive metal, dangerous with manly purpose, shiny and sharp. She did not like it about the house. She knew it belonged in her husband's pocket or deep in Die Bybel. Yes, she could see it and feel it, but he had just said it was gone. Janet could not make it go. She tried, but the image would not go pop, like some of Pieter's silly comics. There was no Aaargh sound, or a Pop!!! with three exclamation marks, to make it vanish. It is gone, he said, but it was still in her head. Janet raised a hand to her forehead. Did it look like she was saluting the thought of the knife.

Gone, she said, unconvinced. The thought would not go.

Poof, said Hektor-Jan demonstrating the vexing disappearance with his hands. Then his eyes switched from her, to look up at Alice-Lettie.

Jy het nie my mes gesien nie, he asked. The Afrikaans, with its emphatic double negative, seemed to insist that Alice-Lettie had not seen his knife, no. The soapy sounds stopped and her maid's soft voice said, Nee, my Baas. Ek is jammer. I am sorry.

The children would not mess with it, Hektor-Jan said significantly. Not after the last time.

Janet saw little Pieter's bottom now. The redness of the knife became thick red stripes on her son's bottom. Pieter would not touch his father's special knife again. Of that she was certain. But then the scene softened to an evening image of her son standing at her husband's side of the bed looking as forlorn as sin. Her son, sin. Janet did not know what to do. She thought of the mirror in the hallway staring blankly at the world, but cunningly reflecting all that passed before it: the furniture, which did not move, the light and the shadows and the dust and the people who did. She tried to offer Hektor-Jan more than a reflection of his concern. She tried to think, tried to feel. She should not just mirror his words. She should think for herself. But there were songs too. Not simply difficult images of knives – or red bottoms and shrieks of loud pain. What would bonnie Jean do. What would her Frank say.

I need to find that knife, Hektor-Jan said. It is my –

Special knife – Janet murmured.

That my mother –

Your mother gave to you, on her –

Deathbed – said Hektor-Jan.

With her dying breath – said Janet.

Maybe not –

Her death, her breath, her knife. She died with a knife on her lips – her lips were a knife, said Janet.

Janet, said Hektor-Jan. Janet.

Janet looked up, but her husband had disappeared. He had gone and Janet could hear the Poof sound, just like a comic book when someone vanished, disappeared off the edge of a cliff. Janet leaned past her big belly and looked at the kitchen floor beneath the table.

There was no husband beneath the table. And no knife either.

When she resurfaced, Alice-Lettie was looking at her, her arms sunk in the sink, as though half-swallowed by the mouth of the sink.

These men, Janet managed to say. Then her cheeks were warm and stupidly wet.

Hau, said Alice-Lettie, My Madam, she said. And she pulled her hands free from the dishes and bowls, knives and forks, and brought her soap-sudded arms to her little Janet. Janet felt their warmth, almost heard the tiny bubbles pop so crisply in the dry air. Beneath Alice-Lettie's warm touch, Janet let herself cry.

She brushed away her tears fiercely as the children came to kiss her goodbye. Pappie was taking them to school – special treat. Wasn't that nice. Sylvia skipped off, Pieter let go of her reluctantly and Shelley stood there for a while. She was not fooled. Mommy was not suddenly coming down with a cold. Her older daughter went to the kitchen door and whistled. New-Jock bounded into sight and burst into the room.

There you go, said Shelley. You look after Mommy whilst we are gone.

Janet squeezed her arm and Alice-Lettie patted Janet on the shoulders, patted the damp spots where all the bubbles had died.

Hektor-Jan rumbled something, and then they were gone.

Some tea, my Madam, said Alice-Lettie and Janet nodded.

New-Jock's ears were soft. He liked to be scratched just behind his ears.

Then she took her tea and her dog, and left her Alice-Lettie in the kitchen. She did not have much time. She pulled her dressing gown about her bump and breathed in the cold air in the back garden.

The willow tree was a nervous tangle of thin, skittish branches. They would rattle in the wind, send clattering signals across the garden. But there was no wind. The air was hard and cold, but still. Janet breathed sharply. The edges of the cold morning smelled burnt, tasted charred. No doubt there were veld-fires. There were always veld-fires at this time of year. Dry grass, like tinder. Just waiting for a cigarette flicked from a car, then all that yellow crackled in an instant and became black and burnt. Somewhere there were fires – had been fires.

Janet stood on the bleached lawn, her mug steamed and her breath came in misty trails. New Jock snorted beside her, then trotted off behind the pampas grass. Janet did not want to look where he went; she did not want to see the pool with its bump, its own gravid mask of stretched tarpaulin.

She wandered over to the wall on her left. The rhododendrons fringed the concrete wall, still green. They gleamed in the thin sunlight against the strained blue sky. She stood by the wall. Her tea steamed.

Where was her odd neighbour. Had he gone into sudden hibernation. How strange that he did not –

No. There was a scampering sound. That was Nesbitt, surely. A little bark, then a snuffle. Janet looked up and sure enough, there came the head of Douglas van Deventer.

Ja, he said, looking down at her.

She looked up at him.

You called, he said.

Her tea breathed calmly in her hand, a warm and reassuring presence.

I don't think I did, Janet said. I did no such thing.

Desperate Doug smiled and shifted his position on the ladder.

We have got a new maid, he said. Finally.

I know, said Janet. Very young.

Just right, said Desperate Doug. We can train her. She is not set in her ways. We can teach her what to do.

Like Emily, said Janet. Then she looked down at her tea. Emily would have a bouncing baby right now. Why did babies bounce. She had not come to the wall to talk about Desperate Doug and Noreen's new maid, or to wonder about the offspring of their previous maid after her miraculous pregnancy, how she came to be with child, but without gentleman callers.

Pieter, she said. The rest of the sentence lodged in her throat. The air was dry. She did not like naming her son to this man, who never seemed to work, who just fiddled about in his garden, fossicking amongst his plants. She took a sip of tea and tried again.

My son, she said. What have you been saying to my son.

Pieter, said Desperate Doug with unpleasant enthusiasm. Klein Pietertjie.

My son, Janet said again.

What a little character, said Desperate Doug. What –

Have you asked him about a knife, Janet said. A penknife. Hektor-Jan's penknife.

Desperate Doug did not flinch. The man was brazen. Quite bold and brazen.

He is so – Desperate Doug paused for the right word. He consulted Janet's garden. He seemed to read the sky. His mouth moved again. Enthusiastic, he said. We were chatting, he continued after throwing a stick for Nesbitt, whose scampering feet came to Janet from the other side of the wall. It did seem strangely as though the scuttling sound came from Desperate Doug when he next opened his mouth. Janet tried to follow what Desperate Doug was saying, but the words scuttled and growled and he kept throwing the stick. He was hardly paying attention.

So, there you have it, Desperate Doug smiled and waved the stick, which was chewed at both ends.

Janet tried to rescue words from her memory. Had he said, Show him, Show off to him, Show it off to him. Janet cleared her throat. Why would Pieter suddenly want to show off his father's knife.

Why would Pieter suddenly want to show you his father's knife, said Janet. Her mug was heavy in her hand. Her voice made it up to the top of the wall. Desperate Doug reached out and took her words, one by one, seemed to fold them neatly and file them in the pocket of his long-sleeved shirt. Perhaps he would pop them in his ears a little later, and then reply.

He winked at her.

He leaned over the wall and tapped her lightly on the shoulder with Nesbitt's ragged stick.

I don't think you should be asking me these questions, he said. I think there is someone else who knows the answer. And I do not mean your son.

Janet tried to look into his eyes. She tried to ignore the tap of the stick that was touching her shoulder, stroking her shoulder. Desperate Doug seemed to fill the sky, and Janet felt her arms become weak, as though the stick were tapping into her life, draining her. Now it was touching her chest.

For a moment, Janet thought that her waters had broken. There was a warm trickle below her – no, beside her. Then she realised that she was spilling her tea. It pooled at her feet, a rusting stain on the yellow grass.

I think, said Desperate Doug again, with his slow, deliberate words propped up by his stroking stick. I think that there is someone else you should ask. When does our garden boy have his tea. Is it ten o'clock for you, like it is for us.

Janet shrugged off the stick. She was not good with time. It was sticky. It made her hands sticky and she got stuck. The hands of the clock in the kitchen were difficult to read. They barely moved. They seemed mired in long minutes, glued to the face of the clock, and they were so thin that they might have just been a pair of linked cracks spreading over its blank countenance. No, she was not good with time.

I tell you what, said Desperate Doug. His stick now waved. He seemed to use it to parse his sentence, to make it easier to understand. When your girl takes him his tea – you know, Solomon – then you follow her and ask him. You ask him about that knife. It's a red knife, hey.

The redness of Pieter's little buttocks tore loose to become the special penknife. The silvery gadgets stuck out at angles, like sharp hands pointing to a time when things were different.

Janet nodded. The knife was red. She was getting closer. She would ask Solomon – when Alice-Lettie took him his tea. She would wait.

She did not want to disturb him, whatever he was doing behind the pampas grass.

Her tea was cold and Desperate Doug had disappeared.

It would be a little wait, before the time that he had mentioned. She would bathe. She felt that she needed to clean herself after speaking to Desperate Doug. Not only had the tea splashed her legs, but she felt grubby again beneath his stick. At least he had not mentioned Hektor-Jan and Alice-Lettie. Janet did not know what she would have done had he spoken slyly about her husband and the maid.

Janet felt the mug, hard in her hand. She raised it to her lips and drank the last of the cold, gritty tea.

He closed the car door silently. Often, when problems were unresolved, when the scales could tip either way, he found that silence was helpful. It opened up a space – allowed things to happen. He did not want to have to push too hard. Like a squat Samson amongst the Philistines, he knew that hair grew in silence and that strength could come simply by watching and waiting. Despite his muscles, despite his powerful body, he was very good at waiting.

Also, his father-in-law's house seemed very watchful that morning. And he had no particular desire to encounter his neighbour. Each to his own, and he had just spent a delightful twenty minutes with his children, taking them to school. Listening to their chatter, telling them about Oupa's glass eye, which came out if the old man coughed or sneezed. Hektor-Jan wanted to be distracted from the cares of work. From the reports, the official concerns, the growing unease. He wanted to hug his children, cherish their perfect bodies, send them whole and happy into school. He needed to remind himself that there could be such wholeness and health, such innocence, such schools.

He wished to lock the car, and head straight into the shower, and then to bed. He did not want to see his wife, or listen to his neighbour. As the key turned in the stubborn lock, Doug's voice sounded in his ear. He turned.

Psst, came the urgent hiss from near his neighbour's cypress trees. He looked hard. Was it in the cypresses. About ten foot up the closest tree, a branch slowly parted. Doug was right above him. He could spit on the top of his head if he wanted to. If he really cleared his throat, like his brothers used to, with unerring accuracy. Hektor-Jan stepped back, further down the length of the car. He stood there, then he leaned against the Ford Cortina, looking up at the portion of Doug's face released by the rough green strands.

Doug was shaking his head. Uh-uh, he said. Don't look at me Higher. Look down, look away.

Hektor-Jan looked down. He leaned against the car and looked away, across the low wall, maybe too low these days, and over the broad pavement and road, to the grassy verge, ash-blond, and to the fence of the Bunny Park, seven-foot high and fringed with barbed wire.

Ja, he said. He tried not to be impatient. But his voice was impatient.

There was a reproachful silence. Hektor-Jan almost turned back to look up at his arboreal neighbour. A small, wiry Tarzan.

Today, came Doug's voice in the morning air. Your knife. Your wife. The garden boy. I am sorry, my friend. But if you want my help, this is what we must do.

Hektor-Jan stared for a long time at the distant jungle gym, the hanging swings and the stiff roundabout. He could make out parts of them through the trees, and beyond the mesh of the strong wire fence. His children played on those swings. He and Janet pushed them to and fro, to and fro. First Shelley, then Pieter, and then Sylvia. He had cranked the tiny roundabout so that it lurched around, nearly throwing the children from its metal rails. They had squealed, and when he had suddenly stopped it, they had reeled about as drunk as little lords. One of them had been sick. Was it Pieter. He felt sick. He felt his little world revolving around Doug's cypress tree, around the centre of his voice. And there came again and again the sickening images of his knife, his wife and Solomon. Not a wise king who offered to cut babies in two, but a dark, supple shadow that divided his heart, ripped it apart.

What must we do, Hektor-Jan said. And he turned to look up directly at Doug.

And so it came to pass.

Hektor-Jan told Alice to inform the Madam, who was in the bath, that he was going for a walk, a long walk, to clear his mind. He would be back for lunch. And he put on his boots, the old ones from his army days. And, out of habit, for he was not dressed without it, he tightened his shoulder holster, and checked that the magazine of the gun was loaded. The clip slotted perfectly into place with the reassuring click. Then he was gone. Through the front gates, looking like he was stepping out.

But in ten seconds he was next door, being ushered quickly past Noreen's bedroom window.

The dog, he whispered.

Inside, said Doug.

And then they crouched on Doug's side of their wall, behind the furious tangle of the large rhododendrons. A few of the leaves had wilted after the recent black frosts. Hektor-Jan looked at the ladder that leaned against the foliage. He noticed the worn paths at the base of the big shrubs and the way his neighbour rubbed his hands and tried not to look anxious. Gleeful.

Again, Hektor-Jan could feel his hands wanting to leap at the man's throat, make him prove that he was telling the truth, make him stop telling the truth.

There was a small bucket. It was filled with mud. Do you mind, said Doug. And put his hands in the bucket and drew them out, dripping, dark and soiled. Then he stepped close to Hektor-Jan and raised his hands. His fingers were cold and rough as he wiped criss-cross patterns of mud across his face. He moved back. Good, he said. His face was grim.

Hektor-Jan plunged his own hands into the bucket and brought them hard against the sharp little features of his neighbour. Anyone watching them would wonder at the game. Two grown men in the back garden. Smearing the camouflage. Like some pact, some manly compact, hiding their features to become masked and distorted so that teeth leapt out and the whites of eyes shone strangely. So it had been in the South African Defence Force. Every white South African male got to go into the army. Now they looked at each other. No longer white men. Men of indeterminate hue. Men made brown. Men of the earth, the dark blood and salt of the earth, with strange white patches that peered through the cracks in their camouflage.

Doug checked his watch. There was plenty of time. But they should get into position, get completely ready. Before Hektor-Jan could open his mouth, his neighbour placed a heavy hand onto his shoulder and looked into his eyes. They did not exchange a word. They did not need to.

Then they were perched in the huge rhododendron bushes, veiled by leaves. Hektor-Jan's greater weight was supported by the ladder; Doug nested further down, in the branches.

His garden lay stretched out, familiar yet strange from this perspective. The weeping willow, a scarecrow on the other side of the vast lawn. The bordering shrubs were hunched. They led down to the pool, dark and mute beneath its odd cover. What on earth was Janet playing at with that cover. Then the pampas grass, closer to them, and finally the wall, the back of Alice's kaya and the garage. It all looked like home and yet seemed not to be home. Just as the earth-stained Hektor-Jan was and was not Hektor-Jan. The skin on his face began to pull. The familiar hardening of the mud. If he moved a muscle, it would crack and split. It would get itchy. He knew that it would get very itchy.

It's ten o'clock, murmured Doug's voice through the leaves. Hektor-Jan's breath quickened. It was shallow and fast. He felt a little dizzy. He had been up for a long time.

Solomon appeared from behind the pampas grass with the young Rottweiler. Hektor-Jan stiffened. Would it smell them, sniff them out. But the garden boy and the dog were not coming their way. Instead, they moved across to the swimming pool, and stood there, looking down at the stupid cover. There was silence in the back garden. Hektor-Jan tried not to shift position. Doug was silent. He was good at this. A dove began to coo. Still, the boy and the dog peered down at the pool. There was no sign of Janet.

Then the back door opened. Would it be Alice.

It was Janet.

Hektor-Jan found himself holding his breath. He peered across at his wife, who carried a steaming tin mug before her, as though she was performing some balancing act. For a moment, Janet did not move.

She blinked in the sun. So clear, and yet so cold. It was deceiving. She could not move for a moment. She adjusted her fingers so that the heat from the heavy mug of tea did not burn her hand. There, that was better. Now she could look up, look across the garden at the rhododendrons.

She stared right at him. Hektor-Jan felt hot beneath the stupid muddy mask. He dared not blink. He dared not breathe. Like a cautious steenbok, or a delicate impala, his wife seemed to test the air. She looked nervous all right. A little way below him, Hektor-Jan heard Doug's long intake of breath. At least he seemed to be enjoying this. Janet stepped forward.

Janet felt her legs move. She stepped forward. The garden came to greet her. The crisp grass whispered underfoot and she walked a tightrope line across the huge lawn, straight to the pool and to Solomon.

Solomon, her voice managed to say. Solomon.

But he seemed lost in thought at the side of the pool, and she had to reach out and touch him.

Hektor-Jan watched. Janet raised her left hand, a white bird, ringed with the golden wedding band, the ring he had given her as well as the eternity ring, making doubly sure. The rings glinted in the thin light. And that hand, that tiny hand, reached out and touched the tall black man. Doug's breath came in a low whistle, soft enough only for Hektor-Jan's ears. It was as though the pressure cooker of Hektor-Jan's brain was beginning to steam. Jesus, came Doug's whisper, as Janet handed the garden boy his tea and he took it with a smile, clumsily holding the white woman's hand that could not seem to let go of the mug.

Her hand would not work. It seemed caught in the handle, stiff from the cold, yet fearful of the scalding tin. It stuck there awkwardly. Solomon held the mug in his rough hand, not burning. Janet had to raise her other hand and prise her fingers free. Thanks, Solomon, she said, and she laughed in embarrassment.

Thank you, my Madam, he said and slurped his tea. She stood where she was, unable to move. She had not been this close to the pool for weeks. Just like the tarpaulin, she had pulled her daily routine over her mind and tried to bury any thoughts of the crack. But she could see how it strained. How, beneath the rough material pegged down on either side of the pool, there had been much movement. It looked like the tarpaulin might soon split. Its central seam appeared strained. The rows of makeshift tent pegs almost hummed in the hard earth as the gap must have grown between them, and pulled the tarpaulin unbearably taut.

What the hell were they doing. They stood there. The kaffir looked at her. She looked at the covered pool. He had spoken; she had laughed. They were alone together. That was all. That was enough. Was it enough. A shy laugh. Her embarrassed laugh. And the boy was staring at her. Hektor-Jan felt an odd prickle. From all sides, the leaves pressed down on his body. Here they were. Three men staring at his wife. His skin felt stiff. It seemed as though the dry mud was pulling his face apart. Then Janet turned to the garden boy. She said something. He replied. He nodded, then he shook his head. His hand went to his overalls. He reached inside, deep into his pocket and Hektor-Jan held his breath. Now, he did feel dizzy. Not a sound came from Doug. No breathing, no soft blasphemy. The boy brought his hand out into the light. There, shining in the sun, as brazen and as brassy as his wide grin, was Hektor-Jan's knife. His mother's knife. The knife that he kept safe and sound. *The knife that no one but he was supposed to touch. The knife that nestled against Die Bybel in his bedside drawer. What the hell was it doing in the garden boy's pocket. The ladder shuddered beneath his feet. Hektor-Jan felt as though he was going to fall. His jaw tightened and his teeth ground as he tried not to move. It was not over yet. What more was to come. Would she hug him. Throw her arms around him. Give him a big, open-mouthed kiss. Would she turn, with his child inside her, large and right there in her belly before her, before them all, and offer herself to him.*

Jesus, came Doug's voice again. Jesus Christ Almighty.

Jesus Christ Almighty, his own lips twisted silently, and he swore with Doug's voice. Here he perched like Lazarus, waiting for the healing hand, but all he saw before him was the horror of those black hands and her white hands. And as his lips moved and Doug's Christ gasped in the smothering leaves, Hektor-Jan saw how she started opening the knife. He watched as the kaffir watched her. She struggled. Then the kaffir had the nerve to help her. To touch her hand, to take his knife from her. There. Out came the big blade, the longest, the sharpest. The kaffir handed it back to her. What were they doing. What dreadful game were they playing. Hektor-Jan swayed on the ladder. How long before he could hold still no longer, before he had to bellow and shout and reclaim his knife and his wife. But he bit his tongue. Warm, dark metal slipped down his throat as his mouth bled. He swallowed, and swallowed again, his face cruelly distorted by the drying mud.

The two figures turned to face the pool. Again, they stood there. A strange couple. He knew that it was only a matter of time before they became pillars of salt in the Sodom and Gomorrah of his back garden. Janet bent down. The kaffir stood behind her. Surely not, not there in the daylight, in front of the dog. In front of him and Doug. But his wife raised the knife and slowly sawed through one of the tight cords, which tethered the tarpaulin. It took a while. Maybe the knife was not as sharp as he thought. There was a sudden ping, and the tough string snapped. The tarpaulin shuddered, then lay still.

They watched as Janet slowly raised the loose corner. She lifted it and looked beneath it. Then she turned to the kaffir and he did the same: squatted down beside her and gawped at the dark pool beneath its stifling cover. They did not stand up. The remained there, crouching in the garden, peering at the pool.

Hektor-Jan had the strangest feeling that he could, with a single sharp word, suddenly cut the air and, quickly and terribly, lift the blue sky and the blond garden, roll them back to reveal the terrible bones that lurked beneath it all. And despite the ache in his mouth and the rigid pull of the skin of his face, despite the knuckle-bursting grip on the branches and the way his eyes popped in the dry air, it was the fearful stiffness in his groin that finally released the shuddering groan. God. The Afrikaans, God, coughed up from his chest, his heart. God shot from his throat like wretched phlegm. God spat into the morning air.

But before he could roar in the name of the father, and in the name of his mother's knife and his children's innocence, the hands of Doug pressed hard against his lips. The man materialised right beside him, out of the thick leaves, and smothered him.

No, Doug whispered in his ear. No, no, no. Not here. Not now. Later. Not in the garden. Do it later. Take your time. Take your fucking time, man.

And his knuckles nodded. His eyes tightened and the liquid iron in his throat agreed. He made a sound. Something sub-vocal – a deep sound, deeper than the holding cells in the Boksburg-Benoni Police Station. Deeper and darker than all the writhing, gurning sounds knotted together. Ja. Ja. This time, this time he would take his fucking time all right.

Slowly, with great care, Doug's stifling fingers released him.

Janet tried not to think of it as an omen. As Eileen-the-Understudy smeared make-up on her face in the busy classroom, and the helter-skelter of the opening night whirled around them, Janet tried not to think of the crack. Instead, she tried simply to watch as any tiny cracks or wrinkles on her face disappeared without a blemish beneath the cloying make-up.

At last. It had come to this night. Everyone bustled. Everyone was shot through with delicious, opening-night nerves. Their first real perform-ance. Where had the time gone. It seemed like only yesterday that –

Five minutes, called someone.

Dear God, Eileen-the-Understudy cried out, almost dropping the mascara, which feathered the dark borders of bonnie Jean's eyes. Janet raised a hand to squeeze her neighbour's arm.

Feet scuttled past the classroom assigned to the women.

Someone moaned about the rough tartan and another voice made a silly joke about a rough tart, Anne. Nervous voices shouted with laughter at the ridiculous wordplay. The lights in the classroom were very bright. All the desk lights that they had brought in for the make-up shone like hot flowers. Janet felt giddy. Bonnie Jean, she whispered to herself, Come home to bonnie Jean.

Two minutes, another voice yelled through the open door. Derek wants a word.

It's the best I can do, Eileen-the-Understudy's voice trembled. She handed Janet the little mirror. It was fine. Her face was fine. Quite bright. She glowed. And it was not just the make-up. Everyone said how she glowed. The bun in her oven made her glow. She must be the first bonnie Jean with a bun in the oven, and Janet had placed a protective arm around her belly, and had smiled. The elasticated tartan skirt was a marvel. There were more pins than usual so that the skirt did not split. But that was fine. As long as she could still dance (carefully) and act and sing (heart-ily). She was way too large to be Karen Carpenter; she was bonnie Jean.

There was a great scraping of chairs in the little classroom that spelt out a is for apple, b is for bat, c is for cat, and $1 \times 1 = 1$, $2 \times 1 = 2$, $3 \times 1 = 3$. There were children's drawings on the wall. Firemen and policemen in thick wax crayon, caricatures, angels or Icaruses flying in white heavens with puffy clouds and squiggly birds and suns that were squashed in neat corners with a prickle of yellow rays, bright porcupines shining down with light.

Like children released for a long-awaited break, the women in the cast threw themselves from the innocent classroom, out into the corridor that gleamed with cold neon light.

The last few relatives scuttled inside the Rynfield Primary School hall. Children with gloved hands keeping their applause warm for later, fathers ushering their charges with breath that came like candyfloss in the crisp Highveld night. The expectation was palpable.

Break a leg, called Eileen-the-Understudy's voice. Break your waters, she seemed to add, but it was someone else, a member of the considerable chorus, who shouted about needing more than water during the break. And there were naughty nudges and giggles as they scampered into Derek-Francis's masterful shush at the entrance of the stage door. He looked across at his Highland women from the top of the steps, and smiled. He did not say a word, just raised a funnel of fingers to his lips and kissed them expressively. Then it was thumbs up, and he threw open the door.

The warmth hit them. The hot air and the breath of the big audience, all filling the hall fit to burst. And the Highland men were waiting. All those men in their kilts and sporrans, bristling men ready to burst into song. And the murmurs and coughs and last-minute conversations of their audience welled up and flooded the stage, which they now filled, filing into their assigned positions. The curtain was still down, but beneath it and through it poured the sounds of their real, live audience! It was one minute before Derek-Francis would pull the great curtain across and unleash them – or let the audience swamp them – however you saw it. Then lights would flood the stage, and their singing would burst forth. All their preparation. All that time and effort. All carefully co-ordinated, sculpted and crafted from chaos by the fluttering hands of Derek-Francis. Benoni would become Brigadoon. The highveld of South Africa would become the Highlands of Scotland. What magic would they weave.

Weave your magic, hissed Derek-Francis, and even then, he waved a script, a flutter of white feathers as he wove a nervous flight path through the dim lighting on the stage. Then he drew himself up to his full height, and paused. It is 15 June 1976, he declaimed. We shall all remember this night. Go on, make it a night to remember.

And so they did.

They lay down and pretended to sleep. The slumber of a hundred years. They were now unconscious, and a century had slipped by. They all breathed deeply, as Derek-Francis had trained them. Someone, whose job it was to snore, snored magnificently.

The curtains gasped aside and the overture burst from the little orchestra pit. There was spontaneous applause. What an audience. For a moment the ERADS players were taken aback. For a single second, they seemed to lie there stunned. But the music propelled them forwards, upwards, slowly onto their feet. They stretched and yawned. All those hours of rehearsing took over; the practising saved them.

When Janet rubbed her eyes, then opened her eyes, she was amazed at the big bed of pale flowers. All those pretty faces, soft petals, glowing in the dark. A whole pool of soft mouths and pale cheeks and dark eyes. They moved constantly. As the opening number swelled on stage, the living sea in the hall shifted and seemed to sigh. What a gathering. All come together in the school hall to enjoy their performance. Families and friends, old and young from all the corners of the East Rand. From Springs and Sunward Park and Kempton Park, from Boksburg and Brakpan and even from Nigel, all come to Benoni and Brigadoon.

And before she knew it, it was her turn to be surrounded by excited women. And there was Eileen-the-Understudy, throwing herself with such desperate skill into her non-speaking part. Every gesture was a wild plea for attention, and as the men sang to Janet, sang to their own bonnie Jean, bonnie Jean tried to smile at the nameless Highland lass, her best friend Eileen-the-Understudy.

Then came the part that Eileen-the-Understudy had warned her about. What would her husband, her real husband make of the kiss. Did Hektor-Jan know that she was going to kiss another man on stage. Had she told him. Was it a surprise. Where did the line between art and life begin and end. What would her children say. Such were the challenges when you secured a main part. There was no place to hide. All eyes were on you. Had she considered that all eyes would be on her.

Janet swelled with pride, fit to burst. Her child danced merrily within her as the music flooded the hall again and the great chorus lifted them up on tenor wings and Highland flings. She stood there, bonnie Jean, on the edge of a great moment. Charlie would come to her soon. The chorus of men and women would single her out in a moment. There she would stand, the centre of attention and Eileen-the-Understudy would bow imperceptibly and acknowledge at last that the casting of Derek-Francis had been faultless and that she should be kissed. She would raise her face to greet the lips of her true love, and the audience would gasp as they saw the shocking likeness. Who would have thought. How had they managed that. What were the chances that the handsome Charlie and beautiful bonnie Jean were perfect reflections. Peas in a pod, repeating patterns in splendid tartan.

There would be no power cut. The hall would not be plunged into a sudden abyss of stunned silence that choked the stage and strangled the song. No, the chorus would continue. Janet shook her head. Charlie was dancing closer. He and his coterie of leaping laddies. There would be no sudden darkness. She shook her head again. Hektor-Jan would not leap up. Do you take this lawful man to be your wedded husband. Charlie came closer. Those whom God has joined let no man put asunder. Her husband would not tear himself from the crowd and split the song with his thunderous voice. Surely not. That would not happen. It was a play. All the world, well, at least Benoni, was a stage, and they merely players. It was not real. Surely everyone could see that it was not real life.

For when in real life, does a man in a lovely kilt with a lovely lilt to his voice, your very own handsome shadow, come leaping up to you during the climax of a chorus, and take you by the hand and kiss you. When does your baby flutter his tiny hands and applaud your wonderful efforts from right inside you. When does a song and the presence of a man hold so many simultaneous possibilities. Would the lights continue to burn brightly, would the song continue to be sung. Would the brave world of Brigadoon rebuff the big world. And as Charlie tilted his wilting chin to kiss her, Janet finally let go of the cold darkness outside, let go the sense of a power cut, the jangling keys from the nasty caretaker and the horrendous crack in the pool at the bottom of the garden.

Shelley's Secret Journal

Granny, all of your words begin with in. I have looked in the dictionary the big one in the lounge and every time it means not. Not definite not dubitable not eluctable. Is that because you are stuck in the care home? Is that why you keep saying why is there no room in the inn? It can also mean inn. Like baby Jesus. Is that what you mean? I winked. I winked Granny. You did not see me wink. I see for the first time that the word in is right inside the word wink. Did you say that on purpose Granny? I don't understand. I love you Granny but I don't understand. Pieter is a silly boy. He got some money from Uncle Doug for doing something and he bought some chappies but indubitably he will not share them. He says that there are plenty more where those came from. He also says that he has found a tooth and is going to put it under his pillow for the tooth fairy so that he can get more money. He showed it to me. He is inveterate about money and it is a big tooth. I asked him where he found it but then he started to cry so I did not remind him that there is no tooth fairy or Easter Bunny or Father Christmas and I did not tell him that it is not the stork that is bringing us a new baby brother or sister but that it was the sex act all along. I almost told him about that to make him grow up a bit but then I remembered what you said. Granny why did you not see me wink? I winked three times. Love, Shelley.

4.096M

I hear their spirits marching, marching in a dream
Coming like a river, swelling like a stream.

> – Sifiso Boateng, from 'Human River', translated
> from Xhosa by Hugh Marais

One day our section was summoned by radio to a remote mine shaft to help search a building. When we arrived there, we found two vehicles of the local Dog Unit also at the scene. It turned out that they actually wanted to show us how they train their dogs to attack, using live targets.

Two terrified illegal immigrants, who had been arrested somewhere, were made to get out of one of the vehicles and ordered to run. When they had covered about twenty metres, two dogs were unleashed. The dogs were cheered on loudly, and urged to bring the fleeing men down.

The dogs reached the men within seconds, jumped on them and started to bite indiscriminately. The handlers battled for several minutes to get the dogs off the men, who had deep bite wounds all over their arms and legs. This was not the end, though – the two were made to run again and again, until the poor buggers stayed down, crying and begging for mercy.

After the exercise I noticed that the handlers were crouching beside their dogs. I went closer to see what they were doing and to my astonishment, I saw that the men were masturbating the dogs. To strengthen the bond between dog and handler, I was told.

– Johan Marais, *Time Bomb: A Policeman's True Story*

For a second, she knew she was free. In the mouth of Charlie, bonnie Jean found warm delight even as the sides of the pool split and the tarpaulin was rent asunder. His warm tongue filled her mouth and silenced her gasp and he held her and steadied her as the crack tore their garden in two and stretched right to the steps of the house. Janet felt her legs shift and part. If she did not have Charlie to hold on to, she would have fallen to the stage floor, towards stage left, and maybe even have slid into the deep well of the orchestra pit.

There was a sound from the audience, a formidable sound. Was Hektor-Jan on his feet, was that him catapulting out of his hard chair and leaping to his wife's defence. No. It was the sudden sound of hands smacking hands. It was the deep breath of the big audience. It was applause. They were applauding her and Charlie at the end of the song. They loved it. Janet released Charlie's succulent mouth, pulled herself free, and gasped. A forest of wild hands. Such applause! She brought her legs back together and tried not to cry. Her breath came in little disbelieving squeals, and the cast stood there stunned. Derek-Francis was doing his nut, windmilling apoplectically in the wings. Get on with it, he mouthed, Get on with it, he silently screamed.

She tried to see whether Hektor-Jan was enjoying the show. Were her children smiling. Did they like seeing Mommy on stage, in tartan, in the arms of another man. But there were too many faces and the small orchestra had fallen silent and the play had moved on.

The feeling was back. It had never gone. Where was she. Janet clenched her fists and tried to tear her eyes from the doors at the side of the hall through which, any moment, she was sure the crack would be coming. She knew. She had the same terrible sense. The limp arms, the breathless despair. It wasn't fair. Not here. Not now in *Brigadoon*. And she tried to breathe. The edge of the stage was terribly close and the scene had shifted. The actors moved on, but she was still and Derek-Francis was flapping wildly. Janet turned as he tried to take off in the wings. Move! he mouthed For God's sake move, you silly cow.

Janet was stuck. The sound of splitting concrete, the warmth in the hall, the black coldness outside, the taste of Charlie's rough tongue, the red penknife and the smile of Alice-Lettie.

Jesus, came the strangled gasp.

But then, simultaneously, came the solicitous hands of Eileen-the-Understudy. Taking bonnie Jean by the hand and helping her along.

A fine lass in your condition, Eileen-the-Understudy extemporised with a bold laugh. Ye silly noonoo, she said, and propelled bonnie Jean into the next scene.

And Janet looked up at her and tried to smile, even though her make-up would surely crack.

The rest of the show vanished. In a welter of tender words, anxious exchanges. Brigadoon was under threat. Who would save it.

Would Fiona and Tommy acknowledge their true love. No, it was time for the interval.

They were carried back to the classroom by the hands of wild applause. There was tea and biscuits, organised by Eileen-the-Understudy, and they all crowded into the one classroom, talking at once, and laughing, and passing around the surreptitious little bottles and a hip flask. The whisky was cold fire. The brandy burned. There was even gin for good measure. They deserved it. Janet sipped it. She felt calmer. Kind, darling, dear Eileen-the-Understudy!

Her tall friend, her Samaritan, offered her another little bottle. Someone had brought rum!

They were good. But wasn't the audience great. What an audience. Well done everyone, well done! And they patted each other, and they patted bonnie Jean. What a performance. They laughed about the few missed cues, someone started someone else's line, Beryl missed her entrance, but otherwise, it was going swimmingly, just swimmingly! The little bottles of fiery conviviality flew around the rum – the room!

Then Derek-Francis called them back on to the stage. He had stayed behind to have a word with the small orchestra about some timing issues. He looked tense, but pleased. The orchestra gulped some cold tea and then the overture poured forth and the audience returned from the tables of refreshments at the back of the hall and settled once again. The lights dimmed to blackout. Derek-Francis's voice whispered. They were off.

There was less for Janet to do in the second half. It was more of a chorus role. She lent sisterly support to Fiona, but that was fine. The true lovers parted. Brigadoon was abandoned by the American men and the scene shifted – a couple of bar stools and they were in New York. Life was not good. Brigadoon was gone for another hundred years, or was it. Surely it had fallen into the great chasm of time, disappeared into the Highland mists, for another lifetime. Tommy would be doomed to wander the hills and dales, forever regretting his decision to leave.

Maybe it was the hormones, maybe the strain of the last few days, or the stress of the certain crack, but Janet could not shake that sense of loss. Poor Tommy. Wandering alone. How it made her sad. How it caught at her throat. True love, torn apart. Lovers who had touched and trembled together, now wandering alone, on either side of a century. Tommy would grow old whilst Fiona slept for a hundred years. He would wait while she tossed and turned; he would go grey while sadly she slept. Such yearning. Such loss. Such love. On 15 June 1976, Janet could not shake that awful sense. Even when the power of love brought Brigadoon back. Even when their voices swelled in the final number, Janet was trying not to weep. What if Brigadoon had not come back. It had, but what if it had not. What if Tommy continued to roam amongst the heather, forever exiled from true happiness. The sense of that suffering was too much to bear.

So she cried at the end.

The applause exploded wildly. And everyone thought that she was crying with happiness, but she was not. Her hot, silly tears kept coming. They were not tears of joy. Eileen-the-Understudy was very merry, and even Derek-Francis had forsaken his battered script and wandered around thumping anyone and everyone on the back. Well done! Yes! Wow! We did it! You did it, guys and gals!

And after all the hugs and kisses and handshakes on stage, they were released into the audience. There were friends and family waiting there for them. Waiting to welcome them back from Brigadoon, to slap them on the back and make sure that these fine players were real. What a show! What singing and acting! And Charlie and bonnie Jean, so remarkable. And Janet was flung into the arms of her family.

Sylvia squealed and hugged her mother, the reason she was up so late. Her hot face nestled into the tartan skirt. Little Pieter reached up to touch her lips, run a finger through her make-up, so bold and brassy. Bonnie Jean really was his Mommy. Shelley stood there, unmoved, beside her grandfather – and grandmother. They had come! They were smiling. At least her father was. Her mother looked through her, past her to the stage that still glowed with light and the misty hills of Brigadoon. The old woman sniffed. Why would her mother sniff. Janet bent forward to give her a kiss, and realised that her mother had been crying.

Very good, very good, her father said and laid a hand on her mother's shoulder. Your mother got quite carried away, didn't you, dear.

And Amelia Amis sniffed again and reached for Shelley who still stood there quietly.

Too hilly for Cambridge, her mother announced. Much too hilly. Mist, yes, that was good. But far too hilly. Didn't fool me once, I'm afraid. She held Shelley's hand.

Bonnie Jean looked at her father who smiled and shrugged. I did tell her, he said. I kept saying –

Professor de Laney looked very young, her mother said to Shelley. I did not know that he danced. But did he not dance well. He danced well. Very – she paused. Very nimbly.

With that she struggled under her husband's hand. Janet peered around to find Hektor-Jan and the audience thronged, reclaiming family members, who had just been to Brigadoon.

Amelia Amis – Mrs Ward – got to her feet.

Hektor-Jan, Janet started to say. But her mother had taken hold of a young man to her left, startled him utterly and was propelling him backwards, away from his friends. Mrs Ward lifted her hands and twirled before him. Professor de Laney, she crooned. Oh, Professor de Laney. Professor. De. De. De. Laney.

Granny, Shelley had the presence of mind to say, to shout. Granny! And she caught hold of one of Mrs Ward's gyrating arms and tried to pull her away. People were looking. Janet and her father grabbed other twirling parts of Mrs Ward and set the young man free.

Sorry, tannie, he said looking half-frightened, half-amazed. Jislaaik, sorry tannie, and he was gone. Just like Hektor-Jan was gone, simply vanished. And Mrs Ward set up a howl.

Pieter and Sylvia stared open-mouthed at their granny's open mouth. Sylvia put her hands slowly to her ears as her granny struggled and fought.

Professor de Laney, her mother howled and tried to pull away. Pro – she suddenly lunged forward and her teeth flew past Pieter, who set up his own cry as the dentures bit the floorboards beside his feet.

Mrs Ward's face collapsed, but the rest of her was strangely strong. They did not want to pull too hard for fear of hurting her. Her thin arms, her fragile hips.

Amelia, said Janet's father. Amelia. He tried to be gentle as he clutched at her shoulders, tried to smother her.

Mind that punt, Mrs Ward changed tack as Janet pressed her belly against her, and tried to hug her, to hold her still. Oh, the Cam is cold, trilled her toothless mother. Oh, Professor de Laney, watch that punt, please. The Cam –

Hektor-Jan's powerful arms saved the day – or the night. He appeared breathlessly, and lifted Mrs Ward off her feet.

Oh, Professor! squealed Mrs Ward to the entire school hall. Oooh, Professor!

Car, grunted Hektor-Jan.

Please, said Janet's father. Please, yes.

And Hektor-Jan carried Mrs Ward down the aisle of wide eyes and open mouths. She crooned and called all the way, shouted to the professor to unhand her, sir, and then began to expound on the manliness of her escort.

Such physique, sir, she trilled wetly, flecks of saliva flung to the world. Such strength. Such virility, her gums struggled to seize upon the word. Virility in a man is not something I object to, not at all. No, sir. As virile as you please, Professor. Heathcliff – Darcy – Rochester – Siegfried – Lucifer … the list went on and on until she was secure in her husband's car.

I'll be fine, her father reassured Janet and thanked Hektor-Jan. He took Granny's teeth from poor brave Pieter. He wiped them and popped them in his coat pocket.

Stanley Kowalski … Granny called from depths of the car, her mouth full of sticky syllables. Rhett Butler – Othello … Then they were gone.

Janet left the family at the car. She tried to run back to the classroom behind the hall to get her things. It was a last chance to hug the few remaining members of the cast and to leave Derek-Francis drinking and fussing with Frank in the corner of the little classroom, watched by a few of the women. Frank appeared to be holding a hand over his eye, and shaking his head.

He just walked up to me – Frank seemed to be saying as Derek-Francis clucked like a mother hen.

Bye! called Janet.

And the two men looked up, and the women looked up.

Night night! called Janet again and fell from their confounded stares, down the corridor and into the darkness. She was breathless. Two more shows to go. Two more nights of being bonnie Jean. And she began to sing softly.

Then they were in the car, all snug together. And then they were home and the children had to be chased to bed.

We won't talk about Granny now, said Janet wondering where Hektor-Jan had gone. Was he putting the car away.

No, I have no idea why Granny did that. Yes, it was a bit of a surprise.

Yes, I suppose Granny could have been a very good actress if she had wanted to. Or maybe a dancer if she had not had me. Now, that's enough. Night, night. Sleep tight.

Yes, the water is fresh. Now, go to sleep. No, you have just been to the loo. Go to sleep.

And Janet closed their little doors, and stood in the passage. Make-up or Milo. Should she remove her make-up or sip some Milo. The woollen tones of Lettie-Alice's radio unravelled from the kitchen and Janet was suddenly very tired. Her feet found their way to the light. Her ankles felt swollen.

Lettie-Alice smiled up at her and the kettle switched off with a click.

Madam – said Lettie-Alice. She seemed anxious.

Milo, said Janet. She could not think until she had some soothing Milo. She was back to being a child. Warm, milky Milo. Mother's milk in a mug. So gentle and soft.

Lettie-Alice knew just how to make it. Hadn't she been making it for Janet since Janet was knee-high to a cricket. Wasn't that the saying, and Janet thought about the beaming face of Jiminy Cricket. And she reached up and touched her nose, and then sat down at the kitchen table with Lettie-Alice's portable tribe of African voices, always murmuring inside the little radio, never quiet, always something to say. What busy lives.

The Milo was soothing. Sweet, brown silk.

Lettie-Alice stood beside her. She seemed to be waiting.

Sit down, said Janet softly. She needed Lettie-Alice to sit down. Where was her husband. He had not slept the entire day, and had worked the whole night. That could not be good. Was he not due to start work soon. Had he got permission to go in later, because of the show. Maybe he had already gone, was already at work. What was going on.

Janet made a slurping sound and smiled as Lettie-Alice sat down on the other side of the radio. The chocolaty voices, like the Milo, breathed life into the kitchen. Lettie-Alice reached up to switch it off, but Janet called to her over the top of her mug, No, no, leave them on. For suddenly she was knee-high once again, wandering beside the skirt of the willow tree, when it was a young tree, and Lettie-Alice was much younger too, and it was Friday afternoon and their maid was playing hostess to all the maids around them. It was a murmuration of maids in their back garden, beneath the willow tree, in the shade. She could hear their voices, and the excited radio chatting away in the background. All their voices sounded the same. Happy and full of fun. They were together. A soft, warm tribe of women. Janet stood on the other side of the veil of leaves, listening for Lettie-Alice's voice. The sun was hot and the willow tree was green and cool. She poked in a pudgy hand and parted the fronds. At that moment, something was said, possibly on the radio, and then Janet's small white face peered through the fronds and all the maids laughed to see such fun, and the dish ran away with the spoon. That just popped into her head.

Janet, Lettie-Alice's hands went up to her and her warm smell called to Janet. Sucking her thumb, and clutching her bottle of Milo with her other hand, Janet did not run across to Lettie-Alice. She made herself walk calmly, even stroll, then she nestled against Lettie-Alice and the world made sense once again. She could replace her thumb with the teat of the bottle and forget about her mother who was hidden behind her spectacles and her mutters and her big pile of papers. The Milo that Lettie-Alice had made her was almost finished, but not quite. She was going to savour it, make it last. But she could not stay in her bedroom as instructed. Even though she had set up her own Teddy and Golly and the dollies, Shelley and Sylvia, and the Clown in a tight circle beside her with the pile of coloured blocks to represent the radio and although they chatted using clicks and soft African sounds in the back of their throats, it was not the same. That week, like every other week, she disobeyed her mother's clear, repeated command, and did not remain in her room. While her mother hid behind the snakelike papers – they seemed to hiss, they were called something hissing, ess-haze – her mother would never know. Like every week, Janet left Teddy and Golly and Shelley and Sylvia and the Clown, and found herself on the fringes of the tree where, within its green heart, came the sounds of the radio and the laughter of Lettie-Alice, and Tryphena and Beauty and Francena and Grace.

Now there was just Lettie-Alice, and less laughter.

Janet needed to reach out and touch Lettie-Alice. The Milo was sweet in her throat and sugary on her teeth. The radio was comforting too. Lettie-Alice smiled as Janet reached out and held on to her arm. She sat there. It was late.

Alice did not move. The Madam's face was too much tired and she needed to touch her arm. It was as Alice's own mother had told her. Look after that little Madam, Janet, Lettie had said. She is too much small, that Janet. Try to be making that little Madam happy.

Bonnie Jean, sighed Janet. Brigadoon, she said. The radio burped cheery African sounds, thick Milo voices.

The front door opened quietly.

Janet's hand tightened on Lettie-Alice's arm.

Hektor-Jan stood in the darkness of the passage, just outside the kitchen doorway. She could hear him. She could feel him breathing.

Had he been running. Why was he out of breath. Then he stepped into the light.

This night, he had promised Doug. This very night. No matter what, he would get to the bottom of this. But to do so, he had had to start at the top, the very head and font of the offending.

When his wife had gone to fetch the children from school, he had strolled across the back garden. He found Solomon behind the pampas grass, past the spot where they had buried Jock. The young dog with the annoying bark gambolled over Jock's grave. It seemed drawn to death. He ignored it and spoke to Solomon as he dug up compost. Solomon had leapt to attention. Ja, Baas, he had said clinging to his spade and looking at the big A-frame sieve, which divided the larger debris from the filtered, smaller particles. The fine stuff, decomposed leaves, roots, kitchen waste and rich soil, would find its way back into the garden. Would once again become green plants and bright flowers. For a moment, Hektor-Jan also looked at the compost, and saw how the rough bits, the clotted scraps of bark, peel and even white cut-worms and writhing songololos, remained on the near side of the sieve, whilst the rich compost had filtered through in a fragrant, brown haze.

Dis goeie kompos, said Hektor-Jan. In Afrikaans, he continued. Jy skei die kaf van die koring – you are separating the wheat from the chaff, the sheep from the goats.

Dis goeie kompos, Solomon could only repeat. It is good compost, Baas.

You are separating the sheep from the goats, said Hektor-Jan again, a smile on his thick-set face. The wheat from the chaff.

Solomon hung on to his rake. Kompos, he tried again. Kompos.

Goats, sheep, wheat, chaff, Hektor-Jan said. His words would not fall through the sieve. They kept coming back. Hektor-Jan smiled at the tall kaffir boy with the strong arms and the worried face. Such a display of innocence. But Hektor-Jan could forgive the silly kaffir. Of course, he would not know that Hektor-Jan knew. He would be wondering what the Baas was doing at the bottom of the garden, the garden he seemed to have forsaken because he worked night shifts and because there was always something that needed to be sorted out with the cars, in the front garden. Or else he was a sleeping presence in the house that kept Solomon working quietly in the back so that he did not go whistling or cutting or digging or raking in the front garden close to the Baas's bedroom window. That's what the Madam said.

They stared at the sieve. Solomon could not look him in the eye. Hektor-Jan peered up at Solomon. Solomon, he said. Solomon's hands gripped the spade more tightly. Solomon, I need you to help me with something.

Ja, Baas, seker Baas, said Solomon, glad to be able to move, anxious to please. He leaned the spade against the sieve.

No, said Hektor-Jan. Not now. Just now. Later this afternoon. You keep up the good work. You keep sieving those goats and those sheep. I shall come and get you. Later.

And he left. Solomon watched him walk past the grave, and when the new dog jumped up at the Baas, the Baas lifted a quick knee so that the dog fell back winded, too surprised to yelp. Then the Baas was gone around the other side of the pampas grass, back into the house where he lived. The big white man would be dark and silent inside and Solomon would have to be quiet outside.

Solomon stood there. Then he called the dog. Jockie, he murmured, Jockie. And the dog's ears were soft and he whined and tried to lick Solomon's hands as he stroked him behind his ears. Solomon stroked him for only a short time. The dog continued to whine.

Hektor-Jan blinked in the light. He seemed annoyed by the light.

Janet let go of Lettie-Alice.

Lettie-Alice, as though freed, stood up. She held out her hand to Janet's empty mug.

I wash it, she said.

Janet looked into the mug. Where had all the Milo gone, all the soothing Milo. Her fingers would not uncoil from the mug. She raised it for one last, futile sip. It was empty. Even the radio seemed hollow. There was a long silence behind the murmuring voices.

You can go now, said Hektor-Jan.

Janet looked up.

It was Lettie-Alice, who responded first.

Master, she said. Madam, she said. Then she took her radio. The door and the screen door closed quietly. She was gone.

Hektor-Jan remained standing in the doorway.

Janet peered at the brown rind in the mug. She braced herself.

And Hektor-Jan said, There is something – I need to show you.

There is something – I need to show you.

Where had Janet heard those words. Said in the same way. Decisive, yet somehow sad. Tough, but almost reluctant. Her husband's heart on his sleeve.

There is something – the slight pause – I need to show you.

It was the need. The need nudged her. As needs must.

She remembered.

It was the first time she met Hektor-Jan.

It was in Benoni. Down town. It was in CNA – the Central News Agency. Where they sold books, newspapers, magazines and a world of white paper and stationery. Even toys. Years before, her own Teddy and Golly and Shelley and Sylvia had come from CNA. Purchased to secure her silence no doubt, so that she disappeared away from the ess-haze.

Janet was with her mother. She was nineteen, maybe twenty. They were looking at books, not toys. Perusing the classics. Her mother was loudly berating the paucity of choice, the scarcity of stock, the affront to her academic sensibilities.

Janet was at university. George Eliot was going well. *Middlemarch* was – Janet's forehead wrinkled with the effort of remembering, crooked images ran across her mind – *Middlemarch: A Study of Provincial Life* was, well, long. There was lots to it. So many moving parts, so many connections, so socially engaged. Casaubon lurked in his study. His book of books threatened to fall from her mind. Janet just wanted to touch the white paper in the stationery section. Leave the books with their ramrod spines, so stiff and sententious, and run her hands across the white surface of the A4 paper, so neat. So simple. No words wriggled on the surface of the white pages. She did not have to pore over the blank pages. They were soothing, not vexing. She would not have to write any ess-haze about any of the blank pages. No ess-haze for her mother to mark and to push back at her and to say, Almost, but not quite, my girl. Now, when I was your age, at Newnham –

But Janet had peeled away from her muttering mother. People passing them often stared, and Janet tried to slide from her mother's too-audible imprecations and sidle across to the stationery.

She did stroke the blank pages, so untroubled by lines, or by letters that looped into strings of sentences that cut across the pristine white, that scarred it and scared her. She felt the whiteness. It was soothing. It was calm.

But then came the trouble.

The big policeman.

The man in burly blue, with so many lines running across his body. Belt, bright buttons, epaulettes, neat cuffs. Beside the white paper he was a confusion, an obfuscation of stripes and unspoken sentences. Janet could still hear her heart in her mouth. She seemed unable to speak.

First came the Afrikaans, a rumble.

It was a storm of dark sound in the sky of her mind. She was still stuck in the blank pages. Her mind would not move; it was stationery.

Daar is iets – ek moet vir mejuffrou wys.

Then the translation, for the startled miss.

There is something – I need to show you.

That made an impression. That moved her, along with his arm.

I have been watching you, he said. And he nodded across several aisles, to where the afternoon sun slanted into the window, and threw dust into the air, so that that portion of the shop seemed furious, every dust-mote irate. And in the salt-and-pepper storm on that side of CNA, her mother glanced up.

Look, said the policeman.

Mrs Ward looked down.

The policeman took Janet towards the sunshine. It was as though they were about to plunge into a pool of silver fire. If Janet recalled correctly, she actually held her breath.

They rounded a corner of sunshine.

Just in time to see her mother slip another book through the top of her blouse, into her bra. Then her hand came out, leaving her chest big and square. Her slight mother with a big, square chest. It was ridiculous.

Hektor-Jan looked at her. That is two now, he said.

They stood at the top of the aisle.

Janet's mother turned to another shelf. She still muttered. Her hands fluttered like birds, and she tried to press them under her arms. Maybe she did not want to steal a third book. But they escaped and alighted on yet another paperback, dragging her mother behind them. Mrs Ward moaned. It looked like she was drowning in the busy dust that haloed and auraed around her. She was a floundering angel in a sea of luminous dust. Her chest was awkward and square: maybe wings would sprout from her heart or from her breasts.

I needed to show you, said the big policeman.

His presence was solid, just as her mother's was ethereal. Amelia Amis seemed to be choking in the thick sunlight. Her hands did reach out to another book.

Janet could not move. So the policeman moved.

As Amelia Amis clutched at the third book, her hands shaking, he placed a firm paw on her shoulder. His other hand caught her by the wrist.

Dankie, tannie, he said softly.

Janet blinked. His voice was so soft.

And it could have ended there. It would have been the simplest thing. The policeman would have kindly, but sternly, unclasped her fingers from the book and returned it to the shelf. Then his sorrowful eyes, his polite murmur would have requested that the tannie, the auntie – so respectful, so archaic – remove the books from her bloes, her blouse.

But her mother did not hang her head in shame and slide out the stolen books, which would never become wings.

She stared at the big square man, with his hand on her shoulder and his uniform in her face. In the silver light, his uniform was as blue as oblivion and his buttons sparkled like stars.

Who's there, her mother said. Haughty and correct, her head erect.

The books, said the policeman gently.

Nay, answer me: stand and unfold yourself, said her mother and Janet felt the jolt of recognition of that opening scene on the battlements. CNA had suddenly become the topsy-turvy world of Elsinore. Something was rotten – but who was this policeman.

Tannie, said the man again. He did not remove his hand from her shoulder and he still held her by the wrist. The book was frozen in the fiery air.

Amelia Amis raised her chin. Her words were unashamed, defiant.

Looking up at the policeman, she looked down on him.

You come most carefully upon your hour, she sneered.

The policeman turned to Janet. His soft brown eyes said, Look, lend a hand. If this tannie is your mother, why don't you step in and help here. I have your mother by the shoulder and the hand. This might seem like a complicated dance, but it is not. This is no citizen's minuet or tango. This is an arresting tableau.

But Janet could only stare. The big, kind man. Her fierce, small mother. The slanting air and the way her heart beat just beneath the surface of her eyeballs. And the shelves of books, all trapped, spines in lines, rigid and stiff, their pages pulsing with the thoughts and struggles of countless characters and dead writers. Was this a book shop, a police station or a mausoleum. Was she –

Her mother trembled with rage, and spat at the policeman. Peace, break thee off, she hissed and the flecks of spit did fly up in the late-afternoon sunlight. Yes, she dealt her bitter words like blades.

The policeman let her go.

But only to unclip the handcuffs that swung from his belt. He moved swiftly. There were two clicks and Amelia Amis suddenly stood, still holding on to the book, with handcuffs adorning her wrists. She looked down in distaste, then up again.

She drew herself up to her dignified best, and faced the policeman, her heart square, books beating in her chest. For this relief, much thanks, Amelia Amis said and the savage irony made Janet gasp.

The policeman did not gasp. He grasped her mother and led her to the cashier, to open her heart, then out of the shop and into his car. Janet followed blindly, as she had always followed her mother. In a daze, determined not to see.

There is something – I need to show you, said Hektor-Jan again and he came into the kitchen. Janet's eyes flicked up to the cookbooks on the shelf. Then she glanced at the door through which Lettie-Alice had disappeared. What could it be – Lettie-Alice, or was it the programme for *Brigadoon*. Or maybe, at last, at long last, it was the crack. Maybe he had finally seen it and she did not have to bear the burden alone. A fissure shared –

Her hand flew up to her face. At last –

He stood before her, watching her eyes move. She looked down. His hand was on her shoulder and, as she arose, she pressed up against its downward warmth.

Are you going to arrest me, she almost said, but he looked so sad, she did not speak.

Come, he said. And he switched off the lights –

The house settled into darkness and their children slept in their cosy beds.

And he led her out the front door, which he closed behind them –

The night was cold. Clouds blanketed the sky. Their breath came in tight wisps.

Maybe there was something wrong with the cars. There was certainly something wrong with the streetlights. They were off –

He led her past the cars, parked outside the garage, an arm easing her through the side door, which squeezed between the house and double garage. It did not squeak at all. It must have been oiled –

They stepped into the dark back garden and he led her up to the door of the garage. Lettie-Alice's kaya was on their left. Her lights were already off. The building brooded large and square. Janet could sense it rather than see it in the overcast night. Just as she could feel the crack. How it had come winging its way from the pool. She could not turn around, but she knew it was there. Right there. Her husband stood behind her. His warmth pressed against her. Just as the knowledge of the crack oppressed her –

She held her breath; he breathed loudly in her ear. His child stirred deep in her womb. A memory moved too. Midsummer – the start of the year. A dream. Was he going to sweep her up in his arms. Would he sweep her off her feet and carry her inside the garage. The glimmer of a memory made her smile, made her think about smiling and she turned towards him, his name on her lips –

But Hektor-Jan reached past her and opened the door to the garage. It swung away on oiled hinges, silently revealing a rectangle of blackness, deeper and richer than the surrounding night. And there came the smell –

Stap, he said in Afrikaans. Walk. He was not going to carry her over the threshold. She held her breath –

Hektor-Jan nudged her and Janet stepped into the garage. The oily, manly scent of the place hung in the darkness. Her breath leaked from her. She had to inhale. She tried not to, but she had to. Hektor-Jan closed the door behind them –

Janet waited. The air was thick in her lungs. She coughed just as there came another sound. For a moment, Janet felt as though she had turned ventriloquist and her voice had been pitched to the opposite side of the garage. Stolen by the darkness, which now mocked her. Both cars were in the short driveway. The garage was an empty cavern of sweat and oil, and now a disembodied voice. Still there was no light –

Hektor-Jan spoke.

It was his sad voice.

Hoekom, he said in Afrikaans, yet again. Why had he lapsed into his native tongue.

And as Janet said, Darling, and reached out to touch him where he surely wanted to be touched, for she was bonnie Janet, there came from the other side of the darkness a sigh of, Nee –

No –

But was it the Afrikaans no, nee, or the English near. So similar. So near yet so no. Janet shook her head, was she going mad. She was hearing voices. A voice –

Hektor-Jan moved. She felt his warmth fall away from her back and he was gone into the blackness –

Janet trembled. This was so strange. And after the bright lights of the stage and the camaraderie of *Brigadoon*, now here she was in the pit of the garage with her husband and a voice. Was he possessed. And even as she began to hum Come home, come home, come home to bonnie Jean, she wondered where New-Jock was and why he had not greeted them with snuffles and licks when they came into the back garden, his doggy domain.

A match flared in the blackness and seared Janet's eyes. For a second, the world was bright and the walls of the garage rushed up and at her. The old wardrobes with oily tools and shelves with hammers and nails. Then the darkness slammed shut and Hektor-Jan cursed. She could hear the box of matches and she braced herself, squinting into the great blackness, flinching at the sharp light, which would stab again –

There it came, the swift scrape of a match, but it stumbled to a small splutter and there was nothing. Hektor-Jan did not say a word this time. Why did he not switch on the light. Was there an electricity failure. What was going on. The matches scuttled in the box –

Bonnie Jean strummed in her throat and Janet had the distinct sense that this had become a game of hide-and-seek. Like when the strange policeman had driven her and Amelia Amis home instead of to the police station. He had asked for directions and had followed them to the letter. Then he had helped her mother up the steps to the front door and had removed her handcuffs and had warned them gently. No further action would be taken. But a week later, he was back and asking for a date. And Janet was puzzled, but had tried not to wonder why and before she knew it, he had arrested her heart. They were in the flickering darkness of the bioscope, the cavernous Lido in the centre of town, watching a film that neither remembered. They were too busy in the dark as his hand sought her hand, and his shoulder moved closer. More images winked unseen as she turned to him and met his mouth halfway across the gap in the seats. And they smoothed over that crack with their lips and it was the first time she had tasted a man's mouth. Then their hands looked for more of each other – and it became a game of passionate hide-and-seek. Sudden and exciting. Warmth and soft skin. Silent gasps and the complicit sense of give and take. Amidst the popcorn and the murmuring soundtrack and the pulsing light and the empty seats on either side of them.

Come home, whispered bonnie Janet as her husband struck another match and she felt weak at the knees. Come home, and the match burst into light and stayed lit. Janet clutched at her big belly.

The world leapt backwards now, rushing away from the point of the match and hurtling towards strange shadows in corners and behind the great bulk of Hektor-Jan, who blocked out half the world.

The he stepped aside. And there it was –

What was it –

Christ –

Bonnie Jean Jesus –

Hoekom, repeated her husband as the match gave up its ghost of light and the world collapsed again. The rat-like sound of the matches came –

Janet opened her mouth and another moan echoed from the wall opposite her.

What was Hektor-Jan doing. Why the matches, why the lack of light. What in God's name –

Vrou, he said quietly, Woman. He struck another match, 'n vuurhoutjie, a small firestick –

Before her, crucified on the wooden rack that was nailed to the wall, the rack from which hung saws and rope and old paintbrushes and rags, there now hung the form of a man, a glistening Christ. He glowed redly, then he was eaten by the darkness –

A pause. Another match –

He leapt back at Janet. This red hanging man, his head on his chest, deep in painful thought, his entire body shining red. Was this a game of cowboys and Indians. This red man was spat out of the darkness, summoned by the fire of a tiny match –

Kaffir, said Hektor-Jan quietly as the light retired from its dance with darkness. And as the blackness pirouetted, the figure of the man seemed to be caught up in its movement, and he shuddered and lifted his head and, in the last glimmer of light, Janet saw that it was Solomon. Hanging on the wall of their garage, like a child's picture of Jesus coloured in red by a careless wax crayon, dripping at the edges, was Solomon. Even his eyes were red. The moaning sounds came from him –

Hoekom, said Hektor-Jan again in the deep night of the garage. Why –

This time he waited longer –

The sharp syllables of his Hoekom cut odd shapes in the darkness. Solomon, swathed in red, floated before her, swam on the surface of her eyes. She could see him even though there was nothing to see. The box of matches rattled again as her sight failed her and Solomon disappeared –

Solomon, she gasped. The child spun in her womb as her belly lurched –

And then he was back, sudden and sharp and looking straight at her. He was strung out on the wooden rack like a garden tool, a human implement. Beside the serrated silence of the rusted saws, great steel crocodiles, metallic and flat, somehow dehydrated, surrounded by the limp bats of oil cloths, like the sodden hankies of giant machines, and ropes as careless and yet as binding as rumour and suspicious thoughts, there he hung. Their very own red man. Janet sank to the floor. Would have sunk to the smeared concrete floor, but even as the match died Hektor-Jan had her in his arms and he supported her. He would not let her collapse. No. Nee. Not here –

She had a question to answer and his Hoekom whispered hot and urgent in her ear –

His grasp was firm and big. He was warm and strong –

In that cold garage, she had no choice –

Her mouth twisted and she cried out, but she made no sound –

She tried to breathe in. She tried to find breath, to fill her chest as she hung there, too, suspended on the strong arms of Hektor-Jan. And he was able still to extract a match, and to scrape it before her eyes, and to whisper Hoekom as it flowered in front of her –

She twisted and writhed. The match arced and waved wildly. Still she could not breathe. The match died.

But then she found her feet and had to stand and breath shuddered into her lungs. Hektor-Jan let her go and she crouched, hands on knees and looked up as the strike of the match brought Solomon yet again before her –

His head had sunk once more onto his chest. What was wrong with him. Why was he hanging in their garage. Why was he red. He looked as though he had been peeled. As though someone had carefully and systematically peeled all the skin from his body so that he hung there, a red man, an oozing, glistening, crucified Christ. In the instant of the flame, she could see his muscles and his sinews. His lithe body was delineated as never before. Even his hair was matted with scarlet curls, a crown of tender thorns –

A drop of blood ran down his bent forehead. It gathered stickily on the tip of his nose that pointed to the floor – and then it fell –

The new match caught the splash of that crimson pearl. It sank into the sheen of the little black and brown blanket beneath Solomon's feet. The crumpled mess of the blanket that looked oddly familiar. And, as the silent cliffs of darkness crashed together, Janet saw that it was not a blanket. It was the dead puppy, New-Jock –

Now she screamed. Bonnie Jean withered and died in her throat and the scream shot forth. And she felt herself falling. Dropping as from a great height. Hektor-Jan had let her go. The oily concrete received her. Her knees smacked hard and her wrists jarred. Like New-Jock and Jock before him, she had become a dog. And even as the match whispered against the rough strip and sang with fire, Janet was scrabbling to her feet and screaming. Light seemed to pour from her mouth. She was fighting to stand up, and to wade across the space. To shake New-Jock and to set Solomon free. Her voice, shrieking in the soft glow, summoned them, but New-Jock did not move and Solomon only hung there solemnly –

And before she could reach out and touch either of them, the poor tortured creatures, and before she could turn to husband and ask What, and Who, and repeat his Hoekom, his Why, his free hand gripped her by the back of the neck and she was led into the light, closer to the guttering flame, which wobbled so precariously on the end of the tiny spear of wood. And she was brought face to face with Solomon –

It was Solomon. She could see that now. And his skin had been stripped from his face, peeled back like a dark fruit to expose the fresh juice of his innermost self. What had happened. What terrible accident, what tragedy had befallen him. And even as her face was thrust close to his, she tried to turn to her husband in trembling consternation –

What. Who. Why.

Tell me, said Hektor-Jan's voice. And even as his grip on her neck was hard, his voice was soft and sad. And she was brought right up to Solomon so that she felt the moist warmth, fresh from his open face. And when the words, Tell me, came again, it was with the insidious voice of Meneer Yuckulls, who also had hung from a wall, but he was hard and bristling, whereas Solomon was so soft and silent –

Tell me, said Hektor-Jan, with such sadness, and his finger swam past her and caressed Solomon on his raw cheek. And as his head jolted in pain, Janet did not know whether Hektor-Jan wanted her or poor Solomon to answer him, to tell him. What could they say. Solomon moaned again, his eyes rolled past her in his private agony, and Janet could do nothing but open her mouth in a great silent scream. The blood was going to burst from her own skin. She, too, was going to rupture like fruit, overripe with horror and maternal sympathy for this poor man and the dog, dead at his feet –

Then another match came and Hektor-Jan's hand floated past her face. She looked down and saw it brush against Solomon's broad chest. Then she noticed for the first time, another nub of red, like a broken rib. The protruding red bit, with a little logo, a cross unsullied and still golden. It was the penknife. The one she had reclaimed from Solomon and then returned to her husband's bedside drawer. Her silly husband, so upset about a stupid knife, the sentimental fool. Now it was half-buried in Solomon's chest and even as she stared at it, little bubbles gathered and burst at its base. Solomon wheezed and she saw that the knife must have punctured his lung, for the bubbles came and went as his red chest with the nipples sliced off tried not to heave –

Despite Hektor-Jan's heavy hand on her neck, Janet reached out and touched the knife. Her fingers took hold of its slippery surface. It was warm with Solomon's blood. Her fingers became smeared with the blood of her brave friend. The match flickered with emotion and Hektor-Jan made a strange sound at the back of his throat like a dog. Soon the little flame would burn his fingers and the blackness would come again. Still, Janet's fingers gripped the knife. Her hand tightened on the nub of the knife and, as the match curled and died, she pulled it –

As the darkness leapt forward, Solomon looked up in pain. He must have seen the knife in her hand, the bright metal made velvet with his own blood – or he might have somehow recalled hot tin mugs of sweet brown tea. His vision might have blurred as he tried to smile in that last flicker of light and his lips whispered huskily, Thank you, my Madam –

And as the darkness came again, Janet wept. She wept for the poor man before her. The fine man, who had been so lithe and strong and helpful, who had stood by her in the battle against the crack. She wept for his shining ebony skin, now stripped away. She wept for the honest sweat that would never again glisten on his lovely skin, such a sheen of kind, strong endeavour. And she wept beneath her husband's rough hand for the dog at her feet, another crushed, maimed animal. And for her children, and for her unborn child, and for herself. And also for her strange husband. What. Why. And she tried to turn towards him in the dark. What had happened here in this dark garage. She struggled to turn in the blackness, Solomon's blood sticky on the knife, fusing her hand with its red base embossed with the golden cross, and its blade stabbing the darkness –

He could feel her move, could he not. His hand was right around her throat –

So, it is true, he said –

So, Doug was right all along, he said –

And the breath gathered in her throat and the pressure burst open her lips and she coughed up the dirty sound. Doug!

Something shifted on the far side of the garage in the gap between the old wardrobes –

It was not easy. Who would have thought that a garden boy would be so resilient. Such a tough nut to crack. So he had peeled him.

He had led the limping boy into the garage in the late afternoon, just before he would have used the maid's toilet and tiny basin to clean up and change into his smart clothes. Before his long legs took him off their property and out into the street.

Kom, he had said to him. And the kaffir did as he was told. He came into the garage where Doug was waiting. Hektor-Jan closed the door. Now they were all kaffirs together in the sudden blackness. The world had become kaffir. And the darkness comprehended it not.

Hektor-Jan waited.

It was happening, happening right here in his home. He could feel it. The instant exhilaration, the clean certainty. The energy surged in him, even though he had not slept for a long time and his hands had been shaking. Now they were steady. Like the rock of ages. In the blackness, nobody said a word. Not even a sudden, Baas, my Baas, from the kaffir.

Let there be light, said Hektor-Jan's voice and he switched on the dangling light bulb that suddenly shone very bald and bare from the rough ceiling.

Before the kaffir could pick up a tool, or shout or strike out, Hektor-Jan nodded as agreed and Doug spoke his name. Solomon.

And as he knew that he would, Solomon turned to his other Master and did not see Hektor-Jan's practiced hands. They bunched into fists and his thunderous right struck Solomon just above his ear, in the temple, and Solomon did not even say, Baas, or register any surprise as he fell.

They let him fall.

He was out for the count. It would be several minutes.

He lay at their feet, a pool of limbs, a dark mass on the oil-stained floor.

Doug bunched his hands into fists too, and punched the air just as Hektor-Jan had punched Solomon and felled him. Doug's little right fist flashed in the light and then he kicked the tangle of Solomon at his feet.

No, said Hektor-Jan, holding up a hand. Wait.

Doug did not know what was ordained, what was supposed to happen next. His neighbour had no clue. They had to lift up the kaffir. Slump him onto an old garden chair and tie his hands behind his back and knot his feet together. That is what they had to do. You did not just hit out. You did not just go mad. This was a dance. And Doug watched in wonder as he lifted the limp kaffir and spun with the body, weaving it into position, upright, swiftly secure, knotted into place. Only the kaffir boy's head lolled. The rest of him was roped and ready. There. That was what you did.

Man, said Doug, impressed. Man.

But Hektor-Jan was lost in the subtleties, in the finer nuances of rope and consciousness. He slapped Solomon's cheeks and the kaffir boy stirred. His black Adam awoke.

And then it began. Whilst his wife got ready for her show and his children tackled their homework at the kitchen table, tongues out, pens and pencils clutched in fierce concentration, he, their father, set about his work. He put a finger to his lips, and smiled silence at the kaffir. He brought the penknife glittering up to the kaffir's face, waved it in front of him and dared him to cry out.

Ek wil nie jou tong afsny nie. I do not want to cut out your tongue, he said in Afrikaans. The word, sny, slid into the kaffir's face. It was a sly word, a most significant word. Moenie skreeu nie. Therefore do not scream, he said in his native tongue, so that the native would hold his tongue. And the word, skreeu, swivelled in the quiet garage, like the English screw, but not quite. It was longer and sharper and more menacing by far. Its twisting vowels dug deeper.

Solomon nodded at the knife. He agreed with its silver blade and bowed to the blood-red handle. He ignored the squealing, strange sounds

The Crack

that the other Master was making, the way the little man patrolled the edges of the garage, grunting and squeaking to himself.

Baas, Solomon whispered to the knife. Baas, when I am breaking the old lawnmower, and the new weedeater, I am sorry, Baas.

You are sorry, Hektor-Jan used the same hushed tones. You are sorry.

And – Doug's throttled conjunction added his voice to the fray.

Solomon seemed not to hear him.

You are sorry, Hektor-Jan said again, his voice hardly audible. Seemingly overwhelmed by sadness.

Solomon trusted himself only to nod.

But what about the Madam, said Hektor-Jan still sorrowfully, still leaning forward, having to stand whilst their garden boy sat in state before them. What about the Madam and this business with the pool.

Sjoe, Solomon shook his head sorrowfully. That one, he said, that one. And he did not say any more. It was as though there was nothing more he could say.

Hektor-Jan waited. They always said more. The longer you waited, the more came out. It was a simple law of physics, of psychology, of speaking in tongues.

But Solomon did not say anything more. He kept shaking his head. He breathed in deeply and frequently, but no words came. That is when Hektor-Jan drove the knife deep into his chest, between the ribs, into his lung so that the pent-up sounds would be released.

Baas, gasped the kaffir boy, apparently in disbelief. Baas, was a gasp, a wheeze, a sigh as he looked down at his chest.

That was better. It was something. They could work with Baas. It was the silence that was so frustrating. For in the beginning, there had to be the word. And the word was Baas, and the word was now with the Baas, and Hektor-Jan and Doug saw again that it was good.

But what about the Madam and this business with the pool, Hektor-Jan said a little more loudly for the wheezing sound was worse and the urine splashed noisily onto the concrete floor, and Doug seemed oddly excited about the kaffir boy pissing himself. Hektor-Jan shifted his feet back a little. How many shoes had he given to the maid to polish, to protect from such sudden effusions.

The Madam, he prompted again.

He would have left a fertile silence after that third query. It was better, so often, to keep one's counsel, whilst they pissed out theirs. You held your tongue, and that loosened theirs. It was a good deal. This trade-off with silence.

But Doug was on a roll. His face suddenly swept down beside the kaffir boy's and he screamed, The Madam, the Madam, you fucking kaffir. I saw you. Don't think I didn't see you. He knows, Doug changed tack, pointing to Hektor-Jan, Don't you see he fucking knows.

Thank you, said Hektor-Jan as Doug threw himself back and continued to patrol the garage. The man was hysterical.

The kaffir boy sat in bubbling silence.

Hektor-Jan permitted himself a brief break. He stood upright, and moved over to his neighbour. He placed a hand on Doug's shoulder. He spoke in low reassuring tones, but what he said was decisive. Doug nodded. Ja, man. I'm sorry, man.

Then Hektor-Jan was back. His attention was completely devoted to the garden boy. Tell me, he said, inviting confidence, but scaring the shit out of the kaffir. The smell was unbelievable.

Hektor-Jan saw it coming. The signs were there. First the piss and then the shit. The writing was on the wall. The excrement was in the air. And so, it was written, so it would come to pass, that he would bring in the dog, the new dog. And if the kaffir had a high pain threshold, as they called it, then maybe he would speak whilst the dog screamed with a voice made human by pain. But if that did not work and the dog died with a song in its throat, just like the other one had died because it had kept him awake and simply would not shut up and for other deeper, darker reasons he had not fathomed, then there were additional means, further methods. It would have to be the genitals. He would have to make his *privates public. There were plenty of pliers in the garage. He would not have to send any corporals out and about to fetch new tools. No, there were pliers and rasps and screwdrivers and even the saws with their fine, ragged teeth. And Solomon would have to watch as his future children had their toes trimmed. Were truncated, were suddenly maimed and made lifeless. Or, there was another way. Hektor-Jan knew the sudden surprise if you simply took a kaffir in hand and toyed with his soft tool. How the terror might make him piss-damp and slack, but when you rubbed and teased and coaxed him out of his fucking fear, the results could be oddly surprising. He might respond against his will. He might be hard up with little to offer, but he might bring something to the table. Stare in shock as his revolting excitement grew and came to realise just what a white man in power might do. How it might come to this. Betrayed by his own body. Convulsed by the hideous pleasure of this white man's hands. How quickly his own penis became Judas. And the small Master squealed and choked in the background as his hot seed spilled all over the oily floor. And Hektor-Jan knew that if all those promptings did not do the trick, they could always crucify him. String him up. There was a rack behind him. The penknife was keen. There would be other ways, Hektor-Jan was sure. When you gave yourself to the dance, when you no longer thought but simply acted, when your movements came unbidden and beautiful, when you were in tune, that's when it happened.*

Now, tell me about the Madam, Hektor-Jan said softly, wiping his hands.

The morning would dawn cold and drear. It was going to be an overcast day, that morning of Wednesday, 16 June 1976. There would be no sun –

Janet opened the garage door and peered out into the new world. It was still dark. There was iron in the air –

She eased her belly through the little gap then closed the door behind her. Still dressed as bonnie Jean, with make-up caked and smeared with tears, she seemed to tiptoe off stage, across the little paved area to the

Christopher Radmann

back door. Her movements were slow, but certain. She had little time, but to move took so much effort. Her time was upon her. She dared not look up. The crack was there. It had come –

She reached the shore of the back door, and clung to the handle. Her belly heaved and she had to stop. Was it locked. She paused, then she opened both doors in the darkness and half fell into the house –

Her breath came loudly. She was already hoarse, but her lips still maintained the mantra, bonnie Jean. It was all she had left. Bonnie Jean, the memory of *Brigadoon*, and her children –

Shelley. Pieter. Sylvia.

They were warm and snug. But not for long. The penknife was slimy in her hand. It was warm and slippery and for a moment she thought that she had dropped it, but it was still there. Had it cut her hand too –

First Shelley. Then Pieter. Then Sylvia.

She eased them out of their cosy sleep. It was time. They had to come –

Mommy, said Shelley almost crossly in her sleep and she had to say, Shelley, with the most urgent of whispers. Pieter was rubbing his eyes and asking about Jock and Sylvia needed to wee, but there was no time. No time at all –

They were half-swaddled in their dressing gowns as she ushered them down the passage, through the dark kitchen and out of the back door –

Quickly, quickly she kept murmuring in their little warm ears, but she did not touch them with her bloody hands –

Then they were outside in the black dawn, the last shiver of night. Janet guided them past the garage and Lettie-Alice's silent kaya and along the grass beside Doug and Noreen's wall with the scarecrowed rhododendrons tall and still. What would Doug do now –

Janet bit her lip and held out her arms like a shepherd. Her children moved with her, hunched figures under the greying sky. Janet was a big mother hen –

They slipped past the pampas grass, past old Jock's grave and the thought caught in her throat. Then they veered off across the top of the garden towards the pool. All the time, Janet tried to concentrate on what they were doing, but all the time she kept glancing to her left, to see if they were safe –

They made it –

At the far end of the pool, they assembled. A tiny huddle of dressing gowns and more yawns and half-hearted complaints –

Janet held them to her, and they slumped onto the slasto together, the cold slasto, the crazy paving was damp beneath them. Janet pressed them to her great belly, so full, so gravid. Her tight skin shuddered. Her arms would not reach around all of them –

Shush, she said. Not a sound –

They were good children. Mostly, they were very good children. They would do as they were told. They would hunch down with her, hunker down in the darkness, which was already becoming grey. The air was damp and cold. Their breath came and went, came and went in little wisps. Small ghosts that got lost in the grey of the dawn as they huddled together. Janet steeled herself –

She looked over their little heads, down the length of the garden –

Was it simply darkness. Were there just shadows. No –

No. In the first grey light of the new day, she could see it. There could be no doubt now –

It was the crack. It was huge –

And the empty pool swam into focus as the light came, the lightening of the eastern horizon. The whole length of the ruptured pool was yielded up and Janet pressed her children to her. And even in the hushed silence, with just their little breaths, there seemed to be other sounds. Things were on the move. The fissure was swimming still, the crack was creeping –

And in the burgeoning light, Janet looked down the length of the garden. Her eyes followed the dramatic zigzag of black, the great crack that unzipped the garden, split it into two jagged sides and tore right up to the house. And even as Janet looked, the crack seemed to dive beneath the house with a black sound. They had just made it. She had got the children out in the nick of time. The house seemed to shudder. There was certainly a splitting sound. Janet gasped. Her father's house. Their home –

The sky grew more grey, but that made the crack seem all the more dark. Oh, it was deep. The white sides of the pool were yielded up by the shattered tarpaulin, which had torn, had been rent asunder. The pool was splintered, utterly shattered and the great chasm sheared off into the garden and all that Janet had felt on stage was true. The crack had called out. Or maybe it was the garden or their home. Come home, come home, come home to bonnie Jean. And her face was still smeared with bonnie Jean and now it was wet with dew and with the tears of the new day. Her eyes overflowed. Her heart beat hard, and her arms ached with the effort of hugging her children to her. So hard she held them, so desperately hard that she squeezed a stifled Ow from little Pieter, who wriggled and writhed in his mother's grasp –

Close your eyes, she urged them. Oh, my little darlings, close your eyes. Think, she said, think –

And she stared at the filthy crack growing darker and deeper in the softening sky. The heavens were mother-of-pearl; the crack was the gates of hell –

Janet found it hard to think –

For even as she frowned with the effort, the crack seemed to widen ever more. The skull of the pool trepanned and fell into deep, dark oblivion. Janet could not even whisper, Jean –

For into the desperate crack fell all sense of old Jock. She knew his bones shifted in the heaving chest of the garden. And falling from her were all Noreen's brave headaches and Eileen-the-Understudy's little smiles. Into the crack, the chasm, went Phil and his stupid magazines and Hektor-Jan's side of the bed. The splitting garden rang with the sound of Oupa's eye tearing, exploding with a metal bang, and the shuddering kiss of her other half, Frank. Nesbitt howled, and Lettie-Alice's radio lay weeping in the depths, its African voices ululating into the earth. Even as her arms ached with her children, in fell her stern mother for ever followed by her father. Only the red pen remained, but it was a hot penknife and it was now stuck to her hand. It was bloody with Hektor-Jan's surprise and with Desperate Doug's last wheeze. The entire garden was the mouth of Meneer Yuckulls, and he lay back and grinned at the new day, for it was coming and it was here, no matter what Derek-Francis did with his hands as he waved them goodbye. Oh God, called Janet as Karen Carpenter withered from sight, sucked into the void, and she now tried to reach past her children. But it was too late. She knew that New-Jock was gone, and so was Desperate Doug and Hektor-Jan. And the children were slipping. Just as the crack ran one way, it would stretch and come their way too. Of course, she should have seen that. They had made it out of the house. Yes, they were huddled at the back of the garden, but the tension was tearing the air; it would not be long before it came their way –

Oh God, called Janet again and her arms found her children who were restless beneath her taut fear –

Mommy, called the little boy, his voice trembling.

I don't like this, wailed the smallest child, Sylvia, whilst the eldest, Shelley, was silent and fierce.

And her arms ached, and her throat throbbed as she tried to cling to her children. But the crack kept coming; there was nothing to be done. And even as the edge of the pool on their side split with a sigh, Janet's waters finally broke. With a gasp, she felt the sudden warmth run down her thighs. There was the quick rush then the patter of heavy drops in the grim dawn –

Oh God, Janet tried not to alarm the children for a third time. Oh Lettie-Alice and Solomon. How she needed her two stalwart friends, her dear, dark mother and black father with their strong arms and brilliant smiles. They would know what to do. What could she do. Her hand rushed to her the depths of herself, to her split self. Yes, there was water. Yes, she had also begun to gape –

What a world in which to be born. No high chaparral and little bonhomie. There were rhododendrons though and bald weeping willows. There was Benoni and the lost promise of Brigadoon, now gone for a hundred years. What would the next century see?

And as Janet tried to clutch the children, and ride with the rupturing spasm of the new child to come, the crack gaped wider and deeper –

So much had fallen into it, and yet now, from it, there came – what was coming?

Mommy, their hands were desperate now. Their voices called to her, even Shelley's, especially Shelley's. Could they hear it too? Above their voices and beyond, or was it down, within the very depths of the land? That sound. It was coming. What rough beast, what was it that slouched, that came groaning up from the crack? Or were the real beasts in the garage?

Oh God. The pain was welling up. Things were not falling into the crack; everything was coming out. Just as Janet gaped, the garden opened up, the land parted –

Oh God, Janet did cry out this time. Oh, oh God. The pain was immense, far worse than she ever remembered and her children were aghast; they were holding on to her now. What was Mommy doing? Why was Mommy screaming? Why had Mommy fallen back? They were trying to help her. Quick, came Shelley's voice fighting though Sylvia's shrieks, quick. And there was Pieter, her own brave little Pieter, holding her in his arms like a lover. And they stroked Mommy's forehead and tried to hold her as the sounds came bursting up and she screamed and held on to her belly, the base of herself –

Ow, ow, ow, Janet cried like a child, as the crack tore and she gaped wider and wider. The spasms were moving fast, were becoming one long, wrenching orgasm of pain. All the truth was coming, but it was coming slant –

Mommy, called Shelley. Mommy! Mommy!

And as the garden finally split, as the huge chasm broke open their land, the children screamed and her baby crowned. They were sliding. The earth was trembling. They were falling. And even as they fell, Janet reached out, clutching at their warm bodies through the agony of it all –

Mommy! they screamed. Mommy! she screamed. Mommy, Mommy, Mommy!

South Africa split with gunshots and cries and terror and fear.

There was death and darkness and the shock of hard earth.

Deep in the crack, it was a difficult birth.

GLOSSARY

ag	oh
allawereld	an exclamation/expression of surprise
asseblief	please
assegai	spear
baie	very/much
blankes	whites
bliksem	bastard
blikskotteltjie	little rascal
bobbejaan	baboon (bobbejaan spanner is a type of pipe wrench)
boervrou	farmer's wife
boet	brother (but in the sense of mate/friend)
brak	dog
brandewijn	brandy
broeks/broekie	knickers
dank	thank
dankie	thank you
doek	headscarf
dof	stupid
dominee	a minister in an Afrikaner church
doppie	a dram
dorpsjapie	town dweller
dwaal	a state of befuddlement
egte	authentic
eish	a multipurpose expression of exasperation or disbelief, it can also show excitement, anger or happiness

ek is jammer	I am sorry
Engelse	English
Engelsman	Englishman
fliek	movie
gaan	go/going
gee	give
geen	none
gelukkige verjaarsdag	happy birthday
goeie	good
groot	big
haal	pull/get
hemel	heaven
Die Here	God
heerlik	wonderful
hierdie	this/these
hierso	here
hoekom	why
hok	enclosure
hom	him (or it)
hy	he
impi (in Zulu)	armed group of men
jislaaik	an expression of surprise
jou	you
jy	you
kaffir	insult: a black person
kak	shit
kans	chance
kaya	maid's room, often in an outbuilding
kerk	church
Khoki	a stationery brand name
klein	small
kom	come
koppie	small hill
krag	courage/power
laager	circular camp
lekker	nice

liewe	dear
lobola (in Zulu, Xhosa, Ndebele)	dowry
maak	make
magtig	expression of surprise/exasperation
mal	crazy
mampara	idiot
mampoer	homemade brandy
mannetjie	little man
meneer	mister or sir
mes	knife
mielie	maize
moer	strong, all-purpose swear word
my	me
nie	not
nie-blankes	non-whites
nodig	needed
ongeluk	accident
oom	uncle
oupa	grandfather
paraat	ready
panga	machete
plaas brak	farm dog/mongrel
reg	right
regte	right/genuine
riempe	leather thongs woven to make chair seats
roepstem	a call/calling – also in the sense of 'The Call', the old national anthem
rooinek	insult: an English-speaking South African (literally 'red-neck')
sag	soft
sê	say
seker	sure
sekerheid	certainty
seun	son
sis	yuck
sjoe	an exclamation of surprise

skoonsuster	sister-in-law
skraal	thin/gaunt
slaap	sleep
slasto	a slate-like shale used for flooring and tiling
snaaks	amusing/odd
sommer	just because/for no real reason
songololo	millipede
stap	walk
swarte	black person
takkies	plimsolls
tannie	auntie (a term of respect)
tarentaal	guinea fowl
terug	back
velskoene	walking shoes
verjaar	celebrate a birthday
vlei	shallow pool/lake
voetsek	get lost
vreet	feed
vrou	wife
wat	what
weet	know
witblits	home-distilled grape brandy
wragtig	truly/really

ACKNOWLEDGEMENTS

I am grateful for the permission to reproduce extracts from the following works:

John Marais, *Time Bomb: A Policeman's True Story*. Reprinted with the permission of Tafelberg.

Weizmann Hamilton writing in *Inqaba Ya Basebenzi* (*Fortress of the Revolution*)

Sifiso Mxolisi Ndlovu, *The Road to Democracy in South Africa: 1970 – 1980, Volume 2*. Reprinted with the permission of UNISA Press.

Frank Welsh, *A History of South Africa*. Reprinted with the permission of HarperCollins Publishers.

Nelson Mandela, *Long Walk to Freedom*. Reprinted (hardback and paperback) with the permission of Little, Brown Book Group; reprinted (digitally) with the permission of Hachette Book Group, inc.

I would like to thank first readers, Lesley Radmann, Betty Marais, Glenda and Helmut Radmann, Andrew Murray and Astrid Coetzer (who also helped with some of the Afrikaans phrasing), my agent, Juliet Mushens, editors Jenny Parrott, Charlotte Van Wijk and Juliet Mabey, copy editor, Kate Quarry, editorial production manager, Ruth Deary, Lord Wandsworth College creative writing pupils, Sophia Agathocleous, Ricky Bevins, Beth Harris and Harry Puttock, colleague, Ed Coetzer, and Chris and Jenny Parker, whose kindness has made so many things possible.

ABOUT THE AUTHOR

Christopher Radmann is from South Africa but has lived in England for the last fourteen years. He is Head of Sixth Form and Head of English at a boarding school in Hampshire, England, where he lives with his wife and two children. *The Crack* is his second novel, following his acclaimed debut, *Held Up*.